# PART ONE

# CHAPTER 1

It's almost time. My award's up next.

I sit at a circular table, glass of wine in hand, watching the stage. Willing for the presenter to hurry up, announce the winner and move on to my category.

He's waffling so I glance around the table. To my right sits my literary agent and close friend. She fans her face with the menu. The rest of the seats are taken by various industry bods that I politely chatted to over dinner. I've already forgotten their names. The organisers like to mix guests up and, earlier, I was beyond relieved to look at the table plan and find Nisha and I sitting together. I can make small talk with strangers, listen intently, ask the right questions. But sometimes, like tonight, I really can't be bothered with it.

I'm nervous, that's why. I take a small sip of wine and put the glass down. The alcoholic waft makes me feel nauseous.

To my left, an empty seat. The place card notes 'Tom Darlington', the teen boyband star turned model, turned actor whose face is everywhere.

"Why is Tom Darlington coming to this low-level industry event? He'll be the only celebrity here! It's not exactly the Oscars now is it, Sal," Nisha had exclaimed when I showed her the card during the first course. "And why have they put him next to you? Not that you're not incredibly important, darling, but I'd have thought he'd be at one of the tables near the front, being such a superstar."

"Doubt he'll show up," I had replied, playing it cool and shrugging.

Secretly I hoped he would so I could tell everyone I sat next to him. His more dancey solo stuff is a guilty pleasure of mine. And one of his boyband songs is my karaoke go-to. But it's late now, the ceremony's nearly done and I've given up hope.

A round of applause. It's time. My stomach flips, the disgusting toffee cheesecake dessert crawls back up my throat. I cross my fingers under the table and hold my breath. Please, please, please let me win.

The presenter announces, "And now we come to Best Author of a Novel Adapted to a TV series."

Nisha squeezes my hand as the presenter reels off the shortlist.

When he says, "Sally Speck for *The Deviants*," the other five around the table turn back to me briefly and smile. I'm surprised they remember my name.

"And the winner is…" The presenter pauses and makes a show of opening the envelope and reading what is written there.

I resist the urge to bellow, "Get a move on!" A slight heat tickles my neck and up my cheeks.

The presenter closes the envelope and leans in to his microphone, opens his mouth…

A commotion at the doors to the fancy London hotel ballroom and all attention, including that of the presenter, shoots there.

"Sorry I'm late! Huge apologies. Now, where am I sat?" Tom Darlington sweeps in, an entourage of assistants behind him. He heads towards the stage, but one black-suited assistant with a clipboard steers him towards the back of the room, to my table. Everyone in the room collectively gasps, including Nisha.

Screw the actor. Did I win? *Did I win?!*

"Our guest of honour, the actor Tom Darlington, has

arrived!" the presenter announces redundantly. Everyone in the room has already seen, or heard, this jerk's entrance.

The black suit points to the empty chair next to me.

"There? Really?" Tom Darlington says in what is meant to be a whisper but which everyone nearby hears.

"Yes, Tom. That's Sally Speck, the author. Remember our chat in the car?"

"Ah. Yes." Tom strides to the table, bows to those seated around it and elegantly sits down. The entourage dissolve to take up position around the edges of the room, eyes on their master and poised to assist.

The presenter talks again but Tom Darlington speaks over him, sticking out his hand to me to shake.

"Sally? Tom. Enchanted to meet you."

He releases my hand after a firm, polite pump. I fret that my palm's clammy.

He leans into me. "I'm simply dying for the part of Xander in your next novel adaptation. I understand the script of your book *Dusk* is bouncing around Hollywood at the moment. What do you think?"

"Well…" I feel myself blush at his interest, at his direct eye contact. My voice comes out in a wibble. He's supremely attractive. He's literally the God of Beautiful Men. I steady myself. "I don't really have much say in casting—"

A shout from the presenter cuts me short.

"Sally? Sally Speck! Are you here? You've won the award. Seems Sally's more interested in that dashing actor. You carry on, we'll give it to you later. Right, moving on to the next award, I've got a tight schedule to keep."

OMG I've won. My heart thrums.

"I'm here!" I yell. I stand and wave my arms.

The presenter shields his eyes from the glare of a spotlight. "Well come on up here then. We haven't got all night, even if you are flirting with the world's most eligible bachelor!"

The audience laughs and the slight blush turns into a

poker-hot glow.

I edge out of my chair and discreetly hitch down my dress. It immediately makes me want to hitch up my tights. But I pin my hands to my side. The dress is short and I can feel the gusset of my tights is low. Please not lower than the hem. For thirty-six, I still have decent, shapely legs, as long as they are covered in thick tights. In the flesh, they're blotchy, flaky and always, inexplicably, bruised. The dress is ruched to flatter my belly with long sleeves to hide my wobbly bingo wings. I feel half decent in it.

Anyway, I must get to the stage without making a fool of myself. My tights are fine. I'm sure they're fine. The wine swims in my vision.

I become painfully aware of eyes watching me and lips crinkling into smirks as I totter to the stage, taking great care on the six steps in my heels. I shake the presenter's hand, desperately thankful that a speech isn't required, and pose with him for the photographer, hoping that my burning cheeks will look like carefully applied blusher in the photo. I hate having my photo taken but force a smile, which I'm certain will come out like a grimace. Clutching my award, I tread carefully back to the table. I curse the heels; long for my pyjamas and slippers.

"Well done for hearing your name, darling," Nisha says as I sit. "And who knew you could shout so loud."

I plonk my small, plastic award on the table, grab a bottle of wine and top up my glass. I'm not hanging around for the waiting staff; I need a drink immediately. The actor who stole my big moment, my first award, converses with one of the industry bods. Everyone else is silent, having the courtesy to listen to the presenter, who still has another three awards to get through.

Tom glances at me, effortlessly wraps up his conversation and turns back to face me. "Ah, you've returned. Now, as we were saying. *Dusk*. Xander. Could you put a word in for me? I'd be devilishly grateful."

I press a finger to my lips and stare intently at the stage as if these final few awards are the most important of the night. The actor takes the hint, jerks his chair closer to mine and looks at the stage, legs crossed and leaning into me. Every now and then he turns to look at me and smiles, as if checking I haven't run off.

His closeness sends shivers across my spine.

Tom looks at the stage. A finger pokes me in the ribs. Nisha raises her eyebrows at me. She whispers, "He likes you!"

"No," I hiss back. "He just wants a part in *Dusk* the movie."

"Ah. Still, you might as well enjoy his asking."

The final award, the final applause, the music switches on and Tom turns back to me.

"Care to join me at the bar? Or perhaps somewhere a bit quieter so we can get to know one another?"

I open my mouth to answer but a wave of people washes over Tom asking for selfies, autographs, if he can say a few words into their phones. His entourage moves in to coordinate.

I'm shoved and elbowed.

"Bar?" Nisha says.

"Yep."

Angrily, I shoot up from my chair, forcing groupies to move aside. I pick up my handbag and award.

A hand grabs mine and clasps it tight. Tom looks up at me through the bodies. His thumb brushes over my knuckles.

The crowd melts from my awareness and I'm transfixed by him.

"Wait for me, Sally. Don't leave yet. I'll get rid of this lot and join you at the bar in a few minutes. Please, do me the honour, and wait."

His manner shocks me. It's charming, yet desperate. Almost as if he *really* wants to get to know me and not use me for his own gain. I nod and he grins. He turns back to his fans.

Nisha is efficiently saying goodbye to the industry folk at our table as if they are all best friends. She's a consummate professional. I make my way to the bar at the back of the ballroom.

I order two gin and tonics and pull two high stools close to each other. I perch on one. Nisha climbs up on the other, her short legs dangling.

We both slurp down our drinks and watch as the front tables are cleared to make way for a dancefloor and as Tom's admirers clamber over one another for his attention.

"Thanks, babe," I say.

"What for?"

"This," I lift the award from the bar top, "is for you too. If it wasn't for you taking a chance on me, none of this would've happened."

Nisha raises her glass and I clink it with mine.

I pat her wrist. "Love you, babe." I'm drunk.

"The feeling's mutual, my award-winning author. Now, let's celebrate."

She orders a second round.

I jut my chin at Darlington. We watch as the popstar slash model slash actor glides from his chair and saunters across the room towards us. Suave.

His people fan out around him, deterring the last few groupies from getting near.

"Ladies," he says with a tip of the head, "let me get you a drink."

Nisha gawps, starstruck.

I play it cool and rescue her. "I'll have another gin and tonic please. Nisha, same again?"

"Uh huh," she replies, not able to take her eyes off Tom.

Tom squeezes between us to place the order and his hips brush my knees. A frisson fizzes through my veins.

The bartender serves him within seconds.

Nisha snaps photos of the actor on her phone. Tom moves next to me and puts his arm around my shoulders like we're old friends. My knee-jerk cringe reaction when anyone points a lens at me is overruled by excitement. Wah! I'm having my photo taken with this uber-famous guy! I grin foolishly, force my eyelids open. I know Nisha will post that pic and tag me in it and then everyone will see. Normally I'd demand to vet the pics to find one I don't hate, but guess I can't be too choosy when a celebrity's involved. Jake'll be jealous. Tom is his celeb crush. Has been since forever.

Tom moves to Nisha and they pose for a selfie.

I take a long swig of my G'n'T.

Nisha fiddles with her phone, no doubt posting the selfie on her social channels with some witty comment. Tom turns to me.

"I loved *Dusk*. That part when Xander saves Zia. Wow. Blew me away."

I'm surprised this guy knows what a book is. "You've read it?"

"Yes, of course," he drawls, edging his body closer to mine, "that's why I think I'm *perfect* for Xander. I just *connected* with him from the outset. And I've read *The Deviants* trilogy and watched the show. Magnificent. You are *very* talented."

He makes intense eye contact, as if he can't pull his gaze away from me.

The flattery flutters throughout my body. A delicious shiver dances around my neck and up to my ears. My lobes glow and I have an overwhelming urge to hold my ice-cold drink against my face. His attention melts the frosty wall I've built up around myself and I shift back on my seat to prevent my ridiculously enflamed cheeks from scorching him and scaring him away. In truth, I want more of his attention.

He winks at me cheekily, conspiratorially, as if we have

some in-joke, some exclusive connection. I lap it up greedily, thrilled.

Nisha's phone rings and she answers.

"Seriously? But it's my first night out in months since the baby was born. And Sal won an award! Ok, ok. I'll be right back."

She jumps from her stool, her pint-sized, five-foot-two frame wobbles slightly on landing as the gin reaches her toes. "Gotta go, Sahil's crying and he's driving his Daddy insane. Pleasure to meet you, Tom. And you, darling, congratulations on your award. We'll speak tomorrow."

Nisha dashes off, the entourage parts to let her through. Tom takes her stool, eagerly edging it closer and says, "Now, I want to know *everything* about you. I'm your *biggest* fan."

# CHAPTER 2

"Oh, right," I say awkwardly.

What on earth do I talk to a megastar about? Before Nisha took a chance on my writing I used to work in recruitment and could talk to anyone, about anything. But, after years working from home, I've lost the knack of being around strangers. And to be honest, I like it that way. I'm an introvert. I love being around people I know and love, and then having some alone time. But small talk with a celebrity? No experience of that before. Zero. Zilch. Nada.

But Tom saves me from my fumbling. "So, is it your dream to have one of your books made in to a movie? I mean, I know you've got a TV series, but this is Hollywood, baby."

His eyes widen as he asks and he looks genuinely keen to hear my answer.

"Yes, absolutely. It's my dream. Along with owning a house somewhere exotic. Guess you've got a few of those around the world, hey?" I laugh and then cringe. What a weird thing to say. Bloody nerves. And gin.

Tom lets the weirdness float over him, thank goodness. "I bet it's a dream. Incredible. Such an achievement. You know, one of my dreams is to write a novel."

"Really?"

"Ha, yes, don't sound so surprised!"

I wipe the gawp off my face.

He continues, "I used to write a lot of poetry when I was younger. Embarrassing, I know."

"No, not embarrassing at all. I also used to write poems."

"High five!" He says and holds his hand up.

I can't leave him hanging so I slap it with mine.

"I've never met anyone else who's admitted to that. Stories, yes. Comics, yes. Poetry, goodness no." He laughs.

And I laugh with him, genuinely.

He points to my near-empty glass. "Another?"

I nod.

"Champagne?"

"Go on, then." I did just win my first award, after all.

He raises his hand to the bartender who skips over to serve him. As Tom orders I drain the last of my gin and get knocked in the nose with ice cubes. As I fumble to get the glass down and wipe my face, Tom leans over the bar, grabs a napkin from one of the holders behind the counter and passes it to me.

"I do that all the time, bloody ice cubes."

"Thanks," I mumble as I dab my face.

"Where were we? Ah yes, writing." He shifts on his stool so his full attention is with me again and doesn't even waver when the bartender pours the champagne right next to him. "Tell me, when did you first know you wanted to be an author?"

"At school. I wrote a story for a county-wide contest thing. It won and I got to read it out at this big event. I hated it."

"You hated it?"

"Oh, the reading-it-out-loud-in-front-of-lots-of-people thing. I loved the writing and winning part."

"Yes, performing. People either love it or hate it, don't they? Personally, I love it."

"Figures," I say and gesture to him in a way that's meant to convey: yup look at you, you super-famous performer you, of course you must love it.

He laughs.

"What about your writing?" I ask.

"I composed soppy love poems, you know. And then I started writing lyrics. I wrote some of the Swoon songs."

"Really?" I say with the gawp back on my face. This guy continues to surprise me.

"Yes. And co-wrote some too. But once it all took off I didn't really have time to write anymore. Other people did it for us."

"I see."

His eager body language sags and the twinkle in his eyes glazes over momentarily. "That's one of my biggest regrets – not writing down more of my songs and lyrics when I was at school. Just wasn't the… er… right *environment* for it."

The way he forces 'environment' out with a slight snarl hints at a less-than-idyllic school life. I itch to know more, but refrain from asking. It's not the done thing to ask celebrities too many personal questions, is it? That's nosiness on another level.

But he continues unprompted. "My first love, the one I wrote my heart out for, was a hockey player in the year above. I'll fully admit it, I was obsessed with her, still am in a way – you never forget your first love, do you?"

No. You don't. My first love sent me into a tailspin when he dumped me. Left me hospitalised for depression. I was thirteen. It's a dark, dismal road I never want to go down again. I've had bouts of mental health issues on and off since, but nothing as black as that time.

But I don't mention this. I nod agreeably.

"She burned them all, to make a point. All my many love letters."

"Bet she wishes she'd kept them now. Could've flogged them and made some money."

"That's exactly what I say! More fool her."

He breaks off eye contact to hand me a glass of champagne. He clinks his to mine and the twinkle returns.

"To Sally Speck, author extraordinaire!"

We drink and I keep my glass to my lips a little too long to hide the blush at his praise.

"It's nothing, really. I'm sure you've had plenty of awards…" I'm about to say 'in your time', but that makes him sound old and me sound even older. He's only in his twenties.

"Yes, one or two." He shrugs. "But never for what I find most meaningful in life."

Meaningful? Is this guy for real? On paper he seems like a bit of a bozo blessed with good looks and a half-decent singing voice. I wasn't expecting him to be deep. When he pauses, I can't help myself. "And what's that?"

He considers me for a moment as if weighing up whether to share. What's he going to say? His spirituality? His love of puppies? What would be meaningful to a model slash actor slash singer? I take a long gulp of champagne. The bartender arrives to top up my glass.

"My charity work," Tom says.

"Oh." Not what I was expecting. The champagne is making me bold. To hell with not being nosey. "Like what?"

"I'm the patron for Heart Disease Now. I donate, help them to raise awareness and go to their events."

"Why that charity?"

He swallows and looks at his hands, his shoulders slump and a wetness glitters in the corners of his eyes. "My mother died of a heart attack when I was a teenager. It's… painful to remember."

Oh my. Is he going to cry? Should I call one of his handlers?

He breathes deeply in through his nose and lifts his gaze back to me. "So, I do what I can. I also work with an anti-bullying charity."

Something pings in my mind. It's my bullshit detector going off. No celebrity is this… real? Are they? I decide to probe, with zero subtlety. "And why that charity?"

"I was bullied as a child," he says matter-of-factly.

"I'm sorry to hear that."

"If it hadn't been for my brother protecting me, I swear those boys would've killed me."

Waaaay too dramatic. "Hmm," I reply and swig my champers.

"You know why they bullied me?"

"No, why?"

He tips forward closer to me and pretends to look around to check no-one's in earshot. "For writing the soppy love poems." He bursts out laughing.

My eyebrows shoot up incredulously. But his amusement is infectious and I snort as the laughter tumbles out of me. I clap a hand to my face in horror at the snort and that only makes him laugh more. Which only makes me laugh more.

We're literally crying with laughter. And every time we try to finish, we look at each other and start again. It's a surreal – and utterly wonderful – moment. My cheeks hurt, my chest is tight and my brain is flooded with serotonin.

The moment is broken as one of his assistants politely interrupts and whispers in his ear and gestures to, what looks to be, the chef of the hotel in grubby whites.

Tom turns to me. "Please excuse me for one moment. It seems I have a fan." He nods at the assistant who gestures to the excited chef.

I slip from my stool. "Just going to the bathroom," I answer the alarmed look on his face.

He smiles as I turn from him and my back prickles. I can't know for certain but I feel as if his gaze follows me through the ballroom and out of sight.

I hurry to the toilets, as fast as my high-heeled feet can take me. It's getting late and there's no queue and an empty cubicle.

Sitting on the loo, I get my phone out. I google 'tom darlington charity work'. His Wikipedia page comes up and so does a few lines on his patronage of Heart Disease Now and Beat Bullying.

"Yikes," I mutter. He was telling the truth.

Then I google 'tom darlington songwriting' and scroll through a few results until I find one that confirms he wrote 'Baby, You're Mine', one of Swoon's biggest-selling hits. I breathe out with my mouth in an 'o'.

So, bullshit detector, you were wrong. Tom is actually a decent guy.

I search for the name of one of Tom's more recent solo tracks that stayed at number one for, like, forever. The results confirm that Tom co-wrote 'Toxic Crush' with a list of four other people. I go to log out but see a headline that catches my eye: WAS CAMILLE AND TOM'S RELATIONSHIP TOXIC?

Scanning the few lines underneath, I read:

As 'Toxic Crush' hits the top spot, the supermodel posts – and quickly deletes – series of scathing, cryptic tweets about her ex-boyfriend Tom Darlington.

I resist the urge to click on the tabloid nonsense and finish up in the toilet, pat powder on my T-zone, swipe a slick of lipgloss and smooth down my curls. I look at myself sideways in the mirror, hoik up my tights and hoik down my dress and, when the other lady in there isn't looking, I whisper 'you got this!' and smile brightly. I totter out of the bathroom and back towards the bar, passing people on their way out.

The chef has left and Tom jumps from his stool to help me onto mine. Then gets back on.

"Apparently the bar's closing."

"Oh." I go to get off the stool.

Tom stops me. "Not for us, though. My assistant has pulled some strings. We still have this champagne to finish, that's if you want any more, of course."

"Hit me up!" I grin and push my glass towards him. Tom pulls the bottle from the bucket and pours me a glass as if he's an experienced bartender at a six-star resort. He refills his glass.

I haven't been out in a while, and I like to drink. Not in an alcoholic kind of way, but in a let's-have-a-binge-one-night-a-week kind of way. My problem is, I don't know when to stop. Others have a cut-off switch, knowing which drink will be their last. I seem to lack that. But as I swig at the champagne, my gut twinges with a red wine mixed with gin mixed with champagne gurgle.

"I think it's time for me to go home," I say, or did I slur? Can't tell.

"Absolutely, my driver can take you."

"Oh, no bother. I'll jump in a taxi."

"He's waiting outside. It's fine, honestly."

He grins and it lights up his face. At that moment I want to snog his magnificent face off. But I don't, of course. I know he's only entertained me this long to get a part in a movie of my book that I have zero say in. And anyway, I can't be bothered to try and find a taxi and – YAY – free ride home. They don't happen often these days.

"That's kind of you to offer, thanks." I get down from the stool and go to walk off.

"Sally, aren't you forgetting something?" He has his arm behind his back and a cheeky look on his face that makes me want to do more than just snog him.

I screw up my face in concentration. But, nope. Nothing comes. I've got my handbag and my coat is in the cloakroom on the way out.

"Give up," I say.

He kneels in front of me and thrusts up my crappy plastic award. "Recognition, Zia! Embrace it, my child, for your life shall never be the same again!"

I'm stunned. Actually stunned. I can't move. He takes my fingers and puts the award in them. I clasp it limply.

He frowns at my incapacity to do anything, and then stands looking at me. "That's a line from your book…It's when Zia wins that battle…" He says by way of explanation, his face worried.

Snapping out of my trance, I laugh. "I know! I wrote it, you idiot. You don't need to mansplain my own book to me."

"Sorry." He laughs. "It's just you went like this." He freezes and plasters a wide-eyed look across his face.

I laugh harder. He relaxes and we have another moment of uncontrollable, blissful giggles.

As it subsides, he asks, "Can I hug you?"

Wow, he's a genuine gentleman. "Uh huh."

He embraces me and then cups my face. "Seriously, though, congratulations. You and I are so alike. We're both chasing our dreams, aren't we? We're artists striving to create something. It's an incredible thing, isn't it, that joy of creation."

His nose practically touches mine. My body wants to melt, right there into a puddle on the floor. I relish his hands on my cheeks, his hot breath against my lips. There's a sexual tension between us that sizzles and splutters and is about to boil over. I want him to kiss me.

But he pulls away. "May I?" He indicates my hand. I nod and he takes it. With his other raised he says, "Our chariot awaits!"

# CHAPTER 3

When the world's most eligible bachelor wants to come in for coffee, and your last three Tinder dates have been big fat disappointments, you don't say no.

That's what I keep telling myself anyway. Still foggy from a boozy, fitful sleep, I run over last night's events.

In the car, I kissed him. It got passionate. His driver had switched on the radio.

Why not? I thought in my drunken state. He's clearly using me to try and get a part in a movie, as why would this devastatingly handsome man want to get with me? So, I thought, why not use him right back for a bit of fun?

And now here I am, the morning after. Tom snores. An actual world-famous actor snores in MY BED! I watched one of his movies only last week.

The sun peeks through the curtains and I watch it illuminate his tattooed, gym-honed limbs. "Tattoos were my way of rebelling against my strict father as a teen and fitting in with the rest of the band," he'd told me at some point last night. His blond, wavy hair shines.

One of his heavy arms lies across my not-so-gym-honed stomach and I concentrate on remembering its weight, touch and shape. In etching it on my memory so I'll always be able to remember this moment. Last night is a bit of a blur, to be honest, but it was thrilling. My entire body remembers that much.

I try to ignore the fact that I need a wee. His sculpted

17

arm pushes on my bladder. I don't want to move him, to break this surreal moment. But it's unbearable.

I lift his arm, gently wriggle across the mattress and place it down again.

He grumbles and his sleepy eyes edge open. "Where you going, beautiful?"

"Bathroom."

"Be quick, my arms are lost without you in them."

I tiptoe to the bathroom, hoping he's fallen asleep again and not looking at my naked behind in the unforgiving daylight. I scoop up my handbag on route.

I sit on the toilet and look at my phone. Already 11.12am! Thank goodness I'm a writer and don't need to do anything on a Thursday. Missed my yoga class though, damn. And I wanted to bash out a few chapters of my new book. Sleeping with a superstar puts things on hold, I guess.

'Well???!!!???!!!'

A message from Nisha demands. I tap back:

'Yep!'

I rinse my hands and look in the mirror. I grin broadly, circle my pointed fingers at my reflection and mouth 'WAHHHHH! You go, girl!'

After congratulating myself on bagging a hottie, I silently yelp at the state of my hair. Splash water on my face and smooth my still-wet palms over my armpit-length brown hair.

My phone screen flashes. Nisha is online.

'You shagged a movie star! How was it? You do know he's nearly 15 years younger than you?! Hilarious!!'

'I had fun! One to cross off the to do list... one-night stand with movie star, tick. Hahaha!'

'Wild. You at his?'

'Nah, at mine. He's still in bed... better get back to him ;-)'

'When he's gone, tell me EVERYTHING! xx'

I head back into the bedroom and put my phone on the bedside cabinet.

Tom snuffles in a not-quite-asleep stupor. I snuggle under the duvet next to him. Mould myself around his hot, silky skin.

"So… what shall we do now?" I nibble his ear.

"I have an idea, you ravishing beauty."

Hours later and I'm getting a bit twitchy. I want a shower, some food and to write. When I'm not writing, I feel anxious. He's asleep again.

I nudge his side. "Do you want a drink? Coffee, tea?"

"Tea would be divine," he mumbles into his pillow.

I wrap my dressing gown around me and make the tea in the kitchen of my one bed, ground floor, Islington apartment. I'm proud of this apartment, of being able to afford it. It's an effort to meet the mortgage repayments, that's for sure, but it's testament to my hard work – and it's totally worth a bit of scrimping here and there.

As the kettle boils, I wonder where Tom lives and if I will ever see it. Don't be daft! This isn't a relationship that is going anywhere. I won't be going over to his anytime soon or meeting the parents. Or parent. That's right, the conversation comes back to me in a fog, his mother died when he was young.

I bring two steaming mugs back to the bedroom. He props himself up against the headboard, a big grin spreads across his face and his blue eyes sparkle. He tucks the covers neatly around his six-pack.

I swoon inwardly over that torso. Wrench my gaze up to meet his eyes, hand him a mug, and then get in next to him.

"So, sexy Sally, what's the plan for today?"

This throws me. I was expecting a quick shrug off and a swift exit. He's certainly convinced me to 'put in a word for the movie casting', although I really don't have any say. "Plan?"

"Yes, we could go and get a late lunch at The Huntington, or order takeout. I know the manager; he'll deliver just for me. Or shall we wrap up warm and go to the park? I'll get Bev to bring me a change of clothes and a picnic of sorts. What's the weather like out there?"

"Don't you have anywhere to be?"

"Wherever you are, beautiful."

I blow on my tea and take a sip. "Listen, I know you seduced me to get a part. And I promise to put a word in for you with the producers. I doubt it'll make any difference, but I'll give it a try. You don't need to pretend this was anything else."

His face screws into a frown and he places his mug on the bedside cabinet, looks at me earnestly. "Beautiful, what are you talking about? I'm *totally* into you. Of course, it would be splendid if you did help me to play Xander, but that's not what this is all about. We have a spark, don't you feel it?"

"Er…"

"Come on, Sally, come for food with me." He leans out the bed, flashes his perfect buttocks in my direction, and grabs his trousers off the floor. He searches the pockets and pulls out his phone.

"Bev. Good morning. Oh right, afternoon. Ok, good *evening.* Fine, just fine. Will you book a table for two at the usual place and then bring me some clothes. Yeah, that'll do. And then send Ashraf. Here, I'll give you to Sally for the address." He thrusts the phone at me and, surprised, I reel off my address automatically.

"We'd best freshen up." Tom slides out of bed and stands nude in front of me with a cheeky grin.

"You go ahead." I stumble my words, too busy admiring his groin area and flick my hand in the general direction of the bathroom.

He glides over to my side of the bed, pulls me to my

feet and plants little kisses on my neck, slowly untying my dressing gown and slipping it from my shoulders.

"Come with me," he whispers into my hair and runs his fingers lightly up and down my arms. My skin sparkles.

I melt at his touch, dip my chin in agreement. He leads me to the bathroom. My pulse pounds and I forget all about writing.

Tom's PA arrives. He opens the door to her wearing my dressing gown, insisting I continue to get ready and not worry myself.

He comes back into the bedroom where I sit in front of a mirror applying make-up. Bev, his brisk, efficient, perfectly groomed but insanely trendy-looking PA with an incredible bleached blond afro, follows, holding up four outfit options on hangers.

I blush, concealer poised in hand and scan the room. The crumpled bed, our clothes and underwear strewn about. And it smells of bodies in here. Bev doesn't seem to notice. Has probably seen this plenty of times before.

She gives me a polite nod as Tom flicks through each outfit option and selects one.

"You've got that important meeting Angus set up with Cecil Clark in an hour," Bev says factually without a hint of irritation or judgement.

Tom's face pings with the recollection. "That's today?"

He's going to sack me off. I'm not as important as an important meeting. My heart sinks and I'm surprised at my disappointment. It signals to me that I might actually quite like this guy.

He looks at Bev. "Can you reorganise to after dinner? And let my brother know?" And then to me. "Cecil can wait."

Bev nods, retreats smoothly from the bedroom and closes the door. I hear her voice on the phone from the hallway.

He lays the clothes on the dishevelled bed, stands

behind me and wraps his arms around me, nuzzling my neck.

We lock eyes in the mirror. I blush again, dammit.

In the cold light of day, stone-cold-sober with a hint of hangover, I can't believe that this is happening. He could have any woman in the world. He's made his point, he wants to be Xander, I get it. So, why is he still here? Why does he want to hang out with me? We definitely had some mind-blowing sex. And my memories of last night are of a lot of laughter. And he was right when he said we were similar… both artists striving to create something. There are tons of older men dating younger women, why shouldn't it be the other way around? Maybe he likes that I'm older. I certainly like that he's a toy boy… plenty of energy.

"You don't need this stuff," Tom says, indicating my over-spilling makeup bag. "You are stunning without it."

I laugh and look away, dab concealer under my eyes again. I'm definitely not a stunner.

"I mean it, sexy Sally." He kisses me, catches my gaze in the mirror and holds it intensely for a few moments before withdrawing to get changed.

He's *super* keen. And I fancy the actual pants off him. He's funny, genuine and charming. And drop-dead gorgeous.

Dinner could actually be a success. Why not? We get on. And we definitely have chemistry.

We travel to the restaurant in his car. Bev follows behind in a second chauffeured car, which also contains two burly bodyguards. Tom says a quick hello to his driver, Ashraf, and then fixes his attention squarely on me.

I squirm slightly under the intense gaze. The uninhibited, constant adoration makes me feel awkward. Most blokes aren't like this. At least, most blokes I've dated.

I take a deep breath and push aside my slithering

insides. Enjoy it, Sal. Enjoy being the object of someone's affections. I smile at him and he doesn't look away.

Since we left my apartment, Tom has made sure he is always physically connected to me. Holding my hand, placing one arm around my shoulders and a hand on my knee as we sit in the back seat of the car, keeping a palm on my back when he opened my front door for me.

I hum with excitement. I think Tom genuinely likes me. Stranger things have happened. Perhaps I shouldn't doubt myself or my attractiveness. Perhaps, perhaps, perhaps.

We are papped by photographers during the short journey from car to building. The bodyguards clear the way. Tom proudly holds my hand, turning back to look at me often, constantly making sure I'm ok. I hold my handbag up to try and hide my face. I hate having my photo taken. Being so exposed. I want to try and maintain a semblance of privacy.

I've always hated attention I can't control. And think I can trace it back to when I was hospitalised at thirteen for depression. Mentally, I was poked and prodded and saw a conveyor belt of experts because I was so young. As these were my formative years the goal was to 'fix' me and get me back out into the world as soon as possible. The intense, forced sharing of my emotions, and the knowledge I couldn't escape from that laser-focused scrutiny, still haunts me. One time, when a black cloud was hanging low over my adult head – after mountains of rejections from other literary agents before Nisha took me on and while in the aftermath of a messy breakup – a counsellor linked that traumatic hospital experience with why I don't like having my photo taken. I think they were probably right.

A surreal experience. Being famous. And not one I've ever courted. Anonymity: that's the name of my game. Success not fame. I berate myself. *Of course* there'd be photographers at this world-famous celeb hangout. I should've checked, I should've asked if there was a back entrance or something. No one will know who I am, but everyone knows who Tom is.

He ushers me into the restaurant.

"All over, beautiful," he whispers in my ear as he kisses my hair and keeps a steadying, protective hand on my shoulder. It's a soothing balm. It thrills me.

It's also surreal being the most important person to someone. My insides flutter. I'm excited for this meal with Tom. I want to get to know him and to spend more time with him.

The manager of The Huntington greets us and directs us to a secluded table in a corner.

Tom pulls out my chair and waits for me to sit before sitting himself.

"Shall I bring the menu?" The manager asks.

Tom waves him away. "We'll just have my usual, Baker."

The manager bows and backs away.

The inner foodie in me bristles. The food at this place is meant to be out-of-this-world amazing. "I would've quite liked to have seen the menu."

"Oh, my apologies. I've been here many a time, and trust me, the dish I've ordered you is simply divine and I'd never forgive myself if I let you order something else. And the wine is a perfect match. I'll call Baker back with a menu and you can change your order." He raises an arm and looks around for the server.

"No, it's ok. If you say it's good, then I'd better try it."

He drops his arm and beams at me, studying my face and hair. "You look ravishing." He leans in to me, doe-eyed, and clutches my hands across the table.

"Thank—"

Tom cuts me off mid-sentence. My lips twitch in annoyance. He's oblivious, keeping steady eye contact. "I have an audition next week for a movie where I fall in love with a beautiful woman, and I'll just remember this moment and channel it. I'll imagine looking at you and allow it to flow through me until my body language and facial expressions are just as they are now."

Maybe he's nervous? I decide to forgive him the interruption.

He blows a small kiss at me as a server brings white wine. The server shows the bottle to Tom, who approves and then pours a drop for Tom to try.

He sniffs it, sips it. "Delicious." He indicates for the server to pour.

"Now, what were we talking about?"

I open my mouth to reply.

Tom gets there first. "Ah, yes, your beauty." He picks up his wine glass and holds it to a toast. I clink my glass to his.

I hate white wine, it makes me very drunk very quick. But rather than make a fuss, I make an exception and take a swig.

He holds the wine glass in one hand, and mine in the other. His legs are pressed into me under the table. I enjoy the warm and fuzzy physical contact. It's making up for the less-than-flowing verbal contact.

"I've done fourteen auditions now and got the part four of those times. My agent tells me that's pretty good, but I've no idea. I've made three films and am about to start filming the fourth. I still can't believe it, you know, moving from boyband to solo singer, to model, to actor. It was a wild time in Swoon, I started at fifteen on that TV talent show and boom, it all exploded. Almost as if it happened overnight, but it took a lot of hard work, a lot of graft behind the scenes, you know?"

"Yes, I know how that feels. I had written four books before I had my first success—"

"I was ridiculously nervous about going solo, but my older brother, Angus, was so supportive. He's been the one who has had my back this entire time. He's a nerdy fellow, a maths whiz-kid, but has a big heart. You'll meet him soon, he'll love you, I'm sure. So, what are you writing now?"

"I've started on—"

Tom looks up and beckons a server. "Can we get some olives?"

"Yes, sir," the man replies and scurries off.

Tom turns back to me and smiles and indicates with a dip of his head for me to continue.

"I've started a sequel to *Dusk*, I'm about three quarters of the way through a first draft…"

His eyes glaze, and flick to check if the olives are on their way. He's not paying me any attention so I stop talking abruptly.

After a moment, he notices that I've gone quiet. Fills the gap. "Your writing is honestly spectacular, like your big green eyes. Ah, here we are."

The olives are placed on the table. He pops two in his mouth in quick succession.

Maybe he's just hungry?

I eat a couple and knock back my wine. Top up a second large glass, take two big gulps. Tom smiles his million-dollar smile at me and I soften.

"You're writing a sequel to *Dusk*? Tell me more."

Ok, so he is listening.

"Well, the first book ends with a cliffhanger, right? Zia is stranded on the planet Yestra and—"

"Xander rescues her?"

"Well, yes, but there's more to it than that."

He laughs. "I'm sure there is."

I open my mouth to continue but Tom clasps a palm over it. "No! Don't tell me. Don't ruin the surprise." He moves his palm to cup my face and then stands over the table, his chair scraping so loudly that neighbouring diners look our way, and kisses my nose. "No spoilers, promise? I want to read your remarkable words. I want to follow the story as it unfolds."

He sits back and I can't work out my feelings. Pissed off at being physically silenced, or awed by the compliment and public show of affection.

I decide to be flattered. I was just about to tell him the entire story. And I get it. No one wants to know the twist and the ending. I change the subject. "Delicious wine, you seem to know about wine—"

His phone rings and he holds up a finger to stop me. "One sec."

He puts the phone to his ear. "Hey, bro. On a date with a beauty. Yeah, that author I told you about. Hmm? Sure." Tom holds the phone out. "My brother Angus wants a word. The reception's not great."

I take the phone. "Hello?"

"Hi there," a crackly voice replies. "I'm Angus, Tom's older brother. I love *The Deviants* TV show."

"Thanks."

"I hope you have a good night with Tom, he's a great guy and he seems really into you."

My ears burn. Tom has told his brother about me? After one night together? "Um, right, thanks."

"Better go. Don't break his heart now." Angus chuckles. "Have fun." He hangs up.

I hand the phone back to Tom and he puts it on the table next to his knife. His eyes travel from me to the phone, me to the phone. He taps the button when a notification pings onto the home screen. I shouldn't be frustrated with his phubbing. My friends and family do this to me – take out their phones and look at them while we're having a conversation. He seems on edge. Perhaps the important meeting is preoccupying him.

Without looking at me, he says, "Now, where were we…"

"Tell me about you," I say. Giving him the opportunity to let some things off his chest. I go silent and listen, drink wine as if it's water and occasionally interject with a "uh huh" or a "is that so" as Tom has verbal diarrhoea.

When the food comes – a piece of fish with its eyes still looking at me, caviar and oysters – wine sloshes in my belly and I can only manage two mouthfuls. I'll only eat filleted fish; can't bear to see the face. I also hate slimy oysters and the idea of fish eggs turns my stomach.

Tom wolfs it down. Wrapping sentences around each mouthful.

He talks about himself, his movies, his heady days in boyband Swoon, his body and how long he spends with his personal trainer, his many famous friends in Hollywood, his dietary requirements ("Protein, lots of protein, to build these muscles."), his strict childhood.

He swallows his last mouthful, puts his knife and fork down and looks up at me. There's silence for the first time in nearly an hour. "Sorry, beautiful, I've been rabbiting on terribly, haven't I?"

"Yep, and then some," I say, happy that he's recognised his monologue.

"Forgive me… I'm so nervous."

"This Cecil Clark an important fella then?"

"Very." He takes a steadying breath.

I knew he was on edge; knew there was a reason his behaviour had flipped from charming to self-obsessed.

"But that's not why I'm nervous."

"Oh?"

"It's you, sexy Sally. I'm trying to impress you and being a prat." He looks at me forlornly.

I can't think of anything to say.

"I've blown it haven't I?" he says.

Before I can answer, Bev appears at our table. "Sorry to interrupt, but it's about time we get going, Tom."

"Be right there," he says. Bev slips away. "I'm sorry, Sally, truly. Will you give me another chance? Meet me later? Please?"

# CHAPTER 4

I decide to give him another chance.

He was so attentive at the awards ceremony, over-the-top affectionate. Perhaps he does really like me and this is more than him wanting a part in the *Dusk* movie. He admitted he was nervous at the restaurant; the one-sided dialogue was just a blip. I was being uptight and impatient – it happens! – maybe I was talking too much. I've had worse dinner dates. *Waaaay* worse than that.

Slightly drunk from the white wine, I doll myself up and put on my best 'out, out' outfit. I slip into the waiting car that Tom has said would pick me up.

"Hi, Ashraf, where's Tom?"

"He's already there." Ashraf starts the car.

"Oh, right, and where is that?"

"The Lemonade Club. We'll be there in twenty."

Never heard of it. "Ok, great." I settle back into the seat. "So, how long have you been driving for Tom?"

"Last four years or so. Used to be the driver for his brother Angus' company. Took Angus around a few times and then he hired me for Tom."

"Bet you've seen a few things."

Ashraf scratches at the side of his nose. "This and that. Some of his fans are nut jobs."

"So, you know his brother well then?"

"Yeah, pretty well. I keep an eye out for Tom, you know, bit more than just his driver."

"He get into trouble lots then?" I joke, but realise I've pushed it when Ashraf hawks up phlegm, winds down his window and spits rather than answers.

Silence looms. I ponder what else to say. Ashraf turns on the radio. We hear the tail end of an advert and then he taps his fingers on the steering wheel to the pop music that's just a little too loud to talk over.

London whizzes past. I hope this Lemonade place is decent and not full of up-themselves numpties. The car comes to a stop.

Ashraf turns to me and gives me a card. "That's got my mobile on it. Just in case."

I slip it into the inside pocket of my handbag.

Ashraf waves at one of the black-clad doormen who speaks in his ear piece. A few moments later another comes forward and opens the car door for me. He gives me an appraising look up and down and wrinkles his nose in obvious disgust.

"This way," he says gruffly.

My guts lurch. This isn't a good idea. If the security guard is a dickhead, guaranteed those inside will be too. I've not been to a swanky nightclub in years, and my feet already hurt in the high heels I never wear. The bass booms from inside and the long line of punters queueing to get in eye me angrily as I skip in front of them.

A second security guard unlinks the red rope for the gruff one and clinks it shut behind me. I follow the first's huge, black-suited shoulders up a dark stairwell with red velvet on the walls. I concentrate on each step and hold the banister tight. He waits for me at the top of the stairs, watches my slow progress with an imperceptible shake of the head. When I finally get to the top, slightly out of breath, and hot in my faux fur jacket, he actually rolls his eyes! The wanker.

He opens the door and the music and flashing lights hit me in the face. The club heaves, the dancefloor full of writhing twenty-somethings with booths around the outside. The security guard leads me to one of these booths, unceremoniously shoving people out the way who turn, annoyed at being barged and stare at me.

"Who's that?" I hear one affronted man say.

I stand by a low table with an ice bucket sunk into the middle of it. Stuffed in that is a huge bottle of vodka, one of whiskey and one of champagne. Tom lounges on the low cushions behind this table, talking intently to perhaps the most striking red-haired woman I've ever seen. To either side are men and women talking and dancing. Bev sits off to one side, somehow still looking efficient and perfectly polished amongst all the noise and people.

The security guard shouts her name. Bev looks up from her phone and gives me a curt nod. She leans across the red-haired woman and taps Tom on the knee.

He looks up and beckons me to him. The red-haired woman grimaces. It's the actor Zoe Barns. I wanted her to play the lead part in *The Deviants* TV series, but the producers said she was too expensive.

Tom is still beckoning to me and I assess all the bodies crammed around the table. Which is the best way in? I decide to shuffle around towards Bev, who kindly taps the dancers on their legs so they move out my way.

I edge past and stand near Tom like an idiot.

"Sit," he shouts at me. But all the seats are taken.

He hitches a little to one side and pulls me down practically on top of Zoe Barns, who squeals as if a forklift truck has landed on her. She attempts to move away but can't get far as I have her pinned down. I put all my weight onto Tom and she edges out from under me, but as I drop my weight, she's still squished against me.

I slouch at a weird angle, leaning into Tom, my face wedged against his arm. My other shoulder high against Zoe Barns. Tom puts his arm around me and makes a show of kissing my cheek. "I'm so happy you're here, beautiful, my night can now begin."

Pearls of sweat run down my spine. I attempt to sit

upright to be able to pull off my jacket. This elicits a second squeal from the red-haired actor.

Tom turns to talk to the man on his left. I struggle to take off my fluffy jacket in the confined space. It gets stuck halfway down one bicep and I can't bend my arm behind me to get the other arm off first. It feels like everyone – and I mean everyone – in the club watches this performance. Their gazes prick me with pity and mirth. I finally heave it off, and then, with nowhere else to put it, fold it and put it on my lap. It's so bulky though that I can barely see over the top of it. I look stupid. Even more stupid than I feel. I shift forward to try and stuff it behind me against the wall.

Zoe Barns, jostled by my flying elbows as I attempt to stash the jacket, shouts something in my ear. I blink at her.

"What?" I shout.

Zoe jabs a finger at one of the hovering servers. "Give him your coat already!"

Stung by her obvious irritation, I raise my hand at a server, who looks at me and then looks away. My ears burn. Not to be denied, I wave and shout, "Hey!"

The server ignores me, stifles a yawn.

"Seriously," Zoe hisses. She elegantly lifts a finger and the server whirls towards her with a supplicant expression. She points to my coat and he lifts it out of my hands. He pinches it in front of him like it's contaminated and moves away with his nose in the air. Wanker. All the staff here are clearly wankers.

"Thanks," I say loudly, with my warmest smile.

Zoe ignores me, slips her arm behind my back and pokes Tom, who turns. They chat behind me; Zoe's elbow digs into the middle of my back so I can't sit upright. They laugh and banter, while I press my belly into my knees.

Sod this.

I slide to the edge of the cushion and Zoe's elbow drops away. I reach for the bucket to make myself a large vodka and tonic. Screw the fact that I've already drunk way too much headache-inducing white wine. Screw the fact that I'll have the hangover from hell tomorrow. This situation calls for it.

The dancers around the edge of the table blatantly smirk to each other as I fumble with the huge bottle of vodka. I pour most of it on the table rather than in the glass and look up to see two girls sniggering behind their hands.

This is not my thing at all. Why did I even think it would be? I don't like the music; I don't like the people. I've moved on from this. Although I hate to say it, I'm too old for this nonsense. Give me a bar playing nineties music any day.

I feel Tom's hand on my back and then Zoe Barns squeezes past and leaves the table, the dancers let her through with admiring glances. I sit back. Take a deep breath. Finally, some space.

"Hey, beautiful, I need to go and talk to a couple of bigwigs, I won't be long." Tom kisses my nose, stands and follows Bev through the crowded dancefloor.

Suddenly, I have plenty of space to either side of me and it makes me feel more out of place than ever. I long for the bodies to come back and hide me. Alone, I'm a beacon.

I clutch my drink and bob my head to the beat. The hangers-on dancers, now with the celebrities gone, saunter away to the dancefloor and to other booths.

I'm completely alone in the booth. The club is packed and there's a yawning empty space around me. Nobody comes close. They would rather pack up tight than stand anywhere near me – an out of place woman ten years older than every other patron in the place. Embarrassing. I take out my phone for something to do, see I have zero new messages or notifications, put it away again.

I'll give Tom ten minutes, and then I'm out of here. How dare he invite me out, then leave me on my own. My foot jerks back and forth. I plot an escape route. I look around to see where they might've taken my jacket.

My patience is wearing thin. Just as I'm plucking up the courage to leave Tom slips back into the booth and lounges on the cushions. He hiccoughs. The celebrity hangers-on filter back to fill the booth.

"Sorry, work stuff. I'm all yours now." He slurs his words. He's very drunk. He takes a long glug of his champagne, puts the flute down and clutches my head, works his fingers into my hair. Hair that I spent the best part of an hour tonging when I got back from the restaurant. I angle my head away. I want to scream: don't touch the hair!

He yanks me to him and snogs me with big wet roving lips, a thrusting tongue and a lot of saliva.

I try to pull away as my chin, lips, cheeks and nose are drenched but Tom's hand in my hair holds me steady. My back is rigid and my limbs stiff, and I keep pulling back, attempting to break off the kiss. My resistance spurs Tom on, he's oblivious to my signals that this massive public display of face eating is making me uncomfortable. Instead, he ramps up his efforts. His sloppy tongue roams around my lips.

My lipstick! He'll smear my lipstick. I'm already the club laughing stock, I can't have lipstick all over my face too. I bite his tongue. He takes that the wrong way too.

He pulls away with a grin and a wicked glint in his eye. "I like it rough."

"I'm going home." I adjust my bum and heave off the cushions.

Tom stands with me. "Good idea, beautiful." He grabs my hand and places it on the bulge between his legs. "You need to take care of this beast."

I wrench my hand away and look around, humiliated. Everyone nearby is gawping, giggling, pointing. Tom laughs as I shrink into myself. I need to get out of this hateful place. Now. I need to get away from this hateful celebrity. Right now.

I shove Tom away from me.

Bev gestures to a few security staff nearby who escort us from the booth, through the dancefloor, down the stairs and out to the waiting car. I follow briskly, ignoring the mocking stares. Behind me, one of the doormen helps Tom. He can barely walk.

I sigh with relief as I sit on the back seat behind Ashraf. Tom slouches against the car door talking with Bev. I pull the mirror from my bag and inwardly groan at the mess. My lipstick is smeared everywhere, like a clown's lips. My carefully applied foundation is caking in patchy clumps where Tom's saliva has dried. My chin is red raw from getting scratched by Tom's stubble and one side of my hair is frizzy and mussed up compared to the other, which still holds the sleek curls. I look like a joke. I feel like a joke.

I choke back a sob at the utter humiliation of the evening.

"Everything all right?" Ashraf says.

Pull it together. "Yes, just want to get home."

"Here he comes," Ashraf replies as Tom gets in the car.

"Back to this fine lady's establishment, my man," Tom says and Ashraf sets off.

"Wait," I yelp as we turn the first corner. "I left my jacket behind!"

Ashraf slows the car, but Tom says, "We'll get you a new one tomorrow, don't worry about it."

"But I love that jacket. Can you turn around, Ashraf?"

The driver looks in the rear-view mirror at Tom. He's the master, not me. Tom considers for a moment then says, "Forget that old piece of cheap crap, we'll get you a Gucci tomorrow. Here," he slides across the back seat and puts his arms around me, "I'll keep you warm."

I stare rigidly out the window, jaw clenched as Tom plants slobbery kisses on my neck and shoulder.

Ashraf pulls up outside my building. The street is quiet. Tom scoots along the seat to get out of his door.

"You are not coming in, Tom." My voice is firm, no

nonsense.

Ashraf shifts in his seat. I glance at the driver and then back to Tom. He has a deep frown across his forehead.

He grins. "You're joking. Get her, Ashraf, she's a funny one." He puts his hand on the door handle.

I slap the leather seat between us. The pitch of my voice rises. "I mean it. I'm going in alone and you are staying in this car." I gave you a second chance and you blew it. There will be no third.

Ashraf coughs to get Tom's attention. The driver shakes his head, looking at Tom in the rear-view mirror. Tom takes his hand off the door handle.

"Why?" Tom says, face forlorn. His torso slumps.

"Because I don't think we're suited." I get out the car.

Tom follows me anyway, skipping around the back of the car to stand next to me. I glare at him and slam the car door. "I don't think we should see each other again."

"You don't mean that."

"Yes, I do!" I yell. "Get back in that car and get the hell out of here."

Tom's jovial expression flips into anger. "Aargh!" he bellows and balls his hands into fists.

I recoil. He turns and punches the backseat car window so hard that it smashes.

I jump backwards, my heart racing, as Ashraf is there, ushering Tom into the front passenger seat without so much as a blink at the gaping hole where the window once was. Tom clutches his bleeding hand as the shattered glass crunches under their feet.

I bolt for my apartment and fly up the stairs to put as much distance between us as possible, but turn back before opening the door.

Tom, now calm as if his blast of hot fury had never happened, winds down his window and sticks out his head. "I'll pick you up tomorrow. Bev'll get them to shut the shop just for us. Have a good rest, beautiful."

I shout, "You're not listening to me! We're not seeing

each other again!"

He blows me a kiss, speaks to Ashraf and as the car edges away, says, "Until tomorrow, my sexy Sally." He brings the fingertips of his uninjured hand to his lips and then dramatically gestures to me, as if throwing me his kisses.

I sneer.

In my apartment I throw my handbag on the floor. What a jerk. What an awful night. And what on earth was that punch all about?

I take my frustration out on my make-up as I drag cotton pads over my eyes, scrub my face harshly with cleanser and slap on my moisturiser.

# CHAPTER 5

I wake with a throbbing white wine headache. I tumble out of bed, take a shower, turn off my phone, swallow some paracetamol and settle down at my desk to write.

When my stomach grumbles a few hours later, I save my work. I make an omelette for lunch, sit at the dining table to eat it and switch my phone back on. It pings frenetically, my notifications going crazy.

Nisha has sent me a link for a tabloid news story with the message:

'READ IMMEDIATELY!!!'

I click on it.

Headline: TOM DARLINGTON DATING OLDER AUTHOR! SALLY SPECK IS ONE HECK OF A LUCKY LADY.

I scroll down the page. There are photos of us eating together, with his hand pressed into my lower back while ushering me through the door of the restaurant, hand on my knee in the back of the car when we arrived, looking lovingly at me while I – rather unflatteringly – am helped into the back seat of the car by Ashraf.

The article reads:

Tom Darlington (22), of Swoon boyband fame and now a prominent actor has been spotted getting cosy with science fiction author Sally Speck. The thirty-six-year-old writer of *The Deviants* is an odd choice for the star, who is usually seen out with supermodels. His ex, Camille Charity (20), is a Victoria's Secret model.

I tap out a message to Nisha:

'WTF!!! My bit of fun has blown up into us full-on dating??!!'

I slowly work my way through messages from my sister and friends, all asking about my new boyfriend, how long it's been going on for, and when I'm going to introduce them.

Nisha replies:

'OMGGGG check out TDs insta!'

I open the photo-sharing app and search for the actor. He has one hundred and twelve million followers and his latest post is a sultry black-and-white shot. I choke when I realise it's a photo of the two of us in bed, our heads on the same pillow. I'm fast asleep. How dare he take a photo of me while I was sleeping. That is seriously *not cool*.

What other photos did he take? I gulp down the bile that rises from my stomach. He definitely didn't take any while we were doing the deed – I know that for certain – but did he take some of me naked? He could've easily pulled down the duvet while I was dead to the world, I would've been none the wiser. Why not ask me or tell me? What else has he done without me knowing? My skin crawls with the violation.

My face is scrunched up in the photo but it's clear it's me. Tom looks airbrushed. The caption reads:

'Think I just met the love of my life...'

The post has three million likes and fifty-four thousand comments. I open the comments. I blurt out loud, "For fuck's sake!" then cup my gaping mouth with my hand.

I'm used to the odd nasty review on my books but this is off the charts. His fans are vitriolic. They attack my appearance:

'She looks like a horse'
'Her arms flabby big time'
'Couldn't she wear summin that hid that belly'

They attack my novels:

'Pile of dog turd, my two-year-old writes better'
'Slag must've slept her way thru Hollywood to get that made into movie'
'I DNF dusk. soooooo bad. 0 stars, and that's being generous!'

And they are incredulous that Tom would date such a non-person:

'Camille and Tom for ever!'
'We gotcha back, Cami, this hoe gotta go'
'Who even is this ugly cow?'

The doorbell rings and I jump. I open it and am immediately thankful I decided to get dressed this morning in joggers and a hoodie and am not in my usual pjs and slippers.

Cameras click, flashes flare and photographers jostle outside my doorway. They holler questions and stick their cameras into my flat to take photos.

"How long have you been together?"

"Where did you meet?"

"Was it love at first sight?"

"Is he here now?"

I shut the door in their faces, stunned. My phone rings, a withheld number.

"Hello?"

"Sally Speck? I'm a reporter. Tell us more about Tom

Darlington…"

I hang up. Another call, and then another. I put my phone on silent and message Nisha.

An hour later, I watch through the door's peephole as Nisha pushes Sahil's pram through the sea of media, shouting "Coming through! Lady with a baby!" and hauls the pram onto the first step. Sahil is fast asleep, peaceful amongst this storm.

The sea parts for her and one photographer even does the decent thing and helps her carry the pram up the stairs. Nisha goes to press the doorbell, but I open the door before her finger connects, and hide behind it. Flashes and shouts start up again. Everyone calling my name.

I shut the door behind Nisha and hug her tight.

"Flipping heck!" she exclaims.

We go through to the lounge and sit, Nisha angling the pram so she can see Sahil's face.

"Thank you for coming over, Nish. It's gone insane! I don't know what to do. It was a one-night stand, that's all. What's with the Instagram post?"

"Have you tried calling him? Tell him to take it down or something?"

"I don't have his number. I gave him mine but I didn't take his. I have no intention of seeing him again. He's an arrogant, egotistical arsehole. Everything you'd expect."

"Oh, right."

"I'm debating whether to post something, set everyone straight. Or maybe speak to a newspaper. Tell them we are not and never have been, a couple."

"Listen to me, darling, whatever you do, do not respond. Stay silent, honestly, it's way more dignified. Those Twitter spats between celebrity exes are just mortifying and cause more trouble in the long run. Rise above it. If you talk, or comment, or Tweet it starts a conversation and suddenly you are public property. As your agent, as your friend, I'm advising you to keep it private. Don't air your dirty laundry in public, as they say."

"You're right." I've always valued my anonymity. Much to my publisher's annoyance, I refuse to have my photo on my book covers.

"Plus, every woman needs an air of mystery about her. I'm sure it will blow over in a couple of days. Just think what this will do to your book sales. They'll go through the roof."

"I guess…"

Yells from the pavement catch Nisha's attention and she stands and goes to the window. She pulls back the curtain to look and gestures for me to join her. I peek out the other side.

The media scrum has swelled and there's a scuffle between two photographers, jostling to get prime position. Someone notices us, shouts and points at the window and we drop the curtains in unison to stare at each other.

"What the fuck…" I say.

"Don't swear in front of the baby," Nisha replies automatically, but she's not really telling me off. She's as shocked as I am.

"Sorry." We move away from the window. "Do you want a drink? Wine?"

Nisha returns to the sofa, slips off her shoes and curls her legs up under her. "It's three in the afternoon. Oh, why not, I'm on mat leave and you're the most interesting person in the world right now."

In the kitchen, I fetch two glasses and a bottle of red. As I return to the lounge, Nisha's phone rings.

"Yes I'm her literary agent and no, I don't have any comment, and never will have any comment. Don't call this number again!" Nisha jabs the red phone icon and stares up at me. "They're digging deep on you, darling, you'd better call your parents and sister and warn them."

I bash out a message on the Whatsapp family group.

Nisha switches into action mode. "Right, I'll keep an eye on the media websites and Tom's social channels. I think you should check your social media, there's bound to be posts, comments and threads."

"Yep." I get on it.

I open Facebook and I get the spinning wheel for what feels like forever. I swig some wine and stare into space for a moment and then look back. My profile page finally loads with three hundred and forty-two friend requests.

"Wow. A lot of total strangers want to be my friend all of a sudden on FB. Thank goodness my personal page is private."

"Yes, and now I think it's a good thing you didn't have a professional channel."

I refused to open an author Facebook page when Nisha first took me on, despite her insistence. I hate people knowing my business. As a compromise, I did open an Instagram and Twitter author profile, which I barely ever use.

I open Twitter first and gulp as the notifications load. My follower count has quadrupled overnight and my profile has been bombarded by tweets. People at-ing me just to abuse me. I scan through a few and then temporarily deactivate the account. I'll reactivate it when this has all calmed down.

I switch to Instagram and it's the same story. Hundreds of new comments on the few photos I've posted. I change the settings to private and go about deleting all the abusive comments, working my way through blocking the trolls so that when I put it public again, they can't hassle me anymore.

The invasion of my online space rankles. But I know I'm in control and feel better about deactivating, deleting and blocking. I could easily get sucked into reading all the abuse, but I'm feeling strong with Nisha here.

"Jeez, he's posted more photos on Insta," Nisha says.

"Seriously?" I still can't process what's happening. This thing… issue?… is mushrooming out of control.

"There's six."

I look at Tom's profile. More photos of the two of us in bed. Me asleep, unaware of the photo being taken. In one, I'm on his chest, my sloppy breasts just covered by my duvet but one bulges out the side. I groan, I'm mortified.

My face is out of shot, but there's Tom, smiling wide in an apparent state of bliss. The caption reads:

'My favourite place to be… missing my SS.'

Nisha jumps up and grabs my phone. "Don't read the comments."

"Nish?"

"It's just silly little girls being bitchy. They're jealous. Don't read them. Promise me?"

I nod, knowing full well I'll read them later. My online space I can control, but I have no control over Tom's. Nisha taps on my phone to get out of the app and hands it back. Before I take it from her, it rings.

She looks at the screen. "A mobile number."

"Media?"

"Probably."

"Can you answer it?"

Nisha puts it to her ear. "Hello, who's this?" She looks up at me. "Tom, right." She puts the phone against her chest to muffle the sound and gestures at me to see if I want her to handle it, but I'm angry and take the phone.

"Tom! What the hell are you doing? It's all gone mental. You took photos of me while I was sleeping without me knowing. And then you posted them online. That's a really shitty thing to do. Take them down RIGHT now!"

"Calm down, beautiful, what's happened? Why are you mad? I'm sorry about all the media shenanigans, just ignore it. You'll get used to it. Those photos are exquisite. I've been thinking about you all day. We'll hit up Gucci and get you some new frocks and a jacket – screw it, a whole new wardrobe! – then we'll go for dinner and come back to mine. I want to show you my insane view of London."

"No, Tom. I told you, I'm not seeing you again. We're not a couple. We had a bit of fun, that's it."

"Oh, Sally, come on. I knew I should've checked with you about taking those pics. You just looked so incredible in the moment and I couldn't bear to wake you up. I'm sorry, forgive me? But I want the world to know, I'm devilishly into you. Don't you feel the same? I'm convinced you do."

"It was sex, that's all. You wanted to convince me to put you forward for Xander, and I will. So this… this can all stop."

He laughs. "Stop playing hard to get, you little hussy, you. I'll send a car to pick you up at eight. Wear whatever, we'll dispose of it at the shop and head for dinner in some new threads."

His voice muffles as he shouts to someone else with him. "Bev, where can we go for dinner after Gucci? Will you book us a table. Oh, c'mon, they'll shut the entire restaurant if I ask them…"

"Tom!"

"Sorry, I'm all yours, beautiful."

"You're not listening to me. I'm not coming out tonight. I'm busy. Don't send a car."

"You're killing me! I'm flying to the US tomorrow for a few weeks. I *must* see you tonight. Anyway, gotta go, Bev's nagging at me. Wait… maybe you can come with me? All expenses paid of course. I don't know if I can stand to be apart from you for more than a few hours at the moment, let alone weeks. We'll discuss later."

"I am not coming out! Delete those photos!" I yell, but he's already rung off.

"He's persistent," Nisha says.

"Did you hear all that?"

"Yep. Loud and clear. What a wa—" she looks at the

baby, "plonker. But, the question is, did he hear anything you said?"

The reporters and photographers are still outside. I sit in my apartment with the curtains closed. I don't dare move or make a sound. The steady, never-ending murmur of voices clogs up my flat. The presence of people, all looking in my windows, all watching my door like hawks, is suffocating.

Nisha left at around five to go and feed Sahil and I sat down to write, put in ear plugs, determined to bash out a chapter or two. But the noise in my mind was deafening and I couldn't concentrate.

So, I paced the lounge like a caged animal. Scared to go out my own front door. I spoke to Mum, then spoke to Nisha to make sure she got home ok.

And now I'm sitting staring vacantly into space. Why did I let myself be seduced by Tom at the awards ceremony? Why am I so weak? I should've known what drama it would cause. Should've known it wouldn't end well. Stupid woman to be flattered by his interest, to allow it to swell my confidence and make me think I could hang out at that club, fit in, be down with the kids. Fool.

I feel trapped.

My phone is on silent, but it flashes on the table. It's Jake. He called me earlier too, but I've avoided talking to anyone but Nisha, my mum and my sister. Why? I'm not entirely sure. Friends' messages all ask me about Tom. Tom, Tom, Tom. Friends who I've not spoken to in months are suddenly crawling out of the woodwork to ask about Tom.

But Jake is a close friend. I've known him since uni.

"Hey," I answer.

"Well, there she is! My little celebrity WAG!" Jake exclaims in a singsong voice.

"I'm no wag. It was a brief fling, we're not a couple."

"Whaaaaat? Don't lie to me, girlfriend! The papers all

say you two are a smoking hot item."

"Don't believe everything you read in the papers, you know that. He's an arsehole. It's done."

"Noooooo, I don't believe you. You do know Sammy from Swoon is gay, don't you? I want you to get Tom to hook us up."

"Ha. Seriously though, I'm not seeing that dickhead again."

"Babe, listen to me. He might be a dickhead but he's a rich, drop dead gorgeous, famous, influential dickhead. And he's really into you, have you *seen* his Instagram?"

"Yes! And he took those photos without my consent."

"Hmmm… but that's kinda romantic don't you think? The captions are like love poems."

"It's all in his head. He's not really all that into me."

"What are you talking about? Why would he say that he's into you when he isn't? You need to give this guy a chance. And if you don't like him… well, use him to your advantage – and use him to *my* advantage too." Jake laughs.

He's not getting it. "Jake, I won't be seeing Tom Darlington again."

"Yeah, you will."

I snap. "He might be a celebrity but he was an arsehole, ok? He might say he's into me, but he treated me like crap. We're not suited."

Jake sighs. "Are you just beating up on yourself again?"

I chew my lip.

"Thinking that you're unlovable and unattractive and that any man who wants to be with you is deluded and lying?"

There it is. He cuts straight to the core. "No."

"I've known you for what? Fifteen years? And you do this a lot. You have men who love you to pieces, who will literally bend over backwards for you. And what do you do? You push them away because you don't think you're good enough. And you convince yourself that they're lying."

I sigh. "Jake, it's not that this time. This is different. This guy… is weird."

"Mmm hmmm."

I hear the disbelief loud and clear.

"And besides, why would a hot, twenty-odd-year-old celeb want anything to do with me? I'm nearly fifteen years older than him, for goodness sake."

I know what he's going to say. And I know I'm not.

"Because you're one hot bi-atch! You are a catch. An award-winning author, no less. And some guys like older women. And you've still got great legs."

"That's true. Anyhoo, how are you?"

"Don't change the subject. I want to hear you tell me that you're seeing him again!"

"Honestly, Jakey, drop it."

"Sal… don't let your insecurities about men screw this one up."

He's like a dog with a bone and I've had enough. "I've gotta go, I'll speak to you soon." And before he can reply, I say, "bye" and hang up.

I feel bad, but Jake's just not getting it. There's something not right with Tom.

To make myself feel worse, for the umpteenth time that day I google myself.

The media has decided I am the most important news story in the world and are voracious in their appetite for information. They've dug up old university photos of when I won a creative writing award. Rerun old work-related photos and given a breakdown of what books I have out and what reviewers and critics have said about them. They claim to have dug up 'close friends' to talk about my 'relationship with Tom'. It's all made up. There are pictures of my apartment building and random personal shots of me, no doubt scoured from Facebook, from friends' who have tagged me with no privacy settings. It's intrusive. But I can't hide.

Tom's fans have decided I am the most hated person in the world and are poisonous in their derision of me. Although I promised Nisha not to look, I can't help it.

All these people I've never met have an opinion of me. Pump vicious words into Facebook, Twitter, Instagram, YouTube, celebrity gossip blogs. I'm a nice person. I don't deserve to be hated on like this.

Weirdly I'm furious with myself for not being able to shut it all out and continue writing. Writing is my life and I love it. I've never had writer's block; the words have always flowed. Until now. It's because I feel like I've just walked around a busy high street completely naked. Exposed for everyone to pick at every flaw.

I check Instagram and Tom still hasn't deleted those photos of me. Every time I see them, my stomach springs up my chest. The intrusion is infuriating.

I'm sure there's some way to complain about a post. I dig around online and find I can report it. I do just that and then wait. Nothing happens. I go and make a peppermint tea, come back to the sofa and look again. Photos are still there. Chill, Sal. It'll take a while for the bots to check, then it'll be deleted. But a little niggle in my head says: 'It's a celebrity with zillions of followers, are they really going to delete any of their posts?'

I turn on Netflix and put on the first movie that I see. I attempt to zone out like a zombie, but I'm clock-watching and on edge waiting to see if Tom actually listens to me.

He didn't. Surprise, surprise.

The car Tom sent to pick me up at eight has been sitting outside now for three hours. The driver has come to the door six times and I haven't opened it.

Tom has called and messaged, telling me to: 'Get in the car, beautiful. I'm waiting for you', but I ignore him.

I lie on my sofa in the dark.

Hopefully if I stay very quiet, the reporters, the photographers and Tom's driver will all just go away.

Cheers and woops and the sound of a car pulling up, the engine idling. I creep to the window and peer out. A black Range Rover is double parked with the car that was sent for me. Out spills four, huge bodyguards.

The reporters go wild, launching themselves against the car hollering question after question. The bodyguards clear a space and open the back door. Out steps Tom Darlington, in dark sunglasses, although it's evening. His hood is up and covers half his face. He's carrying a bulging paper bag, stuffed full of something I can't see.

The photographers surge forward – click, click, click – bellowing his name.

He ignores them and saunters towards the pavement, the bodyguards sweeping a path for him. He jogs up the stairs to my door. The burly men hold back the crowd, so it's only Tom on the steps.

I tiptoe to my front door and squint through the peephole. Tom stops halfway up the stairway, turns to the crowd, waves, and then hops up the last two steps.

He presses his eye to the outside of the peephole and I propel back as if stung. But then I bring my face forward again. He talks to the door, to me.

"Hey, it's only me. Let me in please. Come on, beautiful, don't leave me standing out here in the cold. Let me in. I've been waiting hours for you. I thought you were being a tease, keeping me on my toes, but then you never came. So, I've come here, to collect you. I know the media are a hassle, but you just have to pretend they're not there and get on with life. Ok, listen, if you don't want to go shopping, that's not a problem. Just let me in and we can chill. Come on, beautiful."

He sounds so pitiful, so wretched that I reach for the lock. My heart yearns to look after this distressed human, berating my brain for being so cruel as to leave him out there. As if I've spotted a kitten in trouble in the gutter and walked right past.

But then I stop myself, my fingertips resting on the

latch, and my brain kicks in. No, I do not want him in my apartment again. Ever.

But what if Jake is right? That I'm pushing away someone who genuinely fancies me? I did that with Mike. I did that with Kahlil. Did I imagine Tom's rudeness at the restaurant? Was I just overreacting at the club?

I waver.

He holds the bag up and open to the peephole, pulls my faux fur jacket part the way out.

"I'm sorry about your coat. I got Bev to send someone to pick it up, I know that's why you're mad at me. I should've made Ashraf turn around last night to get it. We were having so much fun at the club, you're an animal, nipping at my tongue like that. Grrrr. And then you turned cold in the car. And it's because of the coat. Let me in and you can have it back."

My heart hardens. Yes, I want my coat back. No, I won't let him in. If he thinks that's what made me mad last night then he truly has no appreciation of me, my feelings, my body language. Nothing. Him leaving me alone in that booth, sloshing his saliva over my face and rubbing my hand on his penis. In front of everyone. That's what pissed me off. The embarrassment of it all.

I count to one hundred. Slowly.

Tom grows tired of waiting and his expression contorts; his eyes harden and he grits his teeth in a snarl. He thumps the door forcefully. A second passes and he rearranges his face, settling it into a million-dollar smile once again.

He turns and bounces down two steps and announces to the horde on the pavement, with a carefree shrug, "I guess she's not in!"

He poses for selfies, scrawls autographs and banters with the media. He gets back in the Range Rover and Ashraf drives off. The photographers rush off on mopeds and in cars after him. The reporters drift away. They know it's unlikely Tom will make a second appearance.

I crawl into bed and look at my phone. Numerous missed calls and messages from Tom.

I resist the urge to read them and instead tap one out to him:

'Leave me alone. I do not want to speak to you, to see you, to hear from you. Do not contact me again.'

My pulse is hammering. I breathe in for four counts, out for four. But it doesn't do much. I know it's going to take hours for my heartbeat to return to normal.

But I'm happy with myself. Happy I didn't let him in. Happy I'll never see him again.

# CHAPTER 6

In amongst all the nonsense, Tom actually said something sensible to me.

His words ring in my ears as I wake the following day. I'm going to get on with my life and pretend the media isn't there. The actor has got the message now – there was no misunderstanding my text last night. Give it a few days and all this will be forgotten.

I take a shower, and decide I'm going to cook myself a slap-up Saturday morning breakfast as a treat. I head to my local supermarket. Not the one closest to me, but a few roads along for a bigger selection. The pavement outside is blissfully quiet and still. No reporters. No photographers. I put my earbuds in, play an audiobook on my phone and enjoy the walk.

The supermarket is empty and I pick up eggs, bacon, sausages, tomatoes, bread and mushrooms. As well as a few other bits. I pay and stuff everything into the two bags that I brought and curse myself for getting too much, as I know my arms will ache by the time I arrive home.

The double doors slide back and I walk from the relative calm of the store into…

Chaos.

Photographers and reporters everywhere, shouting my name. They rush me, crowding around so that I can't retreat back into the store. Cameras are shoved in my face and phones lifted to film me. I attempt to raise my hands to hide my face but the bags are too heavy and cumbersome. Someone knocks into me and my loaf of bread falls out and is trampled under feet.

How did they know I was here? Did one of the staff members tell the media? The guy who served me was totally disinterested and didn't really even look at my face. And there were hardly any shoppers in there to notice me.

I try to push my way through the crowd, but get jostled. My breath hitches and I shout for people to move. They don't. The bags feel heavy in my hands and my legs wobble. I fight to get past, but don't get anywhere.

And then I understand. Parked at the kerb are two black Range Rovers. The door opens and out steps Tom Darlington.

How the hell did he know I was here?

The crowd's attention shifts to him. His bodyguards clear a path to me and he sashays down it, waving and grinning as if he's on a runway.

"Hello, beautiful," he says as he reaches me and then leans in to kiss my cheek.

I'm so stunned that I don't move away. He cups my neck and takes a bag from my hand. I resist and won't let go of the handle. I glare at him.

"Allow me, beautiful." He turns to the crowd and announces, "This incredible woman is making me breakfast. What a lucky man I am."

The reporters react, laughing, swooning and edging nearer. The horde closes in and the bodyguards fight to keep them back.

"Let's go," one shouts and yanks my other shopping bag from my hand and hustles me protectively toward the car. I lose my grip on the first shopping bag as Tom whisks it out of my hand.

I stumble after Tom, caught in the flow of proceedings and following my shopping, and step into the car. The second bag is shoved at my feet and the door closes.

My breath comes so quick that in the cocoon of the car

it thumps in my ears.

Ashraf screeches away like he's in a movie car chase, followed by the second car carrying the bodyguards.

"Always crazy," Tom exclaims. "You'd think I'd get used to it by now. But no. How are you, my sexy Sally? I've missed you."

"Ashraf, please take me home immediately!"

"That's where we're heading, beautiful," Tom answers on his driver's behalf. "I'm meant to be flying, but I just couldn't leave without seeing you."

He reaches a hand across to place on my knee but I slap it away. "I told you to leave me alone! How did you know where I was?"

"I saved you from that rabble. Where's my appreciative hug, hmm?" He leans in and I block him with my forearm.

"Get away from me!"

Tom holds his hands up in surrender. "Ok, ok. I don't want to get in a fight. You're so… vulnerable. It's endearing…" His eyes glaze over and he leans in again.

"Tell me how you knew!" I demand and he snaps to attention.

"I put a tracking app on your phone that first night. It's safer if I know where you are. If my team knows where you are. They're professionals. It gets crazy, as you just saw, and I don't want any harm to come to you. You're precious to me and while I'm away you'll be looked after."

"You *what*?"

Ashraf says, "We're here." He pulls up outside my apartment.

The moment the car slows I open the door. I grab my shopping bags and run for my apartment. At the top of the stairs, I fumble in my bag for my keys and Tom catches up to me.

"Where's my goodbye kiss?"

Before I can respond, Bev is between us. "Tom, we have to go *now*. I can't delay the plane any longer. This tip-off has taken too long. Let's go."

"Bye, beautiful." Tom blows me a kiss and allows his assistant to guide him back to the car.

Bev turns back to me gesturing to the second car with the bodyguards in. "Errol and Ollie will be back in an hour after dropping Tom off."

I let myself into my flat, slam the door and slide down it to sit on the floor. Tip-off? Did someone recognise me and call the media? Or was that whole charade outside the supermarket staged by Tom to manipulate me into getting in his car? He knew I'd never open my door to him after last night.

I pull my phone out of my bag and find the GPS tracking app in a folder I rarely look in. I delete it.

Did he guess my passcode? Or watch me tap it in? How dare he think he could keep track of me. He told me about it, so perhaps he thinks it was an innocent thing to do. Maybe that's the done thing when dating celebrities? Perhaps another woman would think that sweet. But I'm NOT dating this guy. And it's not sweet. This guy is seriously creeping me out and I need to get away from him.

I hastily pack a suitcase, dashing around my flat so frantically that I bump into walls, door frames and furniture edges. I have to get out of London. I have an hour before the bodyguards return. Bodyguards who I know will shadow me even if I tell them to go away and report my every move back to Tom. That's their orders.

I book a taxi and hover by the front door, willing it to hurry up. When the app shows it turning into my street, I leave the apartment.

But the photographers are back, finally catching up after being left at the supermarket. Hearing my door unlock and seeing it open, they stumble forward, haul cameras up to faces and run in front of me as I drag my suitcase down the stairs and onto the pavement. My taxi pulls up and I wave at the driver to pop the boot for my suitcase. I get in the back and he stares at me, trying to work out if he recognises me.

"Waterloo train station, please," I say.

He drives off.

He glances in his mirror at me, and when he can't contain it any longer, says, "You famous, love?"

"No." I look at my phone, conversation closed.

"Well, it's just that we're being followed by photographers on mopeds."

I look out the back window. Mopeds and motorbikes follow. Each with a driver, and a photographer riding pillion, camera up to face.

We stop at traffic lights, the mopeds weave in and out of the cars to pull up beside us. I hold my hand up to hide my face and slouch down the seat.

At Waterloo I head straight into the first shop I see. M&S. The photographers try to follow, but the guard at the door stops them. They hustle and wriggle to take photos of me through the windows. I can't just hang around in the shop, so I pick up a sandwich, some crisps and a drink and take it to the counter. In the queue I scan the magazine rack.

I stifle a gasp as my face screams back from every Saturday tabloid newspaper. Tom's visit to my apartment last night is critical front-page news apparently. Surely there's more important things going on in the world.

The woman serving eyes me, trying to place me, but decides not to say anything other than to ask if I want a bag. My hair is tied back in a low plait, I have a beanie hat on and zero make-up. I don't look in the slightest bit famous but I have a paparazzi tail.

I hurry to buy a ticket from a machine on the concourse and glance up at the screens. The photographers circle me like hunting dogs but I try to be as boring as possible, doing exactly the same as every other person who is stood waiting for their train.

A man invades my personal space, gets right in my face.

"Is your relationship with Tom over?" He thrusts a handheld recorder at my mouth and I know he's a reporter of some kind.

I want to scream, "Get that thing away from me!" and it takes all my will to ignore him, like the 'straight-face' game I used to play with my sister when we were children, trying to make the other laugh. I hold my face in complete stillness and stare up at the screens. Busy travellers are no longer watching the screens, they watch the guy hassling me. My ears burn and I set my jaw as a flurry of questions pour from his mouth.

I look at my watch and dash to the toilets. He follows me, as do the paps, but who wants a shot of author Sally Speck using the toilets at Waterloo? Seemingly, no one, and they back off. In the cubicle I let out a silent scream, whisper "arseholes", regain my composure with a few deep breaths and leave.

They are waiting for me. The platform for my train has been called and I fast-walk to it, put my ticket in the gate, and jump on the train. They don't follow. I find a seat and put my head in my hands, utterly exhausted.

I come to with a jolt at Basingstoke as an older lady nudges me accidentally while attempting to lift her small suitcase onto the overhead rack. I blink away the sleep and stand to help her. She thanks me and we both sit.

I pick up my phone and google my name. I can't let myself get obsessed with reading what people are saying about me. I know it's not healthy. An old photo from my recruitment days has been dug up and used in a few articles. I let out a groan and the lady shifts in her seat.

I switch to social media. Tom has posted another two photos of us in bed together and selfies of him looking sad at the airport on his way to the US with cryptic captions about being lonely and 'missing his SS'. After the tip-off craziness, he has called incessantly and sent messages. I've ignored them all.

How many photos did he take of me while I was sleeping? I tap a few buttons to report these new ones and note that the others I reported are still up. If reporting doesn't work what will? I decide to do some online investigating. To get the police involved I'd need to be a minor, the photos would need to be obscene or some kind of revenge porn. It's none of those, and it's not defamation or character assassination. The photos are – for the most part – quite classy with captions that declare his love for me. So I probably wouldn't have a leg to stand on. The powerlessness curdles in my veins.

As I look at my phone, his name pops up. I stare at it. My phone is on silent. I put it face down on the table and stare out the window. If he leaves a voicemail, I won't listen to it. Definitely will not listen to it.

After a few minutes I look at my phone. He's left a voicemail. I listen to it.

"I'm about to take off, beautiful. I'll have my phone off. I just wanted you to know. I'm guessing you're busy. I understand. But I want you to know that I've really fallen for you. I'm desperate to have you in my arms again. You are all I think about. I see you've deleted that app. And that's fine and dandy. You're headstrong and I'm totally into that. But reinstall it, ok? It's for your own good, beautiful. And means I'll always be connected to you."

There's a pause and I hear a faint female voice. Bev, I suspect, telling him to hurry up.

"I gotta go… I… love you. There I said it. I *love* you." He makes kissing sounds and the voicemail ends.

I hang up the phone. I should delete it. But I don't.

A frustrated scream to shake the carriage off its tracks bubbles up but I clamp it behind gritted teeth and stare daggers silently out the window instead.

Tom will meet someone else in the US and move on. He has women throwing themselves at him constantly. I'm a passing fancy. I just need to lie low at the parents for a few days. Annoying, but doable. This is an irritating little blip that won't mean anything in a week's time, and will be completely forgotten soon enough. Then I can go back to being anonymous.

My sister Mel is waiting in her bashed-up car at the small Hampshire station as my train pulls in. She gets out and hugs me tight, rocking side to side. Mel once played rugby and I appreciate her firm grip. Makes me feel safe and secure.

"What a nightmare," I mumble into Mel's shoulder, the wind blowing her long, poker-straight brown hair in my face.

"We'll deal with it, little sis."

"I'm so relieved to be out of London."

Mel puts my suitcase in the boot and we head to our parents' bungalow, fifteen minutes away.

"How's Mum?" I ask.

"Well, there's a nasty article about you. It's all lies, but you know she loves her newspaper, so it's got to her a bit. She feels cheated, like an old friend has turned on her."

"The media distorts the truth and invades people's privacy. It shouldn't be allowed."

"It shouldn't, but his fans are worse. Steve's Facebook was public and they covered it with abusive comments. It's totally unnecessary, shocking, really. Don't these kids have anything better to do? I'm teaching my girls to have respect for others."

"I need to get a new phone. This one feels tainted."

"Oh, about that. I popped to the shops. Look in my bag."

I rummage in Mel's oversized mum handbag that's by my feet and pull out a new mobile phone.

She glances at me and then puts her eyes back on the road. "Your new number is on the box."

"Thanks, sis, I'll transfer you the money. I'm going to take what I need from my current phone, cancel the contract, turn it off and never look at it again."

"Are you going to bin it?"

"No, I'm going to keep it. Just in case. If Tom's put anything else on it, I doubt it'll work when it's switched off."

"The cheek of him doing that in the first place."

"He left me a voicemail earlier telling me he loves me."

"Loves you! He barely even knows you. What is this guy on?" Mel shakes her head angrily as she pulls into the driveway.

Mum opens the door as I drag in my suitcase. "Hello," she exclaims.

"Hey, Mum," I say and kiss her on the cheek.

"What a palaver. Here." She hands me a glass of red wine with a comforting smile.

Mel follows me into our childhood home.

"Wine? It's a bit early isn't it?" Mel says and closes the front door.

"It's almost midday. And I think Sal deserves it, don't you?" Mum says and embraces me.

"Definitely. I'm so pleased to be home. London was getting scary." I swig the wine gratefully.

"Well, the most exciting news from around these parts is that number forty-four has had a new driveway put in. And over-the-road's cat got run over, survived and now only has one eye."

"Seriously, one eye?" Mel says.

Mum ushers us through to the lounge. "Come on, let's go and sit down and I'll tell you all about it. Your father picked up some Cadbury's Fingers earlier."

"Wine and chocolate biscuits. I knew it was a good idea to come home," I say and immediately feel a weight lifted off my shoulders as the sanctuary of my childhood home envelops me.

# CHAPTER 7

Mum's cooking a slap-up roast for Sunday lunch. Wafts of roasting meat float up into my room.

I drag myself out of bed and throw on some clothes before heading downstairs.

"Morning!" Dad chirrups from the sofa.

"Ah, there she is. Good sleep?" Mum says.

"Yes. Haven't had a lie-in in ages," I say. And it's true. I'm usually up early to write. But not today. Writing has gone out the window since the awards ceremony last Wednesday. "Can I help?"

"No, the table's all set. I'm making your favourite for dessert."

"Apple crumble?"

"Mmm hmm."

"Yes." I punch the air.

I sit next to Dad and notice he's got his feet up on something. It's a pile of newspapers.

He notices me looking. "I popped down the shop earlier and cleared 'em out of Sunday papers. The shop assistant gave me a right funny look. Thought we could have a laugh at your ugly mug gracing the pages."

"Thanks a lot, Dad."

"A lovely mug!" Mum pipes up from the kitchen.

I gesture at the pile and Dad gives me the top paper and then picks one up for himself.

"Oh my," I splutter as I see my face splashed on the

front cover of the tabloid. I'm at Waterloo looking up at the platform screens. I read the caption out loud, "Author Sally Speck ponders life without Tom as the actor jets off to the US leaving her alone in London."

"Ponders life?" Dad says. He holds up a picture of me and Tom outside the supermarket. "This one says, 'Tom Darlington and new girlfriend Sally Speck spotted shopping together'."

"He ambushed me!"

Dad chuckles. "Doesn't quite have the same ring to it, does it?"

I fold the paper and pick up another. I'm the second news story. They've reprinted one of Tom's sad-looking selfies next to a photo of me getting on the train yesterday with the headline: WHILE TOM'S AWAY, SALLY HEADS OFF TO PLAY.

"Bloomin' ridiculous!" Mum says from over my shoulder. She flicks her tea towel at the paper. The gesture makes me laugh out loud.

"It's all so silly, isn't it?" I say.

We continue laughing at the photos, stupid stories and absurd captions until dinner is ready, and then throughout the meal. In typical Speck-family fashion, we decide that humour is the best way to get through this little blip – and go all out on the banter and teasing.

After, I feel much better. I'll head back to London on Tuesday. There's nothing more to say about me, about mine and Tom's 'relationship'.

He hasn't posted any more photos of me to his social media and instead there's pics of him sprawling in the sunshine in a LA swimming pool on a swan inflatable. Another close up where he's in sunglasses and holding a coconut with straw and umbrella.

He's already forgotten all about me. That took a whole weekend. But it's finally over. He's grown bored with his sham adoration and moved on. The media will find a new story to sensationalise and rinse dry.

The dust settles. It always does.

"Next on, The Trevon Williams Show," the TV announces the following evening. I'm curled up on the sofa, full from dinner.

A weight has been lifted off my shoulders, relief to have escaped from overbearing London. I'm always happy with my family. They are safe. They are known. Nothing can happen within my tight family unit. The normality is a balm.

Nisha messaged earlier to say that Tom was on a US chat show that airs here tonight. We'd taken a family decision to watch it when Mel had arrived with her family. If she can't come over for one of Mum's Sunday lunches, she always comes on the Monday instead for dinner, usually a chicken curry with the leftovers.

I don't feel anxious. Not with my family around me. I'm ready to laugh at the fool.

Mel sits on the floor playing with her youngest daughter, five-year-old Ellie. Steve, Mel's husband, sits at the table with Bethany, the eldest at eight. He's tired after a long day at work as an accountant and half-heartedly helps his daughter with a jigsaw.

"Right, let's see what this plonker has to say then," Dad says.

He puts his Screwfix catalogue on the coffee table and picks up a glass of port and a plate of cheese and biscuits, which he balances on his belly. Apart from that belly, Dad still looks pretty trim. His six-foot frame, bald head and ex-builder's brawn keeping him looking strong and spritely.

Mum pats my knee. "I'm sure he'll be talking about his movies and that's all. Keep reading that he's got one coming out. That's probably what this whole charade is about, Sal, publicity and such like."

"That's if the idiot can even string a sentence together," Dad replies.

I remain silent. I have no idea what might come out the actor's mouth. His presence on screen makes my insides all confused. He looks polished and handsome. A proper English gentleman. But I know he's an arrogant, inconsiderate prat. I scratch my face as if some of his saliva still lingers there.

The interview begins normally. The host asks about Tom's latest movie and he charmingly tells a funny anecdote about a filming mishap. There's some banter with the studio audience. Steve even chuckles.

But then it takes a turn for the worse.

"So, I hear you're in love?"

Everything goes very quiet in the lounge. Even the girls hush, sensing something momentous is about to happen by the way the adults are all frozen, gawping at the television.

On screen, Tom's face lights up. "Oh, Trevon. I'm in a relationship with the most incredible, funny, intelligent, creative woman. We are just perfect for each other. I knew from the moment I set eyes on her that she was for me."

"That's great news, Tom."

"It is. But… well… can I say something?"

"Yes, go ahead."

Tom turns from Trevon and looks at his hands. The camera zooms in on him. His entire face melts into one of bliss. He does something with his eyes to make them go all big and gooey that actually makes him look lovestruck.

"Sally, I love you. I want the world to know that I'm yours and you're mine. I'll see you soon, beautiful," Tom announces.

Dad leaps to his feet and shakes his fists at the telly, his plate of food tips over Mel who shouts, "Ow! Dad!"

"Oh my," Mum utters and brings a hand to her mouth.

"What a bleeping bleep." Steve thumps his fist on the table and the jigsaw pieces bounce.

"Mummy! Daddy's swearing. He said bleep but that means it's a swear word," Bethany says.

"Shit," I say.

Ellie points at me from the floor. "Aunty Sally's swearing too," she declares.

"Ummmm, that's naughty," Bethany says.

On the telly, Trevon stands and Tom does too. The host shakes Tom's hand. "Sally, if you're watching, we're all rooting for you and Tom. He's a great guy and he deserves a great gal." He grins at Tom, pats his back and says, "See you after the break, when we speak to—"

Mel switches off the telly. All the adults look at me. I sink deeper into the sofa. What do they want me to do? Nip across the pond and tell Tom off? There's something not right with him. He thinks we're a couple when we're not. I told them that already. His behaviour is freaky. He won't take no for an answer, doesn't seem to understand it.

"I'm going for a bath." I stand abruptly, in a trance, and walk through to the bathroom, sit on the bathtub. I can still hear my family.

"What is wrong with the lad?" Dad says.

"Not so loud, Graham, Sal wants some quiet," Mum says.

"I want to give him a thump, Janice."

"I know, we all do."

"She won't be able to go back to London for a while," Mel adds.

Steve's voice, "It's all kicking off on Twitter – there's celebrities getting involved and all sorts. Wishing the happy couple joy and blessings. Saying that the age gap doesn't matter, that Tom deserves the best. And there's a Facebook page been set up already, called Sally, Darlington's Darling."

I turn on the tap, the gush drowning out the world. I imagine it drowning out Tom Darlington's ridiculous words. I picture holding his insane head under and the water filling up that handsome mouth.

My phone lights up with a text. Jake.

'Wow, that boy has got it bad for youuuu! Do you believe that he's into you now? You can't not after that Oscar-worthy performance – he declares his undying love for you on a massive TV chat show no less. Are you going to give him a second chance? I reckon you should. He looked sooooo loved up.'

I reply.

'You don't think that was weird?'
'Sweet, not weird.'
'I'm telling you. He's deluded.'
'No, Sal, YOU are deluded. That man is SO in love with you – and you're doing your usual. There's only so much chasing a man can do before he gives up, you know.'

I chuck my phone on my discarded clothes where I can't reach it and submerge my head under the water. Does everyone think that? Think that I'm playing hard to get? That I'm denying myself a chance at happiness by denying Tom Darlington? Does no one else think his behaviour is downright strange?

No. My parents believe me. And my sister, and Steve. They've got my back. They will always have my back.

Tom's performance-of-a-lifetime has brought the parasites to my door. Except this time, the pests are at my parents' door. In the back-end of the county of Hampshire. It's scary how they found out the address so quickly – literally overnight – and how out of sorts I feel that my sanctuary, my sacred safe place, has been discovered.

The bloodsucking media are sitting outside in cars that clog up the road. I eye them out the window of my road-facing attic bedroom. The kerfuffle outside woke me up at 6am and no amount of chanting 'ignore the media, pretend they're not there' helped.

The shrill ringing of the landline echoes through the still sleeping bungalow. Dad grumbles and I hear him stomp to the phone in the hallway downstairs.

"Hello," he says.

A few moments later he slams down the phone.

"Who was that, dear?" Mum says from their downstairs bedroom.

"Some numpty offering a ridiculous sum for a tell-all interview with Sally."

The phone rings again. Dad slams it down a second and third time. "I'm unplugging it for now, lovey."

"I think that's a good idea," Mum says.

I put my dressing gown on and head downstairs. "Morning." I force a happy tone into my voice as I switch the kettle on. "Anyone want a hot drink?"

"I've just made us one," Dad replies.

I take my mug into the lounge and Mum hastily switches off the news.

"It's ok, Mum. I doubt I'll be on BBC Breakfast." I blow on my coffee.

"I know, but you do seem to be everywhere at the moment. That actor has really got everyone stirred up about you."

"It won't last." I'm determined to be positive. "Is it ok if I stay a bit longer?"

I'd planned to return to London today, but not with all the media outside.

"Stay as long as you like," Mum replies and I know she means it.

"Thank you. I'm heading into my little writing cave to finish my book and by the time it's done, the drama will all be over."

"I'm going to finish my crunchy nuts and then I'm going out there to tell all those parasites to bugger off," Dad says, spooning up his cereal. I smile at his use of the word 'parasites'. Just how I'd thought of the media earlier. Great minds… and all that.

"I don't think that's wise," Mum says, alarmed.

I back her up. It's not wise. "No, Dad, they'll get bored

and go soon enough."

"They're blocking the neighbours' driveways. You know how that old fart at number twenty-five gets all uppity about that."

"Dennis is perfectly pleasant to me," Mum says.

"If Dennis the old fart wants them to move, then let him ask them, Dad. Promise me you won't do anything. Promise?" I'm insistent. I envision some kind of incident with Dad emblazoned across the front pages tomorrow. I give him a serious look.

Dad waggles his head. "Promise."

"Right, I'm going to get to work." I take my drink back up to my bedroom, set up my laptop and notes and settle down, fingers splayed on the keyboard.

But I can't write. My focus wavers and I stare at the blank screen and that insistent flashing cursor. I'm not able to conjure up a sentence, let alone an entire book.

Instead I search for my name online and read article after article about my 'relationship' with Tom from 'friends of the couple'. My blood boils as the lies and 'eyewitness' accounts pile up.

I used to love reading celebrity gossip, lapped up the trashy mags and latest 'news' about who was dating who. But now I'm the one the media's fixated on and I've become a commodity, I realise just how invasive it is. I have no control over my public persona anymore. People can make up whatever they like about me, and because it's 'gossip' it doesn't get challenged. It scares and angers me.

The entire world has made me their business. And the enormity of that makes me feel miniscule. Like a mote of dust in the vast sky.

I glance at the clock. 11.15am! What a waste of the morning. It's useless. Writing is clearly not going to happen today. I switch off my laptop and settle on the bed to read a book. But the words jump about on the page and I read the same sentence over and over.

I put the book down and stare at the ceiling.

Tom. That's all I can think about. Might as well think it out of my system and then I'll be able to move on. Why is he acting this way? Why does he think he's in love with me? We have nothing in common, we knew each other a matter of days. Is he still hoping I'll help him get the part of Xander? Does he really think this pretence will aid his cause?

These questions circle in my mind until I'm actually sick of it. I turn on the small telly in my room, switch over to some mindless daytime show and look at it without seeing. Nothing goes in, it's background noise. I'm too busy in my own head.

The doorbell rings. I check my phone. Midday. I mute the telly and listen as Mum opens the front door, hear the familiar creak and swish from my childhood.

"Hi, are you Janice, Sally's mother? Can we speak with Sally?"

"No, you cannot, young man. Do not come to my door again, do you understand?" Mum says in her primary school teacher voice. She retired last year, but she still has that air of authority about her, even though she's five foot three. "I'm not at all happy with you loitering and harassing me on my own doorstep."

"I'm not harassing you—" But the journalist's voice cuts off as Mum closes the door in his face.

The doorbell rings again and Mum mutters, "For goodness sake." She opens it.

"Didn't I tell you… Oh, yes. Thank you. I guess you'd better leave it over there."

I strain to hear what's going on. After what feels like forever, the front door shuts.

Mum calls up the stairs, "Sally, for you."

I spring from my room and trot down the stairs to see Mum surrounded by bouquets of red roses. She's staring up at me wide-eyed and gestures to them.

"Who are they from, love?" Mum asks, excited as if I've received them from a new boyfriend.

"The delivery person didn't say?"

"No."

"Probably someone out there who wants to persuade me to sell my story," I say bitterly.

"There's thirty-six of them, apparently."

"Seriously? There has to be a card somewhere," I say and rifle through the bouquets nearest to me. The fragrance is so strong my head aches. Mum checks those nearest her.

"Here it is," she says and holds a card in an envelope in the air. I lean across the sea of petals to take it from her.

I sit on the bottom stair and discard the envelope. I open the card and read the contents. "Urgh."

Mum holds out her hand and I give her the card. She realises she doesn't have her reading glasses on, holds it at arm's length and squints. She reads out loud, "'I wish I was there with you. Sorry about the media hounding you. I can't wait to hold you again – my arms are lost without you in them. A beautiful bouquet to celebrate every beautiful year of your life. All my love, T.'" Mum hands the card back to me. "That's him?"

"Yeah." Thirty-six flipping bunches of flowers. From him.

"You're sure?"

"That's what he said to me before, 'my arms are lost without you in them.'"

"Well it's him that's doing the hounding, not just the media." Mum purses her lips. "What on earth are we going to do with all this lot? I'd better find some vases." She carefully steps over and between bouquets and walks back to the kitchen.

The letterbox in the front door flaps and I jump, my breath catching in my chest. The post is pushed through and tumbles to the doormat. I count to ten, to make sure the postman is well and truly gone and then scoop it up and take it through to the kitchen.

"Here's your post, Mum. Should we bin the flowers?

Send them back?"

"Well, it's not the flowers' fault that their sender is a twerp. We'll find homes for them all, can probably give some to friends, and maybe take a couple of bunches when we visit your Nana. They're very pretty, be a shame to bin them. When they're past their prime, Dad'll put them on the compost."

Mum sifts through the post as I pick up one of the vases she's found and fill it with water in the sink. I put it on the side and move to get the first bunch from the hallway but Mum hands me an envelope. "There's one here for you."

My mouth goes dry. A handwritten envelope. The postmark shows it was sent from London on Saturday.

"It might *not* be from him," Mum says hopefully.

No. It might not. But I bet it is.

I rip open the envelope, unfold three sheets of handwritten paper and turn to the bottom of the final page. Tut. Sigh. "It's from him."

Dad steps in from the garden. "What's all this?"

"It's a letter from the actor," Mum says. "And he sent a lot of roses."

"A love letter and flowers? The chap's smitten. Poor lad won't take the hint. But why did you give him this address, Sal?"

"I… didn't."

Mum and Dad exchange glances as I slouch onto the sofa. The letter weighs heavily in my hands. I know I shouldn't read it. Shouldn't poison my mind with more of his toxic words. He's all my mind is full of anyway. I don't need more of him hurtling around in there, blocking my imagination and focus.

And yet, a part of me has to know what it says. Plus, it's a handwritten letter. Who gets those anymore? Even if it's from a deranged singer slash model slash actor.

Dad must sense my internal struggle. "Well, are you going to read it? Or shall I put it through the shredder?"

I gape blankly at my parents. I can't make a decision.

Mum stands and taps Dad on the arm. "Let's give her a moment, Graham. I think that shredder is buried under a pile of your old magazines, let's see if we can dig it out."

Dad follows Mum into the small study.

I read the first paragraph:

> You are my entire world, sexy Sally. You are the only thing that keeps me breathing, keeps me living. When I'm in a dark place, you are my light. I yearn for you, your touch, your smile, your laugh, your lips. YOU. Everything about you is beauty, joy, radiance. I picture you and my entire body glows. An aura of white light surrounds me when I think of you.

I scan down the page, and then glance over the second and third. Much of the same crap. I stand and walk into the study.

Dad has the shredder on the desk and is demonstrating to Mum how it works. Her hands are on her hips, a bored expression on her face and I can tell she's had this lecture a few times before.

"Here." I give Dad the letter.

He feeds it into the shredder page by page. Good old Dad, never questions me.

"What did it say, dear?" Mum asks.

"Three pages of nonsense about how much he loves me and misses me. Blah, blah, blah."

Dad pats the shredder like a proud father. "Right you are, then. Well that nonsense is now in little pieces and you'll never have to read it again."

# CHAPTER 8

"Where is that darn paper boy?" Dad grumbles into his tea five days later. "He's always late on a Sunday."

We sit in the lounge. It's overflowing with past-their-prime cut flowers. There's been no more letters or roses. That wound has closed finally, thank goodness.

I've done nothing since I arrived last Saturday. A break, Mum says. A waste of time, I say. A waste of precious writing hours where I could be bringing a new story to life. Instead I've slept, allowed hours of my life to be sucked away by mindless daytime telly and binge-watching Netflix. A week where I've not left the house as the horde of photographers and reporters is STILL outside.

They've been watching and lethargically snapping pics of Mum and Dad coming and going. Pottering about as they always do: unloading the supermarket shopping, heading to the tip, going for lunch at a garden centre and invariably coming back with a plant or two, or taking books back to the library.

I'm suffocating. The bungalow is getting tight around me. Crushing my chest. It's been miserable all week, raining and damp so I've not even ventured into the garden for some fresh air. I miss my London flat, my London life. Yoga and drinks with Jakey or going to some literary event with Nisha.

Mum and Dad are the best. They've left me to it. Left me to wallow in my pyjamas. They don't demand anything of me.

But later today Mel, Steve and the kids are coming for a roast, so Mum has got me up, told me to shower, put some clothes on and given me the task of setting the table to prepare for their arrival. She's given Dad the job of 'staying out the way'.

I lay the table, and I make Dad a cup of tea. 'Staying out the way' generally means 'out the kitchen'. But I'm allowed in, of course.

We can hear Mum clattering pans, prepping the chicken and chopping vegetables.

The clunk of the letterbox and thump on the doormat announces the paperboy's arrival.

"Ah, talk of the devil." Dad goes to fetch the paper and brings it back into the lounge.

He arranges himself on the sofa and hands me the magazines. He opens the main paper. I quickly flick through the gossip section, avoiding any potential photos or mention of Tom Darlington – or me – and find the fashion pages.

"What the…" Dad's voice is strained, and he slowly lowers the paper.

"What is it, Dad?"

The colour drains from his face and he stares into space shaking his head.

"Mum," I call. "You'd better come here."

Mum wanders through from the kitchen wiping her hands on her apron. I point at Dad.

We squeeze next to him on the sofa and look at the open newspaper on his knees. He doesn't move, he continues to stare into space. His knuckles are white from the grip he has on the edges of the paper.

Mum puts a hand to her mouth and the other on Dad's shoulder.

Next to a picture of an angry-looking Dad unloading shopping bags from the car boot in the driveway, the headline of the newspaper blares: TOM

DARLINGTON'S LUCKY ESCAPE FROM BENT
SPECK FAMILY.
I read on:

> Actor Tom Darlington might be down in the dumps about
> the strains of his long-distance relationship with sci-fi author
> and older woman Sally Speck, but he's lucky he's not been
> found dead in the dump. Graham Speck was accused of a
> gruesome murder at age 26. He was acquitted in dubious
> circumstances when evidence that placed him at the scene of
> the crime was inexplicably 'lost' by police handling the case.

> Sally's stepfather, now sixty-two, was the prime suspect in
> the death of Spike Thomas, whose body was found
> dismembered in Jenkins Lane dump. Graham, thought to be
> part of Eastside Firm, the notorious gang who terrorised east
> London at the time, is related to a PC Robert Speck,
> suspected to have tampered with the evidence, although no
> charges were brought against him.

Mum grabs up the paper from Dad's clutch, smashes it
on the dining table, disturbing the cutlery, plates,
wineglasses and napkins I laid earlier and tears the full-
page story out. She rips it to pieces, throws these on the
floor and stamps on them. "How could the paper print
those lies?"

I stare open-mouthed at this vehement display from my
calm, even-tempered mother. She pants with the effort and
glares at the torn newspaper under her feet, fists bunched.

This is new to me. I know not to believe what the
papers say… but… "Dad was accused of murder?"

"It was a very long time ago, Sally. And not something
you or your sister needed to ever know about," Mum says
firmly. She thumps a fist on the table and the wineglasses
teeter precariously. "And not something you will ever
repeat again. It's not good for your father's heart to
remember that dreadful time."

Dad hasn't moved. His hands are still on his knees

clutching a newspaper that is no longer between his fingers.

Mum mouths "never" at me and pinches her fingers and drags them from one side of her lips to the other and then gestures as if to throw the key away. I stare at her.

Her voice goes as sweet as honey. "Would you like another tea, Graham love? I'll get you a tea."

I follow Mum into the kitchen.

"Why did you never tell me this?" I whisper.

"Because it doesn't matter." Mum slams down the kettle switch. "Your fling with this damn actor has dragged up all this dirt that was best left buried and forgotten. Your poor father. I've got a roast to get on, so get out of my kitchen."

I back away, my hands held up. "I'm so sorry. Shall I clear up the newspaper?" I ask gingerly.

"No. Just leave it. I'll do it."

I retreat to my bedroom, find my phone and read the article in its entirety.

My beloved stepfather, the only father I'd known, who I call Dad, had been accused of murder? Had once been part of a notorious London gang?

I can't process this information. My heart feels as if it's lodged in my throat and I notice my phone shaking. I put it down and look at my hands quivering.

A commotion. Mum and Dad are arguing, voices raised. I go down.

Dad is stood, mobile phone in one hand, the other holds back Mum who grabs at it frantically.

"We have to fight back. I want to set the record straight! I'm calling those bastards and telling them the truth."

"No, Graham, leave it be. It will only stir up more trouble," Mum pleads.

"Dad, it's better if you leave it. The media will just twist your words and then it'll become a bigger story," I insist, remembering Nisha's advice. "You don't want to air your dirty laundry in public, do you?"

Dad lowers the mobile, grumbles.

"The media have said all kinds of things about me which are completely false, but I've not spoken to them. Don't do it, Dad."

It takes a while, but Dad deflates.

Mum takes the phone from him and drops it in her apron pocket. "We're cancelling the paper and from now on no more trashy magazines for me or reading all that rubbish online. They are invading our privacy, but if we don't read what they are writing then it can't harm us, can it?"

Dad huffs his agreement.

"Sally? No more, agreed?"

"Agreed." Although I know I'm likely to break that promise.

"And don't you think any less of your father because of those lies, you hear me? He's a great man. He doesn't deserve anything less than respect and love, understand?"

I give Dad a hug. "I'm sorry this has happened. It's all my fault."

He looks miserable. It's heart-breaking. This bear of a man is usually such a jolly soul. He slumps on the sofa and switches on the telly to some old western movie.

"Ah, look, Sal, it's John Wayne," he says.

Mum heads back to the roast. I re-lay the table noisily. Taking out my anger by slamming the cutlery down. Not satisfied with trashing me, the media now lie about my loved ones too? It boils my blood that they've managed to upset Dad so much. Scumbags.

A few hours later, Bethany and Ellie bundle into the house as if it's the most exciting thing that's ever happened to them, ever. Mum has her hand on the door, Dad stands behind her and I'm to one side.

Dad gathers up his grandkids in an exaggerated hug. The stress from earlier lingers under the surface. The girls turn and hug Mum's knees.

"Grandma, Grandma! We went to Marwell Zoo yesterday and saw a giraffe," Bethany says.

I watch as Mel and Steve close up the car doors and follow their children in. The atmosphere in the house has been… strained. After setting the table for the second time, I watched the old Western movie with Dad, feeling the shockwaves through his forced laughter, until I heard Steve's Volvo pull into the driveway.

We greet each other with hugs and start moving towards the lounge but Mum says, "Graham, why don't you show the girls the tadpoles in the pond."

"Baby frogs!" Bethany claps her hand. Ellie grins.

"Come on then, tiddlers." Dad ushers them through to the back garden. Mum flicks up her hand briefly. It's enough. Mel, Steve and I don't move.

Mel folds her arms. "What's going on, Mum?"

Mum shakes her head and listens. When we can't hear Dad or the kids anymore and it's clear they are outside she gathers us to her in a circle.

Steve shifts awkwardly into position and thrusts his hands into his jeans pockets, looking at his feet. He's been part of the family since he and Mel started dating at eighteen after meeting at a rugby tournament, but he's still on the periphery of the core family unit.

"Your father's been in the paper," Mum says, looking at each of us in turn.

Steve glances up to catch her eye and then back at his feet. Mel openly stares.

I chew the insides of my cheek and fiddle with the dangling drawstrings of my joggers.

"They've dragged up some old nonsense from his past and I don't want any of you," she sweeps her finger around the three of us and back, "to mention it."

"What nonsense?" Mel says.

Mum purses her lips. "That is not important."

Mel frowns, insists. "What nonsense, Mum?"

Steve fidgets with his car keys.

"It says that he was accused of murder and was acquitted," I say to Mel.

Mum tuts at me.

"Well, she's going to find out! She just needs to look online," I retort. It's true. Mel is the nosiest person I know.

Steve blows out a puff of air that catches behind his lips and swells his cheeks, his eyes wide.

"Really?" Mel says. "Is that true?"

Mum shakes her head and sweeps between us towards the lounge.

Mel grabs her arm. "Mum, for fuck's sake. Is it true?"

Mum sighs. "Language, Melissa." She turns to us. "It happened. Dad was accused and acquitted. It wasn't a pleasant time in his life. It was long before he adopted you two. Now, no more about it. Let's have lunch."

"But why did they think that it was Dad who did it?" I blurt, unable to just let this go.

Mum purses her lips.

"And how was the evidence lost?" I persist. "Was his cousin Bobby something to do with it?"

Mel flicks her gaze between me and Mum, eager for information. Steve keeps his eyes on the floor. Mum attempts for the second time to head towards the lounge.

"Mum!" I shout and she stops in her tracks. "Was Dad part of a gang?"

Mel is suddenly disinterested. "Come on, Steve," she says and they leave me and Mum to it.

Mum folds her arms. "It was a long time ago. And it all worked out in the end. And that's all you need to know. Now, *no more*, understood?" She angles her head to skewer me with a look. "Understood?" she repeats and I know I won't get anything else from her. I also know that I won't ask Dad about it after seeing how badly it affected him earlier.

"Understood," I reply.

"Well this is nice," Nisha coos two weeks later as I show her my temporary workspace in my parents' small dining room.

"Yeah, I always dreamed of having a writing space that overlooked a nice garden," I reply.

"And so close to the New Forest. Gorgeous scenery on your doorstep."

"Yep. Some great walks nearby." I wouldn't know though, because I haven't really left the house since I arrived.

"Are you missing London?"

"More than anything."

She nods in understanding. Nisha is a Londoner through and through, anything outside the city is alien to her. She changes the subject. "How many bedrooms is this bungalow then?"

"Three. It's my childhood home. I'm back in my old room."

"How's it going with the parentals?"

"Absolutely fine. They're very relaxed, like housemates really."

"There's no way I'd ever move back home. My parents are definitely not as chilled as yours." Nisha gives me a look and I know she means that she loves them very much, but they're traditional, strict and unforgiving. She's told me about them before.

"It's only temporary. Until everything calms down. Come on, let's have a sit down." I usher Nisha back towards the lounge.

"Where are your parents?" she says on the way.

"They've popped out for a bit of lunch at the local garden centre."

"At a garden centre?"

"Yep, that's all the rage down here. Not much else to do, to be honest."

We settle ourselves on the sofa and pick up our mugs of coffee that are still just about warm after the tour of my new 'office'.

Nisha gives me one of her looks, and I know she's about to say something that's going to make me feel uncomfortable. She's honest to a fault.

"How you doing? I mean, seriously?"

"Not bad. The whole Tom thing has died down. I haven't heard anything from him since all those flowers and the media have got bored and finally disappeared. I've been lying low."

Nisha grins. "Well, your novel sales certainly skyrocketed."

"Silver linings and all that."

"Indeed. Ok, I'm just going to say it, Sal. There are two reasons I came today. Well, three, if you include me just wanting to see you, to make sure you're doing ok and everything, and to say Happy Birthday for next Thursday. So, do you want the good news or the bad news?"

"Good," I say without hesitation. I always want the good first.

"Well, they've commissioned a third series of *The Deviants*!" Nisha claps and points her index fingers at me, circling her hands.

I pump my fist in the air. "Woo, woo!"

"Well done, darling. You'll get a token payment as per the contract. And we've been invited to the second series launch party later in the year."

Nisha's face turns serious.

"Go on, what's the bad news?" I ask.

"Well, with the massive increase in sales recently, they want the next book ASAP. They won't extend the deadline, Sal."

"Oh." My good mood vanishes. I've been so distracted with the whole Tom drama that I've not been able to write. The deadline for the first draft of my *Dusk* sequel is this Monday, two days away, and there's zero chance the editor will get it.

"I know all this crap is going on, so I told them that

your focus is a bit out of whack."

"And then some." I take a deep breath. "It's just not going to happen for Monday. I'm sorry."

"Ok, I'll try again to push the deadline back."

"Thank you. I'll make it brilliant, promise."

"I'm sure you will," Nisha says. She sips her coffee and puts the mug back on the coffee table. She turns to me and locks my eyes. "Look, we're friends and I'm just going to say it. After the peak in sales because of all that," she waves her hand to indicate Tom, "the publisher is insisting on a publicity campaign. I know you've been lying low, but you're contractually obliged to do a certain number of appearances per year."

A lump lands squarely at the top of my throat. I try to cough to clear it but it comes out as a strangled groan.

"I'm not sure," I say. "What if the media shows up and hounds me? It's all just about on an even keel again."

Nisha notes the uncertainty and says gently, "I know, darling. That's what I keep telling them. I'll tell them again. Don't worry about it. We'll work it out. You need some more time, I understand."

I see the strain across Nisha's face. First, the missed deadline, and now the refusal to do publicity. I know she'll have a rubbish time managing the publishers on my behalf. She understands, yes, but I know they won't. And I don't want them to drop me. All my hard work these past few years, down the pan. I won't let that happen. "When's the first event?"

"Two weeks' time, in Bristol. It's a small one to ease you into the circuit again. You'd be guest of honour."

I chew the insides of my mouth.

Nisha continues, "I doubt any of Tom's fans will be there. He was in that sci-fi movie that tanked. No one remembers that." She wafts her hand as if the movie is a bad smell.

"I'll do it."

A wash of relief sweeps over Nisha's face. Me doing

publicity will appease the publishers for a while and make them more inclined to push back my deadline.

"You're sure?"

"Yes. I need to get on with my life. I can't let this Tom stuff distract me forever. It's all pretty much over now, anyway." The last media articles dragged up dirt on Dad. There's been nothing since. "What's the worst that could happen at a sci-fi and fantasy convention, anyway? A sci-fi fan going to swipe me in half with their lightsaber?"

"Ha. Good for you. Sod that guy. What about the dating scene down here? There were a couple of serious hotties getting off the train with me earlier."

I laugh. "I've sworn off men for a while, they're nothing but trouble. I need to focus on my writing."

A few moments pass and Nisha takes another sip of coffee. She gets up and looks out the sliding glass door at the garden. She turns back to me. "Have you tried going out recently? I know your parents are cool and everything, but just to get a change of scenery and perspective, before you go stir-crazy."

I nod. I've become paranoid that if I step out the front door that everyone will recognise me. That photographers will spring out from behind trees and lampposts, or something, and shove cameras in my face. But, really, why would they? I'm yesterday's news.

Nisha continues, "There must be someone around here that you still trust?"

# CHAPTER 9

My leg taps under the table. The pub is busy for a Wednesday night. Liz went to the bar while Hanna and I found a table. I headed immediately to the darkest corner, and sat facing the wall with my back to the room.

I'm wearing an oversized hoodie and as I walked across the pub, I pulled the collar up over my nose to hide half my face. I scanned the place for anyone who might be looking at me, who might show a sign of recognition. Not one punter paid me any attention, too busy with their drinks and conversations.

I pull the collar down. Hanna gets comfy on her chair, hangs her handbag off the back and looks around.

"Wow, I've not been back in here since we were teenagers. Still looks the same." Hanna takes her index fingers and edges her long black hair away from either side of her face. It falls in perfect curls to her elbows. Her makeup and nails are immaculate and her dark-brown skin glows.

"Here we go," Liz says from behind.

I jump and Hanna eyes me. A slight frown creases her smooth forehead, then dissolves.

Liz leans in and places our drinks on the table. She squeezes past me to get into the corner seat. "Well this place hasn't changed much."

"That's what I just said," Hanna replies.

I hunch into myself and my eyes dart left and right,

taking in what's in my periphery vision. My knee bounces. If Dad was here, he'd tell me that my engine's running.

Hanna puts a hand on my forearm. "Sal, you're fine here, honestly. You look so different to when we were at school, no one is going to recognise you. No one is even looking at us."

"If anyone's looking our way, they're looking at Hanna," Liz says. "Look at her, she's gorgeous."

I force myself to relax my shoulders and let out a long, slow breath.

Hanna was always the pretty one. The three of us were thick as thieves at school. Liz was the sporty one and I was the bookish one. I stayed in touch with them both on Facebook but haven't seen either for many years. Liz and Hanna remained close friends after school, neither having left the area.

I reached out to Hanna following Nisha's visit at the weekend, after convincing myself I could still trust my closest school friends. After all, we'd shared so many secrets back then and gone through so much together. It was Hanna's idea to come back to this old haunt because we'd spent many of my birthdays in here before and it seemed fitting to come back to celebrate again.

"If anyone comes over Liz will kick their ass, she's black belt in taekwondo now." Hanna grins at Liz.

"Wow, black belt?" I attempt to ignore all the people flitting about behind me and focus on the conversation.

"Yes. I'm a personal trainer now at my own CrossFit gym. Run it with the wife. Mary Simmons, do you remember her from school? She was the year above, used to do athletics."

"Oh, wow, yes, Mary Simmons, I remember. You got married? Congratulations."

"Cheers. Yeah, she's a goodun."

"I didn't see that on Facebook." I'm slightly perturbed, how could I have missed that? Damn Facebook algorithm making decisions on who is and isn't important and getting it wrong.

"Nah, the missus doesn't like to put personal stuff up there, likes to keep stuff like that private." Liz sips her wine. Her reddish-brown hair is pulled into a low ponytail and she doesn't have a scrap of makeup on. She's as lean and muscular as Hanna is curvaceous. Both look good. Happy.

I feel like the stressed, miserable, haggard mate now. If only they'd seen me when I was in London, when I was happy and carefree. I reach for my drink and take a long slug of gin and tonic.

"How are your little ones, Hanna? And how's your other half," I ask. I've totally forgotten the names of her husband and children.

"Tim's great. And the kids aren't so little anymore. Josh is eleven now and Angelina is nine. Here I'll show you some pics." Hanna rummages in her bag for her phone and holds it in front of me. She scrolls through photos giving me a running commentary about where each was taken. Liz scopes the pub with interest.

I feign enthusiasm and say "aww" and "so cute" more times than I can count. I'm out of practice. I've forgotten how to pay attention to others, all I can think about is if anyone is looking at me, if anyone has recognised who I am.

When Hanna finally puts her phone away, Liz taps her forearm and points subtly. "Look, that's Phil Taggert from school isn't it? Wow, he's huge now. Must be working out something chronic."

Hanna looks but I resist, I can't risk Phil recognising me.

"So it is! Why don't you call him over?" Hanna says.

Liz starts to stand.

"No!" I say abruptly, then softer, "Please don't."

Liz cuts a glance at Hanna, who has her pristinely manicured eyebrows raised.

"Yeah, sure, no worries, Sal." Liz settles back into her

seat.

I bite my lip. "Sorry, it's just, I need to remain anonymous. I don't want anyone to know I'm here. All that business with that actor…"

"Yeah, that was pretty insane for you, I bet. I was reading all about it in the papers. And that story about your dad, wow," Liz says eagerly, forgetting Phil Taggert in an instant.

I wince at the mention of the dirt dug up on Dad. "Yes, it was insane. That actor is a one-night stand gone wrong who I've managed to finally get away from."

"A one-night stand? Papers said he was desperately in love with you. How come you didn't get together with him?" Liz probes.

I take another long gulp of my drink. "He's a bit OTT, I knew him for a couple of days and suddenly he was in love with me. It's been a tough time."

"Right, so having a famous superstar in love with you is sooo tough." Liz laughs.

Hanna laughs too, but they stop when they realise I'm not laughing with them. My face is stone cold. I knew it was a bad idea to meet them. No one understands.

Hanna's mirth transforms into concern. "Sorry, Sal, I guess we didn't realise the full picture."

We sit in awkward silence for a few minutes, fingering our drinks.

Liz downs her wine. "We're still getting picked up, right?"

"Yes," Hanna replies.

"Well I'm going to get another drink. You want one?"

"I'll have another," Hanna replies and finishes her vodka tonic.

"No thanks, I'm driving," I reply, although I want another ten gins.

Liz shuffles out of the corner and heads to the bar.

Hanna watches her go and lowers her voice, "I didn't realise it was that bad."

"Yeah, well." I shrug. "I haven't been out in three weeks. Scared someone will recognise me and post something online or tell the media. His fans have really had it in for me."

"It's all over now, though?"

"I hope so." I shift on my chair and fiddle with the sleeves of my hoodie to avoid Hanna's questioning gaze. "Where's Liz with your drinks?"

A moment passes before she breaks her fix on me to look over my shoulder. "She's talking with Phil."

I throw a glance over my shoulder to see Liz pointing in our direction and Phil smiling at us. I swivel round quickly to show him my back. Hanna waves.

"You don't think Liz has told him who I am do you?"

"I doubt it, and if she has, it'll be fine," Hanna says. She places her hand on mine in a reassuring motherly way and I immediately feel better. "Phil wasn't the brightest spark; doubt he reads newspapers. Do you remember that time in assembly when he fell asleep and snored?"

"Oh yes, and old Skitten was so mad." I feel energised by the memory. "And told him to come to the front, but Phil was still asleep and didn't move."

We laugh and it feels good.

Liz returns with the drinks, takes a seat and says, "Wow, Phil's done well for himself. Owns a carpentry business. Do you remember when he fell asleep in assembly?"

Outside the pub, after laughing and reminiscing for a few hours about school, Liz grabs me and Hanna for a big hug. After four wines, the personal trainer is tipsy. She stumbles as she pulls out her phone from her jeans pocket. "C'mon, let's take a photo, the three amigos back together after all this time."

I pull away from her grip, turning my face from her phone. "No, no photos."

"What? C'mon Sal," Liz insists, already lining up her

phone as Hanna leans into her.

"You know I hate photos."

"It's just for me, for us. I'll send it to you on WhatsApp," Liz says. "I'm not going to put it anywhere, promise."

Hanna holds me close and Liz snaps a few photos. A car pulls up next to us and beeps.

"Here's Omar," Hanna says. "Come say hello, Sal, you remember my older bro?" Hanna winks.

Yes, I remember him. We dated for a year and a half when I was fifteen and he was seventeen.

Liz clambers into the back seat and Hanna opens the passenger side. I bend down and smile.

"Omar, you remember Sally, don't you?" Hanna says, just as mischievously.

"Yeah, of course. How you doing, Sal?" Omar says.

His voice is deeper and smoother than I remember. He's tall and skinny, his skin the same golden tan as his sister's. His black hair is short and he's got a neatly trimmed beard. His brown eyes are still slightly crossed. Back at fifteen I thought his quirkiness made him all the more attractive. And, as I take in his smiling face, and my stomach flips, I know I still do.

"Yeah, I'm good, thanks, you?" My voice comes out a little higher than usual.

"Can't complain. You want a lift home?"

"No, I'm driving tonight." I point to Dad's Peugeot.

"Right, so I'm just taking you two pissheads home then." Omar smacks his sister's hand away from fiddling with his car radio. I find myself checking if he has a wedding ring on. He doesn't.

Hanna cuffs his hand back playfully. "You and Tim are off on a stag do tomorrow until Sunday! I deserve to let my hair down a little before I'm stuck with the kids all weekend."

"True." Omar laughs. It's the sweetest honey in my ears.

"Did Tim sort the bedding out for you in the spare room?" Hanna says.

"Anyway, I'll be off," I say, before the conversation turns too domestic. "See you."

"Byeeee," Liz shouts from the back seat and thumps the window.

Omar leans across his sister to lock his brown eyes on mine. "Really good to see you. Happy Birthday for tomorrow."

He remembered my birthday... after all these years! My insides do a somersault.

"Oh yeah, Happy Birthday, babe. See you soon," Hanna says. She blows me a kiss and shuts her door.

Two days after my night out, my phone pings with a Whatsapp message:

'Happy Birthday for yesterday'

It's an unknown number and I see that they're typing another message.

I groan.

It's Tom. It has to be. He's found my new number. It's been a couple of weeks since the flowers and I thought I was done with him. But if he could find my parents' address so easily, I guess he could find a private mobile. I swallow the bile that floods my mouth. He'll call and message me incessantly again.

I move my thumb to switch the phone off, but a message pops up.

'It's Omar. Got your number from Hanna. Hope you don't mind. Was good seeing you on Weds. You had a good birthday?'

Omar! My insides fizz. Not Tom. Of course not. Tom is done. I type back.

'Hey Omar. Great birthday, thanks. Didn't do much. Mum made a cake. Had some prosecco. Ok, a lot of prosecco ;-)'

I see that Omar is still online, and then the two ticks turn blue to indicate he's read the message. A second passes before I see that he is typing again.

'That's what birthdays are for – booze and cake! Glad you enjoyed. You remember your 16th? Although that was white lightning and not prosecco. And that involved a head down my mate's bog...'

I laugh out loud at the memory.

'LOL! How could I forget. Never drunk cider since.'
'Yeah, I can understand why!'
'You did a great job of holding back my hair.'
'It was more me making sure your mouth was over the toilet. Sam would've killed me if you'd got sick on his mother's carpet'
'Is that right?!'
'Hahahaha'

The quick-fire conversation stalls and I think what to say. But Omar beats me to it.

'So, I was wondering if you wanted to catch up sometime? If you're down this way for a while, I mean. No worries if not. Just thought I'd ask.'

I pause. Should I go out with Omar? After all the drama with the last guy, is it worth it? I told Nisha that I'd sworn off men for a while.

But I know Omar. I used to date him when we were younger. He's a genuine, decent guy. I shouldn't let the Darlington Disaster stop me from dating indefinitely, or put my love life on hold. That was one blip.

I can take precautions to not be recognised again. Suggest somewhere quiet, just to be on the safe side. If Omar makes a fuss, then he's not for me. And if we meet up and get on? Well… that's cool. I'm not getting younger, as my 37th birthday yesterday reminded me.

Why not?

I look at my phone. Omar is no longer online. Dammit. I panic I've made him wait too long and made him feel awkward. I quickly tap out a reply.

"Shall we go for a walk along the seafront?" Omar asks as I put down my empty coffee mug.

We've been nursing our large coffees for an hour now and have exhausted the chat about the stag do he just went on and the movie we've just seen. Omar works weekends at his insurance firm and has Mondays and Tuesdays off. I suggested an early Monday movie because the cinema would be "nice and empty". I don't like the idea of being surrounded by crowds of people. Or any people, truth be told.

The cinema was indeed quiet, as is Starbucks and I feel at ease. I'm enjoying spending time with Omar.

It's a chilly day, but dry. "Yeah, let's go and see the sea."

Omar opens the coffee shop door for me and we stroll through the gardens towards Bournemouth Pier.

"I'm pleased you said yes to meeting up," Omar says, breaking the amiable silence.

"Me too."

"Why did we split up again?" Omar says with a cheeky grin on his face. It's the first mention of our teenage relationship.

I cringe. "Because I decided I didn't fancy you anymore and I fancied Jack Britt."

"Yeah, that was it." Omar steps behind me and pokes either side of my waist.

The contact feels natural. I don't flinch, I laugh and playfully swat him away.

He moves back to walking beside me. "Yep, and do you remember how you dumped me?"

I groan. "Noooo, I really don't recall…"

"You asked Hanna to tell me," Omar says. "My sister knew I'd been dumped before I did."

"Eeesh…"

"She came in my room, all solemn like, made me sit down on the bed and then sat next to me, her hand on my knee and told me. It was as if she was dumping me." Omar laughs.

"I'm sorry." I manage through my laughter.

"I was mortified, and then she shouted down the stairs to Mum who had been waiting there, 'I've done it, I've told him!', to which Mum said, 'How did he take it?', and Hanna was like, 'Well, I think'. So, my Mum knew I'd been dumped before I did too."

I stop by a bench, reach a hand out to the back and double over with laughter. I haven't laughed like this in a long time. Uninhibited and unforced. It feels like a gust of fresh air, like the last few weeks or so have been scooped out and discarded, the hole filled with hilarity and happiness. "Oh goodness! I didn't know that."

"You laugh about it now, but it wasn't funny then."

"Will you ever forgive me?" I say. My cheeks ache.

Omar puts an arm around me and pulls me to him. With his other hand he ruffles my hair, just like he used to do when we were teenagers, although back then I got annoyed that he'd messed up my perfectly coiffed 'do. Right now, I don't care about my hair so much, but I squirm anyway, just like old times.

"I forgive you," he says into the back of my head.

He holds me for a beat too long and I hold on, elated. Could this be a thing? Could we get together again? Could he be my… boyfriend? The effervescent fizz in my belly works its way into my chest and I brim with the possibility.

I haven't been with a man since… Tom.

And there it is. Can I trust another man after that disaster? Am I ready for this? To put myself out there again. The excitement fizzles to nothing like a spent firework and a wall goes up.

He must feel my body tense, as he releases me. I straighten up and we continue walking.

"Wanna sit?" Omar says indicating a free bench overlooking the sea.

"Uh huh." I let Omar sit first. I stall and pretend to gaze at the sea for a moment. I can do this. I've had boyfriends before and been on numerous dates to know I fancy this guy. He's no dud. But can I trust him?

Screw it.

I sit close to Omar. The length of our sides touching. The tickle in my belly reignites with an explosion. It's windier by the sea and I shiver and lean in to him some more.

Omar picks up on the signal, and doesn't leave me hanging – thank goodness – and puts his arm around me. He pulls me in to his armpit, closer to his chest, wrapping his warmth around me. I don't resist.

"And you want to know the funniest thing?" Omar says.

I look up at him. At his quirky yet handsome face. "Go on."

"A week later I started dating Casey Percy. Do you remember her?"

"No way! She was Jack Britt's ex!"

"Yep." Omar laughs his big, warm guffaw.

I can't help but join in. Carefree, happy, light.

My phone buzzes in my pocket. I pull it out with the intention of turning it to silent so I can enjoy this moment some more but see it's a call from home. Why would one of my parents call me now? They know I'm on a date with Omar. They'd save their nosey grilling for when I got home. Worry percolates through me.

"Sorry, gotta take this," I say and stand and walk a few steps from Omar.

"Hello?"

It's Mum. "Sorry to interrupt, but are you on your way

home any time soon?"

"Do you need me to come home?"

"Well, it's nothing, really…"

"Mum! What's happened?"

"I think it's best if you come home right now."

I apologise to Omar and drive straight home with every kind of scenario running through my head. The media are back, there's been more dirt dug up about my family, Tom's fans are going crazy online again. Perhaps thirty-seven bouquets have arrived this time.

I park in the driveway and fling myself through the front door.

"Mum? Dad?" I yell.

"In the lounge," Dad replies.

I run through to the lounge and find them both sat on the sofa staring at a huge artwork that has been propped against the sliding glass doors, with the brown paper covering ripped half off it.

"What is that?" I ask, in awe.

"It's a Rokas Whelan. She's pretty famous," Mum says not taking her eyes off the stunning abstract painting. She's clutching a card so tightly her knuckles are almost as white as the skin on her face.

"What's it doing here?"

Mum shakily lifts her hand with the card and I take it from her and read:

Dearest Janice, you brought a gift into the world 37 years ago and this is my gift to you. A painting named *Mother and Child*. I hope you enjoy its beauty as much as I enjoy the beauty of your daughter. With all my best regards, Tom.

The card falls from my hand. "Tom sent you a painting?"

"Not just any painting, Sal, this one's worth about fifteen thousand quid," Dad says.

"Whoa."

"And that's not all," Dad says. He stands and edges around the painting and opens the sliding glass door. "Come with me."

I follow him into the garden. Mum stays put, mesmerised.

He turns the corner to the side of the bungalow and points. There are two massive boxes. "That's a luxury hot tub and that's a massive gas BBQ. Together worth as much as that painting."

I mutter a faint, "Oh my goodness."

He pulls a card similar to the one Mum was clutching from his pocket. I read the contents:

Dearest Graham, I noticed your garden was lacking these essential items. Now you can cook and enjoy a soak with my heartfelt and unending thanks. While Janice birthed the perfect woman, you helped to shape her into the wonder that she is today. With all my best regards, Tom. PS. please tell Sally that I haven't forgotten her birthday. I've got a surprise for her.

Alarm clangs between my ears. A surprise? What the hell might that be? I look around me stupidly as if the surprise will suddenly materialise out of nothing.

"How would he know that our garden doesn't have these things in it?" Dad asks.

I shake my head, alarmed.

Dad continues, "I can only think it's that Google Maps thingamajig. Your sister was looking at that when she was buying her last house. Looking at the area and nearby properties."

I get an itch as if I'm being observed from above. "Let's go back inside."

We find Mum in exactly the same position.

"Are you all right, Mum?"

She turns to me wide-eyed. "I love it," she says breathlessly.

"And I've always wanted a hot tub. And a fancy BBQ.

How'd he know?"

My mind races through many sinister explanations but settles on the most obvious. "Pure luck, that's all. We have to send them back."

"We do," Mum says sadly and turns back to gaze at the painting. "But the couriers wouldn't take them and there's no address or anything."

"I don't know his number. It's on my old phone. And I don't want to contact him even if I did."

I sit on the sofa and pull out my phone. I google and find a name of Tom's agent and an email address. I bash out an angry email, but then I mellow, and rewrite it in a professional, unemotional manner. I press send.

"There. Hopefully someone will get back to us." Then my chest fills with dread. I don't want to have to deal with Tom. I don't want *him* to get back to me. I swallow it down. He won't contact me. It'll be some minion.

"In the meantime, can I set up the hot tub?" Dad says hopefully.

"Don't be daft, Graham," Mum replies.

"It's going back," I snap, then soften. Tom has got me seriously riled up. "What the hell was he thinking? If he thinks he's winning me over by sending extravagant gifts to my parents, then he's even more deluded than we thought."

"Very odd," Mum agrees.

I check my emails; no reply. I sit and look at the painting, in the same way as Mum. It has a way of drawing your eye. The doorbell rings and I jump out of my seat. Shit. Tom's surprise? Whatever it is, I don't want it.

Dad goes to the front door. I can hear a few mumbles but nothing clearly. He comes back into the lounge and I perch on the edge of the sofa straining to see if he's holding anything.

"Just someone asking if we want our drive tarmacked," Dad says.

I breathe out a sigh of relief, but the tension doesn't

leave my muscles. The surprise. What is it and when will it arrive? I need to stop thinking about it. Can't let it dominate my every thought. Can't jump every time the doorbell goes. It's a weird kind of unhappy anticipation. What will Tom do next?

I pick up my phone and message Omar before my alarmist over-thinking gets out of control. He's something good to think about.

# CHAPTER 10

"Wait here, I'll find the organiser," Nisha says and leaves me in the Bristol hotel lobby.

I watch as fantasy and science fiction fans filter into the rooms and bar area dedicated to the convention. Quite a few people are dressed up. I spot a brilliant Wonder Woman, a half-arsed Gandalf and a few costumes I don't recognise.

I usually went to these things by myself, but I said I needed Nisha's support for this one, and she agreed. But I'm sure it'll be fine. I did loads of these things before… Tom… and I was good once I got into the swing of it. It took a while to get used to people looking at me and being the centre of attention – because I hate that – but I soon got comfortable with talking about my writing, my passion. The audience wasn't there to poke and prod at my inner emotions, but was there because they loved what I'd created. And I was in complete control of the attention. That settled my nerves.

I got up early and did my hair and put some make-up on, and bought a new top to wear. Mel even came over yesterday and painted my nails bright pink. Bold. Brave. That's exactly how I'm feeling.

It's been five days since the extravagant gifts for my parents arrived and nothing came for me. No surprise. I've convinced myself that nothing will come. Perhaps the surprise was the flowers and some minion messed up the timings so they came before my parents' gifts instead of after.

The management company never replied to my email. I tried three more email addresses for publicists, agents and other contacts. As yet, no response. They possibly think I'm a crazed fan looking for attention – it's a bit weird sending emails asking for celebrities to come and take their gifts back.

On Monday, after an hour of admiring the painting, Mum wrapped it up and Dad put it with the hot tub and BBQ under a big tarpaulin in the garden to keep the rain off.

I take my phone out and see a message from Omar.

**'You're going to be brilliant xxx btw it's going to be dry and overcast in Bristol today'**

Omar has a thing about the weather. He likes to check and let me know every morning. It's become a thing. Our thing. He's the reason I'm feeling good. His attention, his care, his kindness makes me feel alive, like I can do anything, like I have nothing to fear.

A second later another message comes through. Omar has sent me a pic of a young Bill Murray pointing with the words 'You're awesome'.

I laugh out loud and tap back 'No, YOU'RE awesome!'

Nisha appears in front of me. "This way. The first panel starts in five."

As we walk, she hands me a lanyard with an ID card hanging from it. I put it over my neck as we enter the room. It's dim, with a long table at one end and rows of seats split into two with a walkway down the centre. The chairs are almost full and there's a low murmur and rustling of programmes. The other authors and the moderator are already behind the long table.

Nisha boldly walks down the centre towards the table and I follow, wishing she'd gone around the outside edges of the chairs. I feel like we're making some kind of grand entrance and my nerves churn.

I see my name written on a card at the front of the table and edge behind an already seated author to take the chair next to the moderator. Nisha settles herself a few rows back on my right-hand side, so I can still see her but she's not so close that I get distracted.

I say hello to the other authors and then look out at the crowd. There are bright lights shining at the table so I can't see too far, but the faces that look back at me are happy to be there.

And I feel happy to be here too.

The butterflies in my belly flutter in a good way and I can feel sweat forming behind the backs of my knees and under my bum. But it's ok.

There are five empty seats in the front row on the right. They've been bagsied with jumpers and bags left on each. Keen bean fans who want to be right at the front.

"Right," the moderator says looking at her watch, "time to get this show on the road."

As she's introducing me as the guest of honour, the back door opens and in shuffles some latecomers. They hurry down the centre walkway and to the front five chairs. They're dressed up all as the same character. They're aliens and have painted the skin on their arms a bright Homer Simpson yellow. As they sit, I notice they're all girls. They look at each other and, in unison, each pull a cardboard mask down over their faces.

My lower jaw drops open.

The masks are of Tom Darlington's face. More specifically, Tom Darlington as the yellow alien from the rotten tomatoes sci-fi movie he was in.

"Sally," the moderator says and my attention jerks back to her. She's indicating to the room.

I smile and wave. "It's a pleasure to be here today. I'm looking forward to this panel." I hope that's what she's just asked me. My eyes go straight back to the line of Tom's sitting right in front of me.

They whisper to one another behind cupped hands and point at me.

I scan the crowd for Nisha's face. She scowls at the latecomers. Then she uses her index fingers to trace the corners of her mouth turning up and grins exaggeratedly.

I get the message and smile. I focus on what the moderator is saying. The discussion has started and I need to pay attention. It's just some girls dressed up as Tom. Ignore them.

The author at the other end is talking about why made-up languages are annoying and why he doesn't use them in his work and as he starts to tail off, I chirp up.

"I think fictional languages contribute to solid worldbuilding, they help to immerse readers in the world and bring a sense of uniqueness to the story…" I'm in full flow. This is a topic I know, that I've spoken about before, but something is distracting me.

The five Toms murmur to each other. They were silent when the other author and the moderator were talking. Then one pulls an A4 notepad from her bag and a felt-tip pen. I try to look away, to stay focused on what I'm saying, but my point trails off as I watch the girl scribble.

The moderator picks up on my idea and throws it to another author who hasn't spoken yet. The Toms respectfully go silent while he's speaking.

I force myself to turn and look at the author. I watch his mouth to tune in to what he's saying. But out the corner of my eye, the notepad is raised.

The girl holds it against her chest and points at me. On the page is scrawled:

We love TD. We hate you!

She sees me looking and runs a finger across her neck.

The gesture shocks me and I feel very, very hot. I go to pick up the full glass of water that's been set in front of me but my hand shakes so much that I can't hold it properly and water sploshes over the side. There's no chance I'll get it to my mouth without causing a scene. I put it down again.

The conversation about languages is going on without me. The moderator has done her job and got everyone talking, it's my job to contribute at a relevant moment. But I can't keep up, I can't find my voice. I laugh at a few moments when the crowd does.

My brow sweats under the lights. My top lip dampens and I rub my palms down my jeans. The Tom masks are staring at me. I feel like a rabbit caught in the headlights.

"And how did you come up with your language in *Dusk*, Sally?" the moderator asks, obviously conscious that I – the guest of honour no less – haven't contributed anything for a while.

"Um, well I…"

The Toms start to talk quietly to each other. Not enough to get them kicked out but enough for it to distract me.

Someone shushes the Toms. I guess it's Nisha.

They quieten.

I take a deep breath and relay the story I've told numerous times before about how I came up with my fictional language. It's a great anecdote. It involves a Tolkien reference. Usually it gets laughs. But today, it comes out in a flat monotone with a quivering voice. There's no laughter or appreciative murmuring, there's no other author chipping in with supportive comments. When I stop talking there's a horrific pause before the moderator swiftly asks another author a question.

I sit quietly after that, pretending to be listening and the moderator doesn't pull me back into the discussion. It washes over me.

At the end, the Toms jump up, pull up their masks so they can see where they're going and are some of the first to leave the room.

Nisha comes over to me. I'm stunned, latched to my

seat. Nisha thanks the moderator and other authors and I mumble my thanks as she lifts me off the chair.

"What was that, Sal?" she whispers as we leave the room.

"Did you see the Narans? At the front?" I use the name of Tom's character in the movie. Somehow I remember it.

Nisha tuts. We go through the door and she scopes the hallway before guiding me towards the next room. "It's the book signing now."

As we move in that direction, I take a few deep breaths. Pull it together, Sal. *Pull. It. Together.*

Out of nowhere the five girls dressed as Naran jump in front of me in the corridor and surround me, edging Nisha out of the way.

"Sally Speck!" they caw at me through their Tom/Naran face masks. They close in and I instinctively put up my arms as if they're about to attack.

"How'd *you* manage to pull Tom Darlington?" one asks.

"Sally isn't here to discuss her private life," I hear Nisha insist loudly from behind the circle. "She's here to talk science fiction."

The girls peel away, Nisha might be petite but she's ferocious. She grabs my arm, glares at them and leads me towards the signing room.

One shouts my name, she's right next to me, on the other side to Nisha.

I turn to look at her.

Pop!

A glitter canon goes off right in my face.

Nisha lets go of my arm, and I glance to see the girls surround me again, pushing Nisha out the way.

Pop! Pop! Pop! Pop!

Four more go off, all aimed at me. Silver, pink and gold glitter rains down. The girls laugh. Howl.

"Wooooooo!" one shouts. "We were saving those for

when we won the cosplay competition but this is much better."

In shock, I stand stock still, as if drenched with freezing water. My head hangs and I stare at my hands. I'm covered in glitter. I blink and can feel it scratch my eyeballs. I open my mouth and it's stuck to my lips and mixes with my saliva. It's itchy on my scalp. I can feel it around my nostrils as I breathe in. It's stuck to my sweat-damp top and it chafes in my cleavage.

An organiser, a young guy, probably a volunteer, comes dashing towards us. Nisha collars him.

"These attendees are harassing my client. I insist they leave," she says in a tone that brokers no argument.

The girls giggle and smile at the organiser. The guy stares, alarmed at the mess.

"We're just having some harmless fun. It's only glitter," one girl says, pouting at the organiser. "They're meant to be Naran's laser guns."

He doesn't seem to know what to do. Nisha clears her throat and cuts him a stern look.

"No more glitter. Or you'll have to leave," he says to the girls.

"Ms. Speck, the book signing is this way," he says apologetically to me.

"Shitshow," Nisha mutters under her breath, but we all hear it. She beckons me forward as the organiser gets on his walkie talkie to declare a minor cosplay incident and order a cleaner with a decent hoover that'll suck up glitter.

Each step I take glitter flutters off me. Nisha pauses outside the door to look at me.

I rally myself. "It's glitter. That's all. I can sign some books for my fans and then we'll sort it out in the toilets."

But I know glitter never comes off.

Nisha doesn't reply. She knows too. We've all been there, putting it on our faces at festivals and still finding it weeks later.

"I'll shake it off a bit here," I say.

She stands in front of me, as if that'll stop the gawkers in the hallway from watching. I shake like a wet dog. Sparkles snow onto the carpet, but it barely makes a difference.

I attempt to tap it off, brush it, but no use. My heart pounds in my ears and an odd pattering sensation runs around my chest in circles.

"Come on," Nisha says.

In the room, authors are already signing books for fans. We're late. Little queues form in front of the more popular authors.

Another organiser looks me up and down and then gestures to an empty seat in the centre of the room. It's a comfy, upholstered chair rather than the plastic seats the other authors are on. A position of honour for the guest of honour.

I sit and Nisha gives me a biro. My fancy book-signing fountain pen is in my bag but I can't face rummaging for it and spilling more glitter in there. I sit carefully on the chair, but still blanket it with shiny flecks. At the sight, a vice clamps down on my lungs, restricting my air intake so all I can manage is shallow gasps. I force myself to hold it together. I'm here for my fans, sod Tom's fans.

"Sally Speck is here if anyone would like their book signed," Nisha announces to the room. She turns to me and does her smile gesture.

"I've just had a run in with some glitter, ha ha." I fake-laugh, to try and make light of it, and plaster on a grin. Glitter grinds in my teeth like sand.

A few heads turn and people start to walk over. A guy pulls off his backpack and retrieves a dog-eared copy of my book and heads my way.

But before anyone gets near, the five Narans burst through the door and head straight for me. They pull their masks down and cluster around me, standing in front of my chair, blocking me from fans, making people feel uncomfortable.

"Get out the way," Nisha says, but they ignore her.

One girl's arse is so close to my face, I swear she's about to sit in my lap. Nisha stomps over to an organiser and I can see her through yellow-painted skin pointing back at me and 'having words'.

The lad with the backpack thrusts his arm forward through the noisy Naran barrier and hands me his book. I take it, fumble and almost drop it with my shaking fingers, and shout, "What's your name?"

"Tom," he shouts back.

Nooooo. I flick my eyes up to the Narans.

"We love Toms," one says.

The others chant, "Tom, Tom, Tom."

Backpack guy edges backwards. I sign his book quickly, but he's too far away for me to hand it back. Nisha returns and takes the book from my hand. She hands me another. "Ann." She beckons forward a lady, and people start to queue behind her.

Backpack guy breaks free from the Narans and Nisha holds out his book. He grabs it, stuffs it in his bag and hurries away.

With a quaking hand, I scrawl an illegible signature in Ann's book as the Narans drape themselves across the back of my chair, sit on the armrests and one kneels in front of me while another pushes up her mask to take a few photos with her phone.

Everyone does what they always do when someone's taking a photo – they move out the way. Ann steps to one side. I hold my hand in front of my face. But this only makes the charade go on longer.

"Smile!" the photographer Naran says. "C'mon, won't you smile for your fans?" she does an exaggerated frown.

A bristle goes through Ann and the people stood behind her. Doesn't Sally Speck engage with her fans? Tsk tsk, it says.

I lower my hand and smile half-heartedly.

"Move along now," Nisha says standing in front of the

photographer. "There's other people waiting to meet Sally."

The Narans take a while to get moving.

"That's it, time's up! We need this room back for the next seminar," an organiser shouts.

Nisha grabs Ann's book off me and hands it back to her. She asks the next in line what his name is.

"Simon," she says to me as she hands me the book. I sign it quickly and she's already got the next.

The queue of my fans is hanging on as the other authors and people start to leave the room. They clutch their books and shift on their feet.

The organiser comes over to us. "Sorry, guys, but time's up. We need the room back."

"Just a few more," I insist, beckoning forward the next in line and taking the guy's book.

The organiser sighs, looks at his watch and then at his clipboard. He says to the crowd, "Sorry, that's it." Then he turns to Nisha, "Ms. Speck is needed for the fantasy holiday worlds panel in the other room."

Nisha grabs one more book and hands it to me to sign but my fans seep away.

As the room empties, a few more organisers spill in to change the seating for the next event. I stand and move next to Nisha. She's glowering at nothing in particular, but I expect she's furious that I only managed to sign six books. At one signing, a couple of years ago, I did two hundred.

"We're going to need a new chair," the organiser says to one of his staff and points at the chair I've just been sitting on.

I touch Nisha's arm and she jolts to attention. "Right, your next panel."

Feeling lightheaded, I say, "Toilets..."

The corridor is empty as most people have found their next event.

"I'll wait here," Nisha says as I go into the toilets.

There's no one in there and I go straight to the mirror.

I look ridiculous. My heart hammers in my chest so hard that it hurts. I take a couple of deep breaths in an attempt to steady my pulse, but my airway is constricted and I wheeze.

I turn the tap on and wet a paper towel and try to wipe some of the glitter off my cheeks. Big mistake. The wet towel clumps in little white blobs on my face and I smear my blusher. I scrub and scrub but the paper disintegrates and my skin goes red raw.

I shake out my hair over the sink. Glitter falls, but I'm still riddled and I muss up my hair in the process.

The image reflected back at me is a joke.

I grasp the edge of the sink as my legs turn to jelly and my body shakes. A nauseous tornado swirls around the pit of my gut. It's not harmless, it's not funny. It's intrusive and frightening. Glitter bombs fired at me and girls invading my personal space is worse than Tom's fans trolling me on social media. The intrusion is suddenly very close, no longer at arm's distance, no longer from behind a computer or phone screen. Shame and embarrassment blazes through my organs.

I slump to the ground, gasping for air, rubbing at my glitter-scratchy eyes. I pull my hands away and they're splotched with black. I smudged my mascara.

Nisha comes into the toilets. "Come on, Sal, this is where you get to talk about holidaying with ewoks."

I choke on my reply, feeling disorientated. My heart is hammering so loudly in my head I scrunch my eyes. I feel Nisha's hand on my knee. She's saying something to me but I can't make out the words. I can't breathe. I hunch over as dizziness hits and I think I might vomit.

I open my mouth wide, desperate to inhale some air into my lungs. My heartbeat jammers and then stops in an irregular pattern. It's excruciating. I've got a gacky mouth and my skin crawls with a roving clamminess.

"I think… I'm having… a heart attack," I stutter as I

clutch my chest. My heart feels as if it's being wrenched from between my lungs, as if an unseen hand has grasped it too tight and is twisting and pulling to detach it.

Everything's a blur as Nisha keeps one hand on me and shouts urgently down her phone. I can hear the fear in her voice.

# CHAPTER 11

"Sally," Nisha says.

My brain adjusts to the dim room. I'm in a hospital bed with the curtains pulled around me. I go to sit up but Nisha pushes me back gently.

"Just rest, darling. You're all right. It wasn't your heart. It was a panic attack. They're just running some tests and you should be out in a couple of hours. I've spoken to your mum and she's spoken to Omar. Your mum was all ready to come up to Bristol, but I told her I'd take care of you. But then she called me back and said Omar would come. He should be here soon."

I blink at her. Not yet able to form words. I feel shrunken, overly fragile. My ribcage feels bruised. Breathing hurts and there's a lingering pinch in my chest, just under my collarbone. What happened between the hotel bathroom and here is foggy.

Nisha rummages through her bag. "Ah, here we are." She pulls out a near-empty, flattened pack of baby wipes. "Always have some of these handy for Sahil."

She gently wipes my face. I sit still and stare at the ceiling while she tends to me. When the wipe's overloaded with glitter, she gets another and continues her clean up. She balls up the used wipes and places them on the bed.

She looks shaken, her eyes bleary and red-rimmed. I frightened her. I frightened myself.

"What a fucking fuck up. I honestly thought I'd lost

you," Nisha says.

"I've never had a panic attack before," I mumble. My voice sounding as if it hasn't been used in a century.

And then I notice it: the big black dog pawing at my consciousness; the depression creeping back up on me. It's been a constant fight to keep at bay ever since I was thirteen. I can't lose and be hospitalised again. I just CAN'T. It was the most awful time of my life. I've had a few glitches since but mostly years of clear skies. I can't allow this Tom nonsense to tip me over the edge and send me spiralling out of control.

"Doc asked me if you were under any stress. I said yes," Nisha says.

"It all got too much. Tom's weird behaviour, the media and then his fans so… close." Just the thought of the Narans invading my privacy makes my heart race again.

"Shush," Nisha says and pats my hand. "You've had a crazy month. We thought it was all done with the Tom crap, but clearly not."

"I don't want anything to do with him."

"I know, darling."

"I just want my life back to normal."

The curtain pulls back and a nurse ushers in Omar.

"Are you ok?" He dashes straight to my side and takes my hand.

"I'm ok." I smile up at him and his presence fills me with a sense of safety. "Omar, this is Nisha." I gesture to my literary agent. She stands and holds out her hand. It takes Omar a beat to draw his attention away from me to look at her. "Nisha, this is Omar." They shake hands.

Nisha looks at her watch. "Right, if you're ok now Omar's here I need to get going to catch the next train back to London." She gives me a look as if to say, I can stay if you want me to.

"I'll be fine, Nish, you head home."

She leans across the bed and gives me a hug. She whispers, "He's a hottie," in my ear before departing.

Omar takes Nisha's seat and drags it as close as possible to me. "How you doing?" he asks, a look of concern on his face.

"Better now you're here."

"Good. I feel better now I'm here too. That really gave me a fright."

"You didn't need to come all this way. Nisha would've brought me home or organised a car or something."

"I know. But I wanted to. Your mum called and I told work it was an emergency. I couldn't stay knowing you're in hospital in another city a long way from home. I wouldn't have been able to think about anything other than you anyway."

I squeeze his hand.

He continues, "I know it's not been long since we reconnected, but I'm here for you, ok?"

"Thank you. All I want is to move on and live my life. I thought this event would ease me back in, I was so excited for it. And then…" I trail off. I don't want to relive the incident.

Omar seems to sense this. "Nisha gave your mum the lowdown, and Janice told me. But I'm all ears if you want to talk about it."

"My work means everything to me. I've already missed one deadline. I can't miss another."

"You're going to feel a bit out of sorts for a while, I imagine, but you can get your focus back. Just tune out this Tom guy. Don't spend any more time thinking about him, or his fans, or the media. These kids who threw glitter at you. They're nothing. You're an incredible author with incredible things to say. Don't let anything or anyone stop you from saying them."

This pep talk soothes my frazzled ends and suddenly I feel bold. I beckon him forward and kiss him on the lips. It's our first kiss. It takes him by surprise but then he kisses me back. His lips are slightly scratchy but gentle. He cups my face and when we pull apart he kisses the tip of my nose gently.

He sits back and smiles at me. "Well, I'm really, *really* glad I came, now."

I stroke his cheek. "And you're right. I need to just tune it all out. I think I need to head back to London. The words always flow when I'm at my flat."

"That's a great idea," he says tightly and his face sinks.

His vulnerability is endearing. All of the men I've dated have been so closed off emotionally, but Omar is different. He's really putting himself out there and not hiding his true feelings. I reckon my unlucky-in-love dating history is about to get a shakeup. And about time too.

"I know you're in Bournemouth, but we'll make it work, ok? I can get the train down or you up. And, to be honest, I can work from wherever there's Wi-Fi. Me going back there isn't the end. This is the beginning for us."

His eyes light up. "I've lived and worked in Bournemouth since leaving college. I've always thought I should broaden my horizons and move to London. Perhaps this is the right time."

"Maybe," I say. I beam. This guy would move cities for me? I feel elated. "We'll see how it goes."

"Indeed," he replies.

There's a pause as we take each other in. I think the term is googly eyes.

He breaks the moment by standing to kiss me. My body is swept with warmth and lust. The feeling of impending doom from hours before long gone. He keeps his face close to mine as he holds my gaze. "I'll never do anything to hurt you, Sal, never."

I study his eyes, his face, his entire demeanour. And I believe him.

115

# CHAPTER 12

It takes a week for my panic attack 'hangover' to subside; for the drained, exhausted and spaced-out feeling to pass.

It's replaced with a buzz of excitement. I feel ready to write again. Although the panic attack leaves a scar, I'm convinced it's a minor one. I've spent the week in bed or on the sofa in front of the TV with Mum and Dad pottering around me, or over at Omar's. His loving attention and the incredible sex helping to heal my wounds in rapid time.

"I can't wait for a few drinks," Mel says as we get out of the tube and haul our suitcases along the road to my flat. "Those cans of G'n'T on the train were a great idea, Sal."

She's slightly merry. I told the fam I was heading back to London and Mel said she'd come. For support. And for a Saturday night out on the town with her sister. But also because she wants a night away from the kids. She'll catch the train back tomorrow and then straight after work on Sunday Omar will come up to stay overnight, still having Mondays and Tuesdays off work.

So, I won't have to be alone until Tuesday night. And then Nisha is coming round for dinner. And then on Wednesday night I've organised to see my twin cousins who live in London for a drink. It's not like me to want to have company all the time, I love my alone time, but after the panic attack I feel like I want to ease myself back into

London after so long away by being with people I know and trust. At least for a few days.

"Jeez, I don't remember your place being this far from the station," Mel puffs. It's a warm spring day and Mel's wearing her practical mum coat. Padded and hooded, ready for anything.

"Few more steps," I reply.

We turn a corner onto my road and drag our suitcases along the pavement until I come to a halt, Mel pulling up next to me.

"Here we—" The words curdle in my throat as I look up at the stairs to my apartment.

"What the—?" Mel sputters.

I gawp at my apartment, frozen to the spot. In weird slow motion, my hand falls from my suitcase handle and finds its way to cover my gaping mouth.

My apartment, my wonderful apartment, has been attacked, abused, molested. The stairs up to my front door are covered in rubbish. Abandoned handmade signs and print-outs of Tom Darlington photos strewn across the steps. There's rubbish everywhere. The front door is smeared with something. I look closer and see a pile of broken eggshells lining the top step.

"Who would do this?" Mel breaks the silence.

"Tom's fans," I manage.

"Why?"

"Who knows. The same reason they swarmed me in Bristol. Tom is public property and they think they have a say in who he dates and doesn't date."

"Dickheads," Mel replies with a shake of her head.

I lurch forward, desperate to somehow protect my apartment, although I know the damage has already been done. I take a couple of steps and the smell of rotten egg engulfs me. I gag, but push on. Eggshells crunch under my shoes.

"Be careful," Mel says behind me. I hear her take out her phone and snap some photos.

I pull out my key and slowly put it in the lock that has been covered in shiny egg, carefully as if the slime trail might give me a disease. But as I touch the key to the door it swings back a few inches, the catch off.

"Shit, it's open," I shout to Mel behind me.

"I'm coming up."

With my fingertip I push open the door. But it's wedged on something. A spike of fear leaps up my backbone. I push harder and it gives. Something rustles behind the door.

Post.

Of course, it's just my post on the mat.

But as the door widens, I see my mat and the remains of my post. There's a blackened patch. A smoky waft hits my nostrils, overpowering the rotten egg. And then a tang of something far worse. When the gap is wide enough, I step into the flat.

"What the hell is that smell?" Mel says behind me.

When I see, my insides flip and I think I might vomit. I retch and swallow back the sick.

Some little bastard has put dog poo in a plastic bag, lit it and pushed it through my letterbox. It's singed the mat, and burnt the edges of some letters and a flyer from the local supermarket. I look around, but there's no other signs of damage. The fire didn't take hold, thank goodness.

"They could've set the whole building on fire," Mel exclaims. She's carrying the suitcases and puts them down in the hallway, past the singed mess. She takes her phone from her pocket and takes more photos.

"I need to check the rest of the place." I take a deep breath to rally myself; to bolster the bravery that is currently lacking… And get a mouthful of dog crap stench. I tamp down the throw-uppy feeling and take a tentative step into my hallway. "Stay here, ok?"

"Nope, I'm coming with you," Mel replies, clearly as spooked as I am.

She moves until she's practically on top of me and I'm

overwhelmed with relief that she's here with me.

With Mel shadowing me, I slowly walk through the hallway and scan up, down, sweeping my gaze to take in everything. From what I can tell, the hallway hasn't been touched. I decide to head into my bedroom first. I'm not sure why, but something in me says that anything bad that I'm going to find is going to be in there.

I tentatively push open the door, dreading what I might find; as if I'm going to disturb some lewd scene or have a dark figure jump out at me from the wardrobe. Bizarrely, an image of a snarling tiger leaping up at me with claws out flashes across my mind. I scrunch my eyes and then take a step in. I open them and brace myself.

But it looks exactly as I left it. I think. I've been away for five weeks; I can't really remember. But there's no obvious signs of vandalism or abuse. My bed is still made messily with the pyjamas I flung on the edge still resting there; the piles of 'to be read' books still stacked on my nightstand. My wardrobe door hangs open in exactly the same way as I always leave it so I can see the full-length mirror on the inside. The rug looks undisturbed and the curtains still hang partly open from when I left in a hurry.

My heart thumps in my ear and I turn to Mel. "Looks ok."

I gesture for her to back up and we head into the kitchen. We silently creep there, as if we'll definitely find someone or something sinister in that room.

But the kitchen looks fine too. The half-drunk bottle of red wine that I opened with Nisha on the day the media first arrived outside the apartment is on the side. The bathroom looks untouched too.

Next the lounge. This will be the room that's been damaged. The rest of the place seems untouched. But why break in to not do anything? No, there has to be something in this room. My brain scans through possibilities of what I might find, each scarier or weirder than the next. More dog crap? A dead body?

Mel senses my apprehension about this last room and clasps my arm. We step into the lounge together.

I glance around quickly. At the small dining table, the sofa, the telly, the coffee table, the windows, the curtains. All looks ok.

Did someone pick the lock to open the door just to scare me and then not come inside?

I breathe a sigh of relief and look out the window onto the street to collect my thoughts. My house has suffered on the outside, but the inside is still intact. The front door mat is burnt and covered in dog excrement, but the rest of the house appears to be unmolested.

Did I leave the front door unlocked? I rack my brains trying to recall the day I left. I was in a hurry to get in the taxi and get past the waiting media. I can recall that. But the memory of locking the door? Non-existent. But I do it on autopilot. Doesn't everyone? Most of the time I can't remember doing it, but when I go back to check, it's always locked.

That niggling feeling is back, though. Something isn't quite right. Did someone break in to just look around? The thought of someone going through my things, touching my stuff, nosing in my fridge chills me to the core.

"I need to look again." I go back into the hallway and look more closely. Then into the bathroom, kitchen and bedroom. I pause for a long time in my bedroom just looking at everything. Then my gaze lands on my laundry basket.

I pounce on it and rummage through. Then turn and open my underwear drawer.

Mel comes in. "Has your underwear been taken? Seriously?"

I stare at the drawer. It's nearly empty. But that makes sense because most of my knickers and favourite bras I took with me and are currently in my suitcase in the hall. I look carefully and don't immediately see anything gone. But, truly, I have so many knickers that I really wouldn't notice. All the ones left in the drawer are those that I've had a while and are holey or overstretched or slightly uncomfortable. I wear them as a last resort when my favourites are in the wash. I grimace at the thought of someone taking a pair of my emergency knickers.

I sigh. "No… I don't think so. And my laundry basket looks the same. But I can't really remember what was in it."

"Did anyone else have a set of keys?" Mel asks.

I shake my head.

"Could you have left it open?"

"No," I say with zero conviction. I backtrack. "There's a chance."

Mel nods. "There's no sign of forced entry, and it doesn't look like anything has been taken. Perhaps you left it open and nobody's been in here apart from us now."

"Mmm, yeah, perhaps."

Mel heads into the lounge and takes out her phone as if that's it, case closed. But I pace again through the apartment. Even slower this time, taking it all in. It feels as if something's not quite right, but I can't tell what it is. Perhaps it's just the state of the outside that has shaken me so much. I stand in the doorway to the lounge.

Mel indicates her phone. "Steve says, do you reckon there were any witnesses. To the egging and dog poop thing."

"I doubt it. The flat above is owned by an Emirati family who only come to stay during the summer months, and there's nobody there the rest of the year. And the basement flat is currently empty and up for sale."

Mel taps out a reply on her phone then looks up at me.

"You want a tea?" she says.

I nod. We head into the kitchen and dance around each other to find mugs, teabags and put the kettle on. We lean against the counter drinking our brews in stunned silence. When I put my empty mug in the sink, I feel an overwhelming urge to retreat. To get away from this broken place. But I decide to be proactive. Running away from the situation won't change it.

"Shall we tidy up a bit and then have some wine?" I say.

"Good idea," Mel says. "You can deal with the dog poo, because, I know I'm your sister and everything, and I love you, but I don't love you *that* much."

Her humour breaks the tension and I laugh.

She continues, "I'll get started on clearing up outside."

"Thank you." I pull off my jacket, put on my washing up gloves and find the roll of black bin bags from under the sink. I hand one to Mel and we head back to the front door. She sidesteps the mess to head outside while I carefully kneel down next to it.

The burnt poo smell makes my lunch-plus-gin-plus-milky-tea swirl. I pick through the remains of the post, and pile up the untouched letters to one side. I pull open the bin bag and scoop up the doormat, burnt pooey bag and singed post mess and shove it in. I gag at the stench, open the door and drop it on the doorstep. I head back to the kitchen, find my cleaning products and return to give the whole area a wipe down.

The bottom of the door is burnt and peeling. I'm so lucky this entire house didn't go up in flames. Who the hell puts burning dog crap through someone's letterbox? At least, I hope it came from a dog. I thought that was a prank played by kids. And that's who did this. Kids. No sane adult would be so petty, would they?

I drop the used cloth and the gloves in the bin bag. I'll buy new ones. I don't want to use them again with traces of faeces on them, thank you very much. I get the dustpan and brush and sweep up a few burnt paper fragments. I drop the contents of the pan into the bin bag.

I quickly sift through the pile of post. There isn't much: a letter from Boots with vouchers, a letter for the previous occupier. I don't get much these days as all my bank accounts are paperless and everything is done online.

I jam it all in the bin bag with the shitty mat, tie the handle, open the front door, pass Mel picking up egg shells, and take it down to the wheelie bins next to the pavement and throw it in. Good riddance. I even wipe my hands in satisfaction.

But when I look back at my egged stairs, a lump of ice lands in my chest. I'm trying to be strong, but my emotions are bouncing from despair to bravado and back again and I'm struggling to keep up. Deep breaths, Sal, deeeeeep deeeeeep breaths. I need to find some kind of steadiness.

Mel deposits her bin bag and indicates the eggy smears that cake my steps.

"We'll clean this up tomorrow. Let's order a takeaway and have some wine, huh? Don't think either of us are up for going out now."

I nod and dash up the stairs quickly so I don't need to see the abuse they've suffered for any longer than necessary.

The takeaway menus are attached to the fridge with a magnet. I retrieve them and hand to Mel.

"Don't mind what we have. You choose."

Mel flicks through them and we both slump on the sofa. The comfort of my own sofa soothes me. I pull the blanket from off the back and tuck it around me. I snuggle back into the cushions and pick the remote off the armrest to switch on the telly. I don't get further than putting my finger on the button because before I can press, Mel drops the menus in her lap.

"What is that?" she exclaims.

I follow the direction of her pointing finger to the wall behind my telly. I hadn't seen it before because it was so innocuous, hidden amongst the other pictures, paintings and crap that I stick on my wall. In all my walk-throughs of the apartment I hadn't noticed it, hadn't looked carefully at the walls. My sister jumps up and moves nearer. I stare at what she's staring at.

Seriously, though, how could I have missed it?

A huge, framed photograph hangs on my wall. All my other wall hangings have been carefully moved and rehung around it, so it's the centrepiece of the wall. It's one of the photos of me sleeping that Tom took without my consent. His face is in the photo, looking blissful and tucked next to my own oblivious face. The photo is in black and white, with some tasteful visual effects added to highlight areas in colour or sparkle.

"That… that's not mine," I stutter.

"You didn't put that on your wall?"

"Definitely not."

"So someone broke in here to hang a photo on your wall?"

"Looks that way."

Mel shakes her head. "Freaky." She pulls out her phone and snaps a photo.

A word pops into my head.

"Surprise," I say out loud.

"What?"

"I think this is Tom's surprise. He put on Dad's gift card that he had a surprise for me. This must be it. I'd totally forgotten about it with all the panic attack stuff."

"You're sure?"

A niggle in the back of my mind flashes. "No. Could just be a weirdo fan."

I'm suddenly overwhelmed by terror. I freeze and hold my breath, as if I'm in a crime scene. As if this isn't my home anymore now that it's been invaded. As if there are traces of other people – Tom? – everywhere.

My skin crawls.

Did Tom sit on my sofa and admire this photo? Did he go through my dirty laundry? Or take something from my underwear drawer? Did he use my toilet or lie on my bed? My heart beats rapidly and I breathe deeply to stave off a panic attack, in the way the doctor at Bristol hospital told me. Think of something else, distract yourself.

But I can't catch my breath. A sensation as if the walls are closing in and suffocating me hits hard. I try to stand but stumble, my legs tangled in the blanket. Mel catches me and looks intently at me, worry etched across her features.

"That doesn't belong here!" I kick free of the blanket, yank the framed photo off the wall, push through the front door and fly down the steps. I shove it in the bin and the glass shatters. I smash down the lid of the bin on it and then stumble away.

Mel comes after me and I turn to her. "I need to get out of here. I can't be here."

"Ok, Sal, it's ok. We'll get a train back to the parents."

"No," I say but it comes out as a desperate whine.

I can't face being enclosed on a train again for two hours. I need air. I take a few steps down the pavement and away from my apartment, that is no longer *my* apartment. I hang onto some metal railings and bend forward trying to catch my breath.

Mel clutches my arm and moves her face so that she can see my eyes. So that I look at her and understand. "Stay there, Sal. Just breathe. I'll lock up and we can go find a hotel and we'll sort all this out, ok?"

"Ok," I mumble.

As Mel runs back to the apartment to get our bags and suitcases that still sit in the hallway, I slump down on the pavement, desperately trying to control my breathing. Dread tugs at my skin, making me shiver uncontrollably. It doesn't feel safe here anymore. My wonderful home has been invaded, dirtied, touched. I feel exposed. Worse. Violated.

Who would do that? Go to that much trouble to reorganise my wall hangings to hang a massive framed photo of Tom and me? It has to be him.

# CHAPTER 13

"Hey, Sal, you ok?" Steve says the following morning over his shoulder at me in the back seat.

I can't get a word out in reply.

"She's ok, bit shaken up." Mel replies on my behalf. "Let's get her back to the parents."

Steve puts the car in gear and drives away from the station. I zone out as they talk about the kids. I'm exhausted. Mel sorted us a cheap hotel room last night after helping me to stave off another panic attack.

I haven't eaten anything since lunch on the train up to London yesterday. Mel popped out to a nearby shop to get sandwiches and wine after we'd checked in, but I couldn't face anything. Mel necked the wine, ate her sandwich and fell asleep almost immediately, lightly snoring.

But I didn't sleep a wink. Every time I closed my eyes I pictured Tom sat on my sofa looking at that photo. My guts would squirm at the thought and grumble so loudly I thought I'd wake Mel. I couldn't face eating any breakfast this morning either, or a snack on the train.

"Thank goodness you didn't stay at the flat," Steve says.

"Why's that?" Mel replies.

"You've not looked at the news?"

"No, Steve," Mel says in a way that tells her husband to get on with it already.

"Well, it seems that Darlington idiot got back from the

US on Friday night and was at Sally's flat last night. There's been some right weird articles."

Tom was at my flat *last night*? My immediate reaction is to find my phone but it's in my bag that's in the car boot with my suitcase. Mel has the same urge, tapping her pockets. But her phone's in her bag that Steve slung in the boot.

Was Tom there on Friday night too? Was that when he desecrated my home and adorned it with that monstrosity of a photo?

She looks at me from the front seat with a look that says, WTF.

"Here we are," Steve says as we turn onto our parents' driveway.

As soon as he parks, I jump out the car, open the boot and yank out my handbag and suitcase. I fly towards the front door. I can't face finding my house keys and press the doorbell just as Dad opens it.

"Hi, Dad," I say as I squeeze past him, dump my suitcase at the bottom of the stairs then take the stairs two at a time and head up to my attic bedroom and tip my handbag up on the floor to find my phone. I stab in my pincode and go straight to a new browser, cursing how slow my phone reacts.

The tabloids and a few other celebrity gossip sites are carrying the same pictures of Tom outside my flat. He staged the whole thing, it's obvious. The photos are posed, they are not paparazzi shots. A headline reads: TOM DARLINGTON MISSING HIS DARLING.

Swoon boyband member, Tom Darlington, seems to have mislaid his girlfriend. The singer turned actor has returned from a modelling job in the US to find Sally Speck not at home. He's appealing to his fans to help him convince her to forgive him.

"We've been going through a bad patch," Tom explains outside Sally's London apartment. "It's my fault for being away so long, and I want to make amends."

*A bad patch?* What the hell is this guy going on about? I shout at my phone, "We are not together!"

I click into the Sally, Darlington's Darling Facebook group.

Oh. My. God.

I gape at the ceiling for a moment, attempt to rein in my galloping heart. Today's post pinned to the top of the page has received 42k likes and 22k comments:

> Hey guys, it's me, Tom. I'm missing Sally. She's mad at me and I need to convince her that I'm sorry. Will you help me? I know you guys have got my back! If you can get through to her, if you can get her back in my arms, I'll make it worth your while ;-)

That bastard has stirred up a hornet's nest by inciting his fans. The incident at the Bristol convention was minor compared to what the horde might do. I'll never hide from the swarm. It'll engulf me and deliver me up to him. It's a matter of time before they plot a course to Hampshire.

I'm being hunted.

"There's a right hubbub going on outside," Dad says as he looks out my window at the road below the next morning. "They've got signs and everything."

I'm groggy, but hear the voices, cars, music. Immediately alert, I whip out of bed to look out the window with him. A cheer goes up from the vultures gathered outside the bungalow when they spot me. There's about thirty of them with more arriving. They stand on the pavement, and – surprisingly respectfully – don't cross the threshold into our driveway. I duck away and sit on my bed.

It happened. Tom's fans have made their way to the back end of beyond to lobby me on Tom's behalf. I feel vulnerable, stripped bare for all to see. I hide my face with my hands, screw the heels of my palms into my eyes. They're playing his music. A chant starts up of "Take Tom back, be Darlington's darling!"

Dad shuffles away from the window. "It's a lovely day, Sal, perhaps you should come and sit down the end of the garden where you can't hear them. Your mother and I popped out earlier, before that mob arrived, and I've got you a Belgian bun." He's not fussed by the crowd outside, or if he is, he's not showing it.

He moves to the door and an unseen string pulls at me. The need to stay close to a loved one tugs at my chest. I quickly put on my dressing gown and slippers and follow him downstairs, not wanting to be on my own.

Mum is sitting in the garden in the sunshine, reading. Dad goes out and potters about the flowerbeds. Weeding and doing whatever it is he does. I make a coffee and put the bun on a plate and go out to join them.

Our garden is long and secluded. The noise from the street is distant, not so intrusive.

"We deserved some sun after all that rain," Mum says.

I 'mmm' as I eat my iced bun greedily, saving the glacier cherry until last. Dad and I have always loved them. I lick my fingers as a buzzing gets louder.

"What on earth is that?" Mum says and points at a blip in the sky. It flies towards us over the roof of the bungalow from the direction of the road. "Sounds like a swarm of bees."

Dad shades his eyes to look up at it.

As it nears me, it jerks from side to side and I get a clearer look.

"It's a drone!"

I leap up and the plate on my lap smashes on the patio. I sprint the few metres into the house and into the hallway, diving under the stairs, where there's no windows and cower there, like a hunted fox down its hole. Someone has launched a drone to record video and take photos of me in my own back garden. The blatant intrusion makes me shake. The bun is lead in my stomach and the aftertaste turns bitter in my mouth.

A few moments later, Mum stands by me and rests her hand on my head. "Oh, Sal," she says softly. "What was that thing?"

"It's remote-controlled. It has a camera." I dread to think what shots it took of me – in my dressing gown and slippers at 11am, hair a mess and makeup free, gorging on a bun and making a mad dash across the garden – where they'll be plastered, and when.

"That's terrible," she says and goes to the front room to look out the window. She calls back to me, "Do you think we should call the police?"

Would the police help? Would that just stir up the hornets even more? They're a noisy, nosey, but good-natured swarm right now. There's a festive mood. They're having a party outside the house. The drone stung, that's for sure, but I'm certain their stings could get much, much uglier if riled up. I don't want things to turn nasty, for them to kick in my parents' fence… or worse.

But then, it's a horde outside our house. It's intrusive. And it's a public nuisance, surely.

"Yes, call them," I say.

Mum nods, picks up the phone in the hallway and goes through to the lounge.

Does Tom really think that invasion of privacy will win me over? I'm terrified in my own home. I stay crouched in the hallway for a long time. Fearful of going anywhere near any windows in case that drone is there looking in at me. First my apartment, and now my safe place, my childhood home, has been desecrated by that obsessed man and his insane fans.

Dad comes in. "I've cleaned up that smashed plate."

"Thank you. Sorry about that."

"It's just a plate. We've got plenty more. You staying there for a while? Can I get you anything?"

I'd like to ask him to go back in time and erase the

night of the awards ceremony. And I know he would, if he could. "Any chance you can close the curtains in my bedroom and bring me down my phone? It's on the bedside cabinet."

"Right you are."

As he heads up the stairs, I uncoil from my tense crouch. My muscles yowl at me angrily and repay me with pins and needles.

Dad hands me my phone and heads back outside. I doubt the drone operator wants footage of Dad's builder's bum as he weeds the flowerbeds, so might give up the pursuit.

Either way, I don't feel like moving from this shadowy spot under the stairs right now. Ridiculous, I know. I feel like a child playing hide and seek and make as little movement as possible. I trawl YouTube for my name but there's no drone footage or photos uploaded just yet.

I look at the Facebook page. The fans gathered outside have posted various pictures of them standing in front of my house. And there it is. Tom's liked all the photos. He's written something that makes me fume:

Thanks y'all! You're doing me proud. She's hearing you, I'm certain. Keep it up. I can always count on you guys to be there for me. My assistant will be in touch.

Who does that? What kind of freak encourages others to harass someone?

"Police are here," Mum shouts to me from the front room where she's been waiting for their arrival.

I take a deep breath and leave my hiding spot. My legs are numb. I limp over to Mum and watch as a police car pulls up outside our house and two officers step out to talk to the crowd.

Mum opens the window a crack but we can't hear what's said. There's some gesticulating from one of the officers who's doing most of the talking and the crowd lower signs, get to their feet, switch off the music. The other officer takes out a notebook and pen and takes down each individual's details. Slowly they disperse, the officers overseeing the proceedings. I'm surprised to see it's all relatively tame. No screaming or resistance. I'm not sure what I expected – a full-on riot?

After a while, I decide I don't need to see any more and head into the kitchen to make another coffee and then go and sit in the lounge to drink it. When I'm almost done, the doorbell rings and Mum answers it.

I can hear a murmur of conversation and the door closing. Mum brings the two police officers through and introduces them to me. She calls Dad in from the garden.

The two officers smile warmly at me. A man and a woman.

"I'm PC Dawn Cole and this is PC Andy Hawkins," the female officer says.

PC Hawkins nods at me. I smile back at them and shift on the sofa, feeling super self-conscious in my pyjamas and dressing gown, with crazy bed-hair.

"You must be Sally Speck, correct?" PC Cole says.

"Yes," my voice comes out as a squeak. I clear my throat and try again. "Yes, I'm Sally." I can't tell if I should stand and shake their hands, and I'm paralysed with indecision.

Thankfully Dad arrives and saves me by introducing himself. Mum offers the officers a drink. They politely refuse. She asks them if they'd like to take a seat. They both sit on the sofa opposite the chair I'm sitting on. The female officer closest to me.

"May we call you Sally? Or Ms. Speck?" she says.

"Sally is fine," I reply.

Mum and Dad hover behind them as PC Hawkins pulls out his notebook and a pen and PC Cole leans closer to me.

"So, Sally, we just want to understand why those people were gathered outside your house. Mrs. Speck said we should speak to you about it," she says with a friendly glance at Mum.

"It was Tom Darlington," I blurt.

"The celebrity?" she asks as PC Hawkins stares at me for a heartbeat and then scribbles in his notebook.

"Yes."

"Can you explain?"

"He put something on a Facebook page asking his fans to come to my parents' house."

"Did he share your address online?" she asks, a note of real concern in her voice.

"No. But he must've shared it privately somehow."

"Can we see this post?"

I pull my phone out from my dressing gown pocket and find the Facebook group. But yesterday's post from Tom and the one from just moments earlier is no longer there.

"Looks like he must've deleted it… But this is the page I was talking about." I hand my phone to PC Cole who looks at it and scrolls through. She hands it to her colleague who takes a few notes while looking at the screen and then puts the phone on the table.

"So, there's a Facebook page that seems to be about you, however there's no proof that Tom Darlington definitely posted anything."

"His fans also trashed my apartment in London."

"Did you tell the police?"

"No."

"Why not?"

"It was a few eggs and some dog poo through the letterbox. I didn't think it was serious enough to call the police."

"The same fans as outside today?"

"I've no idea. Maybe."

"We took the names down of everyone outside and told them if they returned to the area, they could potentially be arrested under anti-social behaviour or public order offences."

"Wow, arrested." For some reason this sounds incredibly serious and it surprises me. "A group of them also bothered me at a work convention thing recently too."

"So today wasn't an isolated incident, in terms of his fans bothering you?"

"No. Sadly not. And it's all over social media. There's not one fan. There's millions."

PC Cole glances at PC Hawkins who hasn't said anything, but continues to write what I'm saying, occasionally flipping over a full page. He catches her eye and some kind of unsaid communication darts between them.

"It might be an idea to block nuisance people on social media, report anything offensive and also, if it's getting really bad, to take a break altogether for a while."

"That's pretty much what I've done. But it hasn't made any difference."

"Why are these fans so interested in you?" she asks.

"Because I had…" I pause as my hovering parents' presence looms and I can't bring myself to say one-night stand. "… a date with him, which was put in all the papers. His fans took umbrage at that."

"Umbrage, great word," PC Cole says with a smile. "I can tell you're a wordsmith. An author, is that right?"

"Yes, did Mum tell you?"

"No. We often discuss the news in the break area at the station, and there was a story today about Tom Darlington and…" she gestures her hand as if unable to find the right words.

"And you're the woman it refers to," PC Hawkins finishes his colleague's sentence.

I cringe at the thought that they've read all the lies about me from the media. What must they think? And now they're looking at the supposed love of Tom Darlington's life still in her nightwear at her parents' bungalow. Hardly glamorous. Hardly who anyone would expect a superstar celebrity to be in love with.

PC Cole recovers herself. "Has Tom done anything? Or is it just his fans?"

"He broke into my apartment in London and put a framed photo on my wall."

Dad tuts. This revelation riled him up no end when I told him. And clearly, he's still riled up about it.

PC Cole glances at Dad and he purses his lips and shakes his head.

"I see," she says, turning back to me. "Is this picture still on your wall?"

"Um, no. I binned it…"

The female officer glances at her colleague, his face is neutral and he doesn't look up from his diligent transcription of the conversation.

"Was there evidence of a forced entry?" PC Cole continues.

I shake my head.

"There's been other things – flowers, gifts and a letter," Mum chips in.

PC Cole looks at her. "Do you have any of these?"

Mum frowns. "The flowers died, we shredded the letter and the gifts are out the back. Sally's tried to get them picked up and taken away but no one is taking any responsibility. Oh wait. We have the cards he sent with them."

Mum hurries off to retrieve the cards.

"He was also calling and messaging my mobile, but I switched phones and numbers so he couldn't reach me anymore. He also put a tracking device on my phone, which I've since deleted."

"I see, when was this?" PC Cole says.

"More than five weeks ago now. We had our, er, date, and then he hasn't left me alone since. He took photos of me which I didn't know about and posted them on his social media. He was at my apartment on Saturday night – there's media coverage of it."

"What contact have you had with him?"

"None whatsoever. I haven't spoken to him since a few days after the date."

She frowns. "Do you feel harassed by his behaviour?"

"Absolutely."

"Is it causing you serious alarm or distress?" she asks.

"Yes," I reply.

"She had a panic attack at the convention because of those stupid fans' antics," Dad says, getting angrier. His sense of injustice blooming on my behalf.

Mum returns and hands the cards to PC Hawkins who hands them to PC Cole. She takes them but doesn't look at them, still intent on me.

"Does Tom's behaviour put you in fear of violence?"

This makes me pause. I think back to the smashed car window outside my apartment on the night I went to the Lemonade Club and wouldn't let him in. Although that anger wasn't directed at me, it was still there. "Potentially, yes."

"I see," PC Cole says. "Is there anything else?"

My mind goes blank and I don't reply.

PC Cole clears her throat and looks down to read the cards. She places them on the table next to my phone. "It seems as if you're saying this celebrity's behaviour is getting out of hand. Although there's no hard evidence that he posted in that Facebook group, or put a photo on your wall in London or even sent the gifts to your parents – unfortunately this card is printed so could be from anyone who has just signed off as Tom."

She pauses a moment to let that sink in before continuing.

"We suggest you keep a diary of everything that has happened, and happens. And try to keep hold of any evidence. If he's sending you flowers that can be construed as an innocent, isolated gesture. And sending extravagant gifts to your parents could be a romantic gesture on a par with his level of fame and wealth. But if each of those things is one part of a lot of other inappropriate and unwanted attention, then it could be really serious, Sally. Especially if it's affecting you emotionally and physically – I'm assuming you're staying here because you don't feel safe in your London apartment?"

"Yes," I say. "And I thought I was safe here until all those fans showed up outside."

PC Hawkins puts down his pen and looks at me. "We'll make a note of all this. And as my colleague says, please keep a detailed record. If anything else happens, call 101 to log the incident. And if it's an emergency call 999."

He looks at PC Cole and she nods. They both stand and Mum shows them out.

"Well, that's that, then," Dad says and heads back into the garden.

I sit in a stupor. *Really serious.* It's true, Tom has persisted in hassling me when I've made it clear that I'm not interested. It is serious. His behaviour has shifted from strange to outright bizarre. Is Tom harassing me? Or is it his fans? Or is he encouraging his fans? Is that even the same thing? And what about the media? Can they just claim they're reporting the 'news'?

# CHAPTER 14

I snap to attention, dash upstairs and fire up my laptop. I open a blank document and start writing down everything that has happened, starting with today. I then go backwards, starting with the egging and photo in my apartment.

But when it comes to dates before that I pause. I know the date I met Tom Darlington was the same date as the awards ceremony, and the date of the Bristol convention is also easy to find. But what about everything in between? I rack my brains, stare at my phone for a while and then it hits me.

The family Whatsapp group. I open up the app and scroll up and up through hundreds of messages. And… bingo. I find the date that I told Mel about the flowers. And the date that the extravagant gifts arrived for my parents.

After slotting in the dates, I screenshot the Facebook page, note down tons of media coverage links, and see that there's been nothing new since yesterday. I take some screenshots, including one of the article that shows Tom stood outside my flat two days ago on Saturday night.

The action of finding 'dirt' on Darlington thrills me. I will not be a passive bystander in all of this. PC Cole is right – it's not one isolated incident. The more I write and find evidence the more I feel my strength coming back to me.

I rush downstairs into the study, find Dad's shredder and open the lid. If the pieces of the letter are still in there I can try and stick them back together somehow. But unfortunately Dad's already emptied it and no doubt tipped the contents into the recycling bag. So, long gone.

Disappointment stabs through me, cutting my buzz in two.

But the cards. The gifts to my parents. I grab my phone, then head into the garden where the hot tub and painting are stored under a waterproof tarpaulin next to the shed.

"Dad, can you help me?"

Dad looks up from the flowerbed he's tending, stands with an ooh and ah as his knees click into place, wipes his grubby hands on his trousers and heads over to me.

"I just want to take some photos of these things. But need to get this off first."

Dad fiddles with the bungee ropes that are holding the tarpaulin down. They ping apart and together we pull off the plastic sheet. I then take photos of the hot tub box and pull the painting out of its cardboard box and take some pics. Dad waits patiently, scanning his garden, no doubt wondering what needs his attention next.

"Done," I say and together we put the tarpaulin back and Dad secures the bungee ropes.

I thank him and head back into the lounge. The cards are still on the coffee table where PC Cole placed them.

I photograph them and then pick them up. I look at them and realise I need some kind of evidence box. I head back into the study and look through the cupboards stuffed with all the old stationery that Mum once used in her teaching job and is now a free-for-all if anyone needs anything. I find a big black box file that is a bit tatty at the edges from use. It's perfect.

I pull it down, open it and drop in the two cards. I rifle in the tub of marker pens and highlighters and find a black chunky marker. Along the spine in the white box, I write

'Dirt' and it makes me feel better.

I head back upstairs clutching the folder as my phone pings.

It's Mel asking how the police situation went. I tap back a reply, giving her a rundown and telling her about my evidence collecting.

She replies:

'You might want this then. I didn't send it before cos didn't want it to upset you.'

And then a photo follows. It's the one she snapped of the framed photo on my apartment wall before I snatched it down and binned it. I fist-pump the air. "YES!"

I email myself the photo and save it on my laptop, insert it into my timeline and also print it out to include in my Dirt box. I do the same with a photo I'd taken of the 36 bouquets.

The flowers… I search online for florists in our local town. There's only two. I dial the number for the first and ask if they remember delivering a lot of roses to one address. They don't. I try the second. Bingo.

"Do you happen to have a note of the sender?"

The man on the phone hesitates.

"The flowers were for me. I live at the address. I just wanted to surprise the sender by sending some flowers in return but I don't have the address."

I lay it on thick but the guy's not budging.

Not to be deterred, I slot the name of the florists into my timeline of events. Perhaps, if it came to it and the police asked, they'd have to reveal the customer's details. It's like I'm plotting a novel and the thrill I experience at crafting stories comes back to me.

In the back of my wardrobe is a shoe box with some tatty old high heels that I've not worn in an age. They were the first heels I wore when I started going out out when I was eighteen and the first pair I spent some serious money on. Well, serious enough at that age. They even came in a

140

shoebox with tissue paper, and after every wear, they went back in the box. I couldn't bring myself to throw them away when I moved out because of the emotional attachment. They've languished here in my old wardrobe at my parents' house for twenty-odd years. I slip off the lid and tucked between the tissue paper is my old mobile phone. I put it there the day I arrived home after Mel gave me a new phone. Out of sight, out of mind and all that.

I sit on my bed and look at my old phone. Should I turn it on? Will it be full of texts and voicemails from Tom? How long do voicemails last for? How would I record them anyway? I look at my laptop and know the internet will tell me, no doubt. But something in me resists.

I'm not ready to see or listen to his voicemails or texts. The thought is actually repellent and my body reacts by tingling in a similar way to the pins and needles earlier.

When I set up my new phone I changed the number on my Whatsapp, deleted the conversation with Tom and blocked his number in case he somehow got hold of my new mobile. But this old phone, with my old Whatsapp might still show the messages.

I know I should turn it on and check. Take screenshots and add to my Dirt collection. I turn the phone over in my hand.

No.

I drop it into the box folder. If I have to, then I'll turn it on. But for now, it can stay off. I can't pollute my mind with any more of his crap. I shut the lid of the box, press save on my document and immediately feel a wash of relief come over me. As if now everything's out of my head and in one place, it's lifted a massive weight off my shoulders.

The fear from earlier has changed into a feeling of satisfaction for a job well done.

The following day, Omar's car pulls into the driveway, the gravel crunches to announce his arrival. I watch him from the study window and rush to let him in.

"Hey you," he says as I pepper him with little kisses and hug him tight.

"Hey you," I reply. I'm beaming, I can't help it. He makes me feel happy. Since my scary Bristol experience, he's been my rock.

I lead him through to the kitchen and turn the kettle on.

"Parents out?"

"Yep. After all the drama with the police yesterday Mum needed a cake and a fancy coffee and Dad needed to blow some cash on compost."

Omar nods. I don't ask him if he wants a tea, as he always does, so I crack on with making it. While the kettle boils I launch into a full rundown about the police and them telling me to write everything down and collect evidence.

As I make his tea and lead him to the lounge I tell him about my timeline. He had to work last night and I didn't get a chance to update him on my news, so it surges out like a rain cloud bursting.

We sit on the sofa and I excitedly tell him about ringing the florists and the Dirt box. He responds with a few hmms and nods, but isn't as into it as me.

I realise that I've spent the best part of an hour talking about Tom Darlington and his fans and Omar hasn't got a word in edgeways. I've literally talked at him since he arrived. I pause and notice he looks a bit off. His eyes are watery and the left side of his face is puffy. And he hasn't touched his tea. It dawns on me and I reprimand myself for forgetting until now.

"Sorry, babe, I've been wittering on. How was your root canal at the dentists?"

He cups the left side of his face gently. "Awful. Really painful. I hate the dentists."

"You on painkillers?"

"Yeah. Can't eat or drink for a few hours. If I dribble,

tell me ok? I still can't feel my face." He grins at me, a little lopsidedly as the left side droops.

"Oh my… you… um," I lean forward to point at some pretend drool on his chin.

His eyes go wide and he touches his chin, mortified. He looks at his dry fingers, then side-eyes me. "You cheeky thing." We both laugh as he pokes at my ribs.

The mirth passes and we sit in silence. He stares off into space. And I realise he's still a bit… off.

I squeeze his knee. "Hey, what's up?"

He turns to look at me and a frown mars his features. "We, er, need to talk."

My throat constricts. Something bad is coming. It's obvious. Is he going to tell me he doesn't want to see me anymore? That the sex isn't as incredible as I think it is? That we're not compatible? That I'm the only one feeling this intense connection between us.

"I was in the waiting room at the dentists. A woman sat opposite me and got a magazine out of her handbag. I nearly fell off my seat when I saw the front cover."

I frown, not comprehending what he's trying to tell me.

"It was you, Sal. Your face staring back at me, along with… *his*."

He says 'his' like a hiss, full of disgust and contempt for who he's referring to. And I realise that he can only mean Tom Darlington.

Omar fumbles with his jacket and removes a folded gossip magazine from the inside pocket. He spreads it out on the coffee table.

"The woman went in before me, and left the magazine on the seat. So, I picked it up. It's dated today."

Before I can be too horrified at my face next to Tom's on the cover, Omar flicks to a double-page spread. I watch him and a wriggling lump of anxiety builds.

He looks up at me and taps the page.

I read the headline: SALLY SPECK DUMPS DARLINGTON FOR GOOD. TOM COMFORTED

BY BROTHER

I scan the article, notice the official author photo of me that they always use, and an old photo of Omar that looks as if it's been dug up from his Facebook page. Omar's standing with a mate, whose face has been blurred out. There's a photo of Tom Darlington with his head in his hands sitting outside a restaurant, with, I guess, his brother sitting next to him with his arm around Tom's shoulders.

And there, in the corner, is the photo of me, Hanna and Liz outside the pub; Hanna's face blurred.

"Liz?" I ask but a painful stab in my head tells me it's true.

Omar places a comforting hand on my back, just like Angus is doing to Tom in the photo. "She sold out."

"I trusted her." I thump the magazine on the table as bitter tears well. "I can't trust anyone anymore."

Omar hugs me into his chest. "You can trust me."

I push him away. "Can I?" I scream.

"Yes, you can. I'll never hurt you," Omar replies, looking intently into my eyes, not startled by my venom. "And you can trust Hanna. She messaged me just before I arrived here, she saw the magazine at the newsagents this morning and didn't know how to tell you. She's just as shocked as us."

"Do you know what this means? Tom, his fans, the media will come after me again. Maybe after you! Does it say where you're from?"

Omar's jaw clenches. "It does."

"Aargh!" I jump up and pace, scrunching up my face and pressing my fists into my eyes.

"Sal, calm down." Omar stands but doesn't approach me.

"Just when I thought my life might get back to normal, that he might finally be gone, that his fans had been shooed off from outside, that the media weren't interested in me anymore." I turn to Omar and bellow, "How could she!"

Omar looks away, like a dog scolded by its owner.

It's not his fault. I shouldn't take this out on him but I can't stop myself. He's nearby so he's bearing the brunt. I thump my hand against the window.

Omar crosses his arms. "They've written a bunch of lies in there about me too, you know."

I turn to him. He studies his feet. He's hurting. "I'm so sorry, Omar. This is not your fault. That awful story about Dad and now you. It's all because of me."

He holds out his arms and beckons me into them. "I'll help you through it. Whatever that joker throws at you, I'm here for you, ok?"

I walk to him and hug him so tight I think I might squeeze the life out of him. He kisses the top of my head and we sit back on the sofa. I curl myself around him.

After a while basking in Omar's protective arms, I reposition my head and kiss him.

His cheeky grin reappears. "And besides, we haven't even spoken about the most important thing this article brings up."

"What thing?"

"Am I your boyfriend then? If the magazine says it's true then it must be, right? Are we… you know… official?"

My cheeks colour and I squirm my forehead into his chest. "Yeah, we're official."

"Woohoo," he says in my ears and tickles me. I kiss him again.

I ram down my anger at Liz's betrayal. Push it right to my toes. It doesn't matter. None of that matters. Omar matters. This love matters. I won't let anyone or anything cut it down.


Omar left soon after my parents arrived home, after lunch. Well, my lunch. He just looked longingly at my cheese toastie, still not being able to eat because of his tooth. I tidy the kitchen and then head upstairs to my bedroom. I immediately pick up the magazine – that Omar reluctantly let me keep for my Dirt box, he wanted to throw it straight in the bin – and read the article in full.

Oh, Liz, how could you?

The initial fury at her betrayal has ebbed and now I feel… disappointed. The article says they asked Tom's people for a comment, but they had declined to give one.

So I do the thing that I keep promising myself I won't do. I look at his social media channels. For evidence, I tell myself.

Tom has posted cryptic tweets about how he's "heartbroken" and that today's news has "shocked and saddened" him. He's retweeted a tweet he posted on the night we met, which says, "I'm in bliSS". The capital SS are my initials, it's so obvious.

I scroll through the replies, and Tom's obsessed fans have worked it out – of course they have. I skim-read through thousands of tweets attacking me.

I click onto his Instagram and he's posted a moody black-and-white close-up photo of a man crying with the caption: #currentmood

I google my name. A mistake. Tom's outpouring of emotion has sparked article after article and rehashed old stories. Gossip website headlines ask WHO IS OMAR? and WHY THIS MAN OVER TOM? Poor Omar's face is plastered everywhere, along with scathing reports that he's 'just an insurance salesman'. I screenshot some of the comments on one of the most vicious articles and WhatsApp it to Hanna.

'Still can't believe Liz did this. This is the kind of hate Tom's fans have for me – and now Omar.'

A few moments later, Hanna replies:

'I spoke to Liz, she was offered big money to talk. She's opening a second gym and needed the cash. Don't think she realised what harm she'd cause. It's a rag of a magazine.

Omar's a big boy. He'll cope. And Tom will get the hint finally that you're NOT interested.'

'I hope so…'

'You've got a new man, and an awesome one at that. Yep I'm biased cos he's my bro! Anyhooo, gotta go, Josh got that vomiting bug that's going round xx'

Tom must've got the hint by now. I want to believe Hanna, I do. And it's true, Omar is awesome. Nothing that Tom can do will break us. We're solid. Thinking about Omar – my boyfriend! – sends a fuzzy warmth under my skin.

I bash out a quick goodnight message to him and then put my phone in my drawer so I'm not tempted to look at it anymore.

# CHAPTER 15

The doorbell rings at around seven the next morning. I'm drowsily sorting my breakfast in the kitchen and the shrill bell makes me jump.

"Probably those shorts I ordered from Dotty Ps," Mum says from the lounge. "Bit early for a delivery, but I'm not complaining. They've come super quick."

"I'll go," Dad says from their bedroom door. "I'm closest."

Mum comes into the kitchen to take her vitamins with some water. We half listen as Dad opens the front door.

"I don't think she wants to see you, lad," Dad's voice drifts down the hallway.

The reply stabs my heart. I drop the knife I'm holding to butter my toast and it clatters against the plate.

He's HERE! At my parents' house!

The voice is charismatic and self-assured. Lovable. A voice that everyone wants to please. "Mr Speck, sir, I'm desperate to see her. Please, sir, I—"

Tom Darlington turns the charm level up to eleven but Dad cuts him off with a brusque tone.

"Like I said, she does not want to see you. And I expect she will never want to see you. You've caused this family a lot of heartache. Now, be off with you. And don't return."

"Will you give her this? Please, Mr Speck." Tom's pleading tone is wretched and wobbly, as if he's choking back tears. "Please."

There's a pause. I imagine Dad battling with his manners.

"Please, Mr. Speck, I beg of you."

"Give it here then. Now, be off with you."

The door slams and I spring into the hallway. Dad holds out the rain-splattered box and I grab it as I pass him and head up the stairs.

In my dark bedroom I creep towards the window and peek out the curtain. There's Tom getting into the back seat of his Range Rover, Ashraf holds an umbrella above him before shaking it off and getting into the driver's seat. Tom glances up at the window and I duck.

Damn! He didn't see me. Did he? No. No, he didn't.

I turn the light on and sit on my bed. The box is flat and square, with a ribbon around it. Tucked into the ribbon is a small card.

I read out loud. "Diamonds for my diamond. Sally, you are my shining light and guide my way. In my darkest times, I think of you and only you. Tom."

Urgh. Cheesetastic.

I undo the ribbon and open the box.

I gasp as the exquisite, twinkling jewellery catches the light. Matching diamond earrings, a necklace and bracelet – which are probably worth more than this bungalow – sit on my knee. Why is it that men think all is forgiven when they buy you extravagant gifts?

I take the necklace and hold it up to my neck in the mirror. Just to see. Then I clasp it on and put the bracelet and earrings on too. I hold back my hair and I sway from side to side, mesmerised by the sparkle.

Is Jake right? I've not contacted him since Tom's appearance on that US chat show. Jake's called and messaged me but I've not responded.

Here it is. I try it on for size: Tom is actually really into me and I pushed him away because of my own insecurities. He's chased me now for six weeks. Made grand, public gestures. Relentlessly declared his love. Spent a fortune on diamonds. Most men would've given up long ago.

You can't help who you fall for. And he's fallen for me. An older woman who is clearly miles away from his usual 'type'. I'm no lingerie model. I'm an overweight geeky sci-fi author in my late-thirties.

I shake my head in the mirror. NO. He doesn't love me. His behaviour is bizarre.

I take off the jewellery and fling it back in the box, as if it has some strange magical hold over me. I snap shut the lid and a sound escapes me like a growl.

I draw back the curtains and Tom's black Range Rover is still there. He looks up at my window and smiles. All this time, he's been sitting there watching the house, waiting for me to come to the window.

The growl comes again but louder, uglier.

I rush out the house, the rain soaking my pyjamas. They stick to my body. My boobs swing without a bra. I don't care. There's no media around, and the fans skulked off home and didn't come back, scared off by the police warning. If there's pedestrians or neighbours or passing cars watching, I don't care.

A rising tide of fury is welling and is about to crash.

The gravel in the driveway cuts viciously at the soles of my feet. Then the hard pavement scratches and a muddy puddle squishes through my toes.

As I stop, the back door of the car opens and Tom steps out. "Beautiful, you're up! Still in your nightwear though, ha! Come for a drive with me. Or, I know, come back to my hotel for brunch, I'm staying up the road in that five-star place. I've missed you terribly—"

"How *dare* you," I explode. My arms flail about, I bare my teeth in a snarl. "How dare you come here. I've told you a million times – I don't want to ever see you again!"

"You don't mean that. Come for a drive." He points to the back seat and shifts to hold out his hand to help me in, like a gentleman. But he's no gentleman.

I throw the jewellery box at his face. It bounces off his chest and lands on the pavement. His look is incredulous. "Don't you like—" He starts but I yell over him.

"Stay away from me! Take your sodding gift and stay away!"

Tom steps towards me, arms outstretched.

I'm about to launch myself at him, claws out, spitting like a cat but Ashraf stands between us.

He has his back to me and pushes Tom into the car. "Come on, boss, I think we'd better go."

But Tom resists his driver. "I love you so much, whatever I've done, forgive me. I'll make it up to you. I know you don't love this other man. He's a pretender, a nobody. Whatever you want, you'll have it…"

"You've ruined my life!" I scream over Ashraf's shoulder.

Tom looks painfully confused. "*Ruined* your life? Beautiful, you are my life, my light, my reason for being."

"Shut up, just shut up!" Spittle flies from my mouth.

Tom baulks at the fury in my voice and allows Ashraf to guide him into the car. He never takes his eyes off me. "Beautiful, forgive me," he mumbles.

Ashraf picks up the box and chucks it over Tom onto the back seat. He slams Tom's door, gives me the briefest of looks, runs around to the driver's seat and speeds away.

Tom watches me forlornly from behind the window, his nose pressed to the glass and a palm outstretched against it. His lips move. He's saying, "I love you."

I glower at him as the car passes me and continue to stare, my fists clenched long after it turns a corner and is out of sight.

I jolt as light fingers brush my arm.

"Sal," Mum says gently. She steers me off the street.

In a hazy blur Mum tells me to go upstairs, take a hot shower and get into some dry clothes before I catch a cold. Her words float around me as if I'm in a room of butterflies dancing and fluttering, and always just out of reach.

I stumble upstairs, turn on the shower in the little attic bathroom next to my bedroom and get in. I sit in the shower in my pyjamas and the warm water streams over me. I hunch and my hair hangs down in rats' tails. It tickles my cheeks and I fling it back over my shoulder angrily.

Tom came to my parents' house! Tom told me he loves me! Tom still doesn't understand that I don't want to be with him. What else can I do? How can I ever get away from him?

I need to be ugly.

I step out the shower and slop into the second small bedroom in the attic opposite mine, which used to be Mel's room. Mum's sewing machine is set up on a little table with her sewing box next to it.

A glint of silver catches my eye and an image of the glittering diamonds flashes across my vision. I dive forward and grab at the sparkle. I pull out Mum's sewing shears. The scissors have long, polished blades and feel heavy in my hands.

I pull them up to my face and glint them this way and that. I test the end. The sharpness doesn't register through the numbness that has swallowed me up. I sink to the carpet, the scissors in my hands.

I just want to write. To get on with my life. To be anonymous. I've never wanted fame. Success, yes. But never fame. Everything was going so well. I'd just won my first award. But now... Tom has ruined it all. I'm hounded, abused, scared to go out. Betrayed by friends. I can't write or think. I can't concentrate on anything. Nowhere is safe; not my apartment, not my childhood home. Everything has been tainted by Tom.

I've had enough. I just want my life to return to normal.

Beads of water run off my wet hair and it suddenly feels so heavy on my head. So, so heavy. And I can't bear it any more. I look again at the glinting steel. Will I ever feel light again? I know what I need to do.

I sit in the lounge at the dining table. It's covered in an old, faded beach towel that used to be ours when we were kids. Mel puts a second old towel around my shoulders and tips a bag full of stuff from Boots onto the table. Mum is sitting on the sofa, intermittently watching us and looking at her phone. Concern etched on her face.

Mel pulls apart the carton and reads the instruction leaflet. She mixes the contents in the small plastic tub provided.

"You really don't remember doing it?"

I smooth my palm over my scalp. Bring my hands to my lap. They're quaking. I hide them under the corners of the towel. "No," I croak. My eyes won't focus on anything. My voice feels stuck behind my teeth.

"What do you remember?"

"I remember screaming at Tom in the street and the car driving away. Mum bringing me in. Then I don't remember anything until you arrived."

"So you don't remember having a shower in your clothes, hacking off your hair in clumps with Mum's sewing scissors? You don't remember calling me to get you some hair dye from Boots? You don't remember Mum giving you a buzzcut with Dad's clippers?"

"No, Mel, I've told you. I don't remember any of it."

It's a complete blank. A black gaping hole where memories should be, but they are vacant. I can only imagine how horrified Mum had been to find me in the spare bedroom, soaked with the scissors in one hand, my phone in the other and my hair everywhere. Dad has made himself scarce. This is outside his Dad realm.

"You sounded so normal on the call. Asked me what I was up to, asked if I wanted to help you dye your hair. If I'd pop into Boots on the way over to pick the stuff up. I told you I'd just dropped the kids at school and I'd be right over."

All I can manage is a shrug.

"I reckon you should go to the doctors. This can't be good."

Mum pipes up, "I think it's because of the stress of seeing that idiot again. I've looked it up." She holds up her phone. The font of all knowledge.

There's zero energy left in me to muster a reply.

"I'm going to call the surgery, see if I can book you an emergency appointment with your doctor. I know you've been in London for a while but I'm sure she's still there," Mum says and she heads out the room to make the call.

"I also need to tell the police." My voice comes out in a whisper.

"You do. I didn't mention it right away because, well, you're… fragile."

She's right. I feel as if I'll crumble into dust at the slightest touch. Break into a zillion tiny pieces never to be put together again.

Mum comes back in and returns to her spot on the sofa. "Right, got you an appointment at eleven-thirty."

"Thanks," I say weakly.

Mel angles my head up. "Let's sort your hair out first, get you to the doctors and then you might feel up for contacting the police. Right, I think this is ready. You sure about this, sis?"

"Yes, I want to look completely different." And then I might feel completely different. Although the hair cutting is a blank, that desire hasn't changed. People won't recognise me; Tom won't know me. He'll leave me alone. "I want my freedom back, to be able to go out, to live my life again. I've been in hiding, from Tom, the media, his fans, but why should I?"

Mel dabs the bleach on my short hair with the small brush. It's cold and my scalp tingles. "You're absolutely right, that prick has no right to fuck everything up for you."

"Mel! Language," Mum tuts.

"Seriously, Mum, he's turned into a *stalker*."

The word pierces the air like a bullet. It's a seismic shift from a weird fixation to stalking.

I take a deep breath and let it out slowly. "I think he understood this morning. He finally heard me."

"Yeah, well. We'll see." Mel concentrates on putting bleach around my ears, then continues, "I agree that you should move in here for the foreseeable."

"What?" I blurt.

"You asked me what I thought when you called earlier. Oh. You don't remember."

"No."

Mel puts down the mixing bowl, pulls off the plastic gloves and looks at her watch. "You told me that you'd never feel safe again knowing that Tom could get into your apartment so easily. He did it once to put that photo on your wall, so what's to stop him doing it again."

Although I don't recall saying that to Mel, I feel a twang and know it's the truth.

Mel continues, "I think it's a good idea. Everyone knows that address and it's not safe for you to be there on your own."

I love that flat. I love my independence. I worked hard to create an amazing life for myself in London. And that's come skidding to a halt. Living with my parents is definitely NOT where I want to be at thirty-seven – no matter how cool they are. Blinking rapidly, I lean across the table and take a tissue. Blow my nose, sniff, discreetly dab my eyes. Mutter, "Wow, this bleach is strong, it's stinging my eyes."

I'm not fooling anyone. Mel pats my shoulder. "Sorry, sis."

Dad comes in from the garden. It's stopped raining, but still overcast.

"Listen, now you're all here, I've got something to say," he announces. "I'm going to put up a six-foot fence all around the house, and wide hedges at the front and some big gates to keep all the snooping media and fans away. To keep that boyband idiot away."

"But we shouldn't have to do that," I exclaim, horrified at my parents being forced to turn their home of twenty-five years into some kind of fortress. "It'll make us feel trapped inside our own home; be overbearing like we're in prison!" I stare at Mum, expecting support. I get none and continue. "I'll contact the police this afternoon. They'll do something. They have to."

Mel squeezes my shoulder. "I'm sure they will, but can they stop millions of fans from showing up at the door? From that knob arriving again? It won't be long before the media set up camp outside. I hate to say it but this address is public knowledge now, too. It needs the extra security."

Mum gestures towards Dad. "Plus, your father needs a new project. There's no more DIY to be done in the house, he's done it all."

I stare at them open-mouthed. No one can meet my eye. I've caused this drama. Sparked this upheaval. Guilt. It settles across my forehead like a heavy veil. My vision swims.

"Just think," Dad says, "I could invite that plonker actor over, your mother could poison him with one of her healthy soups and I could bury him under the new fence." Dad guffaws. He's trying to do what he does best: lighten the mood.

"Don't be a weirdo, Dad," Mel says.

Mum tuts. "Oh, Graham, you do say some very odd things sometimes. There's nothing wrong with my vegetable soup."

"It's the least he deserves. No one upsets my Sal. I knew I shouldn't have taken that bloody gift off him. If he comes near her again, I'll thump him from here all the way to France." He punches an imaginary foe.

"Better eat your spinach first then, like Popeye. Not sure he'll reach France with those puny muscles," Mel teases.

Here we are. Back to normal Speck banter. My little hair 'episode' almost forgotten. The future pretty much decided. It's my family's way of coping.

Dad flexes his biceps and plants a little kiss on each. Then heads towards the bathroom.

Mel checks my hair colour, uses the brush to move the strands about. "Bit longer, still yellow. Listen, I know you won't like this, but I also think you need to delete all your social media profiles and all that you can from the internet. Seriously, everything. All your author stuff."

"I am *not* deleting my entire online life!" Although I don't use my social media channels all that much, they're still my connection to distant friends and travel buddies from over the years.

"Sis, don't freak out," she laughs to ease the tension, "it means that nuts stalker and his deranged fans won't be able to easily track you down by looking at your posts or seeing you tagged by someone else. If you want your life back, you need to be a ghost."

I groan. Everything is changing because of my reckless fling. I'm erasing my physical life in London, I can't bring myself to scrub my online life too. "I hardly use them."

"You've had some kind of weird episode, Sal! Think about your mental health, for fuck's sake!"

"Mel, honestly, your potty mouth," Mum says.

"Sorry, Mum. But look what Sal did when she saw him! What are you going to do the next time, Sal? Chop off your hand? It made you go mental. We can't let that happen again."

They are worried for me. I know. Very, very worried. I don't remember hacking at my hair. Seeing Tom flipped my emotions upside down and the black dog came bounding in through the open door. But have I turned dangerous? I can't tell.

As soon as I sit down, I can feel the tears welling. Gathering in fat blobs in the corners of my eyes.

My doctor from years ago sits across her desk from me. She's older, greyer, but still just as warm and supportive as she was. When my name was called, Mum stayed seated in the waiting area thinking I wanted to go in on my own. But I pulled her up and made her come with me.

The doctor asks what's been happening and how she can help and her nurturing, caring tone sets me off. The dam bursts and tears stream down my face.

"Oh, Sal," Mum says and hands me a tissue from her bag. To the doctor, she says, "She's in a terrible state."

"I can see that," the doctor replies and the concern tips me over the edge again and the tears spill out, drowning the tissue so it turns to mush.

Mum proceeds to give an overview of what's happened, without mentioning Tom's name. The doctor does not seem the type to read gossip magazines or tabloid newspapers and probably wouldn't know who Tom Darlington was anyway, but I'm pleased Mum's chosen to be discreet.

"Sounds like a terribly stressful time, Sally," the doctor says after Mum finishes.

I sniff. "Yes."

The doctor holds out her bin to me and I drop the mushy tissue in it. Mum gives me a fresh one from her packet and I blow my nose.

The doctor asks me another question but I can't stop blubbering long enough to get any words out. I think she's seen enough though and starts to look at her computer screen and talk about the anti-depressants that I was on before, many years ago, and how they should help with the anxiety and stress. She talks about my forgetting what happened with the sewing scissors as something that can happen sometimes when people are under extreme stress or trauma. She calls it a 'clinical episode'.

She prints a prescription off and before she hands it to Mum reels off a list of instructions about the best time to take them, that I shouldn't drink any alcohol while I'm on them, and how they'll take between one to three weeks to kick in. She also starts talking about exercise and healthy eating.

I try to pay attention but the part of my brain marked 'concentration' is well and truly switched off and I zone out as if my head is wrapped with cotton wool. I hope Mum's listening.

We stumble out of the surgery, Mum steering me, into the next-door pharmacy. Mum hands over the prescription and I make an attempt to find my purse in my handbag but it's like my fingers aren't attached to my hands which aren't attached to my body and I can't even manage the simple task of unzipping my bag. I feel the crying bubbling up again. I'm so useless! But Mum gently places her hand on mine and gets out her own purse to pay.

We get into the car and before Mum even puts the key in the ignition, I pop out two pills and swallow them dry. Mum watches me with alarm.

"Best to get started," I say, attempting to be funny but instead frightening her ever so slightly.

She pulls her worried gaze away from me and starts the engine.

I fumble in my bag for my phone. "I'm going to call the police."

"Right now? Don't you want to head home for a bit of lunch and a rest? I think you need to rest."

"No, I need to do it now."

Blubbing in front of the doctor and taking the meds has made me feel slightly better. I know the doctor said I wouldn't feel any effect for at least a week, but it's like a placebo. I need to be strong. I need to let the police know that Tom showed up at my house.

As Mum drives us home, I call 101 to log the incident and a few moments later PC Cole calls me back. I fill her in on Tom's visit.

She's calm and efficient and her business-like tone rubs off on me. So, unlike in front of the doctor, I don't blub. I tell her what she needs to know and answer her questions. She tells me they'll make a note of it but as it's the first time he's come to my house, he's not committed any offences just yet. She advises me to keep gathering evidence, if any, and to let the police know if anything else happens.

"Sounds like you were really firm with him, Sally, and he knows now, without a shadow of a doubt, to stay away. Hopefully that should be the end of it," she says encouragingly.

The conversation is over by the time Mum pulls into our driveway.

# CHAPTER 16

A week passes in a blur. My emotions leap about my body. It's as if they bunch together and fall to my feet like a lead-weight or bump against the top of my head like a helium-filled balloon. I spend this time asleep, on the sofa watching whatever my parents put on, eating or lying in the bath until the water gets too cold to bear.

I can't write. I can't focus on anything. My mind flits from one thought to the next, not able to hold on for longer than a second or two.

Yesterday, Nisha called me to tell me the publishers are unhappy. They want my words. They want me to fulfil my contract. Of course they do. I get it. But I don't have anything to give them. Nisha is understanding, reassures me she'll stall them for longer, that it'll all be ok.

Then my mortgage payment failed due to insufficient funds in my bank account and I had to cobble the money together from my savings account to be able to make the payment. I cancelled my now-pointless London gym subscription, a painful reminder that my hard-fought-for independent life has been shattered.

Today I woke feeling very angry. My eyes pop open and I want to yell. I don't though, that would bring Mum or Dad, or both, up to my room and I can't deal with them right now. I thump the mattress and kick off the duvet.

This is all Tom's fault. He's caused this. He's screwed up my life. I can't write, can't make a living, can't do what

I love doing. All I can do is mope at my parents' house and hide from the world. And what's happened to him? Nothing. He's continuing on with his incredible life, earning his millions, singing and dancing and acting to his heart's content as if none of this even happened. And while he's living the life of Riley, I'm festering away in the weeds.

Screw him.

I grab my laptop off the floor and sit up in bed with it propped on my knees. I read the latest news about him. I methodically go through each of his social media profiles to see his behind-the-scenes work posts and editorial images with captions like:

'Thanks GQ for having me on the cover again! Cool time on this shoot'

Aargh. I'm so mad at his cheeriness and not-a-care-in-the-world attitude.

I type into the search bar 'celebrities who were murdered' and read article after article with a morbid fascination. Mostly shootings, but some strangulations and a stabbing. Some pretty gruesome. And a lot by crazed fans and stalkers. I then read about all the unsolved cases. And end up going down a rabbit hole reading about 'the most shocking murders' of all time.

As I read, I'm shocked, and disgusted and then numb. I'm so engrossed I don't hear Dad coming up the stairs and the knock on my door makes me jolt.

"How you doing in there?" Dad says.

I slap down the lid of my laptop. "You can come in."

The door opens and his head pops around. "It's lunchtime, and we hadn't heard a peep from you. Just thought I'd better check in."

"It's lunchtime?" I look at the clock on my bedside table to confirm that it's past one. I've spent hours in a dark room, reading about dark, awful things. I last looked at the time when I woke up around 8am.

"I'll come down now. Got a bit caught up in… um… online clothes shopping."

"Right you are," Dad says. "Your mother and I are just popping out." He heads back down the stairs.

I open up my laptop, close down all the browsers and switch it off. The stories and images linger in my mind while I make myself a tuna salad and eat it at the table.

I sit on the sofa and switch on some daytime telly. It's banal nonsense and it doesn't register at all as my brain conjures up gruesome deaths for Tom Darlington. But I don't imagine the scene, I imagine all the media headlines and all the articles.

A few hours pass and I drift off into a fitful, nightmarish sleep on the sofa. The sound of my parents coming in the front door wakes me.

Mum comes into the lounge and plonks a pile of library books on the coffee table.

"These should keep me going for a while," she says before heading back into the kitchen to start on dinner.

Dad comes in with a new Screwfix catalogue, makes himself comfortable on the other sofa and starts to flick through.

I pick the top book off the pile and look at the cover. Urgh. A comedy. I go to put it back, but decide to read the back cover. And then the opening paragraph. But I keep going and before long the story makes me smirk, and then 'hmph' and then full-on laugh out loud.

Dad side-eyes me from behind his catalogue and I hold up the book. "It's actually pretty funny."

By the time dinner is ready, a crack of light has brightened the darkness of the day and I think that the anti-depressants might be kicking in.

Another week flies by and every day feels slightly brighter. The anti-depressants are fully operational and my volatile emotions have almost steadied. I'm on more of an even keel but the slightest thing sets me off again. It embarrasses me to think of my blubbery performance at the doctors.

But PC Cole is right. It's the end of it. I can feel a weight lifting. Since Tom's visit to my parents' bungalow baring diamonds, he hasn't contacted me or put anything about me on social media. A nondescript man-with-a-van came to collect the hot tub, BBQ and painting. As soon as those extravagant gifts went, the entire household breathed a sigh of relief.

I attempt to write, but it's still too soon. My thoughts swirl and I can't cling onto anything long enough to form a sentence, let alone a paragraph or chapter.

Instead, I daydream. Or watch random crap on YouTube about dogs; about a dermatologist popping pimples; about a mother's morning routine with thirteen children. And think about going back to my apartment. But the idea still gives me the shivers. I spend time with Omar, and thinking about him. And occasionally, I'll go out and help Dad. The high fences and new hedges are well underway, thanks to Dad calling in favours from a couple of old construction trade buddies.

Each time I see Dad digging up his beautiful garden to make way for a hedge, a whoosh of emotion wells up and crashes, I attempt to steady myself but the anti-depressants can't quite stop the jerky, amped up buzz. Then I'll head back inside, shut myself in the bathroom and the threatening tears retreat just as fast as they had arrived.

In two weeks, I'm feeling excited and happy. More like myself. Not completely back to normal, but getting there.

Omar has been away for work and I haven't seen him all week. Later, I'm heading to his for a 'reunion'. I decide to brave the shops to buy something new to treat myself and to show up looking and feeling great.

I browse the rails in Topshop and pick out a couple of tops and a dress to try on. But before I head to the changing rooms, I change my mind about some trousers I'd seen on the way in and turn quickly.

Someone darts behind a mannequin out of my view.

It's a bit weird, the speed of it. I get the unmistakable feeling that this person was eager to conceal their face when I turned abruptly. I shake it off as ridiculous. I pick up the trousers and chuckle to myself as I head to the changing rooms and don't give it a second thought.

I buy a top and head into New Look next door, and then into another few shops. On the way back to my car I decide to pop into the lingerie section in Marks and Spencer's to pick up something new for tonight.

One underwear set later, and I feel really happy with my purchases. Gotta love a successful shopping trip. As I dodge past people and cars to get to the Peugeot, my skin crawls with the sense that someone's following me.

I spin around. But no one is there.

An arguing couple are loading their car with groceries nearby and paying me zero attention. I stuff my bags in the boot and get in my car, start the engine and back out of the space. I look over my shoulder and then spin my head back round to check I'm nowhere near the car parked next to me and out the corner of my eye, something catches my attention. I hit the brakes to look.

I see a figure hurriedly get into their car and shut the door a few rows opposite me. Nothing unusual about that. But the car doesn't move. I stare harder, but I can't see who is in the car. The sun's reflection on the windscreen hides the driver from view. The car still doesn't move though. Whoever sits in the car is looking right at me.

A horn blares and I realise I'm holding up a line of cars by being half in, half out of my space. I hold my hand up to say sorry, and continue backing out.

Just a weird coincidence, I tell myself. Whoever it was got in their car and made a phone call or decided to eat a sandwich. They weren't waiting for me to leave.

I drive to Omar's later that night in my sexy new lingerie, new top and new jeans. I feel good. I can't wait to see him.

As I slow for a red traffic light, I glance in my rear-view mirror. The road behind me snakes around the corner and I can see two cars. The car directly behind me is a white convertible. It's a sunny evening and the top is down so I can easily see past it to the next car. It's a dark-grey saloon. I can't see who's driving. The light goes green and I head off.

A dark-grey saloon. It bothers me. Something about the car is tickling a memory. I rack my brains. Perhaps I know someone who has one of those? Or used to?

The underwiring of my new bra is digging in to my side and I adjust it. It makes me think of shopping and the car park.

That's it! The car that was opposite me and didn't pull out was a dark-grey saloon.

I glimpse in the rear-view mirror. Once, twice, three times. Is it the same car? Is that even possible?

The white convertible turns off and now the saloon is directly behind me. It slows right down so there's a huge gap between us. But no car fills it. I slow down and the grey car doesn't catch up. It maintains its distance.

Is it Tom? Driving in a bog-standard car to follow me? Am I being paranoid?

I reach a mini-roundabout and lose sight of the car as other vehicles join behind me. Every five seconds I look in the mirror, but as I get nearer to Omar's flat in Bournemouth the traffic increases and unless I swivel to see the cars behind me, I can't tell if the saloon is still on my tail.

I tap in the code to the parking at Omar's apartment block and look behind me but don't see the saloon. That doesn't mean anything though because it could be parked just round the corner with a perfect view of me. The gate opens and I speed inside. I watch anxiously as the gate slowly closes. But no other car comes in after me. I hurriedly park in a spot reserved for guests. I grab my bag and rush to the main entrance, feeling very exposed in the deserted car park.

I repeatedly buzz Omar's flat on the intercom until he remotely opens the front door. He lives in an old converted Victorian building. The remote opening front door is about the only mod con as I then have to slog up three flights of stairs because there's no lift.

"Hey, you," he says from his front door as I finally make it down the long corridor from the stairwell.

"I think I was being followed," I say, with zero introduction.

"What?" he moves out the way and ushers me inside.

I head to his lounge and sit on the sofa. My hands shake.

He crouches in front of me and takes my hands in his. "Are you ok, Sal?"

I tell him about my weird morning shopping, the feeling of being watched and then the dark-grey saloon behind me for most of my journey that slowed right down when I did so it didn't get close.

"How sure are you that it was the same car?" Omar asks, his brow knitted.

"I have a bad feeling about it."

"Do you know the make and model of the car?"

"No, just that it was the same colour."

"Grey is a popular colour. And saloons are everywhere. It could've just looked like the same vehicle, but wasn't at all."

"I know." I sigh. Now I've said it out loud, it does sound far-fetched.

He moves to sit next to me on the sofa and puts his arm around my shoulders, squeezing me into him and kissing my head. "You've got a lot going on at the moment, maybe you're just feeling stressed?"

I relax into his strong and safe embrace; his scent soothing me. "It could be the drugs making me edgy. I'm feeling better, but still a bit out of it."

"Do you want to tell the police? They did say to let them know if anything happened."

I ponder this for a moment. What would I tell PC Cole? That I had a weird hunch that I was being followed? What could the police do without any evidence? Tom had been quiet since I flung the diamonds in his face outside my parents' bungalow. Would he be following me? Could he? Even in disguise I'm sure someone would recognise him.

I shake my head into Omar's shoulder. "No. I'll add it to my evidence timeline doc, but I don't think it was anything. I was being paranoid and silly."

"It was the druuuuuuugs!" Omar says. "All those pills you been popping." He pokes me playfully in the ribs.

I squirm and laugh. "I didn't even say a proper hello to you when I arrived. I'm sorry. Shall we start again?" I give him a big kiss. "Hey, babe, how are you? I haven't seen you in ages. Tell me all about your week and then take me to bed."

"Let's skip the work talk." He springs off the sofa and pulls me up.

"I've got a treat for you," I say as we hurry to his poky bedroom, which is pretty much all bed.

"Oh yeah?"

"I'm actually wearing matching underwear."

"Whoa," he says. "Matching? Really? I should go away more often."

No, I want to say; no, don't you go anywhere, ever.

# CHAPTER 17

Two weeks later, I angle my screen so Omar won't be able to see it when he returns. He's been in the bathroom for quite a while now and, impatiently, I pulled my phone out of my bag.

The pub is bustling, we're sat at a table in the busy restaurant area, but from where I sit, I can see through a doorway into the pub area. It's full of revellers, and someone on a piano singing.

Omar surprised me with this trip to Cornwall after he'd returned from his work trip. He'd printed out a photo of the cottage and written 'We'll be staying here for four days! My treat!' and tucked it into a napkin when he'd made me post-sex dinner. He pre-booked this pub for Saturday night and a taxi back later to our little cottage in St Anthony-in-Meneage.

At first, I was nervous. It was our first trip away together. But, after two days in Cornwall, walking on the South West Coast Path and hiring a little boat to go out on the Helford River, I realised Omar and I just fit together perfectly. We've had the best time. No one has recognised me or bothered me.

We stuffed our faces with fish and chips at the pub and Omar had excused himself. I don't know why but I'm googling things I shouldn't be. It's been just over three months since my ill-fated dalliance with Tom Darlington. I search for my name, for any new news stories, but there's nothing. I check his social media channels. No new posts about me.

It feels good to have his intrusive presence out of my life. I've faded from his fans' memories. I've been out and about with not even a flicker of recognition. The media maelstrom has well and truly died.

All is still. All is calm.

And that makes me nervous. It shouldn't. But it does.

A server interrupts me with our desserts. She places my Eton mess in front of me and Omar's chocolate brownie on his placemat.

A second later, Omar arrives back.

"Yes! I love it when that happens," he says as he slides onto his chair and rubs his hands together at the brownie in front of him.

I click out of Tom's social media channels and press the X at the top of the search browser. Enough's enough. I won't look again. Good riddance. I put my phone face down on the table. "Perfect timing," I say.

He points at my generous helping of meringue, cream and berries. "That's massive! I've got food envy."

His chocolate brownie doesn't look nearly as impressive as my dessert that is piled nearly as high as my wine glass. I pick up my spoon and get stuck in.

I swallow down a few mouthfuls and pause. I touch Omar's hand. "Thank you for organising all this."

Omar swallows his mouthful and grins. "Are you happy?"

"I'm very happy."

"Well, then I'm very happy too."

"Do you want to try some of mine?" I ask, tipping my bowl in his direction.

"Yeah," he says and gestures to his dessert.

We move food onto each other's plates.

"Mmm, the brownie is amazing."

"Meringue is pretty good too," Omar says and then looks back to his empty bowl.

I eat the last couple of mouthfuls and look at him, but something's changed. We've pretty much laughed and had the best time for the past few days, including the horrendous journey down where we got insanely lost among the back lanes trying to find our cottage.

I take a swig of red wine. "Are you ok?"

"It's the perfect evening, isn't it," Omar states rather than asks. He has a dreamy, faraway look about him. He stiffens, clears his throat and glances over at a server and gestures. They head towards the bar.

The server comes back with a bottle of champagne and two glasses. She places them on the table and poises ready to open the bottle.

"What's all this about, Omar?" I ask.

He grins foolishly, takes a breath and slides off his seat. He drops to one knee and takes my hand.

Oh, goodness.

My heart races and my mouth goes dry as he pulls a little box out of his pocket.

He fumbles a bit and pops the top. A ring glitters from the plush cushion. He looks up at me with the most earnest expression I think I've ever seen on his face.

"Sally, will you marry me?"

I gawp. Can't get my words out. Omar fills the silence, as if I need convincing.

"I know we've only been together this time around for a short while, but, truly, I've loved you since you were fifteen. You broke my heart then and ever since you've been the one I thought about, the one who got away. But this time, I'm going to do everything I can to never lose you again.

"My parents met and married within a few months and they're still happily married. I know this feels like a whirlwind, but you're the one for me, Sally. I think you are the bravest woman in the world, and the most creative woman I know. You are kind, funny and intelligent, and if you'll have me, I'd like to spend the rest of my life with you."

A proposal. An engagement. A marriage. I didn't think that would ever happen to me. I'm thirty-seven. Most of my friends are already married. But, well, why not? Our relationship is awesome. We're both too old to play games. We're happy. Otherwise we would've given up ages ago. I love being with him now and I can imagine feeling the same in fifty years' time. It all feels very right.

I cup his face. "Yes! Oh, Omar. Yes, yes, yes!"

He looks relieved. He takes the ring out of the box and places it on my finger. It fits perfectly. He stands as I do and we kiss.

The champagne pops and the server fills our glasses. Another takes photos of us with Omar's phone and I realise he'd been organising this when he told me he'd gone to the bathroom earlier.

Claps and a few cheers erupt from around the restaurant. We hug and laugh and a couple of servers come over to congratulate us, one handing Omar's phone back. Omar gives the thumbs up to a couple on the table next to us.

"Shall we drink this champagne, then?" I say, suddenly wanting to have Omar all to myself.

We both sit and as the ripple of excitement dies down and people go back to their own conversations, I lean into him. "You little charmer, you."

He laughs and clinks his glass to mine. "That I am, Mrs Hedra."

I look at my ring. Hold my hand out with my fingers straight and move my hand from side to side so the diamond glints. Mrs Sally Hedra. I try on my new name for size. Roll it around. "That proposal was spot on."

"Thank goodness for that." Omar laughs again.

I laugh too. "Low key and natural. Perfect."

He leans over the table to peck my cheek and the jug of water wobbles precariously in my direction.

"Watch out, you," I squeal as I catch it just in time.

He reaches under the table to squeeze my knee and keeps his hand there. The warmth and the weight is comforting. Solid and dependable. Not flighty or awkward. When he moves it so he can take a photo of us, the feel of his hand remains. We pose for lots of selfies together, drinking our champagne. It goes down like water. Omar takes some photos of just me and I grit my teeth and let him.

"Let's get married soon," I blurt. "No long engagement, ok?"

"Yes, ma'am," he says in a way that makes me know that was exactly what he was thinking.

Screw my nervousness about life being too good. Screw my foreboding. Embrace the good times, why shouldn't they last forever? I deserve to be happy just as much as the next person.

"Come on," I say as the servers take our dessert dishes away. "Let's finish up here and head into that bit. They're all singing and I reckon we should join in."

"We don't know the words, they're all old Cornish fishermen songs," Omar replies as we finish the last of the champagne.

I haul him up and we squeeze our way through the merry crowd in the pub area. Omar spots a lone stool at the edge of the room and sits on it while I get the drinks.

I zigzag between people to get to the bar. The bar tender comes over and takes my order.

"Hey, you just got engaged right? Congratulations," he says, before asking me what my tab number is.

As I wait for the drinks I glance to either side of me. One side is a couple snogging the face off each other and on the other is a lone guy with what looks like a full glass of coke in front of him. What's odd is that he's leaning against the bar, his elbow on the top and his hand up to cover his face. It's as if he's deliberately hiding from me.

A second later he leaves the bar, turning away from me so I don't see his face. I can't help it, but I watch as he weaves his way through people towards the door. He pulls his phone from his trouser pocket and as he exits, he puts it to his ear.

"Here you are," the bar tender says as he places the drinks in front of me.

I turn back to him and say thanks. Before I pick up the drinks, I shake off the feeling that the man was behaving oddly. Why would he hide his face from me? And leave the bar without drinking any of his drink?

I pick up the bottles of beer. Forget about it, Sal. It's your engagement! Stop being paranoid. I force the thought from my head and make my way back to Omar.

I perch on his lap and he wraps an arm around my waist.

"'Ere," a wizened old man thrusts a dog-eared booklet in my hands. "They'll call out the number of the song before they sing it, an' you can find it in 'ere an' join in."

I thank him and he moves along to the next group of people. I flick through the booklet and jiggle my bottom on Omar's knees. "Oooh," I say excitedly, "we've got the words!"

"I'll follow your lead," Omar says.

One of the group in the centre of the pub shouts out, "Five!" and I flick through the booklet to find the song. The group launch into the Cornish tune, accompanied by the pianist who takes a swig of ale first.

I start to sing the words, a beat behind the regulars because I don't know how the song goes, but I get the hang of it and belt out the chorus. I hold the booklet so Omar can see and soon he's singing too.

At last orders, we stand up with everyone else in the pub and sing one final song at the top of our lungs. We kiss each other and turn to hug strangers, as everyone else is doing. I laugh and laugh and know my life will be different from herein, will be Tom Darlington-free, will be full of wonderful things.

In the morning, I potter in the kitchen of the cottage making a fry-up for us. Omar is sat at the little table looking at his phone.

I put a plate of bacon, eggs, toast, mushrooms and grilled tomatoes in front of him and sit down next to him with my plate.

He sighs and slips his phone back into his pocket.

"Was that your other girlfriend?" I tease. It's a running joke between us that Omar is in a relationship with BBC News. He's always checking it and getting the alerts. He likes to know what's going on in the world. At all times, apparently.

But this morning, he doesn't take the bait and instead takes a grumpy bite of toast and stares at his food.

"What is it?" I ask.

"It's nothing."

"Omar," I say in a low tone of voice and drag out his name for a long time.

He sighs. "I didn't want to mention anything. I don't want to ruin our holiday."

"But…"

He pulls out his phone and taps in his pincode.

"Is it BBC News? Has she dumped you?" I tease.

He smirks, and finds what he's looking for and hands me his phone.

It is indeed a news article.

I read the headline: ACTOR TOM DARLINGTON COLLAPSES AT STAR-STUDDED EVENT AND HOSPITALISED FOR EXHAUSTION

I frown at Omar. I'm not sure why he's showing me this.

"Check out the statement from his brother."

I scan the article. Apparently, Tom was at a party in London last night with other celebrities and media in attendance. And, according to 'eyewitness accounts', received a phone call at around 9.45pm and collapsed immediately after. I get to Angus Darlington's statement.

It reads:

> We thank you all for your well wishes for Tom's speedy recovery. He has been working hard recently on his latest movie and is simply exhausted and needs some time to rest and recuperate. This has nothing to do with his love life or any other part of his private life, other than his desire for perfection in his work and his relentless pursuit of doing his best. He has a strong work ethic and pushes himself hard. Sometimes, he pushes too hard. This rest will do him good.

"Nothing to do with his love life. Do you think that's a reference to me?"

"I reckon so. But why would his brother say that?"

"Maybe he's trying to tell everyone to leave me alone. Saying this isn't my fault."

"Why would he do that?"

"Maybe he feels bad that I always get all the stick. And doesn't want me to get any more. Fingers crossed this means I won't get hounded."

"Fingers crossed."

I reread the article carefully and see there's only one reference to me, and I'm mentioned in passing as one of Tom's 'last-known girlfriends'.

I can finally move on from the whole debacle. Perhaps Tom wants to as well. Maybe he's told his brother to tell everyone to leave me alone. A hospital might be the best place for him, hopefully see some professionals and get his head straight.

Omar still hasn't touched his fry-up.

"Is there something else?"

He sighs. "I'm just angry about this whole situation."

"The Tom thing?"

"Yes. It needs to be over already. They need to leave you alone. It's *us* now. Me and you. Not you and him."

"It is me and you. It'll always be me and you." I touch his forearm, I've never seen my sweet-natured, even-keeled Omar so flustered.

"It's not though, is it. Even on our engagement weekend, he's a part of it. I had to see *his* name while reading the news this morning. I do that every morning. Why did it have to be today that he's mentioned?" Omar shakes his head and then thumps the table with a fist. "I don't want to always be in his shadow!"

I startle at the viciousness of the blow. "Omar, is there something you're not telling me?"

Omar clenches his jaw and sighs. "I was engaged before. I didn't tell you."

I gesture for him to continue.

"She left me five weeks before the wedding. I started noticing something wasn't right months before. Just a feeling of being second best, of her attention being stolen away, of not being her everything. So I checked her phone one night. And she'd been cheating on me for months with a bastard from work."

"I'm sorry."

He waves my empathy away. "Don't be. I dodged a bullet. If all that hadn't happened I wouldn't be here with you, would I? She's in the past, forgotten. I don't want to talk about it anymore. But thought you should know."

"I appreciate you telling me." I pick up Omar's hand and kiss his fingertips. "You are my everything."

"And you, mine."

"Let's just forget about Tom. Forget about that story. I don't care about that – or him – anymore. All I care about is eating our breakfast and then going for a long walk along the beach and maybe finding a secret little spot for a quickie."

Omar flushes. He's not quite as adventurous as me when it comes to that sort of thing. The thought of fast sex distracts him and I see the funk lift from his features.

I continue, "Tom will only ruin our day if we let him. I'm not about to let that happen. Come on, your meal is getting cold and I spent ages cooking it. You might as well enjoy it, I hate cooking normally."

I dig into my breakfast. He pauses for a few moments, takes a deep breath and pockets his phone. He picks up his knife and fork and gets stuck in.

# PART TWO

*Three months later*

# CHAPTER 18

The hen do was meant to be a quiet affair. Bridesmaids Nisha and Hanna, plus Mel, as maid of honour, booked a house on the outskirts of Ascot with a hot tub in the garden.

Before all the drama with Tom I would've invited tons of friends, but I was cautious now, after Liz's betrayal, and instead my party consisted of my bridesmaids, sister and my twin cousins Abigail and Annabel. They're identical and even after all these years, Dad, hilariously, still can't tell them apart. He refers to them collectively as Annagail, which makes my aunty Margaret howl with laughter every time.

The six of us spent the day at Ascot Racecourse, watching the horseracing in big, fancy hats and having a boozy picnic before heading back to the house for some hot tub action.

At around ten o'clock, when we realised we'd finished all the prosecco we'd brought with us, the decision was made to call a minibus taxi and head into Windsor to check out the nightlife.

I climb into the taxi and my pink penis boppers knock on the roof. I grasp the headband so they don't fall off and take a seat, pulling up my 'Bride to Be' sash so I don't sit on it and rip it.

I'm merry, but not all-out drunk. Not quite yet. I'm pacing myself. I want to remember my special night in the morning. I've drunk gallons of water all day and eaten. Most recently in the hot tub I inhaled chicken crisps and hummus. The taste is pleasant on my tongue, but probably not so pleasant on my breath.

"Can you take us to this place," Nisha asks the taxi driver, and shows him the address on her phone.

As the taxi lurches off, the booze and crisps churn and I wind down the window for some air.

"Where we going, babe?" I ask.

"TripAdvisor says it does good cocktails," Nisha replies, the Londoner in her fine-tuned to hunting down the best places to go out.

"Anyone got any gum?" I ask to everyone.

Abigail digs in her bag and hands me some. I chew in a way that I think is subtle in my drunken state but is probably more like a cow chomping grass.

"Got any tunes, Mr. Driver?" Hanna asks and the taxi driver switches on his radio and changes channels until Candi Staton's 'You've Got the Love' blares out.

"YES!" I bellow and we all sing the words at the top of our lungs. Poor driver.

We arrive at the bar and make our way to order drinks. It's busy, but not so packed that it's uncomfortable. We get served quickly.

"Dancefloor's this way," Nisha says. "Follow me!"

We shimmy through people to the small dancefloor. I attempt not to splosh my fresh cocktail on anyone. Nisha doesn't stop until she's right in the centre of the dancefloor.

We all dance, finger-point and twirl to nineties gems.

I'm not entirely sure how long we're there for, but my throat is hoarse from singing. Annabel stumbles mid dance move and splats on the floor. Mel and Abigail haul her up. She totters. I slurp the end of what I think is my third cocktail and the glass suddenly feels very heavy in my hand.

I place it on the side, beckon Mel to me and shout in

her ear so loud that she pulls her head away from me with a sisterly grimace. "One more!"

"No, I think it's time to head home," Mel says and gathers up the troops.

I'm outside sat on the kerb. I don't recall leaving the club. Or sitting down. Oh well. My contacts are doing my head in. I poke myself in the eye trying to get the little bastards out.

Hanna stands behind me, I recognise her shoes. I lean against her legs.

"You're the best husband… the best," Hanna slurs into her phone.

A few paces away Annabel holds on to a big wheelie bin and vomits next to it. Her twin gathers up her hair and rubs her back.

"That's it," Abigail says. "Get it all out."

"I shouldn't have had that second tequila shot," Annabel mutters between retches.

Thankfully I don't feel sick. Yet.

Nisha strides off to find a taxi or two and Mel fumbles with her phone, attempting to call local taxi firms to see if they have any cars that'll come and get us.

The street's busy, it's kick-out time for most of the bars. The cars dodge revellers who've forgotten what the pavement's for. I watch the legs of people as they pass me on the road, in a contact lens-less fuzz.

A group of legs on the other side of the road pauses and gathers together. I look up to see three younger women. They huddle together, point and laugh at something. One of the three has her phone out filming and snapping photos. I look up at Hanna behind me and then to either side to see what's so funny.

"No," I groan. "Not again."

I'm what's so funny. I'm what's being filmed.

Not sure what to do, I pull my handbag in front of my face and collapse in on myself. I go to fall into a foetal position on the pavement but Hanna's legs keep me propped up.

I attempt to cover my ears by flinging my arm over the top of my head, one ear presses into my bicep and my fingers press into my other ear. I can hear them laughing.

Infuriated, I yell, "Piss off!" I drop my handbag in my lap and give them two middle fingers. I see red and attempt to stand. With booze-fuelled rage I want to smash their smirking faces together to a bloody pulp. Come on, legs! They're jelly. They're not working properly.

Abigail and Annabel stand in front of me. Annabel wipes sick splatters from her face on the back of her hand. The twins shield me from the three sniggering harpies who advance across the road.

"Piss off," I shout again. "Just fucking do one."

Mel gives her handbag to Annabel, balls her fists and steps into the road ready to charge at them, earning a honk from an oncoming car that swerves to miss her. But the three women are oblivious and head straight past us, pointing at a guy who's carrying a squealing woman over his shoulders in a firefighter's lift a few paces down the street.

"Oh," Mel says as she watches the trio greet their upside-down friend. "I was all ready to knock them out."

A mini bus taxi turns a corner and stops in front of us. Nisha hops out the passenger door and slides the side door open.

"Get in, Barry here is going to take us home," Nisha says. She gets back in the passenger side and continues her conversation with the driver.

The twins and Hanna heave me up from the kerb and shove me into the taxi.

Mel jumps in and slides the door shut. She sits in the first row.

"Sis," I say from a seat in the back. Mel doesn't reply. The set of her shoulders tell me she's angry.

"Sis." I try again.

Nothing

"Mel!" I yell.

"What?" she snaps and turns to me.

"I thought they were laughing at me," I say. "I thought they were Tom's fans."

"Not everything's about you, Sal."

"Yeaaaaaaaah it is," I drag out the 'a' sound for emphasis. "It's my party and I'll cry if I want to," I sing.

Mel glares at me, but the other girls take up the song.

Mel's face cracks and she laughs. We all laugh. Well, apart from Annabel. Her head hangs out a window as Abigail holds back her hair.

It takes a long while for the laughter to die down. When it does, Mel says, in all seriousness, "Don't tell Mum I was about to flatten those women."

"Pah!"

"I mean it, Sal," Mel says. Years ago, as a teen, she'd been sent home from a European rugby tour for fighting. Mum had not been best pleased and Mel had been grounded for months. "She'll kill me," Mel says but her voice slips and she snorts.

The mirth bubbles up again and I howl, slapping the back of the seat. My side aches. It's true not everything's about me anymore. The world's moved on from the Darlington/Speck flash in the pan. And I couldn't be happier.

When we get back to the house, we all scatter. Annabel has got a second wind and convinces her twin and Nisha to get back in the hot tub. Mel passes out on the sofa and I head up to my bedroom. I sprawl on the bed fully dressed and pull out my phone. I send Omar some non-sensical voice message on Whatsapp and wait for a reply. When none comes, I decide to google Tom Darlington. The last media activity was three months ago on the same weekend I got engaged when he was hospitalised for exhaustion. Perhaps he's still there. Perhaps he's quietly retired or moved to Bali to reconnect with his spiritual side or something.

I check his social media channels. No new posts since the collapse. The Facebook group has had no new activity for months.

I roll over to grab a drink of water and see my antidepressants on the bedside cabinet. I left them there earlier to ensure I didn't forget to take them. I reach for the box and then stop. No. My life is back to normal. I don't need them anymore. I'm coming off the pills tonight.

The few days after my hen do were spent in a hazy, hungover, junk-food blur. Today I'm heading back to London for the first time since finding that framed photo in my apartment. Not that I'm going back there. It still gives me the creeps. I'm staying with Nisha. But I'm excited for tonight.

Mum is out at her watercolour painting class as I head downstairs with my overnight bag and Dad's hanger bag thing with the glitziest dress I own inside.

"Dad," I call, "will you give me a lift to the station?"

"Right now?" comes the reply before Dad arrives in the hallway.

"Pretty much."

"Sorry, Sal, I've got to go and do something."

"What?"

"Never you mind," he says and grins.

"No worries, I'll call a taxi."

"Righto. See you tomorrow then. Have a wonderful time." He heads out the front door.

As I call for a taxi, I hear his car tyres grind on the gravel and the swoosh of the automatic gate opening and closing. A moment later, a car honks from the road and I lock up, wait for the automatic gate to open and get into the waiting taxi.

We head towards Brockenhurst train station. We pass the car park of a local pub and the taxi driver slows to let a New Forest pony saunter across the road.

I glance at the car park and start upright in my seat.

There is my Dad's Peugeot with the boot up. And there in the middle of the car park, being handed a large black box by another man, is my dad. He looks around as he takes the box, as if checking to make sure no one has seen him and then quickly puts it in the boot of his car.

The pony has crossed and the taxi moves on. I strain my neck behind me to see Dad shake the man's hand.

Bizarre.

What is Dad doing in a pub car park taking boxes off strangers? What's in the box?

Something clicks and I remember the newspaper article about Dad's past. I haven't thought about it since it happened. Did I just witness Dad doing something dodgy? Is that why he wouldn't tell me where he was going and did it when he knew Mum would be out?

The taxi drops me off at the station and as I reach my platform, my train pulls in. I find my booked seat and pull out my phone.

I search for Graham Speck. I find the article from five months ago, which claimed Dad had been arrested for murder but then let off. There are a few other articles linked to that one, but nothing new. I click through pages and pages of search results but nothing more about my Dad.

Irritation squawks under my skin and my heart rate increases. I take a few deep breaths. My physical health is suffering just as much as my mental health coming off the anti-depressants. I feel... weird. Not like the emotional rollercoaster that I was before, which was sparked by Tom's sudden appearance outside my parents' bungalow. But I'm anxious. At any hint of turmoil, my heart thumps in my chest and I feel a panic attack waiting in the wings.

But Dad does have a past. Mum said so. She told us not to mention it ever again. Which means *something* must have happened. But it must've happened like she said. That it was a mistake. A misunderstanding. Dad's a gentle giant. He's never been anything other than a wonderful father, and – from what I can tell – a loving husband to Mum.

I'm being silly about Dad. I'm sure it's all perfectly innocent. Maybe I was mistaken. Maybe it wasn't even him and I completely imagined it. The taxi went by pretty quick.

But I can't help myself and I start searching for the name of the gang, the Eastside Firm, and the name of the murdered man, Spike Thomas. Although I find more information, some of it lurid and juicy about the gang's supposed antics, I don't find anything else that mentions Graham Speck.

"We can still turn around," Nisha says a few hours later, a concerned look in her eyes. "You don't need to go."

"I'm not missing this," I say.

I know Nisha still feels guilty about the heart-attack-that-was-a-panic-attack convention balls-up but I'm stronger now, my hen do reminding me that I'm yesterday's news.

Nisha speaks to the limo driver. He takes a corner and rolls up in front of a red carpet meticulously controlled by intimidating security. Outside of the ropes are photographers, onlookers, fans. On the inside, along the sides, linger presenters with microphones and camera crew. There are guests walking up the red carpet and posing in front of the board for the cameras.

My nerves race.

"Well, here we are," Nisha says as a suited woman moves closer to open our door. "The premiere for the second series of *The Deviants.*"

The door opens and the noise slaps me in the face. Nisha steps out elegantly in her dazzling wine-coloured dress.

Here we go. I slide across the back seat and step out of the car.

"It's Sally Speck!" someone bellows. "The author of

the books the series was originally based on."

Nisha takes my hand and guides me down the red carpet. Flashlights go off and people actually lean over the barrier to ask for my autograph. I smile and wave while Nisha leads me to the crowd and hands me a chunky felt-tip pen so I can sign flyers and other things thrust at me.

I walk the gauntlet of presenters and a few ask me questions about the books, the writing process, how I'm feeling tonight. But they're not fully paying me attention. They're waiting for the stars of the series; their eyes continually flick to the next car pulling up to see who'll step out.

I stand awkwardly in front of the board for the photographers. Some call my name and take my photo, others, like the presenters, are glued to the other end of the red carpet to see who'll come next.

Nisha beckons me on and I step into the venue. As we walk through the hallway to the function room, I squeeze Nisha's hand.

She looks at me. "You ok?"

"All good, babe."

Nisha grins, relieved. "I was imagining the worst, honestly, like you'd get tackled by some crazed Darlington fans or something."

"Nope. That was freaking awesome!"

"And just imagine what it'll be like when it's *Dusk*'s premiere. Wow."

I pull her to a stop to look straight at her. "It's happening?"

"Yep. The script is no longer bouncing around Hollywood. It's found a home."

"Wow, indeed!"

I squeeze her hand again and then drop it to take a glass of champagne off a server's tray as we enter the room.

"Have you heard anything about the casting? Or the director?"

Nisha swigs her champers. "Not yet. Although I'm pretty certain that Tom Darlington is most definitely *not* being considered for the part of Xander."

"No? I can't imagine why not. I think he'd be *fantastic* for the part." I drip with sarcasm.

Nisha leans into me as if it's a secret, and says in a mock whisper, "I think it's something to do with the fact that he's a terrible actor."

"Ha." I scan the room. It's still relatively quiet. Full of industry bods and not-so-famous cast and crew members. The big-name celebs arrive later. "Ooooh, look there's canapes over there."

"Let's go."

We make our way to the side of the room where the servers circulate with trays of food. They immediately approach us and we each grab a Caesar salad in a cos lettuce leaf, a mini burger and a chicken satay skewer.

"Honestly, though," Nisha says through a mouthful of lettuce, "well done on this. And on *Dusk* the movie happening. The publishers are happy about that because the announcement sparked a slight upturn in sales for the book. But they're still chasing me for the next book, Sal. It's months overdue."

"I know. I'm feeling so much better now though. I'm going to finish off *Dusk* part deux next week."

"Great news," Nisha says.

"I've just had so much to think about recently," I say.

"I know, darling. But hopefully it's all over now."

"Yes, it is," I reply, but I can tell it lacks conviction and Nisha immediately sniffs the doubt.

"What's happened? Is it dickhead Darlington again?"

"No, just a family thing."

"I thought your family is solid?"

"We are… I'm sure it's absolutely nothing." I take a swig of champagne and put the image of the box in my Dad's hand out of my mind completely and decide to enjoy my night. I change the subject. "I couldn't have done this without you, Nish. You're the best." I blow her an air kiss and raise my glass in a toast. "Onwards and upwards!"

Nisha clinks her glass to mine. "Now, let's get pissed on free booze."

# CHAPTER 19

Three weeks pass in a hive of wedding-planning activity and today's the day. I stand in front of the full-length mirror in my hotel room with my mum. The photographer has taken photos of me with my bridesmaids, Nisha and Hanna, and maid of honour, Mel, and is now fussing with her camera before taking some more of us two. The bridesmaids are back in the room next door putting the final touches to their make-up and hair. Mel has gone to sort out Dad and make sure he's ready.

Mum is all dressed up and beams at me.

"You look incredible, Sal," she gushes.

"Thanks, Mum. I feel incredible." I swish the dress and look this way and that, fiddling with the veil so it hangs perfectly over my shoulders.

"Right," the photographer says. "I'd like you over here, like this." She demonstrates where she'd like us and we move into our positions. There's a knock at the door and Mel comes in.

"Mum, you almost forgot this! Dad just gave it to me. It was still in your room." Mel deposits a large black box on the bed and then heads back out.

"Oh my goodness! How could I forget," Mum says and heads over to the box.

I stare at it on the bed. I've seen it before. It's the box Dad was given in that pub car park.

"What's in the box, Mum?" I say suspiciously. My

entire body tenses, as if whatever is inside will ruin my big day.

But Mum doesn't pick up on my odd tone. She flings off the lid and tucks her hands inside, lifting carefully. "It's my hat, of course!" She pulls out a turquoise hat with netting and feathers and goes to the nearest mirror to angle it on her head. "Your father got it for me. I spotted it in John Lewis, and it matched my dress perfectly. See. But, oh my, was it pricey. So I settled for a rather dull hair band thing for a third of the price. But your father, bless him, took a note of the details and then found one for sale on eBay! He bought it for me as a surprise and gave it to me this morning."

The relief of knowing that Dad's car park rendezvous was nothing more than picking up a wedding hat overwhelms me. I really shouldn't have doubted him. "Wow. That was really sweet. Was that all Dad's idea? Not Mel?"

"Nope, was all your father," Mum says and beams even brighter. She comes to stand next to me again.

"It looks fantastic."

"Ooooh, I feel fabulous!" Mum squeezes me around the shoulders, careful not to move my veil, which the photographer has just spent a good few minutes arranging and draping.

The photoshoot flies by, and for the first time ever, I don't mind having my photo taken. I don't love it, but I'm not squirming every time the lens points at me. Mum heads off to find Mel, Nisha and Hanna and to get in their car. I find Dad in the hotel lobby and we get into the back of a classic cream Rolls-Royce.

Dad stuffs in my skirts as gently as he can manage and the driver, who is wearing a Peaky Blinders flat cap, closes the door for us.

"Here we go," Dad says and chuckles. He squeezes my hand. I grin at him, but am too giddy to speak.

The driver puts the car in gear and pulls out of the

hotel driveway and onto the road behind the car carrying Mum, Mel, Nisha and Hanna.

"Oh, listen to that purr," Dad says.

He starts up a conversation with the driver about the car, the engine, the spec and I tune out, watching the road fly by, swallowing down the butterflies.

It's not far to go from the hotel to the church as we made sure to book them close to each other. Just past the hotel turning is a lay-by. In this is parked a car with its brake lights on.

As we cruise past it, I see there's a man sat in the driver's seat on his phone. He watches the Rolls-Royce pass and then turns his face away from me. It immediately reminds me of the man in the pub in Cornwall. And the car. A dark-grey saloon. It looks like the one I was convinced was following me when I drove to Omar's flat.

No. Stop it. That's just a man on his phone in his car. I thought Mum's hat box was something sinister! I'm just nervous, that's all.

This is my wedding day. The most perfect day of my life. Nothing will go wrong.

When Dad's conversation with the driver dries up, I say, "You all sorted with the speech?"

He chuckles. "Oh yes. I've got a peach of a story about you to tell."

"Not the one about the lemonade?"

He taps his finger to his nose and grins.

Everyone sits waiting for me in the little church on the outskirts of the forest. Omar's at the front, in his suit. A huge grin lights up his face.

Dad walks me slowly down the aisle to 'All of Me' by John Legend and smiling faces turn to me. I pass my family and friends on one side and Omar's huge extended family on the other. For many of his Egyptian relatives this is their first visit to England. I can't wait to meet them at the reception – a big marquee in our back garden that Dad took full charge of erecting, and Mum and Mel of decorating.

I feel as if I'm floating, gliding forwards to my man, my everything. My chest tightens as we make eye contact and I fight down the urge to cry. As I get close to the front, I see Mum brimming with pride in her big hat.

Hanna's daughter Angelina, Bethany and Ellie walk ahead as the flower girls, pretty in lilac, and as they reach the front, Mel ushers them into their seats. My bridesmaids Nisha and Hanna scoot off to the side and settle in their chairs. Hanna squeezes her brother's arm as she passes. Dad kisses my cheek and gives my hand to Omar. I look up at my husband-to-be. I can smell his Issey Miyake aftershave and I take a deep breath so it envelops me.

"You are so beautiful," he whispers in my ear and I glow with joy, feel it beaming out from my skin. We turn to face the vicar.

"Dearly beloved, we are gathered here today..." the vicar starts.

He talks but the words wash over me. I focus on the presence of Omar standing so close to me, on the hum of people sitting behind, on the feel of my big-skirted princess dress and veil on my bare shoulders.

We sing 'Give Me Joy In My Heart'. Omar holds the order of service booklet in front of us with the words and I remember us singing dirty fishermen songs in Cornwall. A rush of love sweeps over me as Mum's voice warbles 'Sing Hosanna' louder than anybody else's.

The vicar smiles and says, "If anyone knows any just cause why this man and this woman may not be joined together in holy matrimony, speak now or else forever hold your peace."

There's an amused pause as everyone holds their breath. The vicar opens his mouth to continue.

A commotion at the back of the church. Voices, scraping, bustle. I continue to look forward. A latecomer, probably one of my family, trying to sneak in. Omar bristles.

The heavy door creaks open and the vicar looks up from his script and frowns.

"I know of a reason!" a voice shouts down the little church.

It echoes off the stained-glass windows, burrows into my ears. The pronouncement is like a clap of rumbling, ominous thunder disturbing an otherwise peaceful night. It is shocking and frightening and earth-shattering. Murmurs ripple across the congregation.

My heart sinks and rests heavy against my gut as realisation pings across my brow. *I know that voice.*

Omar spins around. I hold my breath and slowly, slowly, turn.

Tom Darlington, six camera crew and perhaps ten other people swarm into the church. Tom stops halfway down the aisle, and flings his arms to the sky.

"I love you, Sally, I can't stand by and watch you marry this man! It is a travesty! My private investigator tracked you down, and just in the nick of time! I will do anything, anything to have you back in my arms. Please… I beg of you to take me back. Take me back, Sally, please…"

He drops to his knees, stretches his arms out to me, sobbing, as if this is his award-winning scene. The cameras scan the church, capture every twitch, every startled expression. Some point at him, some at the congregation and some are fixed on me and Omar. It all happens so fast that everyone is rooted to the spot, utterly stunned.

A lady with a microphone shouts from behind Tom, "Omar, how does it feel to steal Tom's love from him?" Another man to one side says, "How can you, an insurance broker, beat a world-famous actor, voted the world's most handsome man no less, to this woman?"

The lady shouts, "Sally, will you take Tom back? The whole world wants you to take Tom back!" and then jabs her microphone towards me over Tom's head.

I'm thunderstruck, frozen in place. It's as if my whole

being has been put on pause. As if I've simply switched off with the shock. My limbs tense, my breath falters, I don't blink. My insides hitch, my cells forget how to function. *This cannot be happening.*

Mum, Mel, Nisha, Hanna, and the twins jump into action and form a protective shield around me, hold bouquets in front of my face, attempt to hide me from the cameras.

Omar steps towards Tom and goes to grab him. His two best men hold him back, but Dad gets to the actor and cracks him across the jaw with his fist.

There's a collective gasp from the congregation. A child cries.

"Graham!" Mum shrieks.

I've never seen Dad be physically violent and the force and precision of the punch scares me. And for a brief moment Dad is completely unknown to me. He's a menacing and dangerous stranger. But as Tom is propelled backwards, landing on his backside with a thud, I remember it's Dad and he's protecting me.

"You slimy little weasel!" Dad yells as aunty Margaret, who happens to be sitting in the pew closest, steps between him and Tom and pushes Dad a few steps away. "What the hell do you think you're doing ruining my daughter's wedding? Get out of here now. And you," he waves his hand at the cameras and entourage over aunty Margaret's shoulders, "Get out of here! How dare you!"

Tom whimpers on the floor. He clutches his cheek and wipes the blood that spills from one nostril.

Instead of backing away, the camera crew jostle to get closer to the action. One shoves his handheld camera in Dad's face, elbowing aunty Margaret in the process, who yelps.

Mel launches herself down the aisle, flies past Dad and Margaret, snatches the camera out of the cameraman's hand and off his shoulder in a brutal yank and then flings it like a rugby ball over Tom's head towards the back of the church. It crashes on the stone floor and shatters.

"What the hell!" the cameraman shouts and sprints after his equipment, dodging Tom, and falls to his knees to gather up the pieces.

The astonished congregation, until now pinned to their seats, stand and block the cameras' view. Omar's family over from Egypt are utterly horrified. His mum is being supported by relatives as if she might faint.

The vicar edges past Dad and Margaret, then Mel, and pulls Tom up by an arm. "What is the meaning of this? Is there a *legal* reason that this woman can't marry this man? Or just your silly fancy?"

"I love her…" Tom sobs, unsteady on his feet and pointing a shaky finger at me.

The vicar turns back at me for some kind of comment.

I gape for a few moments as everyone looks at me. My cells jolt back to attention and a fury is unleashed. It swills in my veins. Bile fills my mouth. "I hate you, Tom! This is not some Shakespeare play for goodness' sake. We are not in a movie. This is my life. You are ruining my life. I wish you were dead!"

The vicar holds up his hand for calm and says to Tom, "You love her, she doesn't love you. She loves this man here who she is about to marry. You have caused an unnecessary scene, leave immediately." He motions to the camera crew and entourage. "Get out, all of you! You are desecrating this sacred place, this sacred union of two people. You should be ashamed."

"Get out, scum!" Mel bellows and for a moment I think she's about to dive on Tom and pummel him to nothing, but then Steve is at her side, clutching her bicep. They share a look and she stands down.

The guests boo and hiss. Some leave their chairs to shoo the intruders back out the door.

"Sally," Tom wails as he's steered out of the church by Ashraf, his driver.

The cameras never stop rolling.

The vicar appeals for order and quickly ushers Omar and I into a back room. My legs are like jelly and I stumble behind Omar who doesn't wait for me. Mum, Mel, my bridesmaids, and Omar's best men all move to follow us but the vicar tells everyone else to stay put.

"What the…" Omar says as the vicar closes the door and it's just the two of us in the little room.

He's livid. His normal laid-back, sweet-natured demeanour is long gone. His jaw clenches and his eyes narrow. He kicks a nearby chair.

I stand in the middle of the room, impotent. I've never seen Omar this mad. He paces around me. I reach out to him but he recoils from my touch.

"Why is he here?" Omar snarls.

"He hired a private investigator and he planned all this, to ruin our wedding… he's hell-bent on destroying my life," I say. Then it dawns on me. "That's who has been following me! I knew it."

Omar stops across the room from me and glares. "Do you love him? Is this, us, just some charade, to make him jealous? To make him chase you?"

"What? Of course not, Omar, how can you even think that? I love you!"

"I don't know what to think any more."

I rush to him and go to put my arms around him. He slaps them away and slips out of my reach to another part of the room. I turn to look at him but I'm rooted to the spot. "Omar? My love, we are getting married today, no matter what. We carry on with the service. He can't stop us from being together. He can't…"

But I trail off as Omar shakes his head. Imperceptibly at first but then big sharp movements as his chin sweeps from shoulder to shoulder.

"No," he says finally. "I… I don't think I can do this. I can't live forever in *his* shadow, forever knowing I'll never live up to *him*."

"What are you saying? Tom means nothing to me!"

"Bullshit. Once again, I'm playing second fiddle. That's what happened with Kiera. And now you. And in front of all my family. So humiliating."

It takes me a moment to twig that Kiera was his first fiancée who cheated on him. He's never before said her name. I can sense that I'm losing him.

"I love you. I want to be with you. Don't do this," I plead desperately as he turns his back on me.

He opens the door to the church and storms out into the chaos. I slump down to my knees and brace myself for another panic attack. But it doesn't come. Instead, I weep hysterically as my entire world implodes.

# CHAPTER 20

Mel scoops me up off the church floor and hurries me out the back door into a waiting car driven by aunty Margaret. Mel talks to me continuously in soothing words but I can't process them. I'm in a bubble, and inside that bubble is a raging storm that blocks out everything. I can't see properly or feel anything.

There's just a painful howling that circles my head. *Omar, how could you?*

I'm shuffled into Mel's house. Steve, Bethany and Ellie are already there. Mel drags me up the stairs and into her spare room. She sits me on the bed.

"Sal, I'm going to help Mum and Dad sort everything out, ok? We'll take down the marquee, distribute the food to relatives, cancel the band. All that. You don't need to worry, ok?" Then when I don't reply, more urgently, "Sal, is that ok?"

"Thank you," I mutter, because, really, what does she want me to say? I can't roll up my wedding dress sleeves, tie back my veil and get stuck in to unravelling my entire wedding with a smile on my face and a can-do attitude, can I? No.

"First, though, let's get you changed," she says.

I'm completely pliant, like a new-born baby, as she takes me out of my beautiful wedding dress and puts me in a pair of her pyjamas and a cardigan. She even puts socks on my feet. I glance at my perfectly painted toes as she does this. Toes that had been painted just for Omar on our wedding night.

The sobs come again. Mel makes me lie in bed and puts the covers over me. She calls for aunty Margaret.

Aunty Margaret comes in with a cup of tea and places it on the bedside table. Bethany trails behind her. No longer in her pretty dress. She carries a book.

"Aunty Margaret and Bethany are going to look after you while I'm out, ok?"

I nod.

Mel leaves and aunty Margaret encourages Bethany to read me a story. I'm thankful that she's not attempting any kind of conversation. I'd be incapable. Bethany sits on the edge of the bed and reads to me. But really, she reads to her great-aunt who asks questions and helps her with difficult words.

This goes on for a while and I turn my head. Not to sleep, but to silently cry. I can't bear the thought of Bethany seeing me crying.

They take it as a sign that I've fallen asleep and quietly go downstairs, leaving the door open in case I need them.

My entire world is shattered and in pieces around me. Eventually I fall into a broken sleep.

I'm woken by Mel fussing over me. I realise she's taking all the clips out of my short hair and running her fingers through it to break up the hairspray.

"Hey, shall I take your make-up off? Your false eyelashes must be irritating the hell out of you."

I blink a few times and realise it's dark outside. I've slept on what should've been my wedding day. Slept through my reception and dinner and toasts and dancing. But I'm all cried out and I nod.

Mel carefully peels off the falsies and then goes about taking off my eye make-up with pads, cleansing my face and rubbing in some moisturiser. She's never done this for me and it should feel odd, but I'm a husk, an empty shell and I have nothing left in me to feel weird.

"We've had a discussion about what to do about Dad."

I frown at her, unable even to say, huh?

"About what to do if Dad gets done for assault; for punching that idiot. It will be a nightmare because of his previous record. But I don't think that stalker's going to press charges. Not after what he did."

There's a knock at the door and Steve comes in with a tray of food. He gives it to Mel then retreats.

She puts it on the floor by the bed and then helps me to sit up, propping cushions behind my back as if I'm an invalid. I don't resist.

"Here, you need to eat something." Mel picks up the tray and puts it on my lap. "It's chicken soup and some toast."

When I don't move, Mel picks up a spoon, dips it in the soup and then puts it to my mouth as if she's feeding a baby. I eat a few spoonfuls and a bite of toast and then shake my head.

"Had enough?" Mel asks.

I stare at the tray.

Mel continues, "Nobody can believe what Tom did. Or, for that matter, what Omar did. We all love you so much, Sal. You know that right? We'll get through this. It hurts like hell now, but you'll be ok. You'll stay here for a few days until we get everything sorted at the parents. We'll take care of everything, ok?"

"Ok," I croak.

"Do you want to come downstairs and watch some telly? Aunty Margaret's gone and I've put the kids to bed."

The idea of a normal Saturday evening watching some movie slaps me across the face. Tonight wasn't meant to be normal. Tonight was meant to be the best night of my life. Laughing and having fun with family and friends. Meeting all of Omar's relatives. We had Egyptian food lined up in the buffet and some of his favourite Middle Eastern songs on the playlist.

I shake my head at Mel.

She kisses my cheek, picks up the tray and heads out, closing the door behind her and turning off the light.

I stare at the ceiling in the darkness. I can't believe this has happened. It's a nightmare that I'll wake up from. It has to be.

"Here you go," Mel says as she hands me my phone the following day. "Are you sure you want to look at it?"

"Yes."

I want to see if Omar has messaged me. It was all a mistake. He didn't mean to ditch me at the altar; didn't mean to walk out. I switch on my phone and wait for it to warm up. Mel goes about unpacking the bag that Mum just dropped over with some of my clothes and toiletries, and to deliver the heart-wrenching news that she'd cancelled my honeymoon. Nisha had been looking after my phone for me yesterday as my dress, my lovely dress that I only got to wear for a couple of hours, had no pockets.

I look at my Whatsapp, text messages, voicemail, missed calls and emails. I skim through messages from friends and loved ones.

But nothing from Omar.

How could he do this to me? Why?

It was Tom's fault. What kind of person thinks they can disrupt a wedding like that? No wonder Omar freaked out. Tom with all his entourage, all those cameras, swanning into the church as if he was entitled to be there, to do what he did. To get his own way. There's something clearly very wrong with him. Why is he still fixated on me after all this time?

He's bulldozed my life. And Omar's. And what would've been our life together. Razed it to the ground.

"Do you want to come down for dinner?" Mel asks.

"No." I still don't feel up to leaving this bedroom, to facing normal, domesticated life again. It's still alien.

"Shall I bring some up?"

"No, thanks. I'm really not hungry."

Mel nods. She saw me eat a plate of Steve's leftover seafood linguine heaped with cheese at lunch and is satisfied that I won't starve in her care.

"See you in the morning, then," she says as she exits. "Just holler if you need anything and if you want a midnight snack, help yourself to whatever's in the kitchen."

"Thanks, sis."

When she closes the door behind her, I grab my phone and search for Tom's name. The top hit is a video on YouTube dubbed 'The wedding invasion'. It's had more than one million views. I watch the video. It's the footage captured on my doomed wedding day edited into a two-minute clip that includes Tom entering the church and begging on the floor and ends soon after Omar and I are ushered into the vestry. It even includes the vicar berating Tom. I see Omar's happiness evaporating, see Dad throw a punch, see the horrified faces of the guests.

I'm sure it's not what Tom had in mind when he decided to bring a camera crew with him. In his warped mind, he probably envisioned it as some kind of big romantic gesture, where he sweeps me up and we head off into the sunset.

The clip ends and I tell myself I won't ever watch it again. But that's a lie. It's a car crash and I'm compelled to look. Again and again and again.

On every view, I re-live the moment my heart breaks. And my heart is carved up some more. It's in tatters. Irreparable. Shards of it have broken off and got lost in the maze of my body, never to be found again.

Truly, I'm mortified. The whole world can now watch the worst day of my life.

My leg is numb from sitting in the same position for hours and I shift, looking up from my phone. It's dark out and the entire house is quiet. I turn on the bedside lamp and see it's nearly two a.m. I've watched the clip for hours, pausing it at the worst moments so that they etch painfully in my mind. I don't think I'll ever be able to sleep again without seeing this video. The moment when my face crumples from pure joy to full of horror when realisation dawns.

My eye lands on my clear toiletries bag that Mel has left out and spot at the bottom an old packet of my anti-depressant pills.

I get out of bed and fish them out of the bag. They'll numb me. They'll stop this endless painful loop from repeating in my head.

The glass by the side of my bed is empty. Lighting the way with my phone, I creep downstairs, packet of pills in one hand and glass in the other, through the sleeping house to the kitchen. I close the door.

I fill the glass with water and then creep through to the lounge. I sit on the sofa and pop out one pill, then take a swig of water. I know that they won't work for weeks, but I need them to kick in now. Right. Now. I need to numb myself. To resist the urge to watch that video again. To stop reliving that awful moment for eternity.

I spot Mel's alcohol cabinet. I lurch forward and pull open the door. I grab a brand-new bottle of cheap gin, unscrew the cap and take a swig. The cold, sharp taste makes me judder as it slides down my throat, leaving a burning sensation.

As soon as the burn fades I take another swig. Then another and another. Then I pick up the packet and pop out another five pills. I swallow them with the gin. In the box is another packet of six.

Sod it.

I swallow six more and keep drinking the gin. I need some air. I stumble through to the hallway, grab Mel's car keys from the little tray on a shelf and let myself out the front door. My legs feel as if they're wading through mud as I get into Mel's car and drive away.

My brain is a muddle but my body takes over as if on autopilot. I don't realise where I'm driving, until I pull into the clifftop car park.

I drink the last of the gin and fling the bottle in the passenger's footwell. I should've brought another bottle with me.

The sea is in front of me. In the distance is the Isle of Wight. But I can't see it. Not at night. It's just a void. A blackness over the edge of the cliff that is so enticing. It welcomes me, promises me oblivion.

The pills and booze are taking too long to kick in. I long for that oblivion. For an end to this pain. I put the car in gear and drive forward.

# CHAPTER 21

Four days after what should've been my wedding day, I sprawl in my bed at my parents' house. The telly's on, some movie, and my phone rests on my belly playing music. I stare off into space, singing the words of the song on automatic.

Tom. Always Tom. That's all I can think about. I feel paralysed in a Tom bubble, unable to get free. I should probably think about Omar. But that's too painful and leads me straight back to Tom.

Mum took me to my doctor a day or so ago. I can't quite remember. She prescribed me some super strength anti-depressants and insisted I get a counsellor. I recall agreeing wholeheartedly, anything to not have to go into hospital again. But I know I won't get one for a while. I'm not ready to be emotionally poked and prodded just yet.

I took the first pill in the car on the way home and lay on the sofa as Mum insisted on a Harry Potter movie marathon. A few hours later I entered this state of strange emotional turmoil, wanting to cry and wanting to laugh at the same time. It came out as a weird choking bawl in the middle of *Harry Potter and the Prisoner of Azkaban*, which alarmed Mum.

So I came up to my room and here I've stayed for the last few days. I move very slowly, to mitigate the threat of a deluge. Tears well behind my eyes and sit there heavy, ready to burst and drown me. Time passes in a blur. I let it.

A knock on my door.

There's a pause and I should answer, but I have zero energy.

Mel sticks her head around. "Hey, sis, how you feeling? Good enough to sing terribly, I can hear."

I don't answer, can't even muster the effort to look at her. She comes in and sits on the edge of my bed. She rests a hand on my ankle. For some reason it feels way too heavy and uncomfortable. But I don't move my leg. That requires a vigour I don't possess right now.

Mel frowns. "What are you listening to?" Realisation dawns and Mel grabs my phone. "Why are you listening to this crap? This is his solo dance stuff isn't it?" Mel fumbles with my phone. "What the hell, you've got a whole Swoon and Tom Darlington Spotify playlist!" She finally stops the music, but I continue to sing, I know the words as if they're imprinted on my tongue.

Mel slaps my foot. "Stop. Sally!" She jumps up and switches off the television. "And you're watching his movies. What is wrong with you? This is unhealthy, sis. Don't you dare get like you did when Greg dumped you."

The 'time that Sal's teenage angst went into overdrive', as Dad refers to it as, is a touchy subject. One that Mel never really understood. I was thirteen, and my first boyfriend ditched me for the girl who lived opposite his nan. It hurt. A lot. And for a long time. So much so that I was hospitalised for a while. It marred my childhood, but Mel was too busy living her teenage years to pay much attention. We barely mention it now, and when we do, we tend to make a joke about it, in true Speck family fashion. I ignore her dig.

She continues, "You need to snap out of it."

"What's the point," I mumble and fight back the choking happy/sad bawl from erupting again. Tom has succeeded in wheedling his way into my thoughts. He's all I can think about. I tried to resist but it's pointless. So I've given in. It's a form of torture, I suppose. As if I need to punish myself for what's happened.

"The point is, that I want my sister back. Yes, that celebrity has really shat on you, but you need to pick yourself up and fight back. Nisha called me the other day, says you've not answered any of the emails sent by your publisher this week and they're getting pissed off. You need to stop moping around and fight back."

"What day is it?" I ask.

"Wednesday."

"Oh."

"Come on, Sal. For fuck's sake."

That's it, I realise. My sister's sympathy has run out. She's never been depressed in her life. Is one for taking action, never wallowing.

"You don't need to be here. You don't need to do anything else for me," I say into my pillow. I still haven't looked at her.

"Don't need to do anything for you?" Her voice rises in pitch and I know there's a lecture coming. "Don't need to do anything for you?" she repeats and leans closer to my face. "I cared for you like you were a baby and you had to go and do that shit." She shakes her head.

"What shit?" I glance at her.

She glares at me. "*What shit?* Has Mum not told you? Don't you remember?"

My face is blank because my mind is.

Mel does an exaggerated sigh. "Sal, you downed a bottle of gin with a ton of anti-depressants and drove my car to Barton clifftop in the middle of the night. You attempted to drive it off the edge, but it got wedged on a small wooden post, and you were found, unconscious, by a police car that just happened to be cruising past. Then you had your stomach pumped at the hospital. You're telling me you don't remember any of that?"

I look off into space as I rack my brains. But nothing comes.

"When was that?"

"Sunday night, Monday morning."

I chew my cheek. There's a void. I have snatches of memories from Omar turning his back on me to now. Being at Mel's. Mum telling me they've cancelled my honeymoon. Coming back to my childhood bedroom. The doctors this morning. Harry Potter. But that's it. There's a lot missing and I've no idea where it's gone.

I cry. Not the weird emotional bawl, I have nothing left in me to manage that, but just silent fat tears that roll down my face and splosh on my neck. I blink a few times.

Mel softens. "Listen to me. I haven't given up on you. Mum and Dad haven't given up on you so don't you dare give up on yourself. I wish I could murder that bastard actor for what he's done to you. But I can't so we're going to find another way. That actor is mentally deranged, he's harassed and stalked you for six months now."

"What's the point." I pull the duvet over my head.

Mel yanks it down. "You've got evidence. And we've got that video he made. That does not help his case. He's going down."

I groan. I'd forgotten that. The video. Scratched it out, but Mel brings it right back to stab at my heart again.

The wedding invasion has been aired on television, on the internet, pretty much everywhere. The YouTube clip has been viewed more than fourteen million times now. The worst day of my life is an international sensation. Comedy shows have re-enacted skits about it. Mortifying. That isn't a fog. That is stark in my mind.

"The police have been in touch. But I've put them off because you've needed to rest and recover after your…" She waves her hand instead of finishing. Suicide attempt, I guess is what she can't bring herself to say. I tried to drive off a cliff. I don't remember wanting to end my life. But that's what I did.

"I just want everything back to normal, Mel," I say desperately.

"We all do. I want my little sister back. My motivated,

driven, creative, passionate, brave sister."

"But how?"

"Fight back, Sal. You wanted to be an author, you fought for it. You want to get rid of Tom once and for all? You know what you need to do."

Mel's spirit rubs off on me. I ball my hands into fists. "He deserves to pay."

"Too right, he does! And you need to redirect your focus. All this," she gestures at me slumped in bed, "will send you crazy. And you don't want to be hospitalised again, do you?"

Hell no, I don't want to go down that dark hole again. That can never, ever, happen.


Two days after Mel's pep talk, I feel strong enough to leave the house and talk to the police. Mum pulls out of the driveway and I direct her to the police station. Neither of us have ever been before and the act of directing Mum calms me down and dampens my frazzled nerves.

Mum parks up and goes to get out of the car.

"Actually, I think I can do this on my own," I say.

"Sure?"

"Yes, thank you."

"Ok, love. I'll be here. I brought a library book with me." She reaches into her bag and pulls out a chunky hardback.

I head into the police station. At the front counter I ask for PC Dawn Cole or PC Andy Hawkins and confirm that I have an appointment.

I'm asked to wait and sit on a cold plastic chair. A ball of nerves race around my chest and my lungs feel tight. It's the feeling I used to get when I had to do any kind of public speaking, before I got used to it. Why am I nervous? I've not done anything wrong. My emotions are all over the place. But I'd rather feel nervous than teary.

My name is called and I look up to see PC Hawkins.

"Would you like to come this way, please," he says.

I walk towards him.

He looks at me for a beat too long and says, "Would you like a drink? You look like you could do with a cup of tea."

"Yes, please."

He leads me through some doors, down a hallway and deposits me in a small meeting room. It's empty apart from a table and four chairs. I sit at one of the chairs and clasp my hands in front of me.

PC Hawkins comes back in with two cups and puts one in front of me before taking a seat. He pulls a handful of sugar sachets from his top pocket and drops them on the table.

"Sugar?" he says.

I look at the grey-tinged vending machine tea and decide I need the sugar to make it palatable. I empty a sachet into my cup. PC Hawkins empties the other two.

PC Cole comes in. "Hi, Sally. Sorry to keep you waiting."

She takes a seat and scrutinises my face. I guess she sees the same fragility there as her colleague because she says urgently, "Everything ok?"

That's it. The concern opens up the floodgates, but mixed with the nerves I'm overwhelmed and my breath catches in my chest.

"It's ok, Sally, just breathe," PC Hawkins says. "Take your time. Here, have a couple of sips of tea." He nudges the cup towards me.

I pick up the cup but my hand is trembling so much that I can't lift it.

"We know about your wedding," PC Cole says gently. "And what happened after. We want to hear it all from you."

And then I erupt. Words spew forth like a fountain and I don't even know what I'm saying and if it's even coming out in order. I hear myself saying 'followed', 'Cornwall engagement', 'private investigator', 'Tom hospitalised', 'wedding crash', 'camera crew', 'Omar walking out', 'clifftop', and 'stomach pumped'. I repeat myself but each time the story comes out jumbled.

The two police officers sit stunned at the torrent coming from out my mouth. They don't move a muscle as my story hits them again and again. The more they stay still the more animated I seem to become. My arms fling about for emphasis. I lean forward, lean back, half stand, shift on my seat so the legs grind against the floor.

I'm actually hysterical. I don't feel anywhere close to a panic attack. It's actually more like extreme, uncontrollable euphoria. As if I've taken an illegal drug that's playing havoc with all my brain cells but in a rapturous way.

The police officers watch and listen, taking it all in.

Eventually I burn out and slump on the chair, utterly spent.

PC Hawkins very slowly picks up his cup and takes a careful sip of his tea, as if any sudden movement might set me off again. Neither speak for a while, but both look at me, clearly processing what I've just told them, and the bizarre manner in which the story was delivered.

PC Cole taps her colleague's arm and they exchange a glance. She dips her head towards the door and he nods.

"Sally," she says, "I'm just going to go out of the room to discuss what you've told us with our Sergeant. I won't be a moment."

"Ok," I mumble.

"Do you want another cup of tea, or some water?" PC Cole asks.

I shake my head no.

She leaves the room and closes the door gently behind her. PC Hawkins smiles at me, and proceeds to cheerily talk about the weather but I can't focus.

I look around the stark room and chew at the sides of my mouth.

The longer I'm in this room, the more tense I get. I grip the sides of my chair and a feeling comes over me that can best be described as 'plummeting', as if I've been tossed out of an airplane at 32,000 feet. My mouth goes dry and a chill settles over my skin, apart from on my cheeks, which burn up. Was I right to come here? Was Tom crashing my wedding to declare his love for me romantic like so many media headlines claim? Are the police going to tell me to be on my way, that there's nothing they can do? All these questions race through my head and it takes me a while to comprehend that PC Hawkins has gone quiet and is clearly waiting for me to respond to a question.

"I said, are you ok, Sally?"

"Yes… I'm… just really shaken up."

"We can see that," he replies with a warm smile. "And we're going to help you."

PC Cole re-enters the room and sits.

"We're going to check Tom Darlington's previous criminal history," she says. "We expect he has no history, so we'll issue him with an informal harassment warning. This notice will inform him about the law in relation to harassment and stalking so it's very clear he needs to stay away from you as his persistent attention is unwanted by you and making you feel anxious and fearful. There's a possibility that he really isn't aware that his behaviour is inappropriate so this warning will make it very clear. And then if he does anything else, you need to report it and we will look at taking further action against him. Are you in agreement with that course of action?"

"Yes. Will it be kept private?"

"We will do all we can to keep it private," she replies.

"I don't want the media, or his fans, to find out. Because then they'll harass me even more."

"We understand," she says.

"We'd like to think that once Tom's public attention is no longer on you, then the media and fans will leave you alone," PC Hawkins says.

PC Cole gives me a warm smile. "We'd like you to go

home, rest and stay safe with your parents. Look after yourself and stay in touch with your doctor. And we'll organise the warning and inform you when it's done. It won't take long."

I nod.

"If anything else happens, it's likely CID or our domestic violence team will take over the case."

"Ok."

They both stand, and I take that as my cue that this meeting is done and it's time for me to leave.

"How did you get here?" PC Cole asks. "Do you need us to drive you home?"

"My Mum is waiting outside."

"I'll walk you out," PC Hawkins says.

PC Cole takes her leave, peeling away through another door. PC Hawkins leads me back down the corridor, through the reception area and outside. I indicate my mum's car and he says goodbye as I walk towards it.

"Well, how'd that go, dear?" Mum says as she puts her book away and turns on the engine.

"They're going to give Tom Darlington an informal warning."

"Well, that's great news."

"Yes. And it'll be kept private."

"Good. Can you imagine the media getting hold of that story – a celebrity harassing a fan? Oh, it'd be scandalous!"

As Mum drives us home, I check my phone and see I have a missed call from Nisha. We wait for the electric gates to open and swing into the driveway.

"I'm just going to stay in the car a minute and call Nisha back," I tell Mum as she gets out.

"Righto," she replies and heads into the house.

I dial Nisha's number and she answers on the second ring. After I fill her in on the police visit and how I'm feeling, Nisha gets to the nitty gritty of why she called.

"The publisher is taking steps to cancel your contract and to get back that massive advance they've already paid you," Nisha says. "I'm sorry, I stalled them for as long as possible."

"No," I say, desperately wishing for it not to be true.

"The royalties have dried up. And as you're not doing publicity, and there's no new book on the horizon, they've lost interest in you and are chasing the next big thing. It's a cutthroat business."

"This is my dream, Nish. That bastard Tom has screwed everything up for me."

"I know, babe, I know," Nisha says and her voice catches. She's as sad as me.

We end the call and I stare at the dashboard for a very long time. My drunken one-night stand strikes again. My dream career is in tatters.

# CHAPTER 22

Two days later, Mel and I sit on a park bench watching Bethany and Ellie play on the swings. After hearing my news, then hearing Bethany's gymnastics club was cancelled, Mel picked up the kids from school and swung by to pick me up.

It's a clear autumn day and Mel is basking in the sun. I wear a baseball cap and sit on the side of the bench that's in shade and am thankful that the park is quiet. I don't want anyone to recognise me.

"So," Mel says as she tucks the girls' water bottle into her handbag, "the police have been in touch with Tom Darlington."

"Yep, they called me earlier. He had his informal warning yesterday and should now stay away from me."

"About bloody time. How do you feel about that?"

"Ok, I guess. I tried to write yesterday but it was no use. And then Mum and Dad dropped a bombshell."

"Which was?" Mel says, flicking her gaze from me to the kids to make sure they're playing nicely.

I breathe out. "I'm broke. I can't afford the mortgage repayments on my flat. I've got no royalties coming in at the moment and I've used up all my savings. The parents lent me some money for the wedding, and I put other stuff, like the hen do and honeymoon, on credit cards – which are now maxed out and overdue. Mum admitted that they're struggling to manage the household bills on their pathetic pensions and need the money back that they lent me. But I don't have it. I didn't realise it was so bad for them, that they don't have all that much in savings. It's got so bad that yesterday they told me they were thinking about breaking their retirement and going back to work. I feel so guilty because they gave me all that money for a wedding that didn't happen."

Mel heavily blows air out of her lips in sympathy.

"It's awful. My publisher wants my advance back. I don't have that money anymore," I say.

"What about from the movie and TV rights to *Dusk* and *The Deviants*?"

"Paid up long ago, and already spent."

"Jeez."

"Uh huh."

"So, you need to write a book and then they'll be happy? What's stopping you from finishing *Dusk* two?"

"Writer's block. I just feel as if I'm asleep. Like everything that's happened in the last few months is a heavy blanket that's suffocating me. Something needs to happen to wake me up."

We both watch the kids for a while.

I continue, "I'm going to have to sell my apartment. I haven't been back in months." And it's not likely I'll be back any time soon, the state I'm currently in. "Any money left over from paying off the mortgage will go to the publisher. I pray it's enough. But that doesn't help with the money I owe Mum and Dad and on the credit cards."

"Sorry, Sal. I know you loved that apartment."

I sigh. "It's just another thing Tom has taken away from me."

Mel re-routes the conversation to stop me dwelling on my misery. "I have an old rugby mate who's an estate agent in London. I'll put you in touch."

"Thanks."

"I know another way you could make some money," Mel says. "Sell your story to the media for the highest price to get some cash in. You've got plenty of evidence."

"What?" I'm astonished. I stare at Mel but she's not looking at me, Bethany's shriek draws her attention.

"Come on. As well as that wedding video, you've got your diary and dirt box. There'll be tons of texts. And all those paparazzi photos of him loitering outside your London flat as well as screenshots of various social media posts – although he's deleted lots of them now, you still have them. Plus, all his published interviews where he calls on his crazed fans to find you. And all the media articles you can find where he mentions you."

"Why would I want to do that? More media attention is the last thing I want right now."

Suddenly Mel is furious and turns to face me, the pitch of her voice raises as she punches her fist into her palm to make a sharp slapping noise.

"You need to take him down! He needs to suffer as much as you have!" She lowers her tone. "This informal warning is not good enough. Your name has been dragged through the mud, but his hasn't. Everyone needs to know about his behaviour, he deserves a trial by media. And you deserve some kind of compensation. If the media want to pay big bucks for your story, I say go for it. You'll be killing two birds with one stone. Destroying that arsehole Tom and earning some cash quickly."

"Just drop it, Mel. No good will come of it," I say.

But Mel's not listening. She's on a roll. She continues on at her million-miles-a-minute pace.

"I want you to tell those media vultures that he's had this warning. I want him to suffer for that wedding stunt he pulled. He's not a national treasure, he's unhinged. They can't say anything worse about you or Dad or Omar, so let them print some crap about him. Let the media turn on him as viciously as they turned on you."

Mel's referring to a hurtful Omar meme that's going around online. It uses his angry face from the church. He's become a minor celebrity in his own right, but not in a good way. I hope he's not seen it. It'd break his heart.

"Mel," I say and grab her arm so she looks at me. "Listen to me. I don't want any kind of media involvement. I just want all of this to go away. Let's just leave it, ok?"

Mel's not paying attention. Ellie has tripped and yowls. Bethany comforts her as Mel picks up her bag and jogs over to them. I shoulder my bag and follow behind. Ellie's knee bleeds.

"Right," Mel says, rummaging in her handbag. "Let's get this cleaned up and get a plaster on it and then head back to Grandma and Grampa's."

"But, Mummy," Bethany whines. "We just got here."

"But, nothing," Mel replies as she expertly tends to Ellie's graze. "You've got two more minutes to go and play and then we're off."

Bethany dashes to the slide. I pull out my phone as Mel soothes Ellie. I've had five missed calls from the same London number. I swallow. That could only be Tom. Or maybe my publisher. Or maybe it's Nisha calling from somewhere else because she's forgotten her mobile. Whoever it is, they're persistent. As I'm looking at the screen it lights up. Another call from the same number. My phone is on silent so it doesn't ring. I could just put it back in my bag and ignore it. But it could be important… I walk a few steps away and answer.

"Sally Speck?"

"Yes."

"This is Angus Darlington's lawyer. I have a message for you."

It takes a while for me to twig. Tom's brother.

"Ok," I say suspiciously. What does Angus's lawyer want? I brace myself for some bad news.

The lawyer reels off a message in an efficient monotone: "Mr Angus Darlington has requested that I contact you to inform that Mr Tom Darlington has moved on and will not contact or come near you again.

This is Mr Angus Darlington's personal assurance. He is deeply sorry for any hurt and upset that his brother has caused and offers his and his family's heartfelt apologies for any of Tom's behaviour that has caused you distress."

"Ok," I repeat because I cannot think of anything else to say, the anti-depressant drugs making my mind slow.

"Would you like me to repeat the message?" she asks.

"No, thank you." I hear the click as the lawyer hangs up.

Mel has gathered up Ellie and leads her toward where the car's parked. Bethany kicks her heels and trails behind.

"Anyone important?" Mel asks as I catch up to her.

I tell her about the call.

She shakes her head angrily. "That's so sneaky! They're trying to keep you sweet. It's so obvious. You need to go to the media as soon as possible to give that family the finger."

"Mel. You heard what I said. Just drop it with the going-to-the-media stuff. I think this is truly over. Tom's got the message. That's what his brother wanted to tell me via the lawyer. The end."

"Mmm hmm," she replies before shouting, "Come on, Bethany, or there'll be no iPad time later."

Bethany does an over-the-top sigh but then skips to catch us up.

Nothing else is said about the media or the call as we drive, the conversation dominated by the kids.

"What's this about, Mum?" Mel says, eyeing our mother.

Mum discreetly ushers Mel and me into the dining room, leaving Dad dozing in his chair while Bethany and Ellie watch cartoons. And leaving the debris of our tea and biscuits on the table, most unlike Mum. She closes the door behind us quietly and turns to look at us.

"Well, there's no easy way to say this, so…" Mum wrings her hands.

"Mum?" Mel says.

"Your father wants to speak with you."

"What? He's just next door," I say.

"No, not Graham. Your biological father."

Mel and I exchange a glance. I have no memory of my biological father, he left when I was three years old. Graham's always been my father.

Mum continues, forcing herself to say the words, "Pat Tanker. Patrick." She visibly wilts after saying the name, as if it took a lot of effort to get it out.

Mel, who's three years older than me and has vivid memories of Patrick, scowls. "What does he want?"

"He wants to meet you both," Mum says.

"After more than thirty years he wants to meet up with us?" Mel shakes her head violently. "No way. You should've told him to sod off."

Mum clasps her hands in front of her. "He got in touch with me this morning and asked me to pass the message on to you both. Who am I to stop you seeing him? It seems he wants to meet his grandchildren. And, well, he saw that YouTube wedding clip when a friend forwarded it to him for a laugh. Then he realised it was Sally and, well, he's angry about it."

"We are all angry about it, Mum. He can stay in Spain," Mel says.

"He lives in Spain?" I say. A sudden curiosity about this man sparks in me. "How long has he lived there? What does he do?"

"We're not seeing him. He should've made an effort when we were kids, not now we're adults. Bethany and Ellie are going nowhere near him. Their Grampa is Graham."

"Righty-ho, I'll tell him," Mum says.

Mel and Mum turn to leave the room as if the matter's decided.

"Wait," I say. "I'm curious."

They turn back to me.

Mel folds her arms. "Seriously, sis? He'll be one big fat

disappointment. What father abandons his wife and young children with nothing but a forwarding address to send the signed divorce papers?"

"Is that what happened, Mum? How do you know that, Mel?" Both Mum and Mel look away and squirm ever so slightly. This does nothing but inflame my interest. "Can you give me his number. I'll meet him."

Mum and Mel share a look. But I don't care what they think. My mind is made up.

"I'll go and fetch it for you," Mum replies, her face set.

When Mum is out of earshot, Mel says, "You're making a mistake. You'll regret it," before heading back to the lounge.

But I'm ridiculously intrigued. For the first time in a long time, I'm not dwelling on Tom Darlington and my marriage-that-never-happened, now all I can think about is this Patrick Tanker from Spain. My biological father. Will I look like him? Will we get on? What's he been doing all these years?

It's a welcome change from thinking about the monster who devastated my wedding. And it might just be what I need to jolt me out of my funk and into writing again. I have to write something and give it to the publishers so they stop demanding their money back. Meeting my biological father will be the spark that ignites my life again, I'm convinced of it.

# CHAPTER 23

I grew my hair out for the wedding and dyed the blond back to my natural brunette. But on Friday – on a whim after contacting Mel's estate agent friend to put my flat up for sale and grovelling to the mortgage company for an extended payment holiday – I decided to get Mum's hairdresser, who's been coming to the house to do Mum's hair for the last twenty-odd years, to chop it short again. I then bleached it and dyed it a bright, in-your-face pink.

It cheers me up, momentarily, to see that vivid, vibrant colour when I look in a mirror. For a second, my reflection doesn't look like me, which is a sweet relief until realisation dawns that I'm still me.

Four days after Patrick Tanker's contact with mum, I wait for him in an Italian restaurant in Bournemouth wearing new heavy-framed glasses purchased online and a ton of heavy makeup. I don't want anyone to recognise me, so I made sure I don't look anything like the Sally in the 'wedding invasion' video. And, although it's only been a couple of weeks since the attempted drive-off-a-cliff episode, the main side effect of the extra strong anti-depression drugs I'm now on is weight gain. Add that to my comfort eating and lying around all day and I've ballooned in weight.

"Alright, love, just looking for me daughter," a booming voice says from the doorway.

I sit with my back to the room, as is my usual habit,

and don't turn around. Anxiety about meeting this man bristles and the tips of my fingers go cold.

"Doesn't look like she's here yet."

"Perhaps that's her in the corner, she said she was waiting for someone," says a server.

I hear the man approaching and look up as he looms over me.

He stares down. "Well, bless me, it is her. She's changed her hair." He pulls off his leather jacket and slings it over the back of the chair but doesn't sit. "Come 'ere and give your old man a hug then." He opens his arms wide and waits.

Cringing, I stand, the chair still behind my knees, and give him a brief hug, trying not to touch chests and skimming my palms over his shoulders. He bear-hugs me and I feel ever-so-slightly abused. I sit quickly and he makes himself comfortable at the table. He beckons for a server.

A female server arrives and he makes no attempt to hide his eyes from travelling up and down her body. They stop on her chest. "Bring us some bubbly, would you?" he says to her breasts. "Me and my daughter here got some catching up to do."

"Prosecco?" she says.

"Perfect."

She scribbles on her pad. She then leans across the table to pick up our wine glasses and Patrick lifts his chin slightly to try and peer down her shirt. She walks off and he watches her go for just a little too long with his head cocked. I wait for his tongue to loll out, but it doesn't.

His attention switches back to me. He places his hands on the table, and the two heavy gold chains around his wrists clunk. In a booming voice, that I'm sure carries across the restaurant, to the road outside, and into the neighbouring buildings, says, "So, then, Sally, tell me what's been happening with that dickhead Tom Darlington."

The entire restaurant goes silent, or so it seems to me, listening intently to what I'll say next. I don't turn around to see if anyone's looking. Instead, I shrink into myself and my cheeks burn. "Please don't mention his name," I whisper at Patrick.

"Oh, right, still a bit raw is it?" he says. He grabs the wrist of our server as she passes and holds on to it for a beat too long. "Here, love, will you bring us the menus?"

The server grimaces at the touch and jerks her arm away. I feel embarrassed and angry for her. She shouldn't be groped for doing her job. She gets two menus from the bar counter and brings them back. She hands both to me and stands as far away as possible from Patrick. I hand one to Patrick and he ogles her as she departs.

I take a sip of water and consider my biological father surreptitiously while he scans the menu. Apart from clearly being a bit of a sleazebag, he's tall; an attribute Mel has inherited from him. Both Mel and I have green eyes like his, rather than Mum's blue. He has over tanned, leathery, sun-baked skin, and a bald head. Although he's almost seventy, his frame is still solid, overbearing, but with a large belly. He wears a short-sleeved checked shirt. It strains against his gut. One too many buttons are undone at the top and there's too much hairy chest on display. A chunky gold necklace pokes out of the white, wiry tufts. I can't see it, but I expect there's a medallion hanging from the end.

He waves his menu in the air to get someone's attention. "You know what you're having? Spag bol and garlic bread for me, don't want any of this fancy stuff. Truffle oil and pecorino, what the hell is that."

His laugh carries across the restaurant. A male server comes to take our order, perhaps the female server complained and they've switched. After we order, the prosecco and two tall flute glasses arrive and the server pours it. Patrick takes a big glug and turns his attention solely on me. I shift in my seat at his intense gaze.

"How's your mam then?"

"She's really well, thanks."

"And your sister?"

"Good."

"Shame she couldn't be here to see her old man, but I get it. I've been a crap father." He laughs again and swigs back more prosecco. "I'd like to see me grandkids, you know, you two were me only kids, so they're blood. And I ain't getting any younger, or healthier." He proudly pats his gut. "And really I want to see 'em before I pass on. Will you tell her that?"

"Yes, sure," I say, although I know Mel won't change her mind.

"Anyway, enough about me grumbling. Tell me about you. So you're an author now then? I've been following your career, believe it or not, own all your books. Haven't read one of them, mind, don't do reading me. Too busy."

"Do you work in Spain?"

"Nah." He laughs. "I'm retired. Play golf mostly. Eat and drink. I'm a silent partner in a few businesses, do a few deals, got a few investments here and there. You know how it is. Few dealings to keep me ticking along."

I nod. I really don't know 'how it is'. I itch to probe for more details but refrain. He doesn't seem like the kind of person to open up about his 'dealings'.

"How long have you been living in Spain?" I ask, on safer ground.

"Since me and your mam split. I left London and went straight to Spain. Had to lie low for a few years, you know, had a few shenanigans back 'ere that needed to blow over. But I liked it too much, the sun, the sea, the sexy expat women," he laughs, "so I never left. Made a life for meself there, owned two bars, a café, a restaurant and a nightclub in Torrevieja at one point."

"Is that what you used to do in London?"

"Christ, no." He chuckles and smacks the table with a palm as if I've said something hilarious. "Your mam never tell you?"

"Tell me what?"

"Ha, probably best left unsaid then."

Our dinner arrives and Patrick digs into his spaghetti Bolognese with relish.

While chewing with his mouth wide open, he says, "So, tell me about this *you know who* then. I was forwarded that video of him crashing your wedding just as a funny thing to watch, you know. I tell you, I laughed me head off at first, until I realised it was you. Your face when you realise it's him. Well, it broke me heart seeing you like that. And your mother's tears. Right pissed me off. And I don't like being pissed off, never have done. It eats away at me 'til I do something about it."

I don't want to talk about it. I'm trying to keep those painful memories buried. "It's in the past," I say, attempting to move him off that topic.

"Nah, it ain't. Janice told me that the fella you were meant to marry walked out on yer cos of it. And it broke your heart. And I can't stand anything that breaks me little girl's heart." Patrick's volume level rises steadily.

"I'm not so little anymore," I reply, quietly, hoping my hushed tone encourages Patrick to lower his voice.

"Graham gave that twerp a proper good smack, didn't he? And I was pleased to see it. But you're my little girl, not his, and I want to be the one giving that twerp a proper seeing to."

"Honestly, Patrick, it's fine."

"Call me Dad." Patrick pats my forearm and my insides curdle at the alien touch.

I force the corners of my mouth up, then slide my arm away to spoon some of my side salad onto my carbonara plate. Not something I'd usually do, but I didn't have any other option to move my arm quickly and with purpose out of his reach. I eat salad and pasta.

Patrick looks to either side of him, obviously checking who's nearby and then leans in close to me.

"I *know* people," he says.

"Er…"

"People that get rid of little problems, if you know what I mean."

I put my knife and fork down and stare at him. "I don't know what you mean." Although I think I do know what he means, but he surely can't be implying *that*?

Patrick sits back in his chair and taps the side of his nose with his index finger and does an exaggerated wink. "Just say the word, love, and I'll get in touch with my people."

"Say what word? What are you talking about?"

Patrick scratches his chest hair. "I geddit. You don't want to think about doing that, but I'll wipe that little prick off this planet for what he did to you."

His eyes narrow and a furrow creases his forehead. His grip tightens around his cutlery and his knuckles go white. Right before my eyes the sleazy retiree switches into a menacing thug and my palms start sweating. I wipe them on my jeans under the table.

"No one disrespects my family and gets away with it," he snarls.

The server comes over to ask if our meals are ok, breaking the odd, tense moment.

Patrick grunts as he devours the last of his spaghetti, but I'm done. I push my plate away.

"Not hungry, love?" Patrick says through his last mouthful of garlic bread.

"Not really."

"I'm surprised. You look like you've got a healthy appetite on yer. Just like your old man." He grabs my plate and switches it for his empty one and proceeds to shovel carbonara into his mouth. Inwardly I seethe at the jibe at my weight. He's not exactly lean himself. But I let it go.

Patrick finishes and leans back to rub his belly.

"Nice?" I say, just for something to say.

"Yep." He pushes back his seat. "Just going out for a

fag. Order me an espresso, will you." He heads outdoors and lights up immediately. He gets his phone out and paces back and forth outside the window.

The server comes to clear the dishes away. I order a coffee. I stare at the wall in front of me, willing this dinner to be over with as soon as possible.

Patrick sits back down, bringing a waft of cigarette smoke with him.

"So, did you marry again? Meet another woman?" I say.

"Nah, one failed marriage was enough for me. Footloose and fancy-free, I am," he laughs. "The single, bachelor life suits me. I've had women come and go and that's fine with me. There's always plenty of takers." He laughs again. "And now, I'm more in demand than ever. There's always a new retiree moving to Spain cos her husband's popped his clogs or they've finally divorced after thirty years and she's looking for a bit of excitement to fill her days."

I cringe and change the subject. "How long are you in England for then?"

"Well I flew in last night to Bournemouth, staying over tonight then up to London tomorrow to catch up with some family and old business associates. Haven't been back here in a while so making the most of it. Then fly back to the sun on Friday."

"You getting the train up to London?"

"Hire car. You should come out and see me in Spain. Got a decent villa with a pool, not far from Alicante airport. Piece of piss to get to."

"Thanks for the offer, perhaps I will one day." I know I never will.

"Yeah, and bring Mel and her family too. The kiddies would love the pool."

I look at my watch as Patrick's coffee arrives. "Can we get the bill please," I say to the server. "I've got some work to do later," I say to Patrick with a forced smile.

"Work?"

"I've got a deadline to meet with my latest book, want to write a chapter tonight," I lie.

"Right you are. Well, this one is on me."

"No, really, we'll go halves." I put my bag on my lap and rummage for my purse. There's no way I want to be indebted to this man.

"Put your money away," he says in a voice that doesn't allow for argument. He necks back his coffee like a shot and pulls out a wad of notes from his jeans pocket. He peels off two fifty-pound notes and places them on the table.

Then he stands, and grabs up his jacket. "Is there a casino round here?"

"Yes, just up the road," I say as I stand, wondering who wants to go to a casino on a Monday night.

"Good, good." Patrick strides to the door.

I follow. "Don't you want to see the bill? I'm sure that's way too much and you'll have change."

He shrugs. "They can keep it. Tip." On the street he turns to me. "Now which way is the casino?"

I point out the direction and he taps two fingers to his forehead in a kind of salute. We look at each other, unsure how to part ways. I want to run for my car, but politeness holds me rooted to the spot. Patrick, in turn, looks uncertain for a moment. Then he embraces me in a tight hug, pinning my arms to my sides. He releases me swiftly.

"Bye, then," I say.

"Bye, Sal, and remember what I said about erasing you-know-who." He pinches my cheek too roughly and walks off up the hill.

I head to the car park in a daze, attempt to process the dinner, to make an assessment about my biological father. Although still curious, one thing's for certain, I never want to see him again.

Before starting the engine I decide to turn on my phone. It's been off over the weekend. The battery went flat and I just never bothered to charge it. But I charged it to bring tonight. Just in case of emergency. It takes a couple of seconds to wake up and then pings with alerts. A few WhatsApp messages from Nisha and one from Hanna.

Then a notification tells me I have a missed call from... Omar? Omar! I've not heard from him since the church. Our families communicated to sort out the aftermath of a cancelled wedding, but we've not had any contact. He ditched me at the altar, what could he possibly have to say to me? Perhaps he accidentally pocket-dialled me? But that's unlikely.

I have an urge to hear his voice. *Screw it.* I dial his number.

"Hey?" he answers. In that voice that I loved so much.

"Hey," I reply.

"You called me back."

"Uh huh."

"I'm so, so sorry, Sal. I miss you so much. It's taken me a long time to realise that I let that bastard win by not marrying you. I should've been there for you, but I made it all about me. Can you forgive me?"

"I don't know, Omar. I really don't."

"What are you doing this week? Can I see you some time?"

I'm silent. Do I want to see him?

He continues, "Please, I'd love to see you, even for half an hour. Just to talk. I miss you."

My gut tugs, attempts to leap through the universe to wherever Omar is right now. I miss him. His steady, agreeable presence, his laughter. But he walked out on me when I needed him the most. Shamed me even more than Tom ever had. Can I forgive that? I reach deep inside to see if today I have that urge.

"Sal?" His voice is desperate. "Please…"

# CHAPTER 24

"I'm actually in Bournemouth right now," I told him, along with the car park and the level my car was on. Twenty minutes later he taps on the passenger side window of my car.

I nod and he gets in.

"Hey," he says sheepishly.

"Hey," I reply. I can smell his aftershave and immediately think I might break in two with the familiar longing of that smell.

"I was such an idiot. As soon as I walked out of the church, I regretted it. But then it was too late. It's taken me all this time to build up the courage to contact you. I couldn't bear the idea of you rejecting me, even though I know you are perfectly within your rights to tell me to sod off. If you never want to see me again, I understand. But I just wanted to see you one last time to tell you I regret what I did and I never meant to hurt you. I want to be with you forever, I still do! I cut off my nose to spite my face. In the moment, my anger flared and I let it control my actions." Omar's voice cracks and his eyes go watery. He looks broken and hunches into himself, while desperately watching me for any kind of reaction.

"You broke my heart! You walked out on me at our wedding. How is anyone meant to forgive that?"

"I know," he says. "I ruined us. I ruined my life. I ruined yours. If I could go back in time, I would've handled it completely differently. I would've waited for the church to be cleared of that bastard and his crew and I would've walked back out proudly with you on my arm and we would've continued with the service. And now we'd have just got home from our honeymoon, blissfully in love and ready to start our life together. I messed all that up. I hate myself for it. I hate myself so much." Omar slaps his cheeks. He jerks back and forwards and thumps the top of his fist against his forehead. The noise frightens me. He's really hurting himself.

"Omar, stop." I reach over the handbrake and grab his fist before he can thump it again. The brief physical contact stings like a wasp bite and I jerk my hand away. "We can all act impulsively. I get it. But, if you were me, would you forgive you?"

He shakes his head. "I know I'm asking a lot. But I'm begging you to give me a second chance. We can take things super slow. I know you need to trust me again. I know I've damaged our bond. But I'm willing to do all it takes to repair it. Please, Sal."

He tentatively reaches out and touches my arm briefly. It's such a gentle gesture that my ice cladding melts. Can I ever forgive him? I don't know. Do I still want to be with him for the rest of my life? My head says no: *He ditched you moments before you were meant to say I do!* But my heart says yes: *You still love him.*

"Ok. But it needs to be on my terms."

His face brightens and the happiness etched there makes my heart soar. "Whatever you want, I'm down for it."

We go quiet for a few moments.

"What were you doing in Bournemouth?" Omar asks and then swiftly adds, "If you don't mind me asking."

"I don't mind." I proceed to tell him about Patrick and we laugh as I recount all the gold chains my seventy-year-old wide-boy father was wearing.

"I've missed you so much," Omar says as we catch our

breath. And I realise I've missed him. Our easy conversation and our similar sense of humour. "What else has been going on?" he asks.

"Tom got an informal warning from the police about the stunt he pulled at our wedding," I say. Although I don't want to bring up that painful day again, I feel Omar has a right to know as it involves him too.

But Omar bristles and the happy moment passes in an instant as the tension in the car heightens. He looks away from me and grumbles under his breath. He shakes it out and looks at me.

"Sorry. That guy just makes me so damn furious." He takes a long breath in through his nose and then exhales through his mouth. He takes my hand. "But I know if I'm going to be with you forever, I need to understand that he's a part of your life right now, but not forever. I'm learning to manage my rage about that guy. You can trust me, ok? I'm learning to control it. For you. I won't let my anger consume me and cloud my judgement again, ok?"

I take in his quirky features, his brown eyes wide and imploring. We all have our flaws. And if we recognise them then we can do something about them. I'm willing to stick with Omar while he works through his.

"Ok," I say.

He brings my hand up to his face and sweetly kisses my knuckles. "I love you so much. I won't let anything – or anyone – come between us again."

"Sal, dinner's on the table," Mum hollers up the stairs.

I message Omar to say I'm off for my Mum's legendary Sunday roast to temporarily end our conversation. We've been messaging and calling every day since our car meeting on Monday. I come to the dining table in my pyjamas and dressing gown. Dad's already sat there, flicking through a home renovation magazine. I take my seat. Mum bustles in and out with dishes full of veg, meat and stuffing.

My parents don't mention my attire for 2pm in the

afternoon, they let things like that slide. Always have. And for that I love them.

The gravel crunches as a car arrives.

"That'll be your sister," Dad says without taking his nose out of his mag. "The kids are with the other grandparents and Steve's off playing rugby."

Mel lets herself in and heads to the dining room.

"Hi," she says brightly. She's carrying her handbag and another tote bag. She takes a seat opposite me and places both bags under the table.

I smile at her as Dad says, "Hello, there. Everything ok?"

"Yep," Mel replies and rubs her hands together as Mum places a dish piled high with Yorkshire puddings on the table.

"Dig in," Mum says as she takes her seat opposite Dad.

We all pile our plates with whatever is in the dishes closest to us and then in an unspoken family rule, we pass and switch the dishes around so that everyone's got everything.

I pour gravy over my plate. But before I can begin, Mel speaks.

"I've got today's papers," she says.

We all look at her. We haven't had newspapers in the house for a long time.

"Why, dear?" Mum says, lowering a fork loaded with stuffing and green beans.

"Because I told the papers about the police giving Tom Darlington an informal warning and it's made the front page."

"What?" I splutter.

Mum and Dad eye each other. This is clearly a surprise to them.

Mel reaches to the tote bag by her feet and pulls out a few newspapers. She holds one up so we can read the headline: TOM DARLINGTON NOT SUCH A DARLING. ACTOR WARNED BY POLICE FOR

STALKING SALLY SPECK.

I gape at her. My parents stare too.

Mel stares back at us. "I've transferred the money they paid into your bank account, Mum. I'm certain it's enough to cover Sally's wedding loan and hopefully have a bit to spare." Without a second thought, she eats her food.

Eventually, Mum and Dad tuck in too, but I just continue to stare.

Mel senses my discomfort. "He needed to be taught a lesson, Sal. He deserves worse than some bad press, much, much worse. I wish I could royally fuck him up. But this," she points at the pile of newspapers balancing on the edge of the table, "will have to do."

"Mel, language," Mum admonishes.

"I told you not to go to the media," I say.

Mel dismisses my words by waving her knife at me.

"I told you specifically not to go to the media," I repeat, louder.

"Well, I did anyway, didn't I?" Mel replies, matching my tone. "It was the right thing to do."

"No," I yell. "It was what *you* wanted to do. It wasn't what *I* wanted."

"Mum and Dad need the money. And you don't have it. Your flat's on the market, but that could take months to sell. I've done you a favour!"

"Girls, calm down," Mum says like we're children again.

Mel shrugs as if I'm getting angry over nothing and gets back to her meal.

I shove my chair back as I stand, grab a Yorkshire pudding from the dish in front of me and chuck it at Mel. It bounces off her shoulder and her head snaps up, her mouth still full. Her eyes widen and her expression is one of complete shock.

"Liz betrayed me to the media. And now you!" I shout as I stomp away.

Mel's lips screw up and she drops her cutlery, grabs a

roast potato off her plate and flings it at me. She bellows, "I'm standing up for you, you idiot, I'm not betraying you!"

I manage to dodge the missile and hear it thud against the wall, and the sliding noise as it smears to the carpet. As I leave the room, I hear Dad using his 'not impressed' voice, which doesn't come out often.

"Now that really wasn't necessary, was it, Melissa?" he scolds.

I'm not sure if he's referring to her going to the media behind my back or her throwing a gravy-wet roastie at my head. I don't care. I'm not sticking around to hear my traitorous sister's reply. I head up to my room and slam my door like a child. I slump on my bed, take a couple of long breaths and then find my phone.

The article attached to that headline is online. Of course it is. It's worldwide news by now. And the spin-off articles aren't pretty. Some media and fans have turned on Tom, many actually express their sadness at the way my wedding was ruined. But I bet they've watched that YouTube clip.

As I scroll through the comments, slowly it dawns on me that I'm not the bad guy anymore. The tables have turned. There's more support for me than Tom Darlington. Finally, his shiny exterior is crumbling. People are waking up to the abuse I've suffered at his hands.

I should be elated. But I feel empty. My own sister went against my wishes. She blabbed to the media. Just like Liz. The list of people I can trust is dwindling. I can scratch off Mel, and by default Steve. My trust in Omar disappeared on our wedding day and will take a long time to rebuild. Nisha and Hanna are close friends, but when I dig deep down, I don't fully trust them with every confidence, every secret.

Only my parents are left. They're loyal. They don't judge and don't care if I stay in the same clothes for days. They'll never lie to me or ignore me, thinking they know better. They've got my back.

There's a soft tap on my door. "I'll put your dinner here, love," Mum says. "Your father's done you some crumble, too." A pause. "Mel didn't mean to upset you." There's a rustle and her footsteps pad back down the stairs.

I wait until I can't hear anything, then open the door. On the floor is a tray with the plate I had loaded earlier with roast dinner but not touched, a bowl of apple crumble and custard, cutlery and a napkin. On top of the roast potatoes is an extra Yorkshire pudding. The food is steaming, and I guess Mum's put it in the microwave before bringing it up.

# CHAPTER 25

I wake with a start as Mum sits on my bed. "Love, it's a nice day. Do you want to come for a walk with me and your father?"

Mum opens my curtains and I blink in the daylight and wrench the cover over my face.

She gently pulls it down and I let her. "Come on. I've finally managed to convince your father to leave his shed. It's a momentous occasion that I think you should witness."

I sigh. My parents have patiently left me to wallow for ten days after Mel's betrayal. Pud-and-spud-gate as Dad now refers to it as. They've deflected any possibilities for Mel to see me, understanding that I'm still too fragile. She's come and gone with Steve and my nieces and I've stayed in my room. Off limits.

She hasn't tried to phone or message me. Not that I was really expecting her to. She won't feel as if she needs to apologise. Mel is always right. This is what we used to do as children. Quarrel and then never apologise, just forget any altercation with zero grudge or bitterness. When I see her next, we'll act like nothing happened. But this time I'll hold a grudge. I'm bitter. It'll take a while for that feeling to pass, if ever.

But Mum's right. It's been too long since I left the house, since I left my bedroom. Omar and I have been slowly picking up the pieces. He came over on Friday and we got a takeaway and chilled in the lounge while the parents went out. He wanted me to go to his and stay over but it's still way too soon for me. He spent the weekend at some family thing in Coventry, which he invited me to, but which I declined. I need some more time to learn to trust Omar again. I can't even bring myself to kiss him again yet. But we're getting there. It's now Tuesday and I really don't know where the time has gone.

"Come on," Mum says again gently.

"Ok, give me five minutes."

She leaves my room and I get out of bed, throw on some joggers, a T-Shirt that has been resting on my carpet for goodness-knows-how-long and some trainers. I put a baseball cap over my unwashed hair and grab a coat as I head downstairs.

My parents loiter by the front door.

"Here she is," Dad says brightly.

We head off into the forest, Dad drives. We travel in companionable silence.

Dad pulls into a petrol station and gets out to fill up the car. He replaces the nozzle and opens the car door. "Anyone want anything from the shop? Something to eat or drink before our epic hike?"

"Yes, I'll have a chocolate bar," Mum says.

"Which one?"

"I'll come with you and have a look." She gets out the car.

Dad rolls his eyes. Mum is notoriously indecisive when it comes to chocolate. "Sal?"

"Twirl, please."

I watch them walk into the shop, and my eye is caught by the newspaper stand outside. His face is right there. Staring at me. I look away, study the petrol pump. But it's no use. I leave the car and walk to the stand, pull out the trashy newspaper.

I'VE MOVED ON! screams the headline.

Transfixed, I open the paper and see a photo of Tom

and a woman. Another of Tom, his brother Angus and the same woman, all big grins. It reads:

> Actor and former teen pop star, Tom Darlington (24), has found love with children's TV presenter Tanith Evangeline (23), putting his troubled past behind him…

"Do you want that?" Dad says, cautiously, as he and Mum emerge from the shop.

"No. It says he's found a new girlfriend."

Dad's eyebrows furrow and he glances worriedly at Mum.

I let out a very long breath, put the paper back and we get into the car. Tom's once again in the public's favour after his fall from grace with the news of the police warning. And this Tanith is now the object of his – and the media's – attention.

It's done. Finally! I can get my life back on track. Get back to writing again. Maybe even try and marry Omar again… A take two on everything that's happened this year.

I gaze silently out the window as we drive, then walk alongside Mum and Dad, listening to them chatter on about nothing in particular and eat my Twirl on the way home.

"Do you want a cup of tea, love?" Mum calls from the kitchen the following Sunday.

"Yes, please," I say.

"I'd love one," Dad says. He closes the front door.

I drop my overnight bags at the foot of the stairs and head into the kitchen.

"Good train journey?" Mum asks.

"Fine," I say.

"She was on time, at least," Dad says.

"Did you have fun?" Mum asks.

"Yes, a great time. Didn't do much, but was so good to

see Nisha. Her husband, Arjun, was away last night so was lots of gossiping and wine."

Mum hands us our tea. "That's great, I'm so pleased you went. You needed to get out and about, and back up to your old stomping ground in London."

"Yes, it wasn't as bad as I thought. People seem to have forgotten who I am, and if anyone is staring at me, then I remind myself that I'm just being paranoid. That whole Tom thing has died down now that he's got a new girlfriend, everything is about her. I'm feeling really good."

"Good. Seems the new medication is working," Mum says.

"I think so." The stronger medication the doc prescribed after the clifftop incident has well and truly kicked in. I feel ever so slightly euphoric at all times. I like the permanent floaty feeling. Bad vibes bounce off me. I'm functioning again.

"Although you shouldn't be drinking on it. That's what your doctor said." Mum gives me a you-should-know-better look.

"Just a glass or two. Hardly heavy boozing. We were looking after Nisha's son."

The buzzer from the front gate sounds and startles me. My hand jumps and tea sploshes on the floor tiles. My heart leaps and then almost immediately calms. It's the drugs.

"I'll go," Dad says. He heads to the hallway and presses the intercom. "Hello, Hanna, I'll buzz you in."

"Hanna?" Mum says with a frown.

It's odd for Hanna to show up unannounced. She has two kids and a busy family schedule and is booked up months ahead.

Hanna's car crunches on the gravel and Dad opens the front door. I watch through the window as Hanna bounds up, not even closing her door.

I should feel anxious or alarmed or worried, but I'm mellow.

"Wotcha," Dad says cheerfully. "Come in."

"Is Sal here?" Hanna says, her voice sharp.

"I'm here," I say as I head to the front door.

"How could you?" Hanna yells from the doorstep, "How could you do this to Omar? My brother is a good man. Is this your sick way of getting back at him?"

"Do what? What are you talking about?"

Hanna pulls open a newspaper in her hand and I look closely.

TOM DARLINGTON SPOTTED WITH EX SALLY SPECK LEAVING LONDON CLUB blares the headline, with blurry photos of Tom guiding a woman holding a floaty scarf over her head on the street and getting into a car.

"What on earth?" Mum mutters from behind Dad, who stands with his mouth hanging open and still clutching the door handle.

"That's not me," I say, vehemently shaking my head. "They must be fake."

"Oh, really," Hanna sneers. "It certainly looks like you. And that certainly looks like the orange scarf I gave you for your birthday."

"I swear to you, Hanna, I haven't been anywhere near Tom Darlington since he crashed my wedding. That scarf is from H&M – it's not exactly a one-off, anyone could have it – or one that looks similar. The photos are fake."

"So where were you last night then?" Hanna demands looking past us at my overnight bag by the stairs.

"I was with Nisha," I say.

Hanna's eyebrows almost shoot off her face. "In London!"

"Yes, but with Nisha, not with that wanker." I take my phone out of my jeans pocket. "I'll message her now, you'll see."

I tap out a message to Nisha:

'Babe, remind me what we did last night?'

While we wait for Nisha to reply, Mum takes the newspaper from Hanna and stares at it with Dad.

"I can't believe you did this to Omar," Hanna says again.

My med-induced calm temporarily gives way to rage. "Why would I go anywhere near that snake? I hate him, I never want to lay eyes on him again." I know I need to get a handle on this emotional yo-yo-ing but right now I can't stop. "They are fake pictures, photoshopped! It's been months since they last printed anything about us and they are just stirring up crap to sell—"

The ping of my phone interrupts me and my bluster falters. I read the message before showing it to Hanna.

'Oh, was it that thrilling a Saturday night that you've forgotten already lol. We had a takeaway pizza, a few drinks and then I went to bed pretty early, an hour or so after I put Sahil down, left you to finish the movie and the bottle of red. Why?'

"See. I was with Nisha," I insist. "Here, I'll give you her number and you can message her yourself. Actually, you can ask her yourself. You're friends on Facebook since my hen do."

Hanna scowls. "Yeah, I'll message her." She narrows her eyes at me, clearly not convinced and walks back to her car. She slams the door. As she backs out, the gate opens automatically for her to leave. She speeds away, her tyres squeal as she turns onto the road.

"Sal?" Mum asks, still holding the paper.

I grab it from her and ball it up. "It's more lies." I stomp through to the kitchen and dump the paper in the recycling bin and then stomp past my parents, who are rooted in the hallway, heave up my overnight bag and head to my bedroom.

My phone pings as I fling my bag against the wardrobe. It's Nisha again.

'Everything ok? Arjun just got home. Don't u remember what happened this morning? Found u still in ur clothes asleep on sofa, lol, weirdly u had your shoes on. U not only drunk what was left in that bottle but had drunk that second bottle u brought up. U total pisshead! Although I know I was a lightweight and went to bed at 9!!'

I tap back:

'Oh yeah! I remember… my feet got cold ;-)'

I slump to the carpet and lie in the Shavasana yoga pose and count four breaths in and four breaths out a few times.

I have absolutely no memory of the evening after Nisha went to bed. I assume I fell asleep too, and that's why there's a blank. The cocktail of anti-depressants make me feel human again, but the doctor warned me not to drink on them. But a bottle and a bit of wine? That's not a lot, is it? I'd been on form with Nisha, telling jokes, making her laugh. I wasn't a misery. I was vibrant, like me again. I felt back to my old self, invincible even. But why would I have gone out to meet Tom? How could I have even gotten in touch with him?

I look at my phone's last called list, and it shows the home phone, Nisha, Dad's mobile. I also check my email sent items folder, although I don't have his email address, and… nothing.

A mobile phone number pops into my head. His number. I don't realise I've got it memorised until that moment lying there in the corpse pose. I guess I looked at it so many times when he repeatedly called me after we first met.

No. I didn't leave Nisha's house last night. Those photos are fake. I wouldn't have done that. It's not me. I'm not like that. And why would Tom even want to spend any more time with me when he has a new girlfriend. It's a ridiculous thought and I brush it aside.

I dial Omar's number and he picks up before it rings once.

"I just got off the phone to my sister. How could you do this to me?"

I have to hold the phone away from my head as Omar's snarling shout reverberates in my ear. "Calm down! Those photos are fake. I was with Nisha."

But Omar's not listening. He's raging, shouting words that I can't make out.

"Omar," I shout back, "listen to me. Those photos are fake. You do believe me, don't you?"

"Is this your way of getting back at me?"

"What? Of course not—"

"No. It's not you. It's him. He made you do it."

"I didn't see Tom. He didn't make me do anything!"

"I thought that bastard was gone from our lives. He needs to be gone. I'm going to get him; he's going to be gone once and for all!"

"What are you talking about? Tell me you believe me. I didn't see him," I plead.

But Omar doesn't respond. I sense that he doesn't believe me. And my heart breaks all over again. I can't let him destroy me a second time. I have to protect myself.

"Omar, are we done? I just can't see us getting past this. We need to be able to trust each other—"

"No. We're *not* done. He's done! He's fucking done!" Omar yells and hangs up the phone.

It's a brutal, unexpected ending. I stare at my phone open-mouthed for a few moments before putting it down.

Perhaps I should've said sorry. For what though? What do I have to be sorry about? I've done nothing wrong. Omar should believe me and not take what the media says at face value. I don't deserve to be shouted at by one of my best friends and then by the man who is meant to love me.

I wait to see if Omar will message me. Hoping that he'll calm down and apologise. But he doesn't. Part of me thinks I'll never hear from him again. I scream into my pillow and then sob. Fluctuating between fury and sorrow as my anti-depressants attempt to stabilise my roiling emotions.

# CHAPTER 26

Five days later, I pull out of the supermarket car park and head home. I've been to the post office, picked up my prescription, dropped off Mum's library books, and shopped for some food for dinner. This morning, I managed to stall the mortgage company chasing for updates on the sale of the apartment, and then my publisher's solicitor chasing about repayment of my advance. I called the estate agent, but still no offers. I feel productive. I offered to pick Mum up from the station too, after her day trip to Winchester with her friend Verity, but Dad's gone as it's in the other direction.

The presenter announces the news bulletins. I'm in Dad's old Peugeot and the ancient CD player has long since stopped working, so it's radio or silence, and I opt for radio. Although whenever the presenters witter on too long, I switch it off, count to ten and then switch it on again hoping for music.

I listen to news about cyberbullying and climate change and an announcement that:

'Actor Tom Darlington assaulted in the early hours of this morning and is recovering in hospital. The police have charged the perpetrator with assault. He's thought to be the man whose wedding the actor crashed earlier this year.'

I swerve and a car on the other side honks me. I

correct the steering, the thud of my heartbeat blocking out the sports news. I speed all the way home, turning in front of cars, not waiting for cars to pass. I rush in the door.

"Hey, sis," Mel shouts cheerily from the lounge. "In here."

This is our first meeting after pud-and-spud-gate but that only registers on my periphery. I've got other stuff to deal with right now.

"Omar…" I manage.

"Yes, we know," Mel says and beckons me over to sit next to her on the sofa. Mum and Dad sit on the other one.

"I just heard on the radio…" I stutter as I perch on the cushion where Mel pats.

"He went to confront Tom in London and they got in a scuffle. Tom fought back and they were both taken to hospital for minor injuries. Tom just had a pathetic cut above his eye. Omar came off worse. But Omar was arrested because he started it," Mel says.

"Poor Omar. This is my fault…" I put my face in my hands.

"It's definitely *not* your fault, Sal, your father is *entirely* to blame," Mum snaps. She purses her lips at Dad and folds her arms.

I squint at Mum, my head suddenly pounding. "What are you talking about, Mum? Omar's in serious trouble because of me. The radio said he's been charged with assault."

"The charges have been dropped," Mum says matter-of-factly.

My voice rises. "But how do you *know* that? The radio literally just reported the news."

Mum glares at Dad who sheepishly looks at his knees. Mel shifts on the sofa and avoids any eye contact with me, glancing at our parents.

They know something I don't. Fury explodes. "Will someone please tell me what is going on?" I yell.

"Omar only knew where to find Tom because of your father," Mum says, still shooting Dad her extremely disappointed look. "The poor lad was desperate after those photos of you and Tom appeared in the paper…"

"*Fake* photos," I interrupt.

"Yes, *fake* photos. Omar said he wanted to confront Tom for breaking up your relationship and persuaded old muggins here," she jerks a thumb at Dad, "to help him. The stupid sod didn't think it through."

Dad mumbles incoherently.

"What, love?" Mum says. "Speak up, we can't hear you."

"I said, I didn't know Omar was going to attack Tom and get himself arrested, did I?" Dad replies.

"What on earth did you think would happen, Dad?" Mel says. "And getting Steve involved." She tuts.

"Steve's involved?" I ask. The thumping between my ears is unbearable. I just want everything to slow down. I can't keep up.

Suddenly Mum, Dad and Mel all start talking over one another. My brain is addled.

"Shut up," I bellow. They go quiet. "Rewind. None of this is making any sense. First of all, would someone just tell me how Dad helped Omar to find Tom?"

Mum eyes Dad, who looks guiltily at his knees again. When he doesn't speak, she says, "Your father *knows people* and they followed Tom and told Omar where he was so he could confront him."

"*Knows people*? That's what Patrick said. What the hell?" I say.

"They probably know the same people," Mel quips.

"That Wanker doesn't have any contacts anymore," Dad grumbles. "Just the funds to pay for them."

"That's beside the point, Graham," Mum says.

"Who are you talking about, Dad?" I say.

"That Wanker, Pat Tanker. That's what we used to call him. Not to his face, mind," Dad says.

Mum rolls her eyes. "Anyway, it was your father's doing. And poor Omar ended up in trouble with the police. Old muggins here felt bad, and admitted what he'd done to me. Well, I hit the roof, as you can imagine so I've spent all morning in London sorting things out."

"London? Haven't you been to Winchester with Verity?" I mutter but the conversation moves on without me.

"And Dad got Steve to get on Twitter and message Tom to get his phone number for Mum to call him and organise a visit," Mel says, arms crossed. Her knee jigs up and down. "Without consulting me first! He's *my* husband, you could've got him into trouble."

"Steve wanted to help, Mel. He and Omar got on well before all the wedding hoo-ha," Mum says.

"Why didn't you speak to me first?" Mel says.

Mum tuts. "I don't know, love, it was all in the heat of the moment. We wanted to get it all ironed out before Sal got wind of it."

"So, Steve got Tom's phone number?" I ask, attempting to catch up. "So you could go to meet him in London? After Dad found out where Tom was for Omar because Patrick has been paying to have Tom followed?"

"Yes," Mum says simply, in answer to all my questions. "We know you and Omar are trying to make a go of things again and we know it's been a bit rocky. The last thing any of us want is for Omar to have to spend any time in prison or have a police record. So, we decided I should go and see Tom and try to smooth things out."

My hands shake. Wrath crawls up from my belly to blast from my mouth. "You *saw* Tom? You went to London today to see that bastard? You lied to me! You told me you were going to Winchester with Verity."

Mum dips her chin. "It was the only thing we could think to do to fix this mess your father had made. We were hoping it wouldn't be reported, or at least, you wouldn't hear about it. You're extremely fragile, Sal. We don't want anything else to rock the boat. We don't want you to try and harm yourself again."

"You went behind my back!" I stand, my entire body quakes. "You spoke to that arsehole and asked him to do us a favour and drop the charges against Omar and now you are indebted to him! I'm indebted to him. What on earth did you say? What did *he* say?"

Mum, unable to look me in the eye, says, "I said that Omar had been having a bad time and that it was unfortunate, and that would Tom please do what he can to get the police to drop the charges, for everyone's sake."

"And?" I push.

"And Tom said that he would do it because…" Mum fidgets and chews on the inside of her cheeks.

"Because what, Mum?"

"Because he still loves you and would do anything for you."

Mel hisses through gritted teeth.

I groan and fling my hands up. "Oh, that's just great isn't it!"

"I told him, very politely, that you were not in love with him and that you didn't want to see him now or at any time in the future," Mum says, matching my anger with composure.

"I seriously hope this doesn't prompt his stalking me again!" I thump the back of the sofa.

"He was distraught, but said he understood and that he wouldn't contact you again. And that was that. Angus was at Tom's apartment too and was very understanding."

"His brother?" Mel asks.

"Yes, a nice young man. Sensible."

"Sensible?" I ask.

Mum nods. "Tom said something bizarre about you contacting him—"

"I have not been in touch with him!" I screech.

"Of course not, that's what I said. And Angus mentioned that Tom gets all kinds of strange fan mail, and it must be some fan pretending to be you."

"Tom won't come anywhere near you again, Sal, I've made sure of that," Dad pipes up.

"What are you talking about now, Dad?" I exclaim.

Mum rubs circles on her temples with her fingers.

"We need to tell her," Mel says to Mum and Dad.

I take in my family. I don't recognise any of them. I have no idea who they are. My family had once been my rock, but now I feel cast adrift. Alone. Very alone.

"You'd better sit," Mum says.

I slump back on the sofa, exhausted. The drugs tell my body to calm down. I curl my legs up under me and clutch a cushion.

"You know that Graham and I met in the bar where I was the barmaid. You were three and Mel was six. Patrick had just walked out on us and I had desperately taken the barmaid position, leaving you two with a neighbour to do my first shift.

"What you don't know is that your biological father left us because a deal of his went bad and he had to disappear for a while in Spain. The last thing he did before he got on that plane was to send me divorce papers. He's ten years older than me and had been working his way up in the Eastside Firm gang since he was fourteen. He used to do street fights.

"Anyway, Graham… well… Graham used to work for Pat every now and then. And… well…" Mum crosses and then re-crosses her legs and fiddles with her necklace, "Graham and I had met before, had seen each other in passing. But I'd always been Patrick's woman and none of his men ever spoke to me properly, said a polite hello and what not but never anything more.

"When Pat left, it was the same time that Graham had just had criminal charges dropped against him for that awful murder. We were a similar age and both had baggage, as such. Me with two young kids in tow and him with this heavy cloud of suspicion hanging over him, so we agreed to a fresh start. We cut all ties, moved from London to this area and here's where we've been ever since."

A brief silence as I digest this. I squint around the room. Dad squeezes Mum's hand and she smiles at him.

I close my eyes and process the information. Eventually I say, "So, you're telling me that Dad and Patrick were some kind of gangsters in the east end of London?" I turn to Mel who sits quietly on the other end of the sofa. "And you *knew* this?"

Mel shrugs simply. "I'm older, I picked up on more stuff than you. I heard things and questioned them."

"So, who are all these *people* that everyone keeps going on about? Dodgy gangsters?" I ask, I untangle my legs and slowly place my feet on the carpet.

"Your father really shouldn't have gotten in touch with them. He's not spoken to any of that old crowd in decades, since we left," Mum says.

"What's done is done, lovey," Dad says.

"What are these people doing, precisely?" I ask.

"They've been watching Tom. If it looks like he might come anywhere near you, or is planning anything stupid, they'll alert me," Dad replies.

"How long has this been going on for?"

"Since soon after the wedding," Dad says. "At first it was a favour to me. But that was only for a couple of weeks. But then Patrick stepped in and offered to pay to keep it up."

I stand up laboriously, all energy ripped from me. "I'm going to bed."

I don't turn on the light in my room, or take off my clothes. Instead, I close the door and sprawl face-first on my bed. I lie still, barely breathing, I don't want my alien family members downstairs to hear me.

How could they keep a secret like that from me? How could Dad help Omar when he deserted me? Yes, I know we were trying again, but still that was a big ask from

Omar. And how could Mum actually go to visit Tom? With the plan not to tell me about it? Everything feels different, things have shifted, swung onto a new course.

And then it strikes me. It's not real, none of this is real. Like those fake photos, that conversation didn't happen. It's false. I imagined it. I'm asleep and dreaming. The idea soothes me momentarily.

But, in the back of my mind, a niggle. A certainty. That happened. Truths and relationships that I hold dear, that I trust more than I trust myself have crumbled in the space of an afternoon.

# CHAPTER 27

The next morning, Mum shakes my shoulder and says something to me, but I can't hear her. It's as if I'm underwater.

My eyes slowly focus as Mum's grip tightens and the tone of her voice becomes more urgent.

"Sally, what on earth have you done?" Mum is saying, she's wrapped up in her dressing gown, eyes bleary.

I gradually take in my surroundings. I'm sitting on my knees on the floor of the dining room. I've been here a while: my legs are numb and my knees are screaming. I unravel my dead legs and spread them out in front of me. Scattered in a haphazard circle around me are old photo albums upturned and flung about, printed photos and an empty bottle of sherry. I look closer and realise that the photos aren't whole. They're torn up, in shreds.

I look down at my hands as if the answer lies there and then up at Mum. An ugly hangover is kicking in. "I… I don't know."

"Well it looks to me as if you've pulled out the boxes of old albums from the cupboard there, drunk yourself stupid and ripped up my old photos," Mum says. She dips her chin sadly. "Most of those photos were one-offs, we don't have the film anymore."

"I'm so sorry," I say, panic tinges my voice. "I don't remember doing this."

"I know you're upset at what we told you yesterday, but

258

that's no excuse for destroying these things. These are my photos, Sal. And your father's. Photos of our families, your childhood."

Mum kneels and starts to gather the fragments of photos in her hand, looking at the pieces. "It looks like all the ones from when you and Mel were small. What a shame."

"I'm so sorry," I repeat but Mum doesn't respond, bent on her task. Each sliver she looks at makes her shoulders slump and adds to the distress writ across her face. I wiggle my toes to test if the feeling has come back and begin to pick up the ripped-up pieces as Mum is doing. "Perhaps we can stick them back together?"

"Perhaps," Mum mumbles, her voice small and thin.

"I think it's the new drugs. They're giving me blackouts."

Mum's patience evaporates. "No. You're giving yourself blackouts," she snaps. "You drank that entire bottle of sherry your father was given for his birthday. Your doctor said no alcohol."

I clutch my head. "I feel shocking."

"I'm not bloody surprised. Serves you right. Oh!" Mum holds a hand to her mouth and stares at a portion of photo in her other hand. "You've torn our wedding photos to pieces. How could you, Sal?" Mum's voice wobbles and I sink into a deep, dark hole. Mum upset is terrible. She's solid, she's a rock. For her to be upset is very, very bad.

"I'll put them back together…" I say in desperation, anything to make her better again.

"No, get out of here," Mum shouts and points at the door.

"Mum…" I lean forward to give her a hug.

She swipes at my arms, distraught. "Don't touch me, don't you dare! Just get out!"

My heart races as I scramble to my feet, my legs still unsteady as the blood returns, and dash to the hallway, pull on my trainers and grab the Peugeot keys.

I fly out of the driveway, clipping the gates as they open automatically with a loud thunk, and head towards the forest. I wind down the window for a blast of air and turn the music up so loud that the bass makes the steering wheel vibrate through my hands.

I have no direction in mind, but head deeper into the forest, until I turn off the road on a whim and into an empty car park. I screech to a halt, startling some of the wild roaming New Forest ponies into a gallop.

I stumble away from the car along a narrow path worn in the grass between two prickly gorse bushes. I keep going, ignoring the mud, ignoring the thorns that tug and catch my clothes. I bring my arms up to protect my face from the undergrowth and push forwards, my legs propelling me on, on, on.

I burst through into a clearing. A tree-dotted plain that stretches away from me and down a gentle hill. I descend the hill in a daze, staring forward at the horizon as if it holds something that I'm striving to reach.

My foot snags under an exposed tree root and I trip. My legs land in a muddy puddle with a splosh and my torso and hands slam down onto the gravelly earth. I manage to keep my forehead from banging but my lips and nose touch the ground. I spit out dirt as sharp stones dig into my palms.

Damp mud seeps through my jeans to sore knees. A graze on my cheek stings. I push myself up slowly to sitting. Scratches on my forearms and hands bleed, and I gingerly brush the dirt and a pebble off my face with the back of a hand. I sit very still.

I glance down at yesterday's clothes. The ones I didn't take off the night before. They're filthy. Like me, like my soul. Soiled. How could I rip up those photos? Those treasured memories from the past? How could I be so cruel? That's not me, I'm not that person.

I start to sob, great racking heaves that travel up from the pit of my belly and erupt out my mouth. I cry until I physically can't anymore. My eyes dry and I sit numb, shivering.

I have no idea how long I sit here. It's early morning and I've not come across anyone else. Or, more precisely, no one has come across me, because I haven't moved. I become aware of a presence nearby, shuffling through the gorse towards me.

A wave of dread comes over me and I look around for somewhere to hide. Could I have been followed? Will an angry Omar or obsessed Tom pop out?

But it's too late as the noise is upon me.

A chocolate Labrador bursts through and comes up to me, sticking its nose in my face, tail wagging. It snuffles my neck and I surprise myself by laughing out loud.

The encouragement makes it bark and excitedly sniff me again, pointing its nose at a ball near my foot. I grab it and chuck it. It's a pathetic throw, barely travelling a few feet away but the dog bounds after it, picks it up and brings it back to me, dropping it at my feet. It nudges my ankle. I throw it again and the dog chases it. At a call from its owner some way away, it runs off, ball poking out the side of its mouth.

I stand up and return to the car. I go home. Relief rushes over me as I see Mum and Dad are out. I shower, change and head out again.

When I return a few hours later I have a black-and-white, three-year-old Cocker Spaniel with me from a nearby unscrupulous private seller looking for a quick sale and a ton of shopping from Pets at Home.

My windscreen wipers flap back and forth angrily. When I left the bungalow there was a light drizzle. Now, it's torrential and the sky has turned a dark, ominous grey. Baxter whimpers excitedly in the back as I pull into a random car park in the New Forest.

"This'll do," I say to Baxter. He barks twice in reply.

It's only been a week but he's settled in quickly. Mum

was reluctant at first, annoyed at the mess, but soon she fell in love. We have developed a routine. I take him out in the morning and evening and Mum and Dad take him out at lunchtime. They'll take him for a short walk and then to a dog-friendly pub or café. Secretly, they love showing him off. He's a handsome pup and draws oodles of attention.

He's saved me, really. Having another being to look after forces me to focus on something other than myself. Baxter's pestering in the morning is consistent. He doesn't care if I'm having a good day or a bad day. He wants – needs – his walkies. And I drag myself out of bed and oblige. Throw his ball, wipe off his muddy paws, pick up his poo. The exercise and fresh air lift my spirits.

Baxter also helped soothe Mum's sorrow. The photo incident hasn't been mentioned again and I haven't seen the ripped-up photos. I don't know if my parents tried to stick them together again or found the old film to get them re-printed. I don't dare ask. I feel awful about it, but best to forget it ever happened and never mention it again.

Like Dad's murder charge. Like Mel's betrayal. Like my biological father being part of some gang. Like Dad telling Omar where to find Tom after having him followed. Like Mum visiting Tom. It's in the past. A flash of light that's fizzled to nothing. You know it happened but you don't see it anymore. That's what my family does, has always done. We don't hold grudges, we let things go.

Mum gave me the cold shoulder for a few days, only talking to me about the dog. And while Mum was ruminating, Dad avoided me – it's always in his best interests to show solidarity with Mum – but he was amiable when we bumped into each other around the house. One day, Mum's funk lifted and everything returned to normal. Although, 'normal' has a slight, lingering tinge of disappointment in my behaviour and overwhelming guilt on my part.

My parents are on holiday in Southend-on-Sea, visiting some of Dad's family. They left yesterday. Back on Sunday morning and then, instead of Mum's Sunday roast, we're going out for lunch with Mel, Steve and the kids to celebrate Bethany's birthday. I have the house to myself for three days and plan to write. Zero distractions. Baxter's getting an extra-long walk this morning so he won't need an afternoon outing and will hopefully zonk out for hours.

I switch my trainers for wellies and get Baxter out of the boot. Even with my hood up, my glasses get so wet in the time it takes to walk from the front of the car to the back that I can barely see anything through them. I open the front door and toss them on the seat before we set off on a soggy walk. There's only one other car parked, most people opting not to walk in the pouring rain first thing in the morning.

A few paces from the car park I let Baxter off the lead. He dashes off and romps through the undergrowth. Without my glasses he's a black-and-white streak. As I stomp through the forest after him, following a muddy path through dense evergreen trees, I muse that it is all-quiet-on-the-TD-front, as Dad likes to say. According to the media, Tom Darlington is smitten with his new girlfriend. We're all moving on from that disastrous episode. Occasionally the media refer to me as the 'reclusive author', but it's in passing. I'm another flash of light that's fizzled.

The demands from the mortgage company, publisher and credit cards got out of hand, piling on the pressure that I just can't handle right now. So I decided – although it tore at my heart – to lower the price of my flat just to get it sold and to pay them off as quickly as possible. Almost immediately, I had an offer. No surprise, it's a bargain. I accepted, and hope it doesn't take too long to go through. Depressingly, I'm well and truly dependent on my parents again: no home of my own and no chance of having another home of my own for a long time. The fury of my situation and the anger at Tom builds again, but I tamp it down.

I turn a corner and realise I've not seen Baxter in a while. He usually stays close, dashing off but then returning to the path. I call his name and whistle a couple of times but he doesn't return. I stop to look around but can't see far without my glasses through the rain and into the murky vegetation between tree trunks. I turn a full circle, continuing to call and whistle, but there's nothing.

Suddenly I feel very alone in this big forest with no one else around. Exposed. I stare harder into the gloom. A twig crunches behind me and I whirl around.

"Bax, there you are!" I exclaim, but it's not the dog.

I see a dark figure in the shadows. But I can't tell for certain. My eyes pop open and I freeze, every muscle rigid. For a long time, the figure doesn't move. It's my overactive imagination, that's all. It must be.

But I feel watched.

Something or someone is looking at me. An intense shiver crawls across my skin and the hair on the back of my neck prickles. I slowly put my hand in my jacket pocket and bring out my car keys. I wedge the keys so they stick out through my fingers when I make a fist.

I scan my surroundings and see a shadow moving beneath the trees, then another, then another. With my other hand I pull my phone out of my pocket and flick my eyes down at it, but have no signal this deep in the forest. I put it away and ball my other hand into a fist.

Barking snaps me to attention and I listen hard. It echoes through the woods and comes at me from every direction.

"Baxter?" I call out weakly.

The barking comes again, but from further away. Then I hear… laughter? I can't tell but I lurch in the direction of the barking, hurriedly retracing my steps back towards the car park, looking over my shoulder to see if anyone is following me.

The sinister trees close in on me, the air tightens and every creak and crunch is terrifying. I jog, then run. My head is filled with the noise of my heavy breathing and the pounding rain. My hood flies off and I feel dangerously wide open, a high-value target on the move asking to be attacked.

Flinging open the gate into the car park, there's more barking. Has the daft dog just gone back to the car? But he's not there. Instead I see a spark of white from across the road. More barks. I hurry down the car park's entrance and stop at the edge of the road.

My stomach lurches.

There's Baxter on the other side and next to him, a man with his hood up. He seems to be holding the dog, but I can't quite see.

The man hurries to his car as he sees me, which is parked up along the road with the front door open and engine running.

"Baxter!" I yell and I quickly glance both ways to check nothing's coming and step out onto the road.

The car's tyres squeal and it shoots towards me.

I throw myself backwards off the road a second before the car hits me. I land in the bramble-strewn ditch by the side of the road.

I swear the car turns towards me, then straightens at the last second and whooshes past in a blur, speeding away.

I catch a fuzzy glimpse of the driver. "Tom?" I blurt.

Thorns prick at my hair and jacket but Baxter's yapping is all I can think about. Shoving aside the shock, I extricate myself from the muddy ditch and crawl up the small bank to the road. I heave myself to my feet and stumble across the road to Baxter.

A broken branch of the fallen tree is wedged through his collar, so he can't move. But he looks perfectly fine, bounding up and down with tail wagging as I reach him and unhook him from the branch. I clip on his lead and then collapse, hugging him to me as I shake in a frenzy, my skin covered in a layer of ice.

"Everything ok?" a woman asks me. She's turned into the car park and has wound down her window to shout across the road. Dogs bark in the branded van and I see she's a dogwalker.

"Did you see another car?" I reply.

"No, not much on the road this morning."

"I think someone just tried to run me over."

She frowns dubiously. "You mean, on purpose?" She stares at me a bit longer, clearly weighing up whether to get out and help but I save her the trouble.

"I'm parked just there. I'll be fine." I scramble to my feet and give her a wave.

She nods, winds up her window and continues into the car park.

I hobble as fast as I can manage across the road leading the dog. Everything hurts from the fall in the ditch and I'm covered in mud. I get Baxter in the boot and run to the front seat, locking the car doors. Terrified that the man might return, I drive like a maniac out of the car park, past the startled dogwalker, and fly home.

Once in the fortress of a bungalow behind the high gates and fence, I lock myself in the bathroom with Baxter and try to process what the hell just happened. Was it an accident and bad timing? Baxter ran off and got himself caught on that branch. A man pulled over to help, saw the owner on their way, decided to leave rather than get any wetter and swerved to miss me as I walked out in front of him.

But why am I so certain that he tried to run me off the road? Or did I just imagine that? There was a lot of water on the road and the car could've skidded, maybe that's why I thought it headed straight at me when I fell in the ditch. And why not stop when I fell? Maybe he didn't see…

Or was it Tom? I didn't have my glasses on. It could've been anyone. But perhaps Tom lured Baxter away and made me follow to the road, secured Baxter to the tree and tried to run me over.

Why though?

Because he's been rejected. He's had a police warning. And Mum said he was distraught when she told him that I wasn't in love with him and didn't want to see him ever again. Perhaps he's finally got the message. Sadness has turned to anger and in his sick mind he's out for revenge.

I shudder. My life would be just another thing he's taken from me. My independence, my freedom, my dream career, my financial security. All gone. He's screwed up all the relationships I hold dear and flipped my mental health upside down.

And now he's out to kill me.

I find my phone. Should I call the police? My parents? Mel? And say what? 'Hi, I think Tom Darlington just tried to run me over and my life's in danger.'

There's no way I read a number plate; I don't even recall the colour of the car. The dogwalker said she hadn't seen any other cars and looked sceptical when I said I'd nearly been run over. Would anyone believe me?

Do I believe me?

I fret and obsess. Tremble with fear for my life, pace with vicious rage, then hold my head in my hands utterly confused. Hours pass before I feel safe enough to venture from the bathroom. Even though it's not even lunchtime I crack open a bottle of wine to steady my nerves and blot out the morning.

Eventually I decide not to mention it to anyone. I can't be certain what happened. My parents were reluctant to leave me to go away but I convinced them I was fine and getting better. Claiming a superstar celebrity tried to run me over does not make me look sane, especially as I have zero evidence.

One thing's for sure, though: I will NOT let Tom take my life.

The next day, I sit at the dining room table and write a

new sci-fi novel. The words are flowing. Clearly there's nothing like a near-death experience to kickstart your creativity. I know what Nisha will say, she'll call it 'dark' and 'too violent to be commercial', but that's what's coming out so I'm getting it down.

I tried to continue with *Dusk* the sequel but it was like hitting my head against a brick wall, so I started something fresh.

Today is a good day. There's been quite a few bad days recently, including yesterday, which was a *really bad day*, but things are getting better, much better. I feel more with it, although I have a layer of jitters under my skin. A constant wobble, as if at any moment I might crumble spectacularly like a tall building being demolished with explosives.

Baxter snores softly. He's curled on a cushion in front of the radiator by my feet completely unaffected by the drama of the day before. I watch as his belly rises and falls. I took him for a walk this morning at a busy local park. I'm avoiding the forest for a while, and anywhere quiet. The more people around the less chance Tom will try to harm me again.

I've just written four chapters and I'm pleased with my progress. I stretch and my stomach gurgles. It's dinnertime. I look at my phone that's been on silent for hours.

Two WhatsApp messages. My chest lurches as I see the first is from That Wanker, Pat Tanker. I've not heard from him since our disastrous Italian dinner. I haven't messaged or called him and he hasn't contacted me. Both of us satisfied with our solo meeting.

Patrick's message reads:

'It's done.'

I stare at it for a few moments. What on earth is the man going on about? Maybe it's meant for someone else. Odd. I dismiss it and flick to the second message from

Nisha.

'Look at the news and then call me.'

I save my work, click open a browser and navigate to BBC News, shutting down the memory of Omar that flares in my consciousness. I haven't heard from him since he hung up on me after the fake photos row. I scroll, not sure what Nisha means. I'm hoping to see mention of one of my novels or the TV adaptation, or perhaps news about the *Dusk* movie, but then I see it:

ACTOR TOM DARLINGTON FOUND DEAD.
*Shit.*

I don't click on the link, I call Nisha. She answers on the second ring.

"What the hell?" I say.

"I know, darling, rumours say it's suicide. Found by his housekeeper this morning. Looks like a drug overdose, there was a note."

"This is going to drag up all that crap about me, isn't it? Just when things were getting back to normal again."

"I expect so, darling."

I groan.

Nisha continues, "I'll call you if I find out anything more. Stay strong."

We say goodbye and hang up. I ache to call Mum. But I don't want to spoil their holiday. And really, is it that much of a big deal? I should feel relief that he's gone. There's absolutely no way he can pursue me anymore – or try to harm me, if that's even what happened yesterday. There'll be a few months of interest in me again but then it'll fizzle and I'll never have to think about that one-night-stand-gone-wrong ever again.

I head into the kitchen to make dinner, refusing to allow this news to derail me, to keep the explosives detonation button from being pressed. Baxter stirs at the movement and trots after me. I feed him first, before making a huge pile of cheesy pesto pasta and slumping on the sofa to eat it. I bring with me a bottle of red wine, glass and bottle opener. I flick through TV channels hunting out news on Tom's death and thumb through social media and online sites for updates. There's mention of me, of course, as part of his 'troubled past' and old pictures of us resurface, but it's brief.

I guzzle the wine. An aching hollow opens in my head, and I can't tell if I actually feel a bit sad about Tom's suicide – 'poor guy' echoes in the cavity – or if I'm simply drunk. It dawns on me that he tried to run me over in the morning and then went home to kill himself, but I shake off the thought. It's over. Baxter paws at me for his night-time ramble, and farts to let me know he needs to go, but all I can manage is to let him out into the garden.

Three days later the home phone rings and I hear Mum answering it. She shouts up the stairs. "Sally, it's your sister on the phone."

I save my work and head down the stairs. Odd for Mel to call me at this time. It's mid-morning on a Monday. I take the phone off Mum and sit on the bottom stair as she heads back to the lounge. "Hey sis, what's up?"

"You know I'm a proud stay-at-home mum and I watch lots of daytime telly. Well, I think you should watch *My Morning* right now. Their guest on in a few minutes is Tanith Evangeline, you know, that arsehole's girlfriend. I wouldn't normally give a shit or want you to give a shit, but apparently she has some big news to reveal about his death."

"I'll take a look, sis. Thanks."

"I'll give you a call later."

I slot the cordless phone back in its base unit as I head into the lounge. Mum reads on the sofa.

"Mel says we need to watch something."

Mum puts down her book and takes off her reading glasses as I sit next to her, find the remote and turn on the telly, clicking onto *My Morning*.

Tanith sits on the studio sofa, resplendent in black. She dabs at tears with a tissue, careful not to smudge her makeup. Her voice wavers.

"It's such a shock, I still can't believe he's gone," Tanith sobs dramatically, "and in such a horrible way. I wasn't there for him, I should've done more to stop him from doing this…"

The female presenter leans in. "Such a terrible, terrible thing, Tanny. But perhaps now he has found some peace."

"I hope so, Omaya, I really do. We were happy together but there was always a third person, a shadow hanging over us…"

"Turn it off," Mum says urgently and reaches for the remote in my hand. I hold it up and away from her before she can get there. Dread floods my belly. I know what's coming.

"No, Mum. I need to see this!"

Tanith continues, taking deep breaths in between sentences. "He never got over Sally Speck. I was always second to her. His note… he left a note…"

"Go on, his note…" the male presenter encourages.

"He said that he couldn't deal with the rejection any longer, and I'm sure he meant her… her rejection of him. I was never good enough." Tanith flicks her lustrous blond hair over one shoulder and continues to speak through great heaves, "He also wrote 'I'm your biggest fan, now and forever' and I think… I think he meant *her*… He was *her* biggest fan." She sobs and Omaya switches sofas to put her arm around Tanith.

"That's enough," Mum says and switches off the telly.

I slide from the sofa to curl in a ball on the carpet. I just want to make myself very small, to disappear from view.

Mum gently rubs my back. "Oh, love. Even from his grave he haunts you."

# CHAPTER 28

Tanith's little performance sparks a new hunger for me. The next morning, media and photographers show up outside my parents' bungalow baying for blood. Baxter barks himself hoarse at the disturbance. At lunchtime they start calling the landline number and keep at it until Dad unplugs the phone.

By mid-afternoon, the fans arrive and things get ugly. It's not the good-natured crowd that once gathered outside the bungalow. This horde seethes and anger crackles like electricity.

Mum, Dad and I cower in my upstairs attic bedroom, peeking from behind the closed curtains as the locked gates to the driveway rattle and groan with the sheer number of people pushing on them. The high fence is scaled but when the person sees thick bushes on the other side they don't jump over. After that first person comes more. The photographers are hoisted up long enough to snap a few photos. The fans cling on and holler and brandish signs that say: "You killed Tom!" and "It's YOUR fault!".

"Let's hope those gates hold," Dad jokes, but his voice wavers and I can tell he's as terrified as me.

What happens if they break through? It's the question we're all thinking but not saying. Would they smash up our home? And if they managed to break in? What then? Would we get dragged out and beaten?

When a smoking missile is launched over the fence and burns out on the driveway, I call 999 and ask the dispatcher to make PC Cole and PC Hawkins aware. It's an agonising fifteen-minute wait until two police cars arrive and four officers move everyone along. Two come to check on us and Dad opens the gate – which, miraculously, is still holding up and working ok. They take details on the incident, reassure us and then head off.

But, within the hour, the crowd re-forms. They're not so aggressive, but mill about. Every now and then the gate shakes as someone tries it again for luck. The fans sit and hold up the signs. Cars beep them to pass on the road. I call the police again.

Mel shifts into action and employs security guards from a firm run by a relative of one of Steve's rugby mates. Three burly men arrive before the police return and stand by the gates to keep anyone from getting close to the bungalow.

The police arrive for the second time and the crowd disperses pronto; jumping in cars or running to hide. One police officer chats to the security guards, while the other comes to check in on us again before they head off. The security guards stay outside the gates, every now and then heading to the patch of overgrown land opposite to relieve themselves.

Mel calls Dad's mobile to say they'll be staying all night.

"I've managed to get mate's rates," she says. "Steve and I will cover this from our holiday savings. No one will get in."

We creep downstairs and Mum and I pace the kitchen as Dad puts Baxter on his lead and takes him into the garden to do his business. We don't dare let him out off the lead, in case someone grabbed him or something awful happened.

My phone pings with a message from Nisha. It's a YouTube link. I read the message first:

'Look on the bright side, and think of the royalties. They would've had to buy all those books $$$'

I open the video. It shows perhaps fifty of Tom's fans around a bonfire. They're shouting and chanting about how I killed Tom by not loving him. How my rejection broke his heart so he took his own life. The video zooms in and I see they're burning a huge pile of my books with an effigy on top that's made to look like me. They've printed out my official author photo and stuck it to the head of the effigy. When the feet go up in flames they cheer and whoop.

Then the person filming shouts from behind the camera with such vehement passion: "You're dead, Sally Speck! You're dead! You killed our Tom! You don't deserve to live!"

The video ends.

"Are all the doors definitely locked?" I ask, clutching my phone to prevent it falling from my trembling fingers.

"Yes. Your father has checked them several times," Mum replies and indicates my phone. "What was that?"

"A I-hate-Sally-Speck bonfire of my books. With death threats."

"Death threats? Oh my," Mum says with a wobbly voice and comes to give me a hug, which I think she needs more than me. Dad wanders over and hugs the two of us.

"I'm so sorry," I mumble into Mum's shoulder. "This is terrifying."

"It'll be ok," Dad says. His phone pings again and we break away from the embrace.

He reads the message and says, "It's Mel. She says to pack some clothes and Bax's stuff and be ready early tomorrow morning."

"I can't live like this anymore," I say. The first words out my mouth for hours.

We sit, shell-shocked, in the little, musty lounge of a tiny stone cottage, overlooking a picturesque valley in the

Vale of Glamorgan.

"I'm so sorry I put you all through this. I thought his death would save us from this, I thought it would help…"

"Shush, love. We're here for you. We'll always be here for you," Mum soothes. "Graham, put the kettle on, dear."

Dad heads into the kitchen. Mel stands at the doorway to the garden, watching her daughters play with Baxter in the light drizzle. It's an idyllic setting but the adults are all too stressed to appreciate it. I feel like a hunted animal, like my family is my pack, swept up in the bloodlust.

That morning, Mel and Steve organised four blacked out Range Rovers to pick us up, driven by Steve's rugby mates. They enjoyed playing at celebrity bodyguards, were jovial and full of banter, until they saw our faces. The security guards held back the swarm as the gates opened and the cars packed onto our driveway.

We waited for the gates to close again before leaving the bungalow. I got in one, Mel went in another, Mum in the third, and Dad and Baxter in the fourth. We each hunkered down on the back seat and covered our heads with blankets. The cars came out of the gates and the media went crazy, holding up cameras to the windows to try and get a picture, stepping in front of the cars, stepping over one another. From under my blanket I heard the security guards shouting in an attempt to keep order.

As we'd agreed, the Range Rovers all drove off in different directions and the media, on their motorbikes and in their cars, were forced to pick a car to follow. The rugby boys drove in circles around the New Forest until the media eventually got bored, or lost, and dropped away.

We met Steve and the kids at the Chieveley services on the M4. He'd driven up in an unremarkable seven-seater hire car. We switched out of the Range Rovers and all crammed into the hire car and continued on to Wales.

The journey was a blur of Bethany and Ellie chattering, or niggling, or singing, or playing car games and Mel overseeing proceedings. Dad fell asleep in the front passenger seat. Baxter fell asleep in the back. Mum read her book – one of the few lucky people who never get car sick while reading – and I gazed silently out the window.

We arrived at the cottage, piled out, picked rooms, dumped bags and let the kids and dog into the garden. Then we sat, and took deep breaths.

Steve looks up from his phone. "There's been a new development."

"What kind of new development?" Dad's voice comes from the little kitchen.

"The police now reckon it was murder."

"Seriously?" Mel says.

Dad comes in, kettle in hand and stares at Steve.

Steve says, "Wait a sec." He takes a moment to read the website on his phone. He looks up. "Initially they thought he'd taken the pills and booze and then fallen over and bashed his head when he was intoxicated. But there's new evidence, whatever that means, that the head injury came first and the pills and booze came second, forced down his throat after the head injury, when he was unconscious, to make it look like suicide."

"Oh my goodness," Mum utters and touches her fingertips to the centre of her collarbone as if guarding her heart from any more drama.

"Whoa," Mel whispers.

I take in the ashy fireplace, the remains of dead wood, the bronze implements to stoke the fire hanging from a small stand, the basket of fresh wood, the stonework. I don't say anything. Perhaps won't say anything again for another few hours. My words are swimming all over my body, fluid but contained within. I have nothing tangible to say out loud.

Murder.

The sun's out the next morning. Mum, Mel and I are wrapped up and sit around the garden table. I feel cosy, safe, lulled by the sight of endless rolling hills.

The kids and Baxter play in the garden. We're digesting after Mum made a huge fry-up for breakfast. It almost feels like we could be on holiday and not in hiding. Dad and Steve are inside watching the telly and talking about drills. Dad's brought his Screwfix catalogue with him.

Mum reads while I stare into space and Mel supervises the kids. The sound of the telly drifts out. I hear the familiar opening tune for the news bulletin.

"Gosh, it's lunchtime already," Mum says, also hearing the sound.

Mel glances at us. "Steve, turn it up," she yells through the ajar door.

The volume increases just as the announcer introduces the latest on the Tom Darlington story and a police appeal. A male voice speaks: "We are looking for the author Sally Speck in connection with the murder of the actor Tom Darlington. Please make yourself known to the London Metropolitan Police."

"Fuck," Mel says.

"Ummm, Mummy, you swore!" Bethany says.

"Go to your room, now. Both of you," Mel shouts. "And take your wellies off first."

"But I didn't do anything…"

"Now!"

Bethany stares at her mother, alarmed by her venom, and then at her grandmother. Mum smiles and signals gently to the door. Bethany trundles inside and pulls Ellie with her. They kick off their wellies as instructed and head to their bedroom. We follow them in to the little lounge. Mel first, me in the middle and Mum bringing up the rear.

"What do they want with you, love?" Mum says.

"This is ridiculous! You had nothing to do with his murder." Dad slaps his catalogue on the rickety coffee table.

I stare blankly at the TV. The news has moved on. Steve mutes it.

"This poor family has been dragged through the mud

already, and Sally has been stalked, harassed and hounded and now this? The police after her? What the hell?" Mel shouts.

Steve stands and brings his phone to me. "I've got the number here."

"What number?" Mel demands.

"For the Met Police."

"She's not calling them!"

"Chill out, Melissa, would you! It's the police. Sally has to speak to them."

Mel looks as if she's about to throttle her husband, but I nod and take Steve's phone.

# CHAPTER 29

Early the following day, Dad drives me in the seven-seater into London and to the police station. He sits in a waiting area with a reassuring look on his face as I'm ushered through to a small interrogation room.

I sit on one side of the empty table and look around the bare, grey, windowless room. I take deep breaths to calm myself. My heart is racing and my entire body trembles. I'm not guilty, I remind myself, so why am I so worried?

Two plain-clothed detectives come in and take the seats opposite. One places a file on the table in front of her. I tuck my hands between my thighs to hide the shakes and force myself to look at them, to make eye contact. I'm not guilty, I have nothing to hide.

"I'm Detective Chief Inspector Alice Adisa," says the detective on the left and shows me her ID. She has a kind face, but hard brown eyes that feel as if they're boring a hole right through me. "And this is my colleague Detective Constable Dominika Pooley."

DC Pooley shows me her ID. Her thin blond hair is scraped into a low ponytail in exactly the same way as in the photo on her ID card.

"We need to ask you a few questions," DCI Adisa says after they put their ID cards away. "But first, let me remind you that you're not in any trouble at all. You're not in custody and you're free to leave at any time."

I nod.

Pooley pulls out a notepad and pen and silently takes notes.

"Thank you for contacting us, Sally," Adisa continues, flipping open her own notebook and jotting words as she speaks. "We are following up all possible avenues in relation to Tom Darlington's suspicious death."

"I understand," I say.

"We've been in touch with Hampshire Constabulary and a PC Dawn Cole who has briefed us on your contact with the police with regards to Mr Darlington."

"Ok," I say because I'm not sure what else I'm meant to reply.

"Where were you last Thursday night?"

"Um… er…" I rack my brains.

The detectives exchange a brief glance.

"Oh wait, that was a few days before my niece's birthday on the Sunday… I was at home, in South Hampshire."

"Yes, we have the address. Were you with anyone? I understand you live with your parents."

"Um, yes I do. They would've been there… No, wait, they were away in Southend when Tom died."

"I see. So you were alone? No one else was with you?"

"No… I was alone. Well, if you don't count the dog." I attempt a little laugh, but the detectives remain straight-faced.

"Did you speak to your parents or anyone else that night, did you send any messages or use your phone?"

"Err, no, I don't think so… I can look at my mobile and check?"

Adisa doesn't reply, so I take my phone out of my handbag and place it on the table. I fumble through apps, looking at my texts, WhatsApp messages, phone records. The detectives watch me intensely and my skin crawls. On first glance I can't see any activity on that Thursday night. "I don't think I used my phone that evening… I'd need to have a longer look…"

"Sure. So, what were you doing that evening?"

"I think I had a few glasses of wine and a long bath, but I can't really be sure. I don't always remember things… you can speak to my doctor…"

Adisa shifts in her seat, unimpressed. She gestures to Pooley, who opens the file and pulls out what looks like a photo and hands it to Adisa. Adisa glances at it briefly and then slides it across the table so I can see it.

"Is this a photo of you, Sally?" Adisa asks.

"Yes, it's my profile pic on my private Facebook, it's really old now. I still have an account but haven't used it in a long time."

Adisa taps the photo. "And this pink scarf you're wearing… it's quite distinctive isn't it. Do you still have it?"

"Oh yes! One of my favourites, I got it in Peru when I went travelling after uni. Oh, wait, no I don't have it anymore…"

"You *don't* have the scarf anymore?"

"No. I take the dog for walks in the forest, the New Forest, near where we live and a while ago I, er, fell."

"Can you elaborate?"

"Yes, I tripped on this stupid branch that Baxter had dropped on the path and straight onto a pile of logs. I sliced my hand pretty bad… it was bleeding loads and I, er, wrapped it in my scarf."

"Do you often trip and hurt yourself when you go out walking?"

"Well, no, it was just me being clumsy. I was probably looking at my phone or something…"

"I see. Did you mention this fall to anyone?"

"Er, no, I don't think so. It was pretty embarrassing to be honest. I think it was when my parents were away, or maybe a bit before. Dog walks tend to blur into one to be honest."

"What happened to the scarf, Sally?"

"The scarf was torn pretty bad on the logs, and as it was so old, full of holes and wearing thin, that when I got back to my car I binned it."

"*Binned* it?"

"Yes. My cut had stopped bleeding by that point, so I chucked it away."

"You didn't think to bring it home and wash it?"

"Well, to be honest, it's alpaca wool. It has to be hand-washed, and as I say, it was so old and tatty that I decided not to bother... Why?"

"Which bin did you place the scarf in?"

"Oh, I really don't remember... it was at some car park in the forest."

"Which car park, Sally?"

"Why does this matter?"

"Which car park?" she insists.

"I honestly don't know, I go on lots of walks, I drive about, see a car park I fancy, and stop."

"Can I see your cut?"

I show the detectives the palm of my hand. Pooley spends a long time looking at the angry scratch that stretches from just under my thumb to the opposite side of my wrist. I absent-mindedly picked at it in the car on the way here and fresh scabs have formed.

Heat flushes my cheeks and I roll up the sleeves of my jumper and push my hair out of my face.

"How did you get that?" Adisa says pointing at the massive bruise on my elbow.

My body is still dotted with bruises from the fall in that ditch. Do I tell them that I was the victim of an attempted hit and run? On the day that Tom died? And that I think it was Tom? They'll think I'm crazy.

"I'm not sure how I got it," I lie. "I bruise easily." Which is the truth.

Adisa writes something on her notepad and underlines it, then asks, "Did you have access to a car on that Thursday night?"

"Yes, my Dad's old Peugeot."

"Can you give us the number plate please."

"I've got no idea. I don't remember things like that. My Dad will know it. He's out in the waiting area."

"How long does it take to drive from your house to London?"

"Not a clue. We always get the train up from Brockenhurst. That takes about an hour and a half if you get the fast train, over two hours on the stopping service."

"And how would you get from your house to the train station?"

"Why are you asking me that?"

"Please answer the question, Sally," Adisa's tone is firm.

"Either get a lift or use the local taxi firm, there's only one that covers the area."

Adisa looks at Pooley. Something unspoken passes between them. Pooley nods. They both stand.

"Are you staying in London overnight?" Pooley speaks for the first time. She has a slight accent.

"Yes, we've got a hotel."

"I'll need the details."

"Dad'll have them. I've got no idea, my sister booked it."

Pooley raises an eyebrow at me. I can't determine what it means.

# CHAPTER 30

The next day, I sit in the small restaurant at the hotel, waiting for Dad to come down from his room. I heaped my plate high at the breakfast buffet and am tucking into my second croissant when something blocks the light.

I look up expecting to see Dad but its Detective Chief Inspector Alice Adisa and Detective Constable Dominika Pooley. And behind them a group of police officers, some in uniform and some in plain clothes and yellow police vests. I force down the pastry in my mouth.

DCI Adisa clears her throat. "Sally Speck, I'm arresting you on suspicion of the murder of Tom Darlington." And she proceeds to read me my rights.

"What?" I blurt as DC Pooley moves closer.

In her accented voice, Pooley says, "What I need is for you to come with us now."

"Come with you where?" I stutter, I can't compute what's happening. I'm getting arrested? Everyone in the restaurant stares at us, at me. The reception staff come in to watch and the two nearby servers are frozen to the spot.

"You are being taken into custody, Sally. We're going back to the police station." Pooley helps me to my feet. "We're going to need to put these on." She brandishes a pair of handcuffs. Stunned, I hold out my wrists.

"Can I get my mobile phone from my room? Or my handbag? Or a coat even?" I manage as the cold steel clasps around my wrists in front of me.

"We'll get those for you. Your mobile phone will be seized as part of the investigation," Pooley says.

"My Dad… I need to tell my Dad…"

"We'll take care of that for you," Pooley replies as she marches me out of the restaurant, the entourage following, bar one who peels off to talk to the receptionist about getting into my room.

"What on earth is happening?" Dad bellows as he comes out of the lift.

Adisa walks across the reception area towards him, holding up both hands as Pooley opens the door for me and ushers me through it to the unmarked car that's parked right outside, flanked by two police cars with blue lights flashing.

"She didn't do it," Dad blusters as he trails behind me. "It wasn't her!"

"Mr Speck, Sally is cooperating, don't make this any harder than it has to be," Adisa says.

Dad shoves past Adisa and pushes Pooley out the way as I sit on the back seat of the car. "Get out the car, Sally!" He makes a grab at me.

Pooley grabs Dad's arm, but he tries to shake free and, in one decisive manoeuvre, she bends it behind his back.

Dad yelps and then shouts, "She didn't do it!"

Adisa pulls out her handcuffs. "Does that imply you know who did, Mr Speck? We are well aware of your background."

There's a scuffle. Pooley manages to shut the car door and I try to open it but it won't budge. I thump the window of the car as Adisa wrestles with Dad and cautions him for obstructing a police officer.

My heart rate quickens and my breath catches in my chest. "Panic attack," I mutter as a police officer sits next to me on the back seat and tells me to breathe.

Adisa gets in the passenger side and Pooley puts the car in gear. As she turns the car out of the hotel's car park I see Dad being bundled into a police van, his wrists in cuffs.

He catches my eye and he looks twenty years older, his cheeks sallow and the skin of his neck drooping. He shouts, "It'll be ok, Sally, you didn't do it. It'll be ok!"

Pooley zips along as the siren blares. Adisa looks at her phone.

The police officer on the back seat has given me a brown bag and I feel my imminent panic attack easing, although it loiters on the periphery.

We weave through London and pull into the Belgravia Police Station, straight into a crowd of media. Pooley beeps the horn, but, like a frenzied mob of hungry zombies, they are on us.

I shrink back as photographers shove their cameras at the windows. Slapping, smacking, banging the car. I try to cover my face with my arms and bend down out of the way, but my seatbelt jolts and I hang there, my head wrapped in my handcuffed arms.

"What's with all this media? How did they know to be here?" Adisa says.

"Someone's tipped them off. Hotel staff?" Pooley replies.

"Or a guest," Adisa says.

I struggle to breathe and pant like Baxter when he's thirsty. I do the breathing exercises my doctor showed me to try and stave off another panic attack.

Pooley says, "We're through it."

She parks and I'm led into the building, up some stairs, into a lift and then to a waiting area. I'm directed to a small booth in front of the custody sergeant, whose job it is to check me in. He asks if I have any mental health issues, if I've had any alcohol recently, if I understand what I've been arrested for. I answer his questions with mumbles and then sign a form. He explains that I'll be kept for twenty-four hours in custody at which time they'll either charge me, release me with or without conditions or apply for an additional twelve hours to hold me if necessary for the investigation.

"Do you want legal advice?" he asks.

"Yes."

"Do you have a particular solicitor?"

"No."

"Do you want a duty solicitor in the meantime? You will be able to instruct your own solicitor at a later date."

"Ok."

A female police officer comes over and pats me down. I have nothing on me, all of it having been left in the hotel room. But my glasses, watch, shoelaces and belt are taken away. The police officer steers me towards an inner door.

I walk down a corridor with the female police officer and am put in a cell. The clank of the door makes me jump and I sit on the edge of the bed and stare at the silver toilet in the corner.

Almost immediately, I'm taken for a medical examination, where a lot of attention is paid to the cut on my hand and the various bruises on my body. Then to have photographs. A lot are snapped of my injuries. Then I'm taken for fingerprinting and to have samples taken of my DNA.

I'm put back in my cell, given a cup of sweet tea, and I sit on the bed. I shiver and clasp the cup.

What feels like a long time later but could be minutes – I have no way of knowing – I'm shown into a similar grey, stark room with a table and four chairs. It's not the same one as yesterday. This one has a small window.

I sit. A uniformed police officer brings in a plastic cup of disgusting smelling coffee and places it in front of me. He's trailed by a small, twitchy man who turns out to be my legal aid. He introduces himself as Doug Davis and we have a few moments alone to talk through what's happened before Pooley comes in and takes a seat opposite me. A few moments later Adisa comes in with four bottles of water. She puts one in front of all of us. Adisa switches on the audio recorder and cuts right to the chase.

"Are you responsible for the murder of Tom Darlington?"

"No," I shoot back, alarmed but adamant.

"Are you in any way responsible for his death?"

"No."

"Do you know who is responsible for the murder of Tom Darlington?"

"No."

"Do you know how he died?"

"Only what I've read in the news. That at first it was suicide and then murder. That they thought he'd taken an overdose and then bashed his head and then it was the other way around, that the head bash came first."

She nods, giving nothing away, and launches into the same questions as the day before about my whereabouts, my scarf, the scratch on my hand. I give all the same answers. But Adisa keeps coming back to the scarf. She's fixated.

"When was the last time you saw the scarf?" Adisa asks.

I feel the heat rising up my neck and my earlobes prickle. "I've told you! In the bin, in a car park in the New Forest. Stop asking me the same question!"

Davis leans into me and says, "You can answer no comment." His breath stinks of stale coffee.

Adisa changes tact. "The scarf was found at the murder scene, that is why it is so significant. It was covered in blood. We're just waiting to confirm whether that is *your* blood, Sally."

"Found? In London? But that makes no sense," I reply, baffled.

Davis nudges me and shakes his head. "Don't say any more than you need to," he'd told me earlier.

Adisa slaps the table and I flinch. My attention jumps back to her. "Did you kill Tom Darlington, your stalker, the man who ruined your wedding, and cut yourself in the process, mopping up your blood with the scarf?"

"Of course not! No!"

"Where's the weapon, Sally? That you used to smash Tom's skull."

"How would I know? I've got no idea! This is absolutely ridiculous."

Davis nudges me again, and I remain silent for the rest of the interview, refusing to answer questions that imply I murdered Tom. Is it the best course of action? I don't know, but words are swimming again, stuck behind my teeth, and nothing solid, nothing tangible forms. I decide it's best to stay silent.

Adisa shouts at me, is kind to me, shouts at me some more, while Pooley remains frighteningly impassive, watching me like a hawk. I retreat inwards and marvel at my quivering hands.

Eventually, Adisa gives up and I'm taken back to the cell. I remain there for the rest of the day. They bring me food and water and confirm that my items at the hotel have been seized for the investigation. They refuse to answer my questions about Dad. When the lights go off, I realise I've been here for more than twelve hours.

I lie on the hard bed in the darkness.

Did I do it? Could I have done it?

That morning I'd nearly been run over in the forest. I rack my brains for any memory of that Thursday night, but there's nothing. A blank. I fill it with terrible daydreams of me killing Tom, of what will happen to me next. I love my vivid imagination when I create fiction, but now I hate it. I can't stop running through Tom's death, like a movie on repeat, how it might have played out, how my scarf had come to be at his home.

I drink-drive up to London in my Dad's car, somehow avoiding crashing or getting stopped by the police. I'm ridiculously drunk, it's one of those occasions where I won't remember anything the next day. I go to his apartment (how do I know the address?). He lets me in.

Maybe he's expecting me, which is why he's not out.

We have a row (about what?), I smash him on the back of the head with a.. vase? … cricket bat? … paperweight? and he passes out. I pull my pink Peruvian scarf off my neck (because I didn't actually throw it in a car park bin) to use it to stem the flow but can't stop the bleeding and I know he'll die.

So I shove a load of pills down his throat and wash them down with whiskey… or white wine… or vodka… (who knows? And can someone who's unconscious swallow?) and then write out a suicide note by copying his handwriting somehow.

Then I get back in my car and head home, for some reason forgetting to take the bloody scarf but taking the murder weapon. I stop somewhere and chuck the… vase? (or whatever) into a river.

I slap my forehead. "Stop," I groan out loud in my bleak cell. "Stop, stop, stop."

But my mind plays out his death on a loop over and over, refining the details until it's perfectly plausible, and until I convince myself that it's somehow the truth.

I killed Tom Darlington. I did it.

# CHAPTER 31

A female police officer sticks her head in my cell and tells me to get up. I'm still in the clothes I wore yesterday and haven't slept all night, so I stand immediately. She takes me to the interrogation room with the small window.

The two detectives are already there, as is my legal aid. As I pull back my chair, I brace myself. This is it; I'm going to confess.

"We are releasing you without charge," DCI Adisa says before my bum even settles on the seat. "And there'll be no further actions against the allegations made."

DC Pooley sneers and Doug Davis smiles.

My brows crease. "Huh?" I'm so groggy that I don't think I heard correctly.

Adisa continues, "An independent witness has come forward who can vouch for your whereabouts on the night in question."

I look at her, too stupefied to say anything. Who could that be? Who was I with? Is someone lying to say they were with me?

Adisa continues, "We had a call last night from a Mrs Gladys Redmond. She works in the call centre of Vodafone—"

"What is the relevance to Sally's case?" Davis says.

"It *appears* Sally had a conversation with Mrs Redmond on the night that Mr Darlington died." Adisa's tone screams irritation and I can't tell if it's at Davis for pointlessly interrupting her flow or at the fact that it means she had the wrong person in custody.

"Huh?" I say again.

"Mrs Redmond saw the news announcement last night that we had someone in custody for Darlington's murder and – although we didn't officially announce it was you – the media printed photos of you in handcuffs in the back of the car and put two and two together. She remembered that she had spoken to you about downgrading your mobile phone contract on the night Mr Darlington died.

"You called on your house landline and spoke to her for thirteen minutes, twenty-eight seconds. She remembers because she is such a big fan of your novels and you had a conversation about her favourite novel, *Dusk*. She also says you were her last call of the evening before she clocked off at 9pm. She said you were pleasant on the phone and slurred your words slightly, as if tipsy.

"Before she left the office, she messaged her husband to let him know she was on her way home and to tell him about the conversation. Do you recall the conversation, Sally?"

"I, er… vaguely, I guess." In a bid to save money I decided to change my phone contract. I knew I'd done it when a letter arrived with my new contract information, but I can't recall any specifics.

"Well, we asked Mrs Redmond how she was so sure you had called on that specific night and she produced the text message to her husband. She also said there was a recording of the conversation and she made a note on your file. Every call they receive is recorded and date and time stamped, you see. So, we seized the files and the audio from Vodafone. And they check out."

"So, I'm not under arrest anymore?"

"No, Sally. This call places you at home in Hampshire on the night of the murder in London at around the time of death. It supports your account of the night."

"How did my scarf get there?"

Adisa ignores the question and glances at Pooley. The blond-haired detective is still sneering. They still think I did it.

I sit back, my body sinks deep into the plastic chair. "What about Dad?"

"Mr Speck has been released with no further action. He's waiting for you downstairs."

I shake Davis' hand as the same police officer who woke me up collects me from the interrogation room, takes me to get checked out – where I'm handed back my phone and handbag – and then deposits me in the waiting area. Dad stands when he sees me. I run to him and we hug tightly.

"They allowed me to collect the car from the hotel and park it in the station," Dad says as he grasps my hand, "but I've got to warn you, it's not pretty once we get outside."

I squeeze his hand and an officer leads us back to the internal car park. We get in the seven-seater and wait to exit through a back gate as four police officers walk out in front to hold back the crowd. But the media swarms us as soon as we're in the open.

They scuffle to take photos, thumping and scratching the car. A few eggs are thrown. Neither of us flinch. Dad concentrates on navigating through the crowd, following one PC's directions, as I face forward, keeping my eyes on a spot of bird crap on the windscreen. I'm innocent. Screw you all.

"Goodness knows how we'll explain any bumps or scratches to the car hire place," Dad grumbles as he breaks free. "It'll cost us a bloody fortune, no doubt. I don't expect the insurance will cover 'attacked by a crazed mob'. Those car hire people are all thieving bastards."

He speeds up to take the corner at the end of the road in front of a van. The van honks, and Dad takes another corner on a just-turned-red light. But we know there's no chance the swarm can run and catch us up now.

"You all right, lovey?" Dad asks. "I know how scary it

is in the cells."

"Yes. I'm ok." And it's the truth. I didn't kill Tom Darlington, the police say so. "Are you ok?"

"Fine."

We stop at a red traffic light. "All your stuff from the hotel is in the boot."

"Thanks, Dad."

"Can you do me a favour and text your mother to say we're on our way back. Traffic's a nightmare so might take a while."

"Sure."

I switch my phone on and tap out a message to Mum. I ignore my notifications and instead scroll through news from the past few days. Photos of me and Dad in the back of the police car are splashed everywhere. I read one article:

> Author Sally Speck arrested on suspicion of the murder of Tom Darlington. Her stepfather, Graham Speck, the man known for viciously punching Darlington at the now infamous 'wedding invasion', accompanied her. It's not clear if he was being questioned about the murder alongside his step-daughter.

"The media will never forget this, I'll always be the one who murdered Tom even though I'm innocent," I say.

"'Fraid so," Dad replies.

Dad's lips purse and a vein throbs on his lumpy, bald head. He stares glumly ahead at the rear end of a red bus.

After we edge forward a metre and come to a stop again, he grunts. "Tanith Evangeline is quoted everywhere. She seems to have become the world's authority on you and Tom. She claims Tom was scared of you, and had received threats from me to 'stay away from his daughter'. What a bunch of lies."

"What bullshit! She's lining her pocket telling fibs."

"It's a disgrace," Dad grumbles. "While I was waiting for you, I spoke to my cousin Bobby in Southend, he's still in the force, you know, pretty high up now, and he called a few people. And the only thing they had on you was that scarf. No other forensics evidence. No fingerprints, not even Tom's, nothing. The entire flat had been scrubbed clean. There are traces of disinfectant everywhere. That scarf was obviously planted. But do they look into that? No, they're too busy barking up the wrong tree. Bloody pillocks."

Dad swears at a cyclist who cuts in front of him and I look back at my phone. I click on an article that includes a short video of a statement from Angus, Tom's brother, at Tom's lavish funeral that took place yesterday while I languished in a police cell. I press play on the video and listen to Angus' grief-stricken voice:

'We are beyond devastated by the tragic passing of our beloved Tom. He shone bright and had a beautiful, creative and joyful soul. He loved life, loved to perform, and loved to meet his fans. We will forever hold him in our hearts and be blessed that he was in our lives. We ask for privacy at this time to mourn and grieve his loss. We request that anyone with any information relating to his death contact the police. Thank you.'

The video shows clips of the funeral procession, celebrities pouring into the church, and all the flowers outside Tom's apartment building, with a running commentary from a voiceover. I press stop.

"Poor chap," Dad says, referring to Angus. "I know that actor put you through a lot of fuss and bother, but he was *murdered*. It's terrible, really."

"It is. It's shocking."

"I hope they buck up their ideas and find his killer soon."

"Me too." For justice, of course, but really to deflect the blame off me. I don't mention that out loud, though, it sounds too selfish even in my mind. But it's true. I'll be considered the murderer until the actual murderer is found. As we leave the stop-start of the city and hit open road, I rest my head against the window and close my eyes.

If I didn't kill Tom Darlington, then who did?

# CHAPTER 32

"I'm taking Baxter for a walk," I say. "Anyone want to come?"

Mum stands abruptly and heads to the bathroom. I know she's gone to cry. All she seems to be able to manage since we returned to the cottage from London last night is cry. Mel, Steve and the kids had already returned to Hampshire by the time we got back, Steve back to work today and the kids to school. And that brief time alone has tipped Mum over the edge.

Dad goes after her.

I find the dog's lead, clip it on and we leave the cottage. It's drizzling, and I pull the hood up of my coat. The damp air in the valley soothes me, the chill makes me feel alive. We walk slowly, Baxter sniffing and weeing every few steps.

My life has turned to shit and it can all be traced back to that awards ceremony. One bad decision has ruined everything. Why did I let myself be seduced by Tom Darlington? It was an ego boost; I knew he was using me. But then why did he think we were in love? It still makes no sense. I amble down a lane between two fields, jumping over mud while Baxter happily splashes straight through it.

I need to know who killed him. Everyone still thinks I did it. Although dropped as prime suspect, the public consensus hasn't wavered: *Sally Speck did it*. I have to clear my name, to wrench free of Tom's grip once and for all.

Even in death he haunts me. He's a writhing cloud of relentless mosquitoes that cluster around my head, that I can't seem to swat away.

I perch on a wet fallen branch in a wooded area, trying not to dampen the seat of my jeans. I let Baxter off the lead and throw a ball for him. He sprints after it, snatches it up and saunters back to me. He gets distracted by a scent, drops the ball a little way off and keeps his nose to the ground.

I pull out my phone, see there's no reception, and put it back in my pocket. I follow Baxter's movements, then whistle for him when he gets a little too far away. He looks up, spots me and continues on his way, determined to reach the end of the scent trail.

An idea pops into my mind and suddenly I have clarity. I need to speak to the world's authority on Tom. I need to speak to Tanith. The thought consumes me.

How can I get in touch with her?

Nisha will know. It's her job to know people who know people. I whistle again for Baxter as I stand and hurry back towards the cottage where there's reception and Wi-Fi.

"Bax," I shout. "This way."

I hear his collar jingling behind me and then he bounds past, ball in mouth.

"Dad, I need to get in the attic," I say as we arrive home.

The circus outside our gates from almost a week ago has retreated back whence it came. I imagine they got bored of waiting for us to come home and realised the story was in London when I was at the police station. The bungalow is still standing, unmolested.

"We've just got in," Mum replies, "can it wait until tomorrow?"

"No," I say.

"What's in the attic that's so important that your father can't even have a cup of tea?"

I don't reply to her. "Dad!" I shout. We're in the hallway. Dad entered first. I suspect he's gone to the loo. I bang on the bathroom door.

"What?" comes the reply. "Can't a man have a tinkle in peace?"

"I need to get something out of the attic. Can you help me open it? Or just show me how it works?"

The toilet flushes and a moment later Dad comes out. "Right this minute?"

"Yes."

"Oh, Sal, just let the poor man have a sit down first," Mum says from behind me.

Dad looks at my face, sees obstinate determination there. "Come on then."

Mum tuts and heads into the kitchen.

We head upstairs and Dad undoes all the screws on the panel to the attic space behind my sister's old bedroom. He pulls it off and switches on a light. He hunches and tentatively steps on the floorboard and tests it to make sure it's firm.

"I can go in," I say.

"What do you want?" Dad replies already halfway through the opening. The attic is his domain. Mum and I have never been in there.

"It's a blue sports bag labelled 'old clothes'."

"Right you are." He disappears into the attic. He rustles around then holds a bag up to the opening. "This it?"

"Yes, that's the one."

He passes it through the hole and I grab it. "Thanks, Dad." I rush to my room, without even waiting for him to exit, and zip open the bag.

I rummage around for a while, through clothes that I used to wear in London when I was a few sizes smaller and couldn't bring myself to bin, but don't allow myself to get distracted.

"Yes," I say as I extract an old black going-out handbag. I kneel and open the bag, my fingers going straight for the inside pocket. Jackpot.

I slide out a business card. It says 'Ashraf Khan, Chauffeur' and then a mobile number. He gave it to me before I went into that vile nightclub. I haven't used this bag since. Or gone to a nightclub, but that's by the by. I admonish myself for getting distracted from my mission. I tap the number into my phone and dial it. It rings. And rings and then I get the flat tone. I'll try again later.

I power on my laptop. I find a new notebook and scrawl 'Killer: Tanith?' on the first page. I'm not sure why, I just have the urge to write notes, so I go with it. It's like the buzz I get when I research and plan a new novel. I google 'Tanith Evangeline'.

I scour through pages of hits about Tom Darlington until I decide to narrow the search to the few years before she met him. I scan through search results until I hit upon something juicy.

The headline link reads: PROMISING PRESENTER CONVICTED OF ABH AFTER TOILET ATTENDANT FIGHT. I click on it immediately and devour the article.

> YouTube star turned children's TV presenter, Tanith Evangeline (19), has been convicted of actual bodily harm after punching a toilet attendant in the face at a trendy London bar.
>
> The new host of children's TV show *BumbleBeeeez* has been fired by Channel 5 due to the incident, after just six weeks on the job. The victim, Ms. Carla Porter (28) suffered severe bruising and a cut to her cheek in the attack. Tanith will have to complete 150 hours of unpaid community service, pay the victim compensation and pick up the tab for the prosecution costs.
>
> Ms. Porter commented: "She just went mental. One minute she's in the queue for the toilet, laughing with her friend, the next she's totally flipped out, screaming and trying to rip the towel dispenser off the wall. I try to stop her and she turns

on me. I feared for my life. It was such a shock. My daughter used to love her YouTube channel, and she seems so sweet-natured. But it's all a front. She's got a real violent streak, that's for sure."

I scan the article and see pictures of the victim's injuries (pretty nasty!), Tanith arriving at court, Tanith leaving court. And read a comment from her manager.

"Tanith is deeply sorry for the hurt she has caused Ms. Porter and has already sought out anger management counselling."

Anger management counselling? Wow. I write copious notes and allow myself to fall deeper into the rabbit hole by following various links to other related articles about Tanith.

There are a few exclusive stories from 'sources' that claim Tanith is a wild child, and has 'two faces'. But one story draws my attention. A previous boyfriend claims she used to beat him and mentally abuse him when they were together. When he was twenty and she was seventeen, at the height of her YouTube fame. He says, "I'm pleased she's finally getting the help she needs."

So, Tanith has violent tendencies. The police must've checked her out. She'd be suspect number one. I know from watching police shows that murders are usually committed by someone who the victim knows. But Tanith's still free. Perhaps she has a solid alibi. Or perhaps the police have missed something critical. As Dad said, they've been too busy barking up the wrong tree – *my* tree. They must've missed something. I'm determined to find out.

I look back at articles of when she and Tom first got together. A few days after that, it's announced that she's been given a presenting job on a Channel 4 children's show after a three-year hiatus following her conviction. I jot: 'TD relshp excellent timing for publicity' and underline it twice.

I jump as my phone rings. It's an unknown number. Usually I ignore those, they're generally bad news, but I'm distracted by Tanith's less-than-rosy past and answer it.

"Hello?"

"Hello," a male voice replies. "I just had a missed call from this number."

It takes a second to click. "Is this Ashraf? Ashraf Khan?"

"Who wants to know?"

"My name is Sally Speck. You drove me a few times when I, er, when I was friends with Tom Darlington."

Silence.

"You drove Tom to my parents' bungalow in Hampshire and I, um, threw a jewellery box in his face."

"Yeah, I remember."

"Ha, yes, that's probably hard to forget." I give a timid laugh.

"I don't drive for the Darlingtons anymore."

"No?"

"No. I drive a mini cab for my cousin."

"Oh, right."

"What do you want, Sally?" Ashraf speaks rapidly, as if he's in a massive rush. It unnerves me.

"I, um, I'd like to ask you a couple of questions. About Tom."

He sighs.

"And, well, about Tanith too."

Silence.

I plough on regardless, attempting to meet his pace, "I'm coming up to London in two days' time, on Thursday. Maybe we could meet, my train comes into Waterloo and I could get a tube to wherever, and buy you a coffee… or whatever, if you don't want to talk on the phone?"

Silence. I wonder if he's still on the line. I can hear laughter and people's voices in the background.

"Please, Ashraf," I plead. "I want to find out what happened to Tom."

"You staying at a hotel Thursday night?"

"Yes."

"You need a taxi from Waterloo?"

"I guess so."

"Text me the time your train arrives." He hangs up.

"Where to?" Ashraf asks as I get into the back seat after he's helped me put my small suitcase in the boot. I asked if I should sit in the front and he said no.

I hand him my phone with the cheap hotel's address. He looks at it, mumbles, "Bit of a dump," then taps the postcode into Google Maps on his phone. I know it's a rough place, but it's all I could afford. I sold some expensive gold jewellery – a treat to myself years ago when I got my first advance – to pay for the train fare and hotel room.

He leans around to me in the back seat. "We'll be taking the scenic route. Ok?"

"Yes," I say.

"And I'll need to take the fare at the end cos this is metered."

"That's fine. I've got some cash."

Ashraf turns back to the steering wheel and starts the engine. I have a million questions but bite my tongue. I don't know where to start so as not to scare him. He drives out of the station, confidently and smoothly taking turn after turn.

As I deliberate my first question, he says, "Terrible business, y'know. Tom's murder and all that."

"Yes, awful. A tragedy."

"Coppers still think it's you."

"Really?"

"Yeah, I got interviewed. They asked lots of questions about you. Tom's old assistant, Bev, went in after me and we saw each other. So, I waited for her and gave her a lift home. They asked her a lot of questions about you too. Seem the police are determined to prove somehow that you did it."

"I didn't do it. I swear to you, I didn't. That's why I'm here. To find out who did."

He eyes me over his shoulder before turning back to the road. "So, what do you want to know?"

I say the first thing that pops into my mind. "When did you stop driving for Tom Darlington?"

"Day after that fella beat him up."

"Omar?" I still can't imagine sweet-natured Omar hitting anyone, but it happened and Mum went to see Tom. Behind my back. I fling that thought away. Forget it, let it go. Focus on the task at hand.

Ashraf leans his head forward to see if any cars are coming and then deftly nips out onto a busy road.

"That's the one," he says as we sit in traffic on Waterloo Bridge. "Angus was pissed. Tom managed to give us all the slip. Me, his bodyguards, Bev. Bev and the bodyguards were even *in* his apartment. And I was waiting outside. But when it was time to leave, for this family dinner thing, he wasn't anywhere to be found.

"While we were chasing our tails looking for him around his apartment, he went straight to his favourite club anyway. And that's where Omar must've found him. It was a few streets away that Omar attacked him. Tom probably decided to walk home. The stupid sod was always wanting to walk places, like an unknown. But he was too famous for that."

Ashraf quietens as he focuses on turning across traffic.

"Never learnt how Tom got away from us until I saw Bev at the police station," he continues. "She reckons that Tom had come across a secret back entrance in and out of his building, one that Angus didn't know about, and had snuck out that way.

"Angus sacked the lot of us. Fair enough, I guess. He hired us to take care of Tom and we'd failed. Tom went and got himself beat up. I got a big pay out, of course. To keep my mouth shut. I'd been driving for the Darlingtons for five-odd years. The others did too. I don't need this job, but helping my cousin out y'know."

Ashraf stops talking, winds down his window, hawks up phlegm and spits it in the road. A nearby pedestrian looks revolted as it lands at his feet. I look away, not wanting to catch his eye. Ashraf is oblivious. He winds the window back up and the roar of London is muted once again as we continue in the moving bubble that is his car.

"Did Tom not want to go to this family dinner thing then? Did he not get on with his family?" I ask. This is off-script. But I'm curious.

Ashraf shifts in his seat, glances at me in his rear-view mirror, then looks back to the road. "Don't repeat any of this."

"I won't."

He flicks his eyes at me again in the mirror. I eagerly lean forward in my seat, rapt, and he smiles. Perhaps he likes an audience, likes to talk. I give him my undivided attention. I'm all ears.

"Used to drive Tom to his father's mansion every now and then," Ashraf says. "Never met the man. Wealthy family, y'know. Tom never wanted to go. On the journey there he would always go on about his unhappy childhood. Abused by the older boys at a private school, brought up by a conveyor belt of nannies, sky-high school expectations, beatings if he ever sung or showed any signs of being 'flamboyant' as his father called it. That sort of thing.

"Father's a recluse now. Tom said he hasn't left that mansion since Tom's mother died of a heart attack just after Tom got famous. Tom was blamed for her death. It was the shock and embarrassment of seeing him on that TV talent show. He went on that show without their consent. They were embarrassed that he became a singer in a boyband.

"So, yeah, Tom had a strict upbringing. And after the mother died and the father went a bit nuts, Angus kept the family together. A lot of pressure. He went into banking like the father, like Tom was expected to do. Angus did everything for his little bro. Was like Angus had two full-time jobs – one at the bank and one babysitting Tom."

"Huge weight on Angus' shoulders."

"For sure."

When Ashraf doesn't say anything else, I take the hint that the subject of Tom's family is now closed.

"So, what about Tanith? Were they happy?"

Ashraf whistles. "Right piece of work that one."

"In what way?"

"She was pleasant enough, I guess, never really spoke to me. Frosty. Don't think she loved him all that much. They were always arguing and niggling at each other in the car. About stupid little things."

"Like what?"

Ashraf chews the side of his mouth, thinking. "Like the time when Tanith was pissed that Tom had decided to wear a green T-shirt that clashed with her red nail polish. I mean, c'mon. She expected him to match her fingernails!"

"Seriously?"

Ashraf chuckles. "But they stayed together so guess there were happy times I didn't see outside the car. She's a looker, that's for sure." His tone turns serious. "And there was one time where she slapped him. Just the once though."

"Oh," I reply sedately. Although I want to punch the air. More evidence of her violent streak!

We drive along a few streets in silence as this sinks in.

"You got anything else you want to know? Or I'll start heading towards your hotel."

"No, I think that's it."

Ashraf nods and performs a white-knuckle U-turn in the road that earns him some honks and a middle finger from a biker. I grab the ceiling handle to prevent myself tipping over onto the seat.

When we're cruising again a niggle crawls across my shoulder blades. "Um, there's one more thing."

"Shoot."

"There were some pictures in the papers of Tom with a woman that was claimed to be me. Were you… um… were you working that night?"

He looks over his shoulder at me and I attempt to keep my face neutral: yes, I am asking you to confirm my whereabouts, and yes, I really should know.

"Nah. My missus went into labour with our third baby and I had the night off. Would've been fill-in drivers that night."

I'm not sure why I asked. I know it wasn't me. "You have three children?"

"Five. Two with my first wife, three with my second."

"Blimey," I say and then feel old-fashioned for using the word 'blimey'.

"We're here," Ashraf says as he pulls into a space outside my hotel.

"Thanks," I say. "How much do I owe you?"

Ashraf taps a few buttons on the meter. "Twenty-two."

I get my wallet from my bag and give him three ten-pound notes from the cash I had to beg Dad to lend me for this trip. "Five back is fine."

Ashraf fishes a wedge of notes from his pocket and gives me a five. Then we both get out the car and he hauls my suitcase out of the boot. He places it on the pavement and pulls up the handle so I can wheel it.

As I reach for the handle, he says, "I'm sorry about your wedding. I took Tom there that day. I didn't know what was happening and then after… well… it was a bad thing to do."

Before I can reply he jumps in his car and drives off.

# CHAPTER 33

My worst nightmare is coming true. I sit, sweating, on the *My Morning* sofa. I told Nisha not to come, but now I regret it. A polished male assistant stands in front of me.

"Paul and Omaya will be finishing up their segment in the kitchen on the other side of the studio, and then we go to an ad break. They'll then head over here and it'll be your interview. Ok? Anything you need? Are you ready? Five minutes."

I take a shaky sip of water. This is the last place I want to be in the world. It's my first ever TV interview, and – hopefully – my last. I rally myself, take a deep breath and pull my shoulders back, sit up straighter on the sofa.

I'd rather be sticking pins in my eyes but I have to speak to Tanith, to get some answers about Tom, about his obsession with me, about his death, about her part in his death. But the children's TV presenter has stubbornly refused all contact. Nisha tracked down her publicist and attempted to get a phone number, address or email for Tanith but it didn't work. And I messaged her through social media, but these were ignored. I also considered hanging around outside the TV studio where she films in the hopes I'd run into her but I don't have the time for that. So I decided to play Tanith at her own game.

By going on television.

On the same show that Tanith is so regularly on. My parents told me not to do it, that it would only bring more attention on myself. Mel and Steve were dead against it too, but I'm determined. It has to work. There's no way she can refuse such a public plea without looking heartless and damaging her new saintly reputation.

"Here they come," the assistant says and the presenters walk across the studio to the lounge area.

"Hi," Omaya says to me as she sits. She elegantly tucks her legs together and to the side and places her hands in her lap as a hair stylist primps her coily hair.

Paul takes his seat and smiles at me as a makeup artist touches up the shine on his forehead and smooths back a grey strand that's out of place. "Don't worry, you'll be fine."

I met them briefly three hours earlier, when I arrived at the studio at 7am to be briefed, sit through hair and make-up and then be briefed again. Nerves swirl in my gut and I clench my buttocks. I roll my shoulders up and down and stick out my chest in a power pose that Nisha once told me about.

The cameras are readied and the assistant steps back, holding his ear piece.

"And you're back in three, two…" and he waves at us and mouths 'one'.

Omaya radiates warmth at the camera. Her skin shimmers, her eyes are friendly and her posture is open. Her lips are parted in just the right amount of smile and seriousness. "Welcome back. We are now joined on the sofa by our guest, the author Sally Speck. She has written nine novels, including the hugely successful trilogy *The Deviants*, which was adapted into a TV series, as well as the novel *Dusk*, which is currently being made into a movie with Kwame Musa in the lead role."

Paul picks up, "But today we're here to talk about the traumatic experience Sally has gone through in the past few months, with regards to her relationship with the late actor and teen star Tom Darlington. Sally, welcome to the show."

I open my mouth and for a split second think I'm about to vomit – thinking of all those eyes from across the country scrutinising me and with nowhere to escape to – but in a wobbly voice say, "Thank you, Paul."

"Now, I understand this is your first TV interview, Sally. So, tell us, why now," Omaya asks sweetly, with just the right hint of concern.

I launch into my prepped response. "The death of Tom Darlington was a shock to everyone, and the revelation that it was murder... well, it was horrific. I, sadly, was caught up in the investigation. I was cleared of any suspicion, but, unfortunately, I was tarnished by the media as being involved. I'm here to let the public know the truth."

"And what is the truth, Sally? I understand you and Tom had a difficult relationship. You had a restraining order against him." This from Paul, his grey-speckled eyebrows knit together in attentive interest.

"No, it never quite got to that... there was a police caution for harassment." I get back on track. "The truth is, we had a very brief encounter. And we were never a couple, or in a relationship. Tom developed a kind of obsession with me after that briefest of encounters, even though I had made it *very* clear to him that we were never going to be in a relationship. I was hounded by the media, and by his fans to the point I had to leave my home in London. I had to go into hiding."

"That must've been a very difficult time for you," Omaya chips in.

"It was. Then came the whole wedding invasion thing—"

Paul butts in, professionally of course, in a way that only TV presenters can do. "Tell us more about the wedding invasion. Tom disrupted your big day and interrupted your service. You and your fiancé never married that day, or after. How did that make you feel?"

"Well, it was the most awful day of my life... but I

don't really want to go into that… just to say that after, the police found enough evidence to warn Tom to stay well away from me."

I change position on the sofa, sweat trickles down my back and I desperately want to wipe my top lip, which I'm positive is glistening like a lake on a sunny day. "I'm here because Tom's killer is still at large, and it's frightening."

"It certainly is. Is there something you can help the police with? In regards to the killer? Is there something you *know*?" This from Paul, sharp. He's probing for an angle.

"No, the police are doing all they can I'm sure… I'd, um, like to extend an invitation to Tom's girlfriend… at the time he died. Tanith Evangeline, to, um, to talk. We can, um, offer each other support in this tough time."

Omaya nods enthusiastically. "We know Tanith well on this show, and I'm sure she would welcome that. She is hurting deeply."

Paul looks to the camera. "Now, let's take some questions from viewers for our guest Sally…" He looks at the iPad in front of him.

My armpits dampen. Please no weirdos, please no hard questions.

"Ok," Paul says, "our first here is from Wayne in Leeds. He asks if you ever loved Tom?"

"No, I never loved Tom. As I said, I hardly spent any time with him, a few hours, really. It was a brief fling, nothing more."

"So, why didn't you make it more?" Omaya asks.

"Because we simply were not compatible."

"You couldn't have grown to love him? Doesn't sound as if you gave him a chance, only spending such a brief amount of time with him," Omaya pushes, a sweet smile still plastered across her lips.

My face flushes. I've heard this so many times. "He wasn't for me. I'm sure you've gone on dates or had boyfriends that you knew weren't right for you. That you knew immediately weren't the one."

"Yes," Omaya says, "but I generally give my boyfriends more than *a few hours* to prove themselves. Right, moving on to the next question. Jenny from Oxford asks if you're planning a *Dusk* sequel?"

I smile with relief, pleased to get off the awkward subject of my encounter with Tom. And opt not to try to explain that *Dusk* two is languishing on my laptop three-quarters written. "Nothing in the pipeline as yet. But never say never. I'm currently working on—"

Paul cuts me off. "Well, this is exciting. We've just received a message from Tanith." He looks pointedly at the camera and then at me. "She has agreed to meet with you, perhaps later today seeing as you're in London."

"That's great…" I mumble. That happened quick. I half expected this ploy to fail.

"Well, I always like to see women supporting other women. Well done, Tanny, I know this can't be easy for you." Omaya beams at the camera.

"Now, we're going to need to wrap up this interview. Thank you, Sally, for joining us today." Paul fixes a smile on his face and looks straight at the camera. Omaya joins him. I try to look at the camera but can't focus and my eyes dart about, finally resting on my hands.

"And we're off-air," the assistant announces. "You have five minutes, then Omaya you're needed for the fashion segment. Paul, you can get ready to announce the competition after."

Omaya stands and briskly walks off set, without a second glance at me.

Paul says, "Well done, that must've been hard for you." He stands and leaves me sitting on the sofa.

The assistant comes up to me and pulls me up by the elbow. "That's it, you're done." He leads me away into the small room where I had my make-up applied. "Wait here, I won't be a moment. I'll get Tanith's mobile for you."

I wait at a table at The Huntington, booked in Tanith's name. After exchanging a few text messages with her, I headed straight here from the *My Morning* studio.

The children's presenter is running late, and I've nursed the same cheapest-thing-on-the-menu coffee for the past thirty minutes. I sip at the dregs for a third time. The servers openly watch me, the guests continually glimpse in my direction and I feel as if I've got a lighthouse beacon flashing on my forehead.

My train home is booked for 4.30pm and I'm eager to leave the capital. I'll give it another ten minutes and then I'm off. I scroll through Twitter, read comments about my performance on *My Morning*. Some are scathing, but some, I'm grateful to see, are positive, sympathetic even.

The chair in front of me scrapes and Tanith lowers herself down. A server appears instantly and she orders a small soy milk cappuccino, no chocolate sprinkles, no biscotti on the side. She's stunning in the flesh, enviably slim, with pristine long blonde hair and bright red lipstick.

She doesn't apologise for being late, but sits upright, her mouth tight. She turns to one side so she can cross her long legs. So long they don't fit under the table that way. She could be a model. She scans the room and then looks at her fingernails, a peach polish on them today.

In a low, conspiratorial tone, she says, "I don't want to be here, but my publicist insisted it would not look good if I refused to meet you. So here I am. Let's get this out the way, shall we? I think twenty minutes should be enough. There'll be photographers outside, my publicist has organised it, so we need to leave smiling, like friends. Ok? And then you'll get exposure for your new book. As I know that's what this is all about."

I put my phone in my bag and match her tone. "Actually, I really want to talk to you. This isn't about publicity for me."

Tanith huffs and flicks the hair on one side of her face behind her shoulder with a swish of a hand.

"Seriously," I insist. "Look, Tanith, Tom stalked me, he harassed me. I did not encourage it or welcome it at all. I hated his attention. And I was pleased when I saw that he was with you. You two looked very happy. I'm sad about his death, truly, I want to know what happened to him. Don't you?"

Tanith scrunches her nose and looks anywhere but at me. The server delivers her cappuccino. She watches him go and then elegantly scoops the foam off the top with a spoon and sucks it, careful not to smudge her lipstick.

I continue, "Tom ruined my life. He stopped me from marrying the man I loved. I was devastated. Am devastated. I can only imagine what you must be going through, losing the man you love."

"That was shitty. What Tom did at your wedding. Really shitty." Tanith sips her de-foamed coffee.

"Yeah, it was. I… I don't think Tom was all there, mentally, I mean. At that time. Clearly when you met him, he wasn't like that. He loved you and you loved him. I really didn't think he still had any feelings for me anymore, now that he loved you."

"Stop saying he loved me," Tanith says quietly through clenched teeth. "And stop saying I loved him."

"Oh… that's what you said in all those interviews and…"

Tanith leans in close over the table and I move forward to meet her.

She looks around to make sure no one is looking at us or eavesdropping. "Listen to me, ok, I met him at a party. He took an interest in me and I was flattered. We went on a few dates. He was tedious, but my publicist said it would be great for my profile to date an international star, which it was, but he was controlling, angry and obsessive. Towards the end, I loathed him. I'm telling you this because no one will believe you if you repeat it. Everyone will just think you're being jealous and spiteful."

Tanith sits back and takes another sip of coffee.

I frown. "So, you were relieved when he…" I stumble over the word. "You know…"

"It was the best day of my life."

My eyes widen and I gulp back an exclaim. Tanith glares at me. Neither of us speak for an uncomfortable few seconds.

Tanith pulls out a mirror from her bag and checks her lipstick, tidying up a non-existent smear. My eyebrows are still as high as my hairline as I continue to gaze at the woman.

Tom's murderer?

Tanith glances to either side and then whispers in a hiss, "I didn't do it, if that's what you're thinking."

"Why didn't you leave him?" I whisper back.

"Believe me, I tried to. But his brother…" Tanith stops herself mid-sentence.

"His brother? What about his brother?"

But Tanith won't say any more. She smacks her lips together to distribute the lipstick. She looks at her watch. "Right, time to go. Put your best game face on for the paps."

"But, Tanith—"

"Oh, don't worry about the bill. I've got an account here." Tanith pushes back her chair and slings her handbag over her shoulder.

"No, not that…" I say as I stand. I follow Tanith to the cloakroom. We both put on our coats in silence. Staff surround us, eager to help. We walk a few steps and when we're alone between the inner door and outer one, I try again. "What about his brother Angus?"

Tanith pauses and turns to me. With a broad smile, as the paps outside are already snapping us through the glass doors, she gives me a friendly embrace.

"Never mention that name again," she whispers in my ear. "Never."

She lets go and a security guard opens the outer door and she sweeps out. I flounder behind in her wake.

Tanith makes a show of waving to me and marches away to the left. Half the pack follow her, the other half hassle me, shouting questions and pointing lenses and microphones in my face. I automatically freeze and hold up my arms, as if about to be attacked by a slathering beast. The security guard comes to my rescue and guides me to a line of waiting taxis.

I clamber into the first one and say the name of my hotel so I can pick up my suitcase before heading to Waterloo. I hide my mouth from the media, so they can't lipread and follow.

# CHAPTER 34

"Hi, is that Angus Darling?"

It's been relatively easy to track him down. Half way back to the hotel in the taxi I changed my mind about going home, cancelled my train and booked another two nights in the hotel using a maxed credit card that won't be charged until I check out. There'll be issues then, and it'll be awful, but for now, I don't think about it. I messaged the family WhatsApp group to let them know my plans and then spent a few minutes on Google and… Boom.

Angus works in the City at a big investment bank and his photo, email and phone number are all proudly displayed on the website, encouraging calls from potential new clients. I remembered Tom blathering on about his brother, saying he went by the surname Darling so he wouldn't be bothered by Tom's fans.

In Angus' picture, he looks like Tom, but uglier. Lips too wide, nose a little wonky and eyes too small. He has a deep crease between his eyebrows, as if his forehead is slipping down his face. His hair is the same blond as Tom's had been, except it's frizzy rather than wavy.

"Yes, this is he. And who do I have the pleasure of speaking to?" His voice is as smooth as Tom's. Public school educated, wealthy and arrogant.

"This is Sally Speck. I want to talk to you about your brother."

Silence.

"Angus, I met with Tanith earlier. I need answers about Tom. I should've had it out with him when he was alive but I hid from him, from his obsessive behaviour. I thought that it was my fault. But now I know, it wasn't."

"And how, exactly, do you *know* that?" he asks.

"I spoke with Tanith. She said Tom was controlling and obsessive with her too."

Silence.

"Can we meet, Angus? Perhaps later…"

Angus coughs and then says, "Certainly, I have a function after work and should be done about nine. We can meet at the London Eye and go for a walk along the Thames."

I hesitate, I don't fancy walking in the dark with a man I don't know.

Angus seems to perceive my reluctance and says, "My bodyguard will be with us, he's superb, very discreet. I've had him ever since Tom shot to fame as some of his misguided fans took it upon themselves to hound me… I'm sure you are very used to that kind of attention."

"And then some."

"Listen, I only suggested a walk along the Thames because that's what dearest Tom used to love doing. I miss walking with him." Angus' voice quavers and I feel sorry for him.

"Sure, nine at the London Eye," I confirm.

When we meet, Angus is alone. "I dismissed my bodyguard for the evening, I thought we could have a nice walk and talk. It's a fabulous evening and I doubt anyone will recognise us. This place is crawling with tourists."

I get jostled by a man who's part of a big group. He's holding a selfie stick and backs right into me. Although my gut warns me this is a *bad idea*, my brain says, he's right. The place is swarming with people. And Angus does not look threatening. He looks tired, big purple bags puff under his bloodshot eyes. His cheeks are sunken and his posture is hunched. He's slim, too, not obviously gym-honed like Tom.

"Ok," I reply.

"I miss him so much," Angus begins as we walk along the river towards Southbank. "He was… *misunderstood*, but he had a heart of gold. Such a kind man."

"He stalked me, Angus. And Tanith said he was controlling and aggressive with her. There was something not right with him."

"Nonsense," Angus' tone is sharp, then softens. "He didn't stalk you. He was in love with you. Truly. He just had a funny way of showing it. That's what fame does. He was famous from fifteen, he was used to people doing what he wanted, and couldn't comprehend when someone didn't feel the same about something as him."

I chew my lips. There's little point debating this, Angus will clearly never believe his brother was mentally unstable. "If he was such a nice guy, then who murdered him?"

Angus visibly winces, then rallies himself, running his hands through his hair. A pang of guilt hits me at my bluntness. He's just lost a loved one. I need to chill out.

"Well, everyone thought it was you," Angus counters. A snide jeer flashes across his features before it's replaced with remorse. "My apologies, that was crass. We are both hurting, and we both have a vested interest in discovering once and for all what happened."

"Is there anyone you think it could be?"

"Well, if I'm brutally honest with you, I thought it could be your father or your stepfather. Both have dubious pasts and links to some undesirables."

I think back to the odd text I received from Patrick on the day that I heard of Tom's death. 'It's done'. And Dad's adamant protests that I hadn't 'done it' when I was arrested. Could my father or stepfather have called in favours with the 'people' they know?

"Absolutely not," I reply with conviction, but a tickle of suspicion loiters at the back of my throat.

Angus nods. "Well, that only leaves Tanith."

"Tanith?" I repeat. So, Angus has also come to the conclusion that the show pony has a nasty side too.

"She's a complete bitch. Treated Tom terribly. He did so much for that money and fame-grabbing whore. The nerve of that woman telling you that he treated her badly."

The venom in his voice startles me. Did Tanith lie to me about how Tom treated her?

"For a long while, I believed it was you. But the police tell me you have an alibi. I want to believe it wasn't you, otherwise why am I here talking to Tom's murderer? I want to believe the police, to trust in their methods and I want to forgive and move on. I don't want to dwell on his death, it's not healthy – my therapist tells me. Do you have one?"

"No."

"I'll give you the number of mine, he's very good."

"Er, thanks."

"I just can't stop wondering though – could you have gotten to London in time? The time of death is between 9pm and midnight. Your call with the insurance company ended just before 9pm, then if you drove fast you could've arrived in London for 11pm—"

"I have absolutely no idea where he lived," I cut in.

Angus rakes his fingers through his hair and stops to look at me. I stop too.

"If you did it, Sally, I really wish you would confess," he snaps aggressively.

I furtively scope my surroundings, to see how many people are near us. Who might come running if Angus turns nasty and I scream.

But he doesn't. He takes a series of noisy deep breaths. "Sorry, I don't want to get angry. I'm trying hard not to let anger control me. It's just... I miss him so much. He didn't deserve to die like that."

He looks desperately sad. His phone rings and he retrieves it from the inside pocket of his overcoat. He looks at the screen. His sadness evaporates. "I'm sorry, I really have to take this… work. Listen, let's stay in touch. I'll help you clear your name. We'll find Tom's killer. I promise to keep you in the loop with the police investigation."

He answers the phone and strides away. I stand on my own for a moment, the crowds parting and reforming around me. I move to the railing and watch the River Thames for a while. When I get cold, I flag a taxi back to my hotel.

On the journey, I pull out my notebook and under all my notes on Tanith, I write: 'Killer: Patrick?' And then, with a skewer through my chest, I scrawl: 'Killer: Dad?'

It's ten-thirty by the time I get back to my hotel room. I've been up since 5am and I'm running on adrenaline. I can't stop now.

I sit at the small desk and pull out my notebook and pen. I dial That Wanker, Pat Tanker, which is the name I have in my contacts list for my biological father. I know it's late, and probably later in Spain with the time difference.

"Sally," Patrick says.

"Hi, Patrick," I say.

"Call me Dad," he says.

His voice is strong, but slightly slurred. He's probably drunk. In the background I hear the hustle and bustle of a busy street. It sounds as if he's outside.

"What can I do for you, little lady?"

"Well, I'd just like to know what you meant by your text."

"Hey, you!" Patrick bellows, his voice is muffled as if he's holding the phone to his shirt. "What the hell was that?"

I hear a second voice. "Piss off, old man…" it shouts in an Irish accent. Then, "Ah, feck, sorry Mr. Tanker." The voice grovels, "I didn't realise it was you."

"Watch where you're fucking going next time, son," Patrick's voice responds.

"Sorry, chief, sorry, sorry," the voice fades.

"You still there?" Patrick says into the phone.

"Yes. Everything ok?"

"Sure. Some git just knocked into me."

There's a pause and I realise I've been given permission to speak again. "I wanted to ask about your text, you said 'It's done'. What did you mean? What was done?"

"Huh? Thought you'd be bright enough to work that one out." He laughs, then in a patronising tone says, "All I meant was that dickhead was dead. It's over. Done. Finito. Good riddance."

I don't reply, processing this. Is that a confession? Or did he just hear about Tom's death on the news like I did?

"And you're welcome."

"What?"

"That's what you called for, wasn't it. To say thanks."

"Err..."

"Listen, am at my bar. Best speak to Graham. Tell your mam we're all square. Behave yourself, kiddo."

He hangs up. A shiver rolls down my spine. Mel was right. I made a mistake getting in touch with Patrick. I do regret it.

But there's no stopping me now. I know it's late, but I call the home phone.

Dad answers it promptly with a brisk hello in the voice he reserves for junk 'there's something wrong with your broadband' callers. I can hear the telly in the background. Either he's still up or they both are. Since they retired, my parents are passionate advocates of napping during the day and staying up later at night.

"Dad, it's me."

"Everything all right?"

"Yes, I'm fine."

"I'll hand you to your mother."

Dad isn't good on the phone, never has been. Will

always hand a call to Mum as soon as he can, unless it's one of his friends or close family. His extended family? Get handed off too.

"No, I want to talk to you."

"Oh, right." He sounds surprised.

"How did you know I didn't kill Tom?"

Silence.

I try again, "I mean, you shouted at the police that I didn't do it. Do you know who did?"

"Sal, you didn't do it, did you."

"No, of course not… It's just… I'm so confused."

There's a pause and I can almost hear Dad weighing up his options.

"That Wanker and I continued to have Darlington watched after Omar," Dad confesses.

"Why?"

"To make sure he didn't come anywhere near you again."

That was not what I was expecting to hear. Something else they've kept secret from me. "When did you stop?"

"When he was found dead."

"So, did your…" I struggle for the right word, 'spies' feels too James Bond, too serious, "watchers… see who went in the night he died?"

"No."

"You were watching his apartment from the front?"

"Yes."

"So, you didn't know about the back way in?"

Dad is silent for a long time and I can hear the canned laughter from a TV show.

"No," he mutters and I know that he wasn't aware there was a second entrance. And I guess that he's now wondering how I know there was a secret way in.

This explains how Tom managed to evade notice and get to the forest to run me off the road. Or perhaps they found out and that's why later that day…

"Did you and Patrick… you know…"

I stop myself. Seriously, what am I asking? Did he and Patrick have Tom knocked off? Did he do the deed himself? Did he do it with Patrick, who flew in from Spain for the occasion?

I hear Mum's voice.

"Your mother wants a word," Dad says.

Mum comes on the phone. She sounds bright for this time of night. "Sal, are you ok? We've been so worried about you. We watched you on telly. Did you meet with that woman? Baxter's been missing you terribly, whining and fussing."

A wave of exhaustion hits me in reaction to her chirpiness. "Mum, I don't want to talk right now." It's not that I don't want to talk to *her*, I just don't have any energy to talk at all.

She must be able to hear how tired I am. "That's fine, you get some rest and we'll speak tomorrow. Love you."

"Bye, Mum."

I write in my notebook:

'All square about what?'

'Hired hitman?'

'Own hands?'

Then I change into my pyjamas, get into bed and switch off the light. My phone pings.

It's a WhatsApp message from Mel, not in the family group but direct. She's clearly just spoken to Mum, who would've called her to let her know she's spoken to me and I'm fine.

'Just leave it alone, sis. It's over. Stop stirring up shit. Let it be. Come home NOW.'

I don't reply. I switch my phone to silent. What is she so pissed about? The streetlight coming in through the edges of the curtains casts a silvery glow across the room. I close my eyes again and in a half-sleep I daydream, imagine ridiculous scenarios, get emotional at events that haven't happened.

Is the reason Mel wants me to stop looking into Tom's death because she did it? She's got away with it so wants me to come home and forget all about it?

I roll over, turn on the light and swipe my notebook off the bedside cabinet. I scribble: 'Killer: Mel?'

Then I sit back and feel ridiculous for suspecting my family. But seriously, they've not helped themselves, have they? They've all gone behind my back. They've all lied. Even Mum went to see Tom and only told me because I heard about Omar's arrest on the radio.

Omar.

I haven't heard from him since he hung up on me when those fake photos were printed in the media. He was so angry at Tom. He beat him up! But would he have gone further? *Could* he have gone further? The man I fell in love with was sweet and kind. But something about Tom enraged Omar and he became a different person. Even when we tried to give it a second go, Tom drove a wedge between us again.

I write my ex-fiancé's name in my notebook and then flip through my notes. Were they all in this together?

I jolt upright, my heart hammering. Mum knew where Tom lived! She said that Angus had also been at Tom's apartment when she'd gone to talk to Tom. She went to his apartment, where he was found dead.

I get up slowly and walk into the bathroom to splash some water on my face. I look at my sallow, tired face in the mirror and the sight of it makes me feel utterly exhausted. I'll work this out in the morning. I get back into bed and fall into a fitful sleep, my imagination running on overdrive in my dreams.

# CHAPTER 35

I wake up late, have a shower and order room service for midday: lasagne and chips. Just another thing I won't be able to pay for when I check out. But I have more important things to think about. I put my pyjamas back on, because, well, why not? I haven't brought any comfy clothes with me and lounging in tight jeans is not so fun.

I need a plan for today; to tick things off a list. I feel motivated. Like I'm making some progress. I sit against the headrest of the bed with my knees up and open my notebook. At some point in the night I've scrawled 'pink scarf' on the page. I clearly did it without turning the light on and half-conscious because it's slanted across the lines and I only have a vague recollection of doing it.

Pink scarf…

Of course. I missed a vital clue. Been barking up the wrong tree just like the police.

My Peruvian scarf proves that no one in my family murdered Tom. Why? Because why would they plant my blood-stained scarf at the scene of the crime? Why would they incriminate me? If they were going to murder him it would be to protect me, to keep him away from me for good. And, how would they have got that scarf in the first place to leave there?

Omar wouldn't have done it because he was angry at Tom, not me. The last thing he said to me was "We're not done", which implies he thinks we'll get back together one day with Tom out the way. So, why would he plant my scarf?

I score heavy lines through my recent notes and laugh out loud at my doubt of my family and ex-fiancé in the first place. Yes, they've done some strange things recently and hurt me – but they're not capable of murder. Never that.

My phone pings. It's a text from That Wanker.

'Even kept the rag. Get it delivered every morning, Spanish newsagent gets it in specially for me. Not without some grumbling though ha ha.'

Attached to the text is a skewed photo of the front page of a UK tabloid newspaper. I click on it to see the headline blaring about Tom Darlington being found dead, suicide suspected. Then check the date. I realise that after our brief phone call last night, Patrick is telling me he found out that Tom Darlington was dead from his morning newspaper and then sent me that 'It's done' text.

So, if it wasn't them that circles me right back to… Tanith. But how would she have got hold of my scarf?

A knot forms in my chest and all warmth drains from my skin. I shiver. Was it me? Did I leave it there? The murder movie I concocted in my cell at the police station switches back on and I play it over and over.

A knock on the door halts proceedings and I let room service in. She leaves the tray on the little desk but as soon as she's gone, I pick up the plate and cutlery and sit on the bed to eat it.

No. It wasn't me. I was at home, drunk, talking on the phone about downgrading my phone contract. It must've been Tanith. I need to persuade her to meet me again.

I finish my meal and grab my phone. I do a little sitting jig. There's to be no persuasion required as I have two missed calls from Tanith, and two texts. The first reads:

'Come round mine later. 8pm. We need to talk.'

And the second is her address.

My bowels twinge. Lasagne springs back up my throat. Not neutral ground. If Tanith is capable of murdering Tom, she's dangerous. But I tap back a message. As if I'll refuse! I'm on a roll now, I'm close, I can feel it.

I cancel dinner with Nisha, message the family group with Tanith's address and, at two minutes past eight, press the buzzer on Tanith's front door.

She lives in a pastel-yellow house in Notting Hill. I hear locks unbolting and the door edges open as far as a security chain allows. Tanith's face briefly appears. She takes off the chain and opens the door.

"Come in," she says.

I step into her hall. It's tastefully decorated in monochrome, with a checkerboard tiled floor. Tanith closes the door and carefully turns all the locks. She walks past me towards the back of the house and I follow. Tanith points to a bright-pink chair and plonks herself down on a lime-green sofa. She doesn't offer me a drink or to take my coat.

I take my coat off anyway, lay it across the back of the chair and sit.

Tanith stares at me for a few moments, I hold her gaze but then study the sleek glass coffee table.

"I can't believe you spoke to Angus," Tanith explodes. "Now he's furious at me. Even more so than usual!"

"Why is Angus mad at—"

"Shut up! Let me finish! You need to forget all about Tom, all about me, all about his brother, ok? Forget about it. Right now. I invited you here to tell you that, it's too risky in public. Do you hear me?"

"I don't understand. What's the issue? Why is Angus mad at you? Does he think you have something to do with Tom's death?"

"Urgh, stop asking questions!" Tanith stands and

stomps around the room, she slaps her palm on her forehead and then bangs her head against the wall.

"Tanith, stop! You're going to hurt yourself." I jump up and yank Tanith away from the wall. She slumps and I hug her. "It's ok, Tanith. It's going to be ok. Let me help you."

"I've told no one, no one," she mumbles. "But he still threatens me, still has me watched. I can't do this anymore. I want my life back…" She cries.

"Let me help, Tanith. What happened?"

Then it gushes out of her in one long torrent. "I was cheating on Tom when he died. I was at Karl's hotel... I met him when I was in America, he's a basketball player. We got together and then whenever he was in London we hooked up. I kept trying to leave Tom, but he would hound me until I agreed to come back. And Angus…" She sniffs.

I grab my coat, hook a packet of tissues out of a pocket and give one to Tanith.

Tanith blows her nose and continues, "Angus had me followed, he was always watching Tom and those around him. Angus found out about Karl. He threatened to expose me to the media, he said he'd annihilate my career and that Tom needed me. Tom didn't function well, his brother kept him together… Angus even followed you himself every now and then. He's just as obsessive as his brother…"

My pulse throbs in my ears. Is she lying again?

Tanith continues, "Was the same with that supermodel before you too. Tom goes off the rails when women leave him, he can't cope with rejection. He needed professional help, but the family didn't want the embarrassment of mental illness, you know? Angus always tried to make sure Tom kept hold of women. The model got away, and you… you got away but I was trapped…"

"But Tom is gone, you aren't trapped anymore, Tanith."

"I am," she sobs. "Angus was my alibi. He told the police that the two of us met at his to talk about a birthday surprise for Tom… So I didn't need to say I was with Karl. Angus saved me from another scandal, and career suicide."

"But you lied to the police."

"I know. I feel so bad about it… And then it was revealed that it wasn't suicide but murder. Murder!"

The doorbell rings, Tanith freezes. There's a thump on the door and through the letterbox, a voice. "Tanith! I know you're in there. Let me in. Tanith!"

"Angus," she whispers.

"Tanith!" More thumps on the front door. "You know I have Tom's keys." Keys scrape in locks. Then more thumps, and kicks.

"I changed the locks," Tanith whispers. We are as still as statues, neither of us dare to move.

The bombardment gradually subsides and all goes quiet.

"I think he's gone," I say.

Tanith brings a finger to her lips. We listen until my back cramps from standing in the same position for too long and I shift my feet.

Tanith's trance is broken at the movement. "I think you're right. Tom bought me this place, but Angus managed it all." She smiles up at me. "Thank you for being here. Do you want a drink? Red wine?"

I bob my head enthusiastically. I want a lot of wine.

Tanith picks herself up and heads into the kitchen. It's an open plan lounge, dining room and kitchen with patio doors through what I assume is a small garden or terrace area outside. There are no blinds or curtains and the glass is black and reflects the room. I catch a glimpse of my reflection and settle back in the pink chair.

From the kitchen, Tanith says, "I've got Malbec or Cabernet Sauvignon, which would you prefer?"

"Malbec."

"Have you eaten? I've not got much… I never have any food in the house… I'm a terrible cook. Do you want some popcorn? I can bung it in the microwave."

"Sure."

The microwave beeps, a bowl hits the worktop and Tanith comes through with two large glasses of wine. "Here you go—"

She screams. The glasses slip from her hands and spill red all over the cream rug. I follow Tanith's gaze to see what she's so hysterical about. And I scream too.

# CHAPTER 36

Angus' face is at the patio door, his fists thump the glass. He's dishevelled, his jacket has a large rip and his shirt is untucked. He fumbles in his pocket and brings out a clump of keys. He finds one and puts it in the patio door lock.

I leap up and grab the handle to the door, my face inches from his, my breath steams the glass. "Did you change these locks too? Tanith! Did you change these locks?"

"No…"

Angus unlocks the sliding door and yanks it back. Tanith springs to my side, together we push against him, so the door only slides open an inch.

"What the hell is she doing here?" Angus yells through the gap. He grits his teeth and tugs at the door.

Tanith shrieks, "Piss off, Angus! Leave me alone. It's none of your business who I see, not anymore. Tom's gone."

With a forceful wrench, Angus jams a foot in the door and squeezes his arm and chest in. He grabs my hair viciously. Tears well at the sting.

"Get off me!" I push harder at the door, but he's strong. "Tanith, go and phone the police, now! I'll hold him off a bit longer. Go!"

Tanith lets go and I hold the door shut with all my strength. I ignore the pain as Angus tugs at my hair.

The door pushes into his chest and he grunts. But he forces it back, and tumbles through into the room.

He wrenches up my head with my hair and – smack – his fist connects with my face. Pain blossoms across my cheek and up my nose and I crumple to the floor. My brain swims and my vision blurs as I fumble around on all fours, trying to right myself. But my limbs have gone dead and are like jelly. I hear Tanith's shrieks and Angus' grunts. I'm aware of a scuffle behind me, but I still can't summon up enough focus or feeling in my limbs to stand. I retch at the smell of burning popcorn.

Firm hands grab under my armpits and I'm dragged across the floor, lifted and propped on the lime-green sofa next to Tanith, who whimpers. Angus slaps my face and my attention snaps back. I glance at Tanith. She has a black eye and a bloody nose that streams down her lips, chin and drips on her blouse. Then I look at Angus. He sits in the pink chair, with a kitchen knife across his knees and another knife resting on the arm of the chair. The sliding patio door has been closed.

"Ah, so the hack writer decides to join us. About time. Tanith here is not great company right now."

I focus on the knife on his knee, I don't want to look him in the eye and provoke him.

He continues, "All I wanted was to talk. And now look what you made me do. Silly women, always so hysterical. But I've come up with a plan. A great plan, in fact. I'm going to fake your deaths. You stab each other, you see. In a fit of jealousy over Tom, my dearest departed brother, and that will wash my hands of you both in one fell swoop. I adore efficiency."

"Why would you do that?" I garble thickly. My pounding nose is swollen from the punch.

"Because, hack, Tanith here is cracking. She can't keep her mouth shut. And you, you were simply in the wrong place at the wrong time."

"But Tanith can say she was with Karl, tell the truth,

face the police and the media's wrath. That has nothing to do with you," I say.

"Oh, you really are naive. And here I thought you had imagination." He picks up the knife from the armrest and points it at Tanith. "If Tanith tells the truth, then I don't have an alibi for the night Tom died."

Tanith gasps.

"Oh Tanny, Tanny, Tanny, don't tell me you hadn't thought about it? No? You really have zero brain cells between those ears."

I goggle him. "You... you killed Tom?"

He slow claps his palm on the knuckles of the hand holding the knife.

"Your own brother..." I say.

"He was a pain in the arse," Angus snaps. "He had an extremely distorted view of the world, from growing up in the public eye. He thought everything was about him. It became utterly boring. That night, he was blathering on about you again, Sally Speck. About getting married and starting a family and a load of other nonsense. I can't even begin to imagine why, look at the state of you. Still, when he got it in his head he was besotted, that was it. Frumpy author or supermodel or that pig-ugly girl from hockey when we were at school."

Angus rolls his eyes.

"We took him to a shrink once, who diagnosed him with something called erotomania," he says the last word with a heavy dollop of disgust, "a delusional belief that the other person is in love with them and that sooner or later they'll respond. He was convinced you were sending him secret messages, telling him you loved him. Pathetic."

He scores the tip of the knife along the armrest, snagging the fabric.

"I thought he'd got you out of his system after that wedding stunt he pulled behind my back. That could've ruined everything, damaged his career irreparably, undone all my years of hard work. I was livid. But not long after that little unauthorised exploit he became obsessed with Tanith so I made sure she stuck around for the good publicity."

Angus smirks at Tanith and she squirms away from his attention. He points the knife at me.

"But then he started pining for your absurd self again. He even paid for a prostitute who looked like you and he took her out – the bloody fool – but it didn't help. Do you know, he still had that scratty coat of yours, the one you left at that nightclub. He'd found it again and that night cuddled it like a blankie, convinced it still smelt like you. Smelt like farts and well-used gym shoes more like."

Angus chuckles, but his mood darkens.

"When I arrived that night, I'd already sent home his bodyguards, PA and driver because Tom planned to stay in. We drank a bucketload of that good whiskey and I demanded he forget all about you, hack, for the sake of his career. But he wouldn't stop prattling on about how you two were destined to be together. On and on and on and on. It turned physical and we fought. I bashed him over the head, rather more brutally than I intended, and suddenly he was barely conscious and bleeding heavily. So, I stuffed him with painkillers and more whiskey, telling him it was for his own good, wrote a little note, planted that revolting pink scarf and left him to it. It was a slow, agonising death apparently."

"You... monster," Tanith stammers.

"You had my scarf?" I blurt.

Angus snorts. "You really should be more careful about where you dump your rubbish. I thought that bloody rag might come in handy one day. And it did. You know, I did enjoy all those little walks in the forest. My hit and run would've been impeccable if it hadn't been for that damn ditch. With you out the way, Tom would've moved on. But alas, it wasn't to be."

I could've died that day in the forest, and Tom would still be alive. But Angus missed me and his brother paid the price. For the second time, my gullet fills with lasagne sick.

"Tom loved you," Tanith stutters. "He trusted you…"

"Enough talking." Angus grabs the knife off his knees and stands. Clutching a kitchen knife in each hand he advances on me.

I find my feet, stumble as my head swims from the earlier punch, and edge around the coffee table. He comes at me, wielding the knives. I dodge, but a knife slices my bicep. I scream as the pain sears my skin and my hot blood spurts out, soaking my shirt. I swallow back vomit and a wooziness threatens to engulf me but I know I must stay sharp otherwise he'll kill us.

Angus lunges again and I brace myself, but he chokes backwards as Tanith puts her clasped arms around his neck and hangs behind him. He stabs at her forearms with the knives and she howls in pain.

I kick him in the bollocks and his knees buckle. I grab a large mosaic candleholder from next to the television and smash it over his head. Glass shards fly everywhere and nick at the skin on my face. He stumbles forward, drops one knife but swings the other at my thighs. It connects in a long slash, rips my jeans and tears open my flesh. Blood spurts and I struggle to take in any air. I collapse as my legs give way.

Tanith clings on, still screaming, still bleeding. Angus lurches to the side and twists so that he can stab Tanith, her side fully exposed as her arms are still up around his neck. Before he can, I grab the dropped knife off the floor and bring it up with all the force I can muster into his belly. He grunts and continues to tussle with Tanith, swiping his knife at me. He slashes my arms and chest. I wrench the knife from his belly and then, with a bravery I didn't know existed, stab his torso again.

I let go of the knife handle as he crumples on the rug, clutching his wounds. One hand is around the hilt of the knife that sticks in his flesh.

"Fucking bitches," he seethes.

Tanith scrambles free of him, gets to her feet and kicks his head. Quick as a flash, he grabs her ankle and tugs. She flies backwards into the huge flat-screen television, smashing the screen to pieces. It falls on top of her with a crack and she doesn't move.

With some kind of superhuman strength, Angus slowly rises, snarling and slides the knife from his body. His murderous eyes narrow on me.

I fumble for the second knife he dropped, and thrust it in his side. I scrabble backwards. Angus' arms flail, but I'm just out of his reach. His eyes flicker and close, finally succumbing to his injuries. He slumps face first. The first knife flies from his grip and skitters across the cream rug out of his reach.

"Tanith?" I yell. "Tanith?" I drag myself to her and shove the television off. She groans.

With all my energy, I push myself up. My legs are in agony. Blood pours from numerous stab wounds. I stagger to my bag, still sat by the side of the pink chair, and with slippery, blood-slick fingers find my phone and dial 999.

# CHAPTER 37

"Could I have that?" I croak at the cleaner.

"It's yesterday's," he replies.

"That's fine."

He scoops the folded newspaper out of his recycling sack, hands it to me and leaves the room. I shift on my hospital bed, organise the pillows so I sit upright. I've already checked my phone and the battery is dead. The past few days have been a blur of pain, police and doctors. Today, though, I'm feeling more lucid.

It's the time between breakfast and lunch. I know this because I ate bland cornflakes not so long ago. Watching the cleaner cleanse my room passed the time for a while, but now he's gone and I'm desperate for information. I expect I'll have visitors soon. I have hazy snapshots of Mum, Dad and Mel in this room from the past few days.

The front-page headline tells me all I need to know: BROTHER CHARGED WITH TOM'S MURDER.

The photo shows Angus being wheeled on a stretcher still hooked up to a drip, and escorted somewhere by two uniformed police officers. He's attempting to cover his face.

The caption reads: 'Angus Darlington is moved to a secure medical unit after being charged with the murder of his famous brother.'

I scan the article and learn that Tom's father has committed suicide, after learning of Angus' involvement.

And that Tanith has officially announced her 'new' relationship with basketball star Karl Johnson with plans to appear in a joint interview on *My Morning* as soon as she's recovered from the injuries inflicted upon her by Angus Darlington.

Tanith and I are billed as heroes for fighting off a 'madman' and 'eyewitness accounts' – I expect Tanith's nosey neighbours – tell of all the blood on Angus, Tanith and me as we were carried out of Tanith's Notting Hill house by paramedics.

I flick through pages to find an article that claims to have 'access' to Angus' private diaries. How they snagged his journals, I've no idea, but I read the 'exclusive' passage anyway.

> I got the nose. The stupid sodding Darlington nose. Hooked with a lump at the bridge. But you have to make the most of these things. Then Thomas came along, adorned with mother's fine features, not a hint of hook in sight. Ever since I can remember I've been jealous of that little bastard. Fiercely protective and loyal, but so bloody jealous.

> My skill is maths and risk-taking – perfect for banking. His is for poncing about making a show of himself. And he can sing. Not great of course, but well enough to get him into that boyband, who only care about his looks anyway.

> I love him, the little toerag. But in a way, I loathe him more than anything.

There's more, but I drop the newspaper on the floor, exhausted by it all.

I notice an envelope on the bedside cabinet with a yellow post-it note on top. I pick it up and see Mum's handwriting: 'From Omar. We got one too.'

I open it and inside is a non-descript floral card. I read Omar's short note in which he says how sorry he is for everything, how grateful he is to my parents for helping him out, and how he wishes me all the best. I put the card back in the envelope and drop it on top of the newspaper.

"Knock, knock," Nisha says a few hours later as she pokes her head around the door to my private room at the hospital.

"Oh, come in, come in," Mum says and stands up to usher Nisha in. She gestures to Dad and Mel. "We were just off to buy Sal some more pyjamas anyway. Those ones she's wearing will be walking on their own soon."

My parents and Mel say their goodbyes and head off. Nisha takes one of the plastic seats near my bed and jerks it closer.

"How you doing?"

I fill her in on how my injuries are healing and she updates me on what she's been up to and how baby Sahil is doing. Then her face turns serious and I know I'm about to hear some straight-talking.

"Listen, darling, I know I said not to air your dirty laundry in public, but I've had a change of heart. I think you should milk this situation for all it's worth. You've been hounded by the media since day one, and now you're a hero. I'm advising you, as your literary agent and friend, to write a book about it."

I squirm on the hospital bed.

She notes my unease but continues, "It'll never be over, Sal. This is your chance to tell your story, in your own words, and to earn money from it. This will help you to recover financially and get back on your feet. Honestly, I could get an *incredible* deal with a publisher."

"I just want my life back to normal," I say.

"I know. But this is normal for you now. Your life will never be what it was before that awards ceremony."

I know she's right. That impulsive one-night stand has turned into a lifetime relationship, whether I want it or not – and no matter that Tom is now gone. Perhaps writing will be like a catharsis. I'll get it all out and then I can move on. I'll be free of Tom by telling everyone everything. If there's nothing else to know, then they'll leave me alone once and for all.

"I'd better be getting on," Nisha says and leans over to give me a hug. "I got this for you." She pulls out a paper bag from her handbag and hands it to me. I look inside and it's a notebook and pen. "I know how you love to write everything down."

I thank her and she blows me a kiss as she leaves. I stare into space for a while, listening to all the busy hospital noises from the hallway.

After a while, I pull out the notebook and write at the top of the first page: 'My time with Tom'.

# AUTHOR'S NOTE

Did you enjoy reading *Her Biggest Fan*? Please could you leave a review on Amazon. Your review will help other readers to discover the novel and I hugely appreciate your help in spreading the word.

Please subscribe to my email newsletter to be notified when my next psychological thriller is released, and for giveaways, price promotions, book recommendations as well as exclusive extra content. You can sign up here: www.noravalters.com/subscribe

Thank you for taking the time to read *Her Biggest Fan* – I'm very grateful for your support.

Nora Valters
September 2020

# ACKNOWLEDGMENTS

Massive thanks to my parents Ann and Brian, and to my sister Kath, for all their encouragement and help. My Mum read this story numerous times in all its different iterations (it started life in 2017 as a very different novella called Distortions) and her feedback has been invaluable.

I'd also like to say a huge thank you to my beta readers Becky, Robyn and Kath who bravely read my early draft and gave me their honest opinions. Also, to my editor Eve for her thorough advice. Plus, big appreciation goes out to my cousin-in-law Andy who gave me incredibly useful insight into police procedure.

And big-ups to all my friends and family who have supported me on this journey and have always been so enthusiastic about my decision to become an author.

Nora Valters
September 2020

# ABOUT THE AUTHOR

Nora Valters grew up in the New Forest in the south of England and has lived in London, Manchester, Bournemouth, Oxford and Dubai.

She studied English Literature and Language at Oxford Brookes University before embarking on a career in marketing and copywriting.

Her debut psychological thriller *Her Biggest Fan* was published in 2020. She's currently writing her next novel, which will be out soon.

Nora loves to travel and has journeyed around the world. She enjoys exploring new places, painting, hiking, and is an avid reader. She's also a bit obsessed with dogs…

Subscribe to be notified by email when Nora's next novel is released, for giveaways, price promotions, book recommendations as well as exclusive extra content at www.noravalters.com/subscribe

Keep in touch:
Website www.noravalters.com
Facebook www.facebook.com/noravalters
Twitter www.twitter.com/nora_valters
Instagram www.instagram.com/nora_valters
Goodreads www.goodreads.com/noravalters
BookBub www.bookbub.com/authors/nora-valters

For more information and to contact Nora, please visit www.noravalters.com

Printed in Great Britain
by Amazon